Katie Mettner wears the title c... her leg after falling down th... decorating her prosthetic leg to fit the season. She lives in northern Wisconsin with her own happily ever-after and wishes for a dog now that her children are grown. Katie has an addiction to coffee and X (formerly Twitter) and a lessening aversion to Pinterest—now that she's quit trying to make the things she pins.

Kimberly Van Meter wrote her first book at sixteen and finally achieved publication in December 2006. She has written for the Blaze and Heroes series. She and her husband of thirty years have three children, two cats, and always a houseful of friends, family, and fun.

THE RED RIVER SLAYER

KATIE METTNER

COLTON'S SECRET STALKER

KIMBERLY VAN METER

MILLS & BOON

First Published in Great Britain 2024
by Mills & Boon, an imprint of HarperCollins*Publishers* Ltd
1 London Bridge Street, London, SE1 9GF

www.harpercollins.co.uk

HarperCollins*Publishers*
Macken House, 39/40 Mayor Street Upper,
Dublin 1, D01 C9W8, Ireland

The Red River Slayer © 2024 Katie Mettner
Colton's Secret Stalker © 2024 Harlequin Enterprises ULC

Special thanks and acknowledgement are given to Kimberly Van Meter for her contribution to *The Coltons of Owl Creek* series.

ISBN: 978-0-263-32222-4

0324

THE RED RIVER SLAYER

KATIE METTNER

For my three Es

Thank you for always supporting and encouraging my
work, even when you have to admit to your friends that
your mom writes romance novels. I couldn't have asked
for kinder, more empathetic kids than you three, and
I'm so proud to see you out making a positive
impact on the world.

Chapter One

They shouldn't be here. Mack Holbock had had that thought since they were first briefed on the mission. The hair on the back of his neck stood up, and he swiveled, his gun at his shoulder. The area around the small village was silent, but Mack could feel their presence. Despite what his commander said, the insurgents were there and ready to take out any American at any time. The commander should have given them more time for recon. Instead, he executed a mission on the word of someone too far away to know how the burned-out buildings hid those seeking to add to their body count. Mack knew the insurgents in this area better than anyone. He'd killed more than his fair share of them. They didn't give up or give in. They'd put a bullet in their own head before letting you capture them. If you didn't get them, they'd get you. Survival of the fittest, or in this case, survival of their leader maintaining his grip on terrorized villages.

That said, the first thing you learn in the army is never to question authority. You follow orders—end of story. No one wants your opinion, even if you have intel they don't have. His team had no choice but to go in. Mack still didn't like it. He didn't join the army by choice. Well, unless you consider the choice was either the military or prison. He chose the army because if he had to go down, he would go down helping someone. In his opinion, that was better than being shivved in a prison shower.

The kid with a chip on his shoulder standing in the courtroom that day was long gone. The army had made him a man in body, mind and spirit. He'd learned to contain his temper and use his anger for good, like protecting innocent villagers being terrorized by men who wanted to control the country with violence. As long as Mack and his team sucked in this fetid air, they had another think coming.

"Secure one, Charlie," a voice said over the walkie attached to his vest. His team leader, Cal, was inside with their linguist, Hannah. They needed information that only Hannah could get.

"Secure two, Mike," he said after depressing the button.

"Secure three, Romeo," came another voice.

Roman Jacobs, Cal's foster brother, was standing guard on the opposite side of the building. So far, all was quiet, but Mack couldn't help but feel it wouldn't stay that way. They needed to get out before someone dropped something from the air they couldn't dodge. He shrugged his shoulders to keep the back of his shirt from sticking to him as the sun beat down with unrelenting heat. The one hundred degrees temp felt like an inferno when weighed down with all the equipment and the flak jacket.

"Come on, come on," he hummed, aiming high and swinging his rifle right, then left of the adjacent buildings. There were so many places for a sniper to hide. He checked his watch. It had been ten minutes since Cal checked in and thirty minutes since Hannah had gone into the complex. She would have to sweet talk some of the older and wiser women in the community to cough up the bad guys' location. Sharing that information would be bad for their health, but so was not rooting the guys out and ending their reign of ter-

ror. If Hannah could ascertain a location, their team would ensure they never showed up around these parts again. There was far too much desert to search if they didn't have a place to start.

"Charlie and Hotel on the move," Roman said. "Entering the complex veranda, headed to Mike."

"Ten-four," he answered before he backed up to the complex's entrance. With his rifle still at his shoulder, he swept the empty buildings in front of him, looking for movement.

A skitter of rocks. Mack's attention turned to a burned-out building on his right. A muzzle flashed, sending a bullet straight at the courtyard.

"Sniper! Get her down!" Mack yelled, bringing his rifle up just as another shot rang out. The "oof" from the complex hit him in the gut, but he aimed and fired, the macabre dance of the enemy as he collapsed in a heap of bones, satisfying to see.

"Charlie! Hotel!"

"Secure one, Charlie."

"Secure two, Romeo."

"Secure three, Echo."

"Mack!" Cal hissed his name, and it snapped him back to the present.

"Secure four, Mike," he said, using his call name for the team. His voice was shaky, and he hoped no one noticed. Not that they wouldn't understand. They'd all served together and they all came back from the war with memories they didn't want but couldn't get rid of. Sometimes, when the conditions were right, he couldn't stop them from intruding in the present.

At present, he was standing behind his boss, Cal Newfellow, dressed in fatigues and bulletproof vest. Was that overkill for security at a sweet sixteen birthday party? Not if the birthday girl's father was a sitting senator.

"Ya good, man?" Cal asked without turning.

"Ten-four," he said, even though his hands were still shaking. It was hard to fight back those memories when he had to stand behind Cal, the one who lost the most that day. "Something doesn't feel right, boss."

"What do you see?"

"I don't see anything, but I can feel it. My hair is standing up on the back of my neck. My gut says run."

"We're the security force. We can't run." Cal's voice was amused, but Mack noticed him bring his shoulders up to his ears for a moment. "Keep your eyes open and your head on a swivel. Treat it like any other job and stop thinking about the past."

Mack wished it were that simple. Cal knew that not thinking about the past was tricky when you'd seen the things they had over there. War was ugly, whether foreign or domestic, and Mack was glad to be done with that business. He liked the comforts of home, not to mention not having to kill people daily.

He glanced at his boots, where the metal bars across the toes reminded him that his losses over in that sandbox were his fault.

At least the loss that ended their army careers for good was his fault. Mack had missed a car bomb tucked away in the vehicle he was tasked with driving. He was carrying foreign dignitaries to a safe house that day, but nothing went as planned. In the end, Cal had lost most of his right hand, Eric had lost his hearing and Mack had suffered extensive nerve damage in his legs when the car bomb shot shrapnel across the sand. Now, the metal braces he wore around his legs and across his toes were the only thing that allowed him to walk and do his job. Something told him that tonight, he'd better concentrate on his job instead of worrying about the past.

"What are the weak points of the property?" Mack asked, fixing his hat to protect his ears better. It was early May, but that didn't mean it was warm in Minnesota. Especially at night in the rain. Sometimes working in damp clothes with temps hovering near forty-five was worse than working in ninety-degree heat.

Cal swept his arm out the length of the backyard. "The three hundred and fifty feet of shoreline. This cabin is remote, but anyone approaching from the road would be stopped by security. If someone wants to crash the party, it'll be via the water. We need to keep a tight leash on the shore."

A tight leash. That had been the story of Mack's life since he'd been four. His mother was the first to make helicopter parenting an Olympic sport. When his dad died in a car accident, and Mack survived, she became obsessed with keeping him safe. His mother would have kept him in a bubble were it possible, but she couldn't, so she kept the leash tight. Sports? Out of the question. He could get hurt, or worse, killed by a random baseball to the head! As much as Mack hated to say it, he was relieved when she'd passed of cancer when he was seventeen. She was more a keeper than a mother, and it had to be a terrible way to live. It wasn't until she was diagnosed with blood cancer when he was fourteen that she started living again. The sad truth was that she had to be dying to live. When she passed away after three years of making memories together, he was relieved not for himself but her. She was with her soulmate again, and he knew that was what she'd wanted since the day he'd passed. Mack was simply collateral damage.

When he was seventeen, he'd stood before a judge after breaking a guy's arm for talking trash about a female classmate. He was told there were better ways to defend people than with violence. If you asked him, the military personified using violence to defend people. He joined the army to find a brotherhood again. He'd found one in Cal, Roman, Eric and his other army brothers. They were Special Forces and went into battle willing to die to have their brothers' backs. Until the one time that he couldn't. It had taken Mack a long time to understand he shouldn't use the word *didn't* when it came to what happened that day when Cal's soulmate was taken before their eyes. It wasn't that he didn't. It was that he couldn't. His mind immediately slid down the rabbit hole toward the car full of people he didn't save. Mack shook his head to clear it. Going back there would result in losing sight of what they were doing here.

Mack eyed his friend of fifteen years and reminded himself that Hannah hadn't been Cal's soulmate. He used to think so, but then Cal met Marlise. Hannah had been a woman Cal loved in youth. Her death opened a path for Cal to start a successful security business and eventually find the woman who centered him. The moment Cal's and Marlise's eyes met while the bad guys bombarded them with bullets, time stood still. Cal used to think he started Secure One Security because of Hannah, but not anymore. They all believed Marlise was the reason. The tragedy that started years before was the catalyst to put Cal on that plane when Marlise needed him.

It had been three years now since they met. They were engaged one month and married the next, which hadn't surprised the team. Marlise had shown Cal that he could love again, but Mack never thought he'd see the day. Not after the scene that spread out before him in that courtyard. Then again, Cal never saw that scene. He never saw his girlfriend with a fatal shot to the head. He never had to drag his friend's body out of the square, stemming the blood oozing from his chest to keep him alive until help got there. Cal hadn't known any of that. It was Mack, Eric and Roman who lived that scene. They were left with the worst memories of a day when they could save one friend but not the other. Whether he liked it or not, Cal had been spared those images, and Mack was glad. There weren't many times you were spared the gruesome truth of war.

Not all wars are fought on foreign soil. The new team members of Secure One had taught him that three times over. Roman's wife and partner in the FBI had been undercover in a house filled with women who had been sex trafficked and forced to work as escorts and drug mules. Mina had been injured to the point that she lost her leg and had come to work at Secure One when she married Roman. Their boss at the FBI, David Moore, was responsible for her injuries by putting her undercover in a house run by his wife, The Madame. Because of the deception, Roman and Mina could retire from the FBI with full benefits.

Marlise was one of The Madame's women in the house with Mina, and when she arrived at Secure One, she was broken and burned but determined. She wanted to help put The Madame behind bars. As she healed, Marlise worked her way up from kitchen manager to client coordinator, but not because she was Cal's girl. She had earned her position by observing, learning and caring about the people they were protecting.

His thoughts drifted to the other woman at Secure One who sought shelter there not long ago. About six months ago, Charlotte surrendered to Secure One under unusual circumstances. She was working for The Miss, the right-hand woman of The Madame in the same house Marlise and Mina had lived. The Miss had left Kansas and moved to Arizona to start her escort business, funded by drug trafficking. Charlotte was one of the women she took from Red Rye to help her. The Miss had made a mistake thinking Charlotte was devoted to her. She wasn't, and she wanted out. Last year, she'd helped them bring down The Miss by providing insider information they wouldn't have had any other way.

Charlotte took over the kitchen manager position when Marlise moved up to client coordinator and fit in well with the Secure One team. She had healed physically from the illness and injuries she'd suffered while living with The Miss, but her emotional and psychological injuries would take longer to scab over. She'd been homeless for years and then went to work for people who used and abused her without caring if she lived or died. There was a special kind of hell for people like that. Mack hoped The Miss had found her way there when he put a bullet in her chest.

Had he needed to kill her that night in the desert? Yes. Her guards had had guns pointed at his team, and there was no way he would lose another friend to her evil. As it were, Marlise took a bullet trying to protect Cal. Thankfully, it had been a nonlethal shoulder wound.

On the other hand, the gaping chest wound he'd left The Miss with was quite lethal and well-deserved. Mack had learned to channel his temper in the army, but he couldn't pretend he wasn't angry at the atrocities that occurred in a country that was the home of the free to some, but not all. He would defend women like Charlotte until his final breath so they would have a voice.

Mack rolled his shoulders at the thought of the woman who currently sat in their mobile command center on the other side of the property. The mobile command center offered bunks, food and a hot shower to keep the men warm and fed when they were on jobs away from their home base of Secure One. A hot shower and warm food were on Mack's wish list at that moment.

The hot shower or seeing Charlotte again?

His groan echoed across the lake until it filtered back to his ears as a reminder that he didn't need to concern himself with the woman in the command center. He could protect her without falling for her. He noticed how his team raised a brow whenever he helped Char in the kitchen or took a walk with her. He didn't care what they thought. She needed practice in trusting someone again without worrying about being hurt. It was going to be a long hard road for her, so the way he saw it, he'd be the one to teach her that not all men were bad, evil or sick. Sure, he'd done some bad things, but it hadn't been out of evilness or demented pleasure. He had done bad things for good people in the name of justice or retribution, making the world a better place to live. She didn't need to know that, though.

His gaze traveled the lakeshore again, searching for on-coming lights and listening for outboard motors. It was silent other than the call of the loons. The hair on the back of his neck told him it wouldn't stay that way for long.

Chapter Two

"Charlotte?" Selina called from the front of the command center. "I need a break for a moment."

Charlotte stuck the pasta salad into the fridge and dried her hands before meeting Selina at the bank of computers in the front of the renovated RV. Cal had spared no expense when he'd gutted it to make it work for his business. Three bump-outs provided a large kitchen and bathroom, bunks in the back where six people could sleep at a time and a mobile command post to put the FBI to shame.

"What's up?" she asked the woman sitting at the computers.

"Hey," Selina said, motioning at the four screens in front of her. "Would you keep an eye on these for a few minutes? I need to use the restroom and get something to drink."

"Sure. I don't know what I'm looking for, but I'll hold down the chair."

Selina stood and patted her on the shoulder. "There's not much going on since the birthday girl is inside with her guests cutting the cake. Watch for anyone who isn't on the Secure One team or teenagers trying to sneak away." She pointed at a walkie-talkie on the table. "Radio someone if you see anything."

"Got it," she promised. "There's pasta salad in the fridge if you're hungry."

"I'm starving. I'll grab a bowl and bring it back up here. I know you don't like covering, but I gotta go," Selina said, hurrying to the bathroom while Charlotte chuckled.

The computers were intimidating, but Charlotte sat in the chair Selina had vacated and watched the screens, looking for interlopers as described. Selina was the nurse at Secure One, which meant she went on every mission as their med tech, but when she wasn't stitching wounds and handing out Advil, she was the team's eyes in the back of their heads. Selina had been trained as an operative when she joined Secure One and was as accurate with a 9mm as she was with an IV needle. Sometimes, Charlotte wondered if she covered for Wonder Woman when she needed a break because that's how pivotal Selina was to the team.

"Mike to mobile command." The walkie squawked with Mack's voice, and Charlotte nearly jumped out of her skin as she fumbled for it.

She had to take a deep breath before pushing the button to speak. Mack Holbock always had that effect on her. "This is Charlotte. Selina had to step away."

"Hey, Char, how's your evening?" Mack asked when she released the button. She wondered if he realized his voice softened whenever he addressed her. Probably not, and she shouldn't be taking notice either.

"Quiet as a church mouse in here. Did you need something?"

"Nope, it was just my check-in time. There's a clipboard to check off my nine p.m. call-in. Do you see it?"

Charlotte released the button and found the board he referred to, searching for his name and putting a check next to 9:00 p.m. "Done. It looks like you're due for a break in thirty."

"Negative. That's when the dance is going to pick up. I can't leave my post on the shoreline. I don't want guests wandering down and falling in the drink."

"Mack, you know how Cal feels about that stuff," Charlotte warned.

"What are you? My mother?" he asked, but she heard his lighthearted laughter that followed. "I'll clear it with Cal."

"Okay, be careful," she said, wishing her voice hadn't gone down to a whisper on the last two words.

"Ten-four, Char," he said, and the box fell silent.

Mack had been calling her Char since she'd arrived at Secure One last fall with her hat in her hand or rather her hands in the air. She had surrendered herself, hoping to gain immunity against The Miss the same way Marlise had when the Red Rye house burned. The night of the fire, she hadn't known Marlise wasn't going with them to the airport. Had she known that, Charlotte would have refused to go as well. Working for The Madame, and subsequently The Miss, had been demoralizing, scary and for some, downright deadly. When she saw Marlise escape their grasp, Charlotte had vowed to do the same if she ever got the chance.

That was the night she'd had her first interaction with Mack Holbock. It was the moment she realized she was safe, and they believed she hadn't been working for The Miss by choice. Exhaustion, fear and relief took over, and she had fallen apart right there in the little room where they'd been holding her. Mack had scooped her up and taken her to the med bay for treatment. She couldn't remember much about that time, but she remembered him. His presence, more than anything. He was smaller than Cal and Roman, but only in the height department. He was ripped, strong and capable regarding his work, but he was also kind, quiet and gentle when the occasion called for it.

When Cal, Marlise, Roman and Mina had left to find

The Miss, Mack stayed behind for a few days to ensure everything ran smoothly. Initially, he was the only one who believed that she had no ulterior motive. She needed that unquestionable acceptance more than anyone understood.

"What did I miss?" Selina asked, carrying in a bowl of pasta salad with the fork halfway to her lips. Before Charlotte could answer, she was chewing, moaning and swallowing the first bite. "This is brilliant. Pepperoni and black olives?"

"And Italian dressing, to list a few." Charlotte laughed as she stood so Selina could sit.

"Seriously, you learned your lessons well from Marlise."

"I'm glad you enjoy it. To answer your question, Mack checked in for his nine p.m. but isn't going to take his break at nine thirty. The dance is about to start, and he doesn't want anyone wandering down to the water and falling in."

"That sounds like Mack," Selina agreed, setting the bowl down and jiggling the mouse. "Normally, Cal has a hardline about breaks, but this isn't a normal job, so I'm inclined to side with Mack."

"Same," Charlotte said, lounging on the back of the couch while she waited for one of the crew to come in looking for something to eat or drink. "It isn't every day that you're tasked with keeping one hundred teenagers safe when the birthday girl is a sitting senator's daughter."

"It's a little nerve-racking, not going to lie," Selina said before shoveling in more salad.

Charlotte kept her eyes on the screens in case she caught a glimpse of Mack. She liked watching him work, which might be weird, but it was true. When he was working, he moved with military precision, reminding her that he had fought his own battles in life. Some of those battles remained with him, she knew. He'd told her that in so many words one night as they worked together in the kitchen.

She'd sensed that he didn't open up much about his time in the army, so she let him talk. While his stories weren't specific, his emotions were. He was struggling with the scars left from those battles as much as she was from hers. Maybe that was what made them immediate friends and easy companions. They understood each other on a level of unspoken atrocities and nightmare-riddled dreams.

Charlotte had only slept those first few nights at Secure One because Selina gave her medication to keep her calm. After that, she slept in fits and bursts. Her psyche struggled to know if the people surrounding her could be trusted, and it took her several months to feel comfortable enough to sleep through the night, at least as through the night as she could when plagued by nightmares of men's hands holding her down. Mack always seemed to materialize in the kitchen at 2:00 a.m. on those nights when she couldn't close her eyes again. He'd sit by the butcher-block counter and share cookies and milk with her rather than scold her about not going back to bed.

"You know it's okay if you want to date Mack," Selina said.

Charlotte's brain came to a full stop and nearly slung her backward off the couch. "Excuse me, what now?"

"I said it's okay if you—"

"I heard what you said, but what makes you think I want to date Mack?" Charlotte had forced the words through a too-dry throat, hoping it sounded genuine.

"Because you like each other, which is obvious. Everyone else tiptoes around you two like sleeping lions, but I'm all about calling it as I see it."

"Clearly," Charlotte said, tongue in cheek. "I don't want to date Mack, but I'm happy to know it would be okay if I did."

"If you say so," Selina answered in a singsong voice that was a bit juvenile as far as Charlotte was concerned.

"We're just friends, Selina. First of all, he's five years older than I am."

"Cal is five years older than Marlise."

Charlotte chose to ignore her. "Second of all, I'm not ready to date anyone. Since working for The Madame, I don't know how to date. I don't know how to be with a man who didn't pay for my company."

"Do you trust Mack?" Selina asked with her back to her now as she watched the screens.

"You know I do, with my life, but that's different."

"I understand what you're saying, Charlotte. You're scared. I get it. I know you don't know me or my past, but suffice it to say that I do understand being afraid to rock the boat. I just thought you should hear from someone on the team that moving on and living your life now that The Madame is in prison and The Miss is dead isn't rocking the boat. You earned your freedom, and you should enjoy it."

The woman who had nursed her back to health fell silent then, and Charlotte stared at the screens as she considered what Selina had said. She had earned her freedom from The Miss and had been pivotal in helping them find her and rescue the other women. She could leave Secure One whenever she was ready, Cal had told her, but he'd also said he wasn't putting an end date on her employment. As long as she wanted to be part of Secure One, the team would welcome her with open arms. They had, which was the reason she wouldn't rock the boat. If she had to leave Secure One and find work in a different city with a different company, she could end up back on the street. That was the very last place she wanted to be.

The man in question walked onto the screen, and Charlotte watched as he made his way down the bank and disappeared from view. She turned away and walked back to the kitchen. Secure One was her life, and while Mack might be part of it professionally, that was as far as it would go. For Charlotte, self-preservation would win out every time, even if that meant being alone for the rest of her life.

THE CABIN OF Senator Ron Dorian was well hidden among the trees until they parted for a view of the Mississippi River. The *cabin* was a six-bedroom, four-bath summer home with a grand staircase and wall-to-wall windows in the family room that looked out over the water. Mack wondered how ostentatious his DC house must be if he called this his *cabin*. Then again, that wasn't his job. His job was to keep a young girl and her friends safe while they were on the grounds celebrating a milestone. Secure One had been in charge of the security on this cabin for six years, and they'd run point on plenty of parties held here. His worry at tonight's party? The sun had set, and one hundred teenagers were ready to pour out onto a dance floor under a rented tent. There was a 100 percent chance a couple or six would sneak down to the river to make out. Having one of them fall in the drink and get swept downstream was not the reputation Secure One wanted.

He'd been patrolling the football field length of shoreline for the last three hours other than the ten-minute break he'd taken inside the command center to grab dry clothes, boots and a snack. He hoped the rest of the crew didn't eat all the pasta salad before he got back there. It was one of the best salads he'd ever had, and that was saying a lot, considering Marlise used to be the resident chef. When he'd tried to compliment Charlotte on it, she'd turned away and acted like she hadn't heard him. He knew she'd heard him when her lips tipped up a hair before she spun away. She'd been fine when he'd done his 9:00 p.m. check-in, so he couldn't help but wonder what had happened in the meantime.

Mack went over everything he'd said to her the last week and couldn't think of anything that would have upset her. Maybe she was just having a rough night. Security at these events required a lot of planning, and even tighter control, which put everyone on edge. She'd be fine once they returned to Secure One and were back in the swing of their usual duties. At least he hoped she would be. Mack didn't like the idea that someone had upset Charlotte, especially if it had been him. Before Charlotte arrived, he'd taken the time to listen to and observe Marlise during her two years at Secure One. He'd understood that women in their situation had a hard time trusting people and had limited, if any, self-esteem. That led to difficulty staying employed or in school, often leading them back to the streets. He didn't want that for Charlotte.

She reminded him a lot of Marlise though. Strong, determined and seeking a better life. Charlotte had been that way since they'd hauled her in off the shoreline the first night. She'd wanted to escape the woman holding her captive and was willing to risk getting shot. Unlike Marlise, Charlotte's scars weren't visible. They were buried deep in her mind and soul, and she rarely let them show. A few months ago, she'd been sketching on her pad when he walked into the kitchen for a snack. She was a skilled artist and had already helped Secure One clients by drafting plans to provide specific problem areas with better security. That night though, her drawing drew his eye immediately. She'd tried to hide it from him, but he hadn't allowed it. His eyes closed for a beat when he thought about it.

The drawing was of a naked woman with bleeding wounds, tears on her face and vulnerability in every pencil stroke. She told him it was a self-portrait of how she felt inside. The slashes across her body and blood pooling by her feet would rest in his mind for always—most especially the wound to her leg where The Miss had buried a tracker not meant for humans. Despite Selina's best efforts, Charlotte had gotten an infection and now had nerve damage in the leg. She'd sketched an intricate tattoo around the scar that spelled out *worthless,* and he'd assured her she was anything but that. Those were just words though, and Mack knew women like Charlotte didn't believe wo—

A scream pelted the air in a high-pitched frenzy that relayed fear in a way Mack had heard only a few times in his life. He started running toward the sound just a few hundred feet ahead. He stopped in front of two teenage girls, no longer screaming, just staring at the water with their mouths open in terror. One girl had her arm pointed out with her finger shaking as Mack followed it to the shore below.

"Secure two, Mike. I need help on the shore, stat!" He turned the girls away from the water just as Eric came running from the other direction.

"What's going on?" he huffed, and Mack flicked his eyes to the water. Eric's gaze followed, and his muffled curse told Mack he'd seen her too. "I'll take them to the command center while you call the cops. We'll need to keep these two separated from the rest of the group until then."

"After that, get the party shut down while I deal with this," Mack hissed, and with a nod, Eric led the two women toward the command center.

Mack walked down to the lakeshore, holding his gun doublehanded as he navigated the rocks and wet sand. What could first be mistaken for floating garbage, on a second glance, was a woman with her long blond hair floating over her red dress. When he stopped along the shore to stare down at her, the woman's eyes were wide open, and her mouth made an *O* as though whatever she saw in the last moments of her life were welcoming her into the new world.

"What do you have?" Cal asked as he came running up behind Mack.

"Young woman. No visible COD. We need to get her out before she floats downstream."

"Cops aren't going to want us to touch her," Cal said as Mack holstered his gun.

"They're going to like trying to find her again in the Mississippi much less." Mack snapped on a pair of gloves he'd pulled from his vest and then grabbed his telescoping gaff hook. Everyone had one on their belt when they worked on the water. You might have to pull a fellow team member out of the drink at any time.

"We need a tarp before you pull her out," Cal said quickly, stopping Mack's arm.

"You'd better get one then," Mack growled and shook his boss's arm loose. "I'm going to hook her dress just to hold her here. If I don't, she's going downstream."

Cal hit the button on his vest that connected him to command central. "Secure one, Charlie. I need a tarp or plastic on the shore directly below the dance tent."

"What size?" Mack heard Selina ask.

"Body size," Cal answered, and it ran a shiver down Mack's spine.

Now secured by his hook, the young woman wasn't going anywhere, but Mack couldn't take his eyes off her. She couldn't be twenty-five, and her long blond hair reminded him of Marlise and Charlotte. He prayed that someone was missing this woman, and she wasn't the victim of The Red River Slayer. His cynical side said the slayer was responsible for this woman's death, and he was only getting started.

Chapter Three

The muted light through the window told her the sun was setting. She knelt by the bed and scratched another line into the wood. It was the five hundred and fiftieth. She knew some were missing from the early days when fear kept her huddled on the bed for most of the day. That was before she realized he wouldn't kill her. Now she marked the end of each day rather than the beginning of a new one. She suspected her end would come at night.

Frustration filled the woman as she stood. She had to get out, but the room was a beautifully decorated and posh fortress. She had all the comforts of home except for a way to contact the outside world. She also didn't have a television or a radio. She'd been *his* captive for too long. Soon she'd be replaced with a new plaything. That was how it worked. What he did with his old playthings, she didn't know. Probably sold them or killed them.

The thought ran a shiver down her spine. She hoped he'd kill her. The last thing she wanted was to be sold to another man in another country. If she had a way to do it, she would kill herself just to steal his joy, but he made sure there were no weapons for her to use. Who was he? She had no idea, but he had money, and he must have power. You don't keep women locked away in the basement of your home for years without the ability to make people look the other way. Then again, she had no idea if anyone lived in this house other than her. Maybe he just came to visit her or lived alone upstairs. In the early days, she'd tried to ask questions but soon learned he wasn't interested in answering them. Her fingers played across the puckered scar on her cheek. The night she pushed him too far with her questions, he showed her rather than told her to stop.

Her gaze drifted to the window above her bed. She'd tried to break it until she realized it wasn't glass. It was layers of plexiglass that no amount of pounding would break. She paused. Were those footsteps?

She moved to the door quietly on practiced tiptoes to listen. He should be bringing her dinner soon. He would sit with her while she ate and engage her in conversation that would be considered mundane in a different time and place. He stayed to ensure she didn't try to hide the utensils or kill herself with them. When she finished eating, he'd want her to thank him for dinner if he were in the right mood. She learned early on to obey that order, or she'd spend a week drinking her food through a straw until the swelling in her face receded from his beating. Oh, sure, he'd always apologize for hurting her and bring her ice and medicine, but he wasn't sorry. He thrived on the power he held over her, and beating her turned him on.

The footsteps stopped at the door, and a key jingled. She was back on her bed as the door swung open, and her monster walked through with a tray balanced on his arm. He was wearing his full leather hood and his smoking jacket tonight. He always wore the mask, but the smoking jacket meant she'd have to thank him properly tonight. Initially, she had nightmares about the mask, but after a few months, she found a way to ignore it and imagine the man behind the mask. She came up with ways she would take him down if she ever escaped.

He set the tray down on the bed and ran a finger down her cheek. She forced herself not to recoil. "Good evening, my angel. Little Daddy brought you dinner. Are you hungry?"

"Yes, Little Daddy," she obediently said while trying hard not to roll her eyes. She stopped being scared of him months ago, but she'd learned if she didn't want a backhand, she'd best comply with his demented fantasies.

"This will be one of our last meals together, angel."

Her breath hitched in her chest. This was it. She had to act tonight.

"Soon, you'll go to your new home with your new daddy. He can't wait to meet you. I'll miss you, but you're ready for him now. Are you ready for a new daddy, angel?" he asked as he set up the food on the table.

She nodded but knew she was out of time. This was it. It was time to put her plan into action. She'd spent months earning his trust, and tonight, she'd thank him properly for all the things he'd given her, but more so for the things he'd taken away.

"How long until the cops get here?" Mack asked Cal as they stood in front of the body. They'd laid her on the shoreline on a tarp, but they didn't cover the body for fear of contaminating it more than it already was.

"At least another thirty minutes," Cal answered while he fielded questions from the rest of the team as they sent kids home with their parents.

Selina was caring for the two girls who had discovered the body. They would wait at mobile command until their parents arrived. The police would need to speak with them, but Mack had no doubt their parents would want to be present.

"Who are we kidding?" Mack muttered. "The tumble she took down the Mississippi left no evidence of her killer for us to find."

"Us?" Cal asked with a brow up in the air. "There is no us. This is for the cops to figure out."

"And they've done a smashing job with the other three bodies they've found in the last few months."

The authorities had pulled three women from three different rivers over the last six months. The first woman had been found in The Red River and was wearing a red dress, which was how this particular serial killer had earned his moniker.

"Not my monkey," Cal said again. "We can't get involved in this, Mack. We have enough on our plates at Secure One."

"We've been involved in this since the day you brought Marlise onto the compound," Mack reminded him. "If this is yet another nameless, background-less woman like Marlise or Charlotte, that means someone is buying and killing women from the street. How long are we going to brush it under the carpet before we *get involved*?"

Cal whirled around and stuck his finger in Mack's chest. "Don't."

"Don't what, Cal?" Mack knew challenging his boss was risky, but they were also brothers, and sometimes you had to call your own family on their crap.

"Don't accuse me of inviting this into our lives. That was not what I did when Marlise came to Secure One."

Mack held up his hands in defense. "That's not at all what I was saying, Cal. I simply meant that we're taking care of women just like this one," he said, motioning at the woman behind him, "while others are still dying. The cops are missing something. How long will we stand by without at least trying to prevent more deaths?"

Cal shook his head and planted a hand on his hip. "Mack,

I wish there were a way to get involved in this case, but there isn't. The FBI is involved and—"

"The FBI can't find their way out of a paper bag!" Mack exclaimed.

"I don't disagree," Cal said with a smirk, "but we still can't go traipsing in like *the Mod Squad* and take over their investigation."

Mack snorted. "The *Mod Squad*. Okay, Grandpa, but I'm tired of women dying because of our inaction."

"Same," Cal said with a sigh. "In each victim, I see Marlise or Charlotte. It was just chance they made it out of The Miss's grasp alive. These poor women."

"All of them," Mack agreed.

As a man, he hated that some men thought they could use a woman and then throw her away like garbage. It enraged him to the point of violence, which didn't solve anything. The only way to stop it was for someone to figure out who was doing it. Unfortunately, Cal was right. With the feds involved, they couldn't be. Cal had been read the riot act after The Miss fiasco when he went rogue, and the woman ended up dead because of it. In the end, it was brushed under the carpet as a problem solved, but Secure One had to tread lightly whenever the feds were around. They didn't like their tiny toes stepped on.

"Secure two, Sierra."

"Secure one, Mike. Go ahead."

"Charlotte is on her way down," Selina said over the comm unit in his ear.

"What?"

"I said Charlotte is on her way down."

"No, don't let her leave the mobile center. She doesn't belong down here."

"Already tried that, Mack. You've met the woman, right?"

"I'll have Eric intercept her. Thanks for the heads-up."

Mack huffed as he grabbed his radio to call Eric. Of course, Charlotte would try to come down here. She felt responsible for these women as much as Marlise did. If Marlise weren't back at Secure One with Mina working the other client security, she'd be down here too. "Secure two, Mike," he said and waited for Eric to reply. Once he did, Mack explained the situation and signed off.

"You're not going to pass me off on someone else, Mack Holbock," a voice said from his left, and he spun in the dark without drawing his weapon. He knew it was her, even if he was frustrated by her inability to follow orders. He secretly loved that she still had some fight left in her. She didn't back down on something she believed in, regardless of what she'd been through in life, even if that personality trait made his job harder.

He stepped to the side enough to hide the woman on the ground, and Cal moved alongside him. "You shouldn't be here, Charlotte," Cal said firmly. "This is a crime scene."

She stopped and stood before them with her hand on her hip. Mack had to bite his tongue to keep from smiling. "I'm not contaminating your crime scene," she said, throwing around air quotes. "The Mississippi is contaminating your crime scene."

"What do you need, Char?" Mack asked, softening his voice as he took a step toward her. She needed to be on her way before she saw the body and realized she was a victim of the same nameless, faceless perp.

"I need to see the body."

"Not happening," Cal said, crossing his arms over his chest. "No one views the body without the police here."

"When the police get here, it will be too late. They'll bungle it the way they always do, and more women will die."

"More women will die? We don't know how this woman died," Mack reminded her.

Charlotte rolled her eyes so hard that Mack couldn't stop the smile from lifting his lips. "She's the fourth woman found dead in a river in six months. More women will die if we don't find the killer, Mack."

Mack turned and lifted a brow of *I told you so* at Cal before turning back to the woman in front of him. "Be that as it may, we must follow protocol, Charlotte. Protocol says we have to wait for the authorities."

"Are you going to tell them?" she asked, both hands on her hips.

"I won't put you through it. I know you want to help, but you can't."

"Don't tell me what I can and can't do, Mack," she hissed, standing chest to chest with him.

Cal's grunt was loud to Mack's ear, and he grimaced. His boss wasn't happy. Cal's flashlight snapped on, and he lifted it to Charlotte's chest. "It's not up to us, Charlotte—"

Her gasp was loud enough to stop him midsentence. His flashlight had illuminated the woman's head by accident, and Charlotte's eyes were pinned on her. Mack grasped her shoulder to turn her, but she fought him.

"I know her," she whispered, dropping to her knee on the muddy shore. "I know her, Mack."

Mack knelt on both knees, not caring that the cold mud soaked through his pants. He cared that someone on his team could identify this woman. "Char, how do you know her?" He could see shock kicking in, and he wanted the answer before she couldn't speak.

Cal switched the light off, and it went dark again just as Charlotte reached her hand out toward the body. "That's Layla."

"Layla who?" Cal asked as Mack put his arm around Charlotte. She was starting to shiver, whether from the cold or trauma, he couldn't say.

"I don't know," she whispered. "I met her in Arizona when I worked for The Miss. She was from one of the small towns around Tucson."

"Wait, she was with The Miss?" Cal asked from behind them to clarify.

Char nodded but dropped her gaze to the ground now that the body was in the shadows. "Layla wasn't there very long. She cried nonstop and cowered in the corner whenever The Miss came around. We woke up one morning, and she was gone. We figured she tried to run, and The Miss killed her. That or she got away."

"Would it be safe to say you met her two years ago?" Mack asked, trying to get some kind of timeline to help the police when they arrived.

Charlotte turned to him with wide eyes as she nodded. "Something like that. Where has she been all this time, Mack?" She grabbed tightly to his coat when she asked, her face just inches from his now.

"I don't know, but now that we know who she is, maybe we can find out."

Charlotte shuddered, and Mack wrapped his arms around her as he glanced up at Cal and mouthed, "Don't tell the cops."

Cal tipped his head for a moment in confusion, but after a long stare, he cleared his throat. "Mack, please walk Charlotte back to the command center. I'll wait here for the police."

With a nod, he helped Charlotte up the grassy hill toward the lights shining in the distance. "I want you to listen to me, Char," he whispered, and she nodded. "Don't tell anyone outside of Secure One that you know the victim."

She tripped on her next step, and Mack steadied her as she lifted her gaze to his. "But, Mack, they have to find her killer!"

"Shh," he said, hushing her immediately. "First, the police will have to decide if she was murdered."

"You know she was!"

His finger against her lips muffled her exclamation. "We know she was, but the cops must *prove* she was. Does that make sense?" She nodded against his finger, and he lowered his hand and started walking with her again. "While they're busy proving she was murdered and searching for her identity, we'll be after her killer."

"But I already know who she is, Mack. If I don't tell them, I'll be in trouble when they find out I knew her."

He squeezed her to him to quiet her again. "You will tell them as soon as they release her image to the press. That won't happen until they determine her cause of death. The same as they have with the other women found dead with no identity, though in this case, they may be able to get her identity if she wasn't washed like you and the women from The Madame's ring."

"That's true," she agreed with a nod. "She was a street girl but had a record, at least according to her."

"Good, good. Then the police will find out who she is without you telling them. When they do, you'll call to tell them you knew her for a few days and the dates she was with The Miss. That's as far as your responsibility goes with this case."

She stopped abruptly, and he caught himself from falling at the last second. "Wouldn't it save time if we could give them her identity tonight?"

"It would," Mack agreed, lowering his head closer to hers so no one overheard them, "but then we have no time to look into it at Secure One."

"But this sicko is out there hurting other women!" she exclaimed, and his finger returned to her lips.

"He's following a pattern. One woman every six weeks, at

least that's been the frequency they've been finding the bodies. We can take a couple of days to try and track down the last knowns on this woman before we turn what we know over to the police. We're trying to prevent another woman from dying by helping the police, not working against them, okay?"

"Why do you think you can help now? Just because you have a name?"

He turned her and started walking toward the command center again. He wanted to get back before the cops showed up so he could hear what Cal told them. "This is the first time we've had the name of the victim, which means it's the first time we can put Mina on the task of following her trail before she disappeared. All we needed was one mistake from this guy, and he may have just made it."

"Killing a woman with an identity?"

"Killing a woman with an identity and leaving her where Secure One could find her. Our record speaks for itself regarding getting justice for women being held against their will."

A smile lifted Charlotte's lips, and he squeezed her shoulders one more time before reaching the steps to the command center. "It's safe to say Secure One has done better than the police, that's for sure," she agreed.

"Then trust us, just one more time, and we'll get justice for women like Layla too."

A shadow crossed her face, but it was gone before he could grasp its meaning. He had shadows of his own that he kept hidden, and he wouldn't judge her for hers. When she leaned in close to him, her scent of apple blossoms filled his senses, and he inhaled deeply. He reminded himself that he had no business liking this woman for any reason other than to keep her safe while on a job. At the mere thought, he laughed at himself. As if that were the only reason he liked Charlotte.

"Isn't it illegal to withhold information?" she whispered, so close to him that he could bury his nose in her neck and fill his head with her. He didn't, but it took every ounce of willpower not to.

"As far as the police know, only four people have seen the body, and only two up close—me and Cal. That's all they need to know. Right?"

She nodded once, zipped her lips and tossed away the key. Then she climbed the steps and disappeared inside the trailer. Mack couldn't keep the smile off his lips as he turned on his heel and walked back toward the shore in awe of the woman half his size with twice his strength.

Chapter Four

Charlotte approached the two girls who sat huddled together on the couch. Selina had covered them with a warm blanket and calmed them down so they could speak rather than just stutter words. Their names were Tia and Leticia, and they told Charlotte and Selina they were best friends.

She handed each girl a mug of hot cocoa and sat across from them on a chair. She'd seen a lot of horrible things on the street, and she remembered her reaction to the first dead body in a dark alley on the streets of Phoenix. Nothing prepared a person for that, and nothing could wipe the image away.

"Your parents are on their way to be with you until the police arrive," Selina said, hanging up her phone. "They're about ten minutes away."

"Okay, thank you," Leticia said before scooting closer to her friend. "What are the police going to ask us?"

"Basic questions," Selina assured them. "Your name and address, how long you've been friends with Eleanor Dorian, if you've ever been here before and what you were doing by the water tonight. It will be simple questions that you can answer easily. They know you didn't have anything to do with the woman's death. They just want to know if you remember anything that might be helpful to their investigation."

"Can we stay together?" Tia asked.

"That I don't know," Selina admitted. "It will be up to the police and how they decide to question you. You don't have anything to hide, so don't worry about it."

The girls glanced at each other again, and Charlotte noticed the fear that hid in their eyes. "What were you doing down by the water tonight?"

Another shared glance confirmed for Charlotte that they were hiding something they didn't want to come out.

"Girls, if you were drinking or smoking down there, the police will find out, so you may as well be honest," Selina said without judgment.

Tia shook her head and held her hands out to them. "No, no, we weren't. We'll do a test to prove it. We weren't doing that."

"Then you have nothing to worry about," Selina said again.

"Are you in a relationship together?" Charlotte asked, the truth evident.

"You can't tell our parents," Tia hissed, tears springing to her eyes. "Please."

Her protective arm around Leticia suddenly made more sense, especially when she pulled her closer. "We just wanted to dance together," Leticia whispered, "so we went down the hill where no one would see us. We aren't out because of my parents."

Selina knelt in front of them and rested her hands on their knees. "We aren't going to tell your parents. Let's take a minute to agree on what you'll tell the police if you're separated. You'll want your answers to match."

"You mean you'll help us hide the truth? Won't you get in trouble?" Tia's gaze flicked between the two women, and Charlotte took her other hand instinctively.

"There's nothing wrong with saying you went down the

hill to escape the noise or see the river at night. Technically, that's what you did, right?" Charlotte asked, and they nodded.

"We danced and then walked out on the fancy lookout dock just as the moon came out from behind the clouds. The moonbeam on the water was magical and something you don't see living in the city, you know?" Tia asked, and both she and Selina nodded.

"Were there any boats on the water tonight?" Selina asked. It didn't surprise Charlotte that Selina would dig for more information when the opportunity presented itself. When she walked in the door earlier, Selina was already on the phone with Cal.

"No," Leticia said without hesitation. "All I heard was the rain falling on the water. I turned to kiss Tia, and that's when I saw the flash of red over her shoulder. When we focused on it, we realized it was a dress, and someone was still in it. She was floating down the river as though it were a sunny summer afternoon." They both shuddered again, and new tears sprang to Leticia's eyes.

"Okay," Selina said quickly, squeezing their knees. "Just tell the police that you were turning to go when you noticed the red dress." They both nodded robotically, and Selina glanced at Charlotte for a moment. "Did you see anyone else on the bank of the river? Anyone walking or running through the trees?"

"No, we didn't see anything, but it was so dark it would have been hard. We wouldn't have heard footsteps with the music playing for the dance."

Selina patted their knees and then stood. "I just ran you through the questions the police will ask. Do you think you can handle it now?"

Both girls nodded, and smiles lifted their lips. "Yes, thank you," Tia whispered. "Thank you for understanding why we don't want to tell the police why we were down there."

"We understand you're in love, and that's a wonderful feeling," Charlotte said, leaning forward to talk to the girls. "Don't let what happened tonight steal that joy from you. Finish high school and then go to college where you can be together without worry. Life is hard, but love makes it worth it. Okay?" They nodded again, and Charlotte stood. "Want a refill?" She pointed at their empty mugs of cocoa and smiled as they handed them to her.

Charlotte disappeared into the kitchen to refill their mugs as her words flooded her head. *Being in love is a wonderful feeling.* She'd never been in love but hoped one day she'd find someone who understood her scars and loved her anyway. She ladled the sweet milk into the mugs and sighed. That was a tall order for anyone. Her mind's eye flicked to Mack tonight and the way he tried to protect her from the ugliness of life. She immediately shook it away. She wasn't here to fall in love with Mack Holbock. She was here to feed him and, if she had her way, heal him, so he could go out and find someone worthy of his love.

THE BRANCHES TUGGED at her skin, leaving red welts across her bare arms as she barreled through the dark, cold night. She'd bested her *Little Daddy* and escaped the prison she'd been in for over eighteen months. She'd found an old pair of shoes by the door and a jacket, but with no phone and no money, she wasn't sure how she would find help. She was surprised how remote the house was when she tore out of the basement like the hounds of hell were on her heels.

She was tired but knew she had to keep going. How far was far enough? She didn't know. She'd been following the river, so she had to run into a town eventually, right? She had to find a car and get far, far away from wherever her current hell was.

Streetlights glowed in the distance, and she slowed to a walk. She had two choices: run past the town while it was still dark and keep going or stop and see what the town had to offer. Her first problem was a lack of money or identification. Her second problem was figuring out if The Miss was still in business without landing on someone's radar who would call the cops. She glanced down at herself and sighed. Her cami and boy shorts would land her on someone's radar, and she couldn't risk the cops finding her or alerting The Miss.

Think, she told herself. *You're in a forest with trees and a river. That means you aren't in the desert anymore.* The thought lifted her head, and she saw the town with fresh eyes. She was a long way away from Arizona. If The Miss was still doing business, she'd need long tentacles to know she'd escaped.

The idea spurred her forward into the shadows. First things first—clothes and then transportation. Ahead was a service station. No lights were on, which meant it was closed or shut down. A glance up and down the dark asphalt showed no cars, and she skittered across the road before sliding behind the brick building. She said a silent prayer as she dug in her coat pocket for the flashlight she'd found earlier. She'd been too afraid to use it before, but the risk was worth it now. Keeping it low to the ground, she searched the area behind the garage. A hulking metal body sat as a sentry next to the building. Focusing the weak beam of light on the license plate told her the first thing she needed to know.

Pennsylvania.

A long way from home, Toto, she thought. She didn't know the town's name, but it didn't matter. She wouldn't be there long. Sliding along the side of the truck, she noticed there was no logo on the side. That meant if she could get it started, it could be her salvation. A glance in the back of the rusty truck bed revealed old coveralls that she balled up under her arm for later. Hot-wiring a truck this old would be a piece of cake as long as the door was unlocked. She needed to get in fast if it was, especially if the dome light came on. With a steady breath, she pulled up on the truck's handle and prayed she'd caught her first big break.

IT HAD BEEN hours since Mack had pulled Layla onto shore, but the property was still buzzing with activity. The police were interviewing kids as their parents looked on in horror, and the ERT team was on the scene looking for any evidence they could pull in and analyze. It didn't take a genius to realize there wouldn't be much left on the body after being in the Mississippi. The medical examiner gave them a time of death between seventy-two and ninety-six hours ago. Whether it was three days or four didn't matter. Trace evidence would have been washed away in the Mississippi within minutes. That was the way The Red River Slayer wanted it.

Mack suspected they wouldn't find any labels in her dress, which would match the MO of the other women they'd found. Even if they could track down the dress, it would likely be from a big box store and sold in every state. The Red River Slayer had repeatedly proven that he wasn't stupid or careless. Mack hoped killing Layla was the perp's first mistake.

When working with the feds—correction, when the feds are running a case—you had to be careful that you don't tamper with evidence. Mack knew that, but before they arrived, he'd felt it was essential to check for vitals, which was why with a gloved hand, he had palpated her neck. He couldn't help that while he was doing that, he noticed petechiae in her eyes and her swollen tongue. While there were no ligature marks on her neck, that didn't rule out strangulation. It was surprisingly easy to strangle someone to death without leaving a mark. Mack would know. The feds were selling the cause of death as drowning, but no one at Secure One was buying. The person killing these women wanted to be hands-on, even if it meant holding them under the water while they struggled. That said, neither Mack nor Cal believed that to be the case.

It was more likely the killer felt these women needed to be beautiful even after their death, which was why they were placed in the river wearing red gowns. The Red River Slayer was helping these women find a better afterlife, whether from their past lives or what they had to do while they were with him.

For the first time, Secure One may have finally got some solid information about the guy. Since Charlotte knew Layla disappeared around eighteen months ago, and the ME put her time of death around three days ago, the math told him the perp kept the women for a long time. To do that, he had to have a home or building to house them without raising suspicions. It was a huge risk to hold someone hostage that long, which meant wherever he was keeping them had to be isolated with no neighbors or regular deliveries. Then again, maybe he kept them bound and gagged when he wasn't home. The idea of it sent a shiver down Mack's spine.

He was itching to return to Secure One headquarters so they could plot all their information on Layla against the other victims of The Red River Slayer. They may not be actively involved in solving this case, but that was the very basis of the Secure One team in the army. They were a ghost team that went in and got the job done. It was starting to look like they would have to do the same this time if they were going to stop this guy.

"Who's in charge here?" The man's brusque tone put Mack on guard immediately. He stepped up next to Cal as the man, nearly fifty yards away, was yelling. "I demand to know what is going on here!"

"Ah, yes, we knew it was only a matter of time before Senator Dorian arrived," Cal said out of the corner of his mouth. "Should we pass him off to the cops or try to pacify him first?"

"Let's take him back to mobile command. We can keep him occupied by walking him through the entire party while the feds do their thing here. I'm sure the feds will want to talk to him, but since he wasn't here to celebrate his daughter's birthday, I might add, there isn't much information he can give them."

"Agreed," Cal said before stepping toward the man to head him off. Mack followed, breaking right of Cal so they could turn Dorian toward mobile command. "Senator Dorian."

"Cal Newfellow! What is this I hear about a dead woman on my property?"

The senator was shouting now, which was unnecessary with their proximity, so Cal took his shoulder and kept him walking toward the motor home. "Sir, let's go to our command center, and we can show you what occurred this evening. Everything was recorded."

"I want to see this woman!"

"Not possible," Mack said as he quickly texted Selina with one word, incoming, before he finished answering. "The ME has already removed the body. We should talk inside."

They'd managed to herd the senator and his protection detail to the command center quickly and efficiently without drawing too much attention to him. The door opened, and Selina stepped out, holding the door for their entourage to enter. Dorian motioned for his team to stay outside, so Selina closed the door behind them.

"Where's Charlotte?" Mack asked her under his breath. The last thing he wanted was for her to overhear them.

"She's overseeing the kids waiting for a ride at the house. I didn't want her here just in case."

Mack nodded, glad Selina had anticipated this situation and acted accordingly. Senator Dorian was difficult on a good day. Tonight, he was going to be impossible.

"What is going on?" Dorian asked, raising his voice again.

"Settle down, Senator," Cal said, motioning with his hands. There were few people Dorian let order him around, but Cal was one of them.

"You'd better start talking, Newfellow. I pay you to keep my name out of the news, not plaster me across the front page!"

"Senator, we cannot control where a body floats to shore," Cal reminded him. "All we can do is control what happens if that situation arises, which is what we've done."

"It was him, wasn't it? The Red River Slayer?"

A shiver went through Mack when he said the name. He didn't know who the guy was, but he was ruthless, and too many women were paying the price.

"We don't know that, Senator. People drown in the Mississippi all the time. We can't jump to conclusions," Cal reminded him.

"Nice try, Newfellow. Do you have any idea how bad this is going to look for my reelection campaign? I can't host a party here now!"

"Why not?" Mack asked with his arms across his chest and feet spread. He wanted the senator to know they wouldn't back down to his demands.

"Why not? Do you think anyone will want to come here for a party when there's a killer on the loose?"

Dorian's voice was way too loud for the small space, and Mack took another step toward him. "If the woman was murdered, it didn't happen here. The ME put her time of death closer to three to four days ago. While it was unfortunate that she washed up on your shoreline, no one is at risk of being killed here. For any future campaign parties you may host, we'll be here with more staff to protect the property from the road, the woods and the shoreline as we always do. There's nothing to worry about, Senator."

The tension in the room was taut, and Mack steeled himself for the tongue-lashing from the man, but it never came. His shoulders slumped, and he wiped his hand across his forehead before he planted it on his hip. "I'm sorry. I was terrified something had happened to Eleanor, and then to find out another young woman had died riled me up. They have to stop this guy."

"We're all in agreement about that," Cal assured him, directing him to a chair in front of the computer monitors. "Let's go over the footage from tonight. Maybe you'll spot something we overlooked."

Cal started the camera replay and lifted a brow at Mack from behind the senator. Mack bit back his chuckle. They didn't miss anything, and he was confident they'd played the entire night by the book. None of that mattered unless the senator believed it as well. The last thing Secure One needed was Dorian bad-mouthing them all over the country. Cal would do anything to make sure that didn't happen.

Chapter Five

"When will my dad get here?" Eleanor asked in a huff.

"He's chatting with Cal and the team now, so I'm sure he will be here soon, Eleanor," Charlotte answered, trying to placate her.

"Chatting," she said with an eye roll. "More like yelling and throwing his name around."

Eric's snort from across the room drove Charlotte to glare at him.

"What? She clearly knows her father." He gave her the palms out, and this time it was Eleanor who giggle-snorted.

"I also know Cal doesn't let my dad push him around. I'm glad about that. You should always stand your ground with bullies."

"You're saying your father is a bully?" Charlotte asked.

"Just calling a spade a spade. My dad thinks he's president of the United States already. He hasn't even run yet."

"Is he planning to?" Eric asked, leaning forward.

"Last I heard," Eleanor said with boredom. "It's all he talks about right now. I'm sure that's what he's planning to reveal at the next party. He needs big bucks to throw his hat in the ring, which means he needs big donors to like him."

Charlotte didn't follow politics, much less Minnesota politics, but she would do a deep dive once they got back to Secure One. Dorian was a long-time client of theirs, and she wanted to familiarize herself with him, his career and his family. Well, his family was easy. He was a single father to Eleanor and spent most of his time in Washington while his daughter lived in Minnesota with his mother. Her grandmother raised Eleanor while Dorian pursued his career. Eleanor's mother was killed in a car crash when she was a baby, and Dorian had never remarried. Eric shot Charlotte a look before he picked up the tablet and started typing. He was probably making notes since the team was busy with Dorian in the command center.

"Why can't I go to my room?" The girl was frustrated, and Charlotte couldn't blame her.

"I'm sorry, Eleanor. Cal wants you to stay here with us until they're done briefing your dad on what happened tonight. I'm sure it won't be much longer."

"Please, call me Ella. Eleanor makes me feel so…" She motioned her hand around in the air until Charlotte answered.

"Old?"

Ella pointed at her. "Ancient."

"I understand," Charlotte assured her with a chuckle. "I feel the same way about the name Charlotte."

"I don't think Charlotte is a bad name, but maybe a little old-fashioned. Do you have a nickname?"

"I used to," Charlotte said, pausing on the last word.

"Well, what is it?"

"I've only told one other person this before." She paused, and Ella cocked her head, fully engaged with her now. Charlotte didn't want to lose that connection, so she took a deep breath and spoke. "Hope. I was an artist in my former life."

"You're still an artist. A damn good one," Eric said without lifting his head from the tablet.

That made both Charlotte and Ella smile. "I'm still an

artist, but I was a street artist back then. Do you know what that is?"

"Sure," Ella said with a shrug. "You tagged buildings. Graffiti."

"I guess some would call it graffiti, but I painted murals on buildings while everyone else slept. They were my way of bringing hope to the other kids on the streets."

"Your tag name was Hope?"

Charlotte nodded, trying to force a smile to her lips, but it didn't come. She noted Eric nodded his head once as though he respected her. No one had ever respected her before, but that was the feeling she got from him and Ella. She could change her name to what it was before The Madame washed her history, but doing that meant she'd have to face her past as Hope. After all, there was a reason she'd jumped on The Madame's offer to change her name and find a new life. She just hadn't expected that new life to be as an escort, drug mule and mercenary against her will.

"That's a cool story. You must be a fantastic artist if you painted murals on buildings."

"She is," Eric said, still without lifting his head. "Charlotte—Hope—should show you some of her work. She doesn't just draw a picture. She tells a story. She has natural talent, and that can't be learned."

"Would you show me?" Ella asked with excitement. "I do some drawing, but I'm not that good."

"Yet," Charlotte said with a wink. "We all get better with practice and time. I don't have my sketchbook here, but I promise to bring it to the next party. We can hang out in mobile command and draw."

"That would be great," Ella said with excitement, but Charlotte also noted a hint of relief in her voice. "I hate his parties. He makes me show my face for a little bit, but then I always find a place to hide to avoid all those people."

"I feel your pain," Eric said, lowering the tablet. "There's nothing worse than a bunch of snobby adults jockeying for the top spot as richest in the room."

Ella laughed while she pointed at Eric. "I like you. Not many people get what it's like to deal with politicians and their donors. It's exhausting. That's why I live in St. Paul with my grandma. I want to go to school and live a normal life. Well, as normal as possible. Yes, I have to go to private school, but I could never live in Washington, DC, year-round. I go in the summer, and that's enough for me."

"I'm ex-army," Eric said. "I know what it's like to deal with the government and politicians. I don't blame you for wanting time away from that three-ring circus."

Eric's phone rang, and he held up his finger, then answered it, stepping into the corner of the room to talk to the caller.

Ella glanced at him and then leaned in closer to Charlotte. "I'm not kidding here when I say I need to go to the bathroom in my room or I'm going to ruin this gown."

"Understood," Charlotte said with a nod. "Let me get Eric."

"He's busy. Besides, I don't want him ushering me to my room to get pads. Please."

Charlotte could see Ella was embarrassed, but she bit her lip with nervousness. They weren't supposed to leave the room on Cal's orders. Then again, he didn't put them in a room with a bathroom either, so she had to assume he knew they'd have to leave for that.

"Okay. This place is crawling with cops. It won't be a big deal to run up there, but I need to tell Eric, and I'm going with you. To your room and back. No other stops."

Ella held up her hands in agreement, so Charlotte walked over to Eric and leaned in to whisper. "She needs the restroom. It's an emergency. I'll take her there and bring her right back. Will Cal object?"

Eric put his hand over the receiver, glanced at Ella and back to her. "Not much we can do other than be careful. There are cops everywhere but stay alert. I'm not expecting any other problems tonight though."

Charlotte nodded and tucked her required Secure One Taser into the holster on her belt. While she was trained on handling a gun, she rarely carried one. Too many innocent people had died from a bullet meant for someone else, and she couldn't live with herself if she were the cause of an innocent person's death.

She motioned for Eleanor to follow her to the door. This was her chance to prove to Cal that she was part of the team, whether she was cooking for them or doing unexpected bodyguard duty on a US senator's daughter. Cal had trained her for this, and when she'd asked him why, his answer was simple: *You never know when you will have to keep yourself or someone else safe in this business. If you work here, you're part of the team, and everyone on the team does this training.* She always thought she'd never need it, but tonight, she was ready to prove she'd learned her lessons well.

CHARLOTTE STOOD OUTSIDE the bathroom door and waited for Ella. She had agreed to let her change clothes before they went back to where Eric was waiting. She was right, it didn't make sense to parade around in a ball gown, but Charlotte also didn't want to be gone too long.

"Hey, Hope," Ella called from inside the bathroom. Charlotte didn't cringe at the name, and that surprised her. "Did you happen to see Tia and Leticia before they left?"

"I did," Charlotte said, reminding herself not to spill their secret. "They left with their parents after they talked to the cops."

"Were they okay?" she called back through the door, and Charlotte heard rustling on the other side as though she were hanging up the gown.

"They were fine. Why?"

"They found a dead woman in the river. I figured they'd be shaken."

The door opened, and Ella stepped out wearing a pair of pajama pants and a long T-shirt. She was ready for bed, and honestly, so was Charlotte, but she dragged a smile to her face and nodded. "They were shaken up, but by the time they left, they'd calmed down."

"I felt so bad when I found out they were the ones who found her," Ella said, following Charlotte to the door.

"Why?" A look left and then right had Charlotte stepping out into the hallway with Ella.

"They go through enough already. It's hard being in the closet. Then, when you finally get some time alone, that happens."

"Wait. You know?" Charlotte asked.

"Everyone knows," Ella said with an eye roll. "We go to a Catholic school, so we all pretend we don't know just to protect them."

"Wow, I wasn't expecting that."

"Why? Because I'm a snobby rich kid who doesn't care about anyone else?"

Charlotte stopped and spun on her heel to face her. "I would never think that, Ella. I've known you barely an hour and know you're nothing like your father. You care about getting to know people. I wasn't expecting you to say that because the girls told us no one else knew."

Ella's shrug was simple. "That's what they need to believe, so as a class, we decided we would let them believe it. We protect them whenever someone starts asking too many questions and always make sure we have parties where there's a place for them to escape together. Did you see them together?" Charlotte nodded but didn't say anything. "Then you know that they've already found their soulmate at sixteen."

Charlotte turned and started back down the hallway, keeping Ella on the inside of her against the wall. "Do you believe in soulmates?"

"I do. I think that's why my dad has never remarried. My mom was his, and when she died, a piece of him did too. He never dated again after she died. Women try, trust me, but he's not interested. I wish he would though."

"Why?"

"It might chill him out a little. He's always wound so tightly that I'm afraid he'll have a heart attack one day."

"I agree with you. Your dad strikes me as an all-work-and-no-play kind of guy."

"He so is, but this summer, when I'm in Washington, I'm going to do something about it."

Charlotte had already messaged Eric to let him know they were on their way back, and as they started down the stairs, she noticed that the house had cleared out and was much quieter.

"What are you going to do about it? Set him up?"

"That's exactly what I'm going to do!" Ella said, laughter filling the stairwell as they stepped onto the lavish parquet flooring. Calling this house a "cabin" insulted the artists who'd poured their souls into it. The view during the day must be breathtaking from the large bay windows that faced the back of it, and the chef's kitchen and extensive library weren't something you saw in most "cabins" in Minnesota. Charlotte hadn't lived in Minnesota long, but she did know that much.

"I'm sure that'll go over well," Charlotte said with a

chuckle just as a man dressed in black stepped out of a hallway and grasped Ella's elbow.

"I'll take Miss Dorian to her father now. Thank you for your help," he said, tugging Ella's arm to follow him.

Charlotte instinctively grabbed Ella's other arm and held tight. "I need to see ID, and I'll have to call my boss before I can relinquish Miss Dorian into your care." She sounded calm, but she wasn't. She was panicking, so she forced the sensation back and focused on her training. *If you ever feel like something is off, hit your all-call button, and we'll come running.*

Mack's words ran through her head, but she hesitated, taking stock of the man again. He wore a black suit and coat, a black hat and had an earpiece running from his jacket to his ear. The tall man kept his head bent low, ensuring that Charlotte couldn't get a good look at him.

"I said, I need to see your ID."

"I'm protection detail for Senator Dorian," he repeated. "I don't have to show you anything."

"Then you can't take Miss Dorian. We'll wait for her father in the designated area. Come on, Ella."

Charlotte tugged on Ella's arm, but the man didn't release her. The girl looked terrified, which told Charlotte that she had never seen this man before. Without hesitation, Charlotte hit the button on her vest and then took hold of Ella with both hands. "You should leave now unless you have ID."

She unhooked the button on her holster, but she never got to pull the Taser before a fist flew at her from her right. She dodged it but not before it glanced off her jaw and tossed her head to the side. She didn't let go of Ella, who was now screaming for someone to help them. Charlotte couldn't worry about help arriving. She had to concentrate on protecting Ella. She was afraid he would punch Ella next, so she yanked the girl to the left and then kicked out with her right leg, landing a hit in the guy's solar plexus. He let out a huff, but it wasn't enough to stop him from hitting her dead in the eye with a sharp jab.

Ella had fallen to the floor and was crab-walking backward as the man went for her. Gathering her wits, Charlotte struck him in the back with her elbow and then hit him behind the knees with a back kick that sent him to the floor. Commotion and shouting filled the house as men came running from all doors, but the man in black wasn't giving up. He turned and swept Charlotte's feet out from under her, and she fell, hitting the floor with her head. Dazed, she knew she had to fight him off long enough for Mack or Eric to get to them. All she could think to do was lift her feet and kick up. A smile lifted her lips when the resounding crack told her she'd made contact with her target. He bellowed and pinwheeled backward, right into Eric's waiting arms, who quickly subdued him.

Charlotte didn't get up off the floor. She just stared at the cathedral ceiling, the colors swirling and spinning in the atmosphere around her. She had to catch her breath before she could move again. The fight had taken everything out of her.

"Hope!" Ella said, her face swimming in her line of sight. "Are you okay?"

Charlotte wanted to answer her, but all she could do was watch the swirling colors above her head.

"Hope, I mean, Charlotte needs help!" Ella yelled. Charlotte could hear the frantic tone of her voice and reached for her, trying to reassure her, but her hand missed its target and fell back to the hardwood floor. "Someone, please, help her!"

A voice broke through the din in the room, and she begged her mind to focus on the sound. It was her name on

Mack's lips as he scooped her up, wrapped her in his protective arms and started running.

"I need a medic!" Charlotte found his bellowing voice more soothing than scary. "I'm going to get you help, Charlotte," he promised, and it was only then that she closed her eyes.

MACK PACED ACROSS the floor of mobile command, where the team had met up after the attempted kidnapping of Dorian's daughter. They'd have lost Ella tonight if it hadn't been for Charlotte. What had Eric been thinking letting them go alone? He would never say it to the man, he felt bad enough, but Charlotte had paid a heavy price.

"I'm fine, Mack," she said from the corner chair where she sat with an ice pack on her face. Not only did she have a concussion from hitting her head on the floor, but the jerk had given her a black eye and swollen jaw.

"You're a warrior, Charlotte, but I can't stop thinking about how close we came to a kidnapping on our watch."

"Me neither," she said, wincing when she held the ice to her eye. "Did anyone get anything out of the guy?"

All eyes were on Cal and Eric. They'd taken the guy aside and had a "chat" with him before the police arrived. "Not much," Cal said with a shake of his head. "I have to hand it to you. You broke the guy's jaw with that last kick. He was twice your size and strength."

"He wasn't taking Ella on my watch. When she looked at me with terror, I knew she didn't know the guy, which meant he wasn't part of the senator's detail. I had to stop him long enough for you guys to wade in and help me."

"I'm proud of you, Charlotte. Hand-to-hand isn't easy for anyone, especially when you're outsized the way you were. That was Secure One protection at its finest."

Mack noticed her chest puff up and her shoulders straighten at Cal's words.

"He's right, Charlotte. You saved Ella, and all of us here know it." Mack glanced at Eric, who was glaring at them with his arms crossed over his chest. Whether he was ticked at them or himself, Mack couldn't say.

"I'm glad she's safe, but we have to find out who this guy is."

"The cops will know that quickly, but so will we," Cal said, holding up a glass slide. "I accidentally got the guy to touch this." He gave her a wink. "I'll get Mina working on it back at Secure One. In the meantime, we have to assume that it's either tied to Dorian's reelection campaign or the body they found tonight."

"I'm leaning toward his reelection campaign," Mack said. "He's got enemies, and what better way to get you to back off something than to leverage the one person you love the most."

"Agreed," Cal said. "I think it was coincidence, or else the person behind the kidnapping got wind of the chaotic events tonight and decided he'd take advantage of it. It was smart to send someone in when there were already so many people in a tight space. You could get away without being noticed."

"Wait," Charlotte said, leaning forward. "The guy we got isn't the person behind the kidnapping?"

"Not according to him," Eric said, finally engaging with the team. "He told me he was hired to get the girl and bring her to a secure location where he'd hand her off for a big payday."

"More likely, he'd trade her for a bullet to the head," Cal muttered, and Eric pointed at him.

"So he was doing someone's dirty work. What does Senator Dorian think?" Selina asked while checking Charlotte's blood pressure.

Mack kept his gaze trained on the readout and was relieved when her blood pressure was normal.

"He thinks it has something to do with his future bid for the presidency," Eric said. "Mack's right. He's made enemies. There aren't many politicians who don't, but Dorian seems especially good at it. Someone saw an opportunity and took it tonight. I shouldn't have let you go alone to her room."

Charlotte brushed her free hand at him and sighed. "I thought nothing of it either," she said, trying to reassure him. "When I took her up there, cops were everywhere. There was no way to know this guy would appear out of nowhere and attempt a kidnapping amid that much law enforcement."

"It was brazen," Cal said. "No doubt about it, but there's nothing we can do until Mina gets me a name and we can look into his past."

"I doubt it will lead us anywhere. I would bet my month's salary that he's got a laundry list of previous convictions and multiple addresses where he's lived," Eric said. It was easy to hear the frustration in his tone, which was mirrored in everyone's body language. It was after 3:00 a.m., and they'd been going for over eighteen hours. Everyone needed rest and food. Good thing their cook turned bodyguard had stocked the kitchen with easy-to-grab meals.

"Most likely," Cal agreed, "but you know Mina. All she needs is one tiny hint of a path, and she will find where it leads. We trust our team at home until we can get there, which won't be until tomorrow. Right now, we all need sleep." Heads nodded, and shoulders slumped at the idea of finally closing their eyes.

"Selina, let's keep Charlotte—"

A knock on the door interrupted Cal. "I want to talk to you, Newfellow!"

Mack heard Eric swear from the corner, giving him a mental fist bump. Dorian was the last person they needed to deal with right now.

"Let me do the talking," Cal said, and heads nodded as he opened the door to the senator and his entourage.

Dorian climbed the stairs and stood with his hands on his hips in front of the team. "How in the hell did that happen?" he demanded, pointing behind him. "I pay you exorbitant amounts of money to keep the security tight on this place!"

Cal held up his hand and nodded. "You do, Senator. What happened tonight was unforgivable. I completely understand if you want to cancel your contract with Secure One. We let you down tonight."

Mack glanced at his boss with surprise and wasn't entirely sure that Cal didn't want exactly that to happen. Cal had grown tired of the senator's dramatics long before tonight. The man was fussy, ornery, demanding and never took the time to understand why or how something did or didn't work before he flew off the handle.

Ron Dorian's shoulders dropped an inch when he shook his head before he spoke. "I don't want to cancel my contract. I realize there were extenuating circumstances tonight that you had no control over. Though, I do want to know how that little thing in the corner was the only one around to save my daughter from a kidnapper!"

He gestured at Charlotte while he glared at the rest of the men in the room. Eric stood and walked toward the man. He wasn't going to follow Cal's no-talking order. "She was with your daughter because you put us in a room without access to necessary facilities. Ella is a sixteen-year-old girl who needed a restroom for reasons I don't think I should go into here. I sent the trained Secure One operative your daughter felt comfortable with and stayed in contact with them the entire time they were gone. I had all the exits covered, meaning no one was getting out of the house without an ID check." Eric held up his hand to the man who was ready to speak. "And before you ask, we don't know how he got inside. He may have snuck in when parents were coming and going with their kids. We will search our camera footage for that. When our operative indicated she needed help, I was there in less than twenty seconds to offer her assistance, though I'm sure it felt much longer to her and Ella. You can be unhappy with what happened here tonight, but our team did what we're trained to do regardless of the situation. So, yes, our trained operative in the corner currently nursing a concussion saved your daughter tonight, as any of us would have."

Eric faced off with the man for a moment and then stepped back and sat in the chair again. If a pin had dropped, everyone would have heard it. Mack couldn't remember the last time Eric had stepped up and taken the lead role. He wasn't sure he picked the right time to do it, but that was between him and Cal.

Dorian turned to Cal. "My daughter wants her," he said, pointing at Charlotte, "as her bodyguard until this guy is caught."

"Charlotte is not a bodyguard," Cal said.

"I don't care what you call her, but she will be by my daughter's side until this guy is behind bars."

"Sir—"

"Don't sir me," Dorian said. "Just listen. I want the girl, Mack, and the mouthy one," he pointed at Eric, "in my house in twenty minutes."

"I'll arrange it, sir," Cal said rather than continue to argue with him. "But Charlotte will need rest tonight. She can't take charge of your daughter until she is no longer concussed."

"That's what he is for," he said, pointing at Eric again. "We both know she's in no shape to protect my daughter now, but Eleanor doesn't, so we'll let her continue to think Charlotte is her bodyguard while he provides the muscle. I want Mack there because I trust him to keep the perimeter safe."

"Eleanor is staying at the cabin and not returning to St. Paul?" Mack asked to clarify.

"I don't want my mother involved in this, so I'm keeping Ella here until they have the guy behind the kidnapping in handcuffs. She's on spring break this coming week, and if it takes longer than that to find the guy, she will do school online for the duration."

"I don't know how long I can be without two of my head men," Cal said, and Mack could hear in his voice that he was dead serious. Leaving Mack and Eric here meant a heavier workload at Secure One for the rest of the team. At least they wouldn't have to worry about Dorian's place, but that still spread them thin.

"Then you better find more guys or tell the police to hurry up. I have to fly to Washington for a vote. I will return to Minnesota once that is completed to prepare for my reelection campaign party. Understood?"

"Understood. I'll need to brief the team staying here and set them up with equipment in the morning. That means our mobile command will remain here until then."

"I'll need to assess Charlotte before we can leave as well," Selina added.

Mack bit back a smile. Everyone was tired of Dorian pushing them around, it appeared. He noticed that Charlotte had remained silent through the entire exchange. He glanced at her and noticed she was sagging in the chair. She needed rest.

"Dorian, I need a room for Charlotte immediately. She needs rest if she's going to hang out with Eleanor tomorrow," Mack said, taking a step forward.

"My staff has already readied a room. I'll see you there shortly."

Before anyone could respond, he turned and left the command center, his entourage closing in behind him and following him back to the house. When Mack turned back to the team, they were all awaiting Cal's orders.

"You heard the man. Mack, carry Charlotte to the house and get her settled."

"I can walk," she said, but Mack didn't like how soft her voice sounded. He glanced at Selina, who gave him a headshake. He'd be carrying her.

"Eric will follow you with bags for the night. Tomorrow, we'll regroup and figure this out. Nothing we can do until we've had some sleep."

Mack walked over to Charlotte and scooped her into his arms, her cry of surprise weak enough that everyone made way for them as he left the RV. Mack glanced down into the battered face of the woman in his arms and smiled.

"I know you feel like you went ten rounds with Mike Tyson, but remember, you were the hero we needed tonight. I'm so proud of you for not backing down and protecting Ella when she needed it."

"I've been Ella, and no one was there for me, Mack," she said as she rested her head against his chest. "I righted more than one wrong with a few of those kicks."

She fell quiet, and soon, her soft even breathing reached his ears. He wanted to rage against the world that she'd had to go through those things, but they had made her the strong determined woman who refused to shrink away from the flame. She had been burned so many times, but she proved to him tonight that she wasn't afraid to walk right back into the fire when it mattered most.

Her past made her a soldier.

What she'd done tonight made her a hero.

Chapter Six

The bus rumbled beneath her as she settled back into her seat and pulled a blanket up to her neck. The darkness surrounding the bus relaxed her. She was one step closer to safety. It had been sheer luck when she clicked on the radio in the truck and heard that news bulletin. Another woman had been found in the river, and she'd bet anything she'd once been in the same house in Pennsylvania. Her first piece of luck came when they mentioned a company, Secure One, had found her while working for a party at Senator Dorian's house outside of St. Paul.

When the sun came up, she ditched the truck and walked into a Salvation Army. They had bought her story that she was trying to return home to Minnesota but lost all her belongings and wallet when she accepted a ride with the wrong person. She had fought hard not to roll her eyes when she said it. She hadn't been given a choice when she took that ride, but she wasn't about to tell them that. They'd fed her, clothed her and bought her a bus ticket to St. Paul. Now all she had to do was figure out how to contact this Secure One place when she got there. She hoped they'd listen to her story and try to help her figure out this mess. Now that she knew The Miss was dead and The Madame was behind bars, she had to take the chance that Secure One could help her. If she didn't, she might as well have died in that room.

MACK TOOK IN the space around him. He was satisfied with the equipment Cal had given him to stay in touch with the team at Secure One. They'd be connected in real-time, and whenever they needed answers, someone would be there to give them. He didn't think Cal would stay gone long, but he did need to get back to Secure One and help Roman sort out their priorities before he returned to St. Paul. Mack was confident that he and Eric could handle any situation that arose. While they were in a holding pattern, he'd look for answers about the river deaths.

Before they left this morning, Selina checked Charlotte over one more time and gave her a list of things she should and shouldn't do with a concussion. Mack and Eric had plenty of experience taking care of head injuries and wouldn't let her do anything she shouldn't for a few days. When Charlotte woke this morning, she was chipper and not in much pain, so Selina was sure the bruises would stick around longer than the concussion. She was in the kitchen with Ella, making cookies and discussing art, which seemed to make Ella incredibly happy.

He hit the button on their quick connect link and waited while the system rang through to the Secure One control room.

"Secure one, Whiskey," a voice said.

"Secure two, Mike," he answered, and Mina's face popped up on the screen.

"Miss me already?" she asked with a chuckle.

"I didn't want you to think I didn't care." His wink made her smile. "I had a free minute and wanted to ask a favor."

"I'll do what I can."

"I know you have a database where you're keeping track of what rivers the women were found in, correct?"

"I cannot confirm nor deny that information."

Mack couldn't help but grin. She had been an FBI agent for years, and old habits died hard. The fact remained that she wasn't supposed to have that information and didn't get it through the proper channels at the FBI.

"Should you have that information, would you be able to highlight the rivers on a map for me? It would help me to see it laid out that way."

"If I have that information, I can send it through our secure channels in about an hour."

Mack pointed and winked. "Thanks, Min, you're the best."

"Are you hitting on my wife, sir?" Roman asked, sticking his face into the camera from behind Mina.

"Wouldn't dream of it," Mack answered with laughter. "I'm afraid of her husband."

"Someone should be since she's not. Are you guys managing okay over there? That was a hell of a night you had."

"We're good. It was a rough night, but it could have turned out worse than it did, so we'll take it as a win."

"How is our young scrappy one?" Mina asked. "I was terrified and proud all at the same time when Cal told us what she did."

Mack knew the feeling well. "I'm not sure if terrified even begins to cover it. I've been in combat situations that scared me less than the events of last night."

"It's okay, Mack," Roman said, leaning on the desk now. "It's okay to feel both of those things and admit you have a connection to her."

A brisk cross of his arms had Roman smirking before Mack even said a word. "A connection of commonality, maybe. Otherwise, that's a negative."

Roman and Mina had to bite back a snort, but Mina recovered first. "I'll prioritize that info and get it to you in a few minutes. Okay to tell Cal?"

"Of course," Mack agreed, straightening his back and letting go of the tension in his shoulders from their razzing. "I'm looking for a pattern, so if any of you find one, shout it out. We have to start somewhere."

Mina pointed at the camera. "Couldn't agree more. Whiskey, out."

The screen went blank, and Mack sighed as he lowered himself to a chair. They were right, there was a connection between him and Charlotte, but it was one he had to force himself not to think about or consider. They both had ghosts, but he wore his every day as a reminder that he had been weak when he should have been strong. He couldn't forgive himself for how those ghosts died, so there was no way she would ever look at him twice once she knew the truth. Being trapped here with her wasn't making it easier to distance himself, especially when he'd been the one to wake her every two hours last night.

The exhaustion wasn't helping him look at this case with a clear lens either. He forced his mind to look at the information analytically. What did they know about this guy? He pulled a pad of paper closer to him and grabbed a pen. In the beginning, he was impulsive but slowly, over time, perfected his presentation of his victims and his timeline. *Why didn't they find any victims for two years?* Mack underlined that question several times. Maybe he was in jail or out of the country? His last victim was found shortly before The Madame was arrested, and his next victim wasn't found until The Miss was in Arizona. Coincidence? Mack underlined that word several times too.

As far as they knew, the guy had to have connections to get the women and hold them somewhere. That is, assuming he'd held onto Layla for the whole of the eighteen months she'd been gone. Maybe he hadn't. Maybe he got her from someone else. Either way, he had to have connections and be cunning enough not to get caught. He would also need money and a vehicle. If he were using the same river repeatedly, it would be easy to pinpoint his location within the river's course, but he never used the same river twice.

He sat up immediately. That had been hiding in the back of his mind somewhere. He'd double-check when Mina sent him the map, but as far as he remembered, the women were never in the same river. Why was their perp driving around the country? Just to throw the feds off his tail? Was he getting the women from the same states, or was he transporting them already dead? Or was he transporting them alive and then killing them near the river?

Drawing a new column, he wrote the traits they knew the perp to have just by what his crimes revealed. He was connected, cunning, well-off, likely narcissistic, controlling and got off on having power over others. Mack paused with his pen on the pad. Maybe they were looking for this guy in all the wrong places. He dropped the pen and grabbed a laptop, then opened an incognito window. Narcissists like to talk about themselves. They yearned for accolades, even when they couldn't come right out and talk about their crimes.

Narcissists were everywhere, but Mack knew one place a lot of them assembled to swap war stories, so to speak. There was a forum for everything, but some forums held darker content than others, and Mack intended to start his search there.

Chapter Seven

Mack stood in the makeshift office and stared at the map projected on the wall. Something was bugging him about this case, but he couldn't put his finger on it.

"Mack?" a voice asked from the doorway, and he turned to see Charlotte peeking in the door. "Everything okay? It's late."

"Everything's fine," he said. "It is late. Why are you still up?"

Her smile brightened his day no matter when she hit him with it, and tonight was no different. Her black eye and bruised chin didn't detract from her beauty. In fact, in his eyes, those bruises reminded him that behind her beauty was an irrefutable strength few people had.

She stepped into the room and walked past the large wooden desk the senator used when he was home. Now it held Secure One computers and link-ups to headquarters. They had a dead body and attempted kidnapping on their watch, and he wasn't any happier about it than Cal. While it was beyond their control, it also put their name back in the media. Cal had tried to minimize publicity about their security service since The Miss was killed, but it appeared the universe was not cooperating with him.

"That or this is still tied to The Madame," Mack muttered.

"What now?" Charlotte asked, her back stiffening at the utterance of her former boss's name.

"I'm sorry." He grimaced at himself. "I didn't mean to say that aloud. I was thinking about how we can't keep Secure One out of the news no matter how hard we try. Cal is frustrated that The Madame and The Miss have kept us on the public's radar."

"And you think all of this," she motioned around the map, "is tied to The Madame?"

"I don't know, but according to Roman and Mina, several women were found in rivers while The Madame was operating." His head swung back and forth in frustration as he tried to see a pattern that wasn't there.

"What is this?" Charlotte pointed at the map of the United States. "Rivers?"

"Yeah," he said, his hand going through his short brown hair in frustration. Unlike Cal, he'd gotten rid of the high and tight hairstyle the moment he left the field on a stretcher. His boss liked to tease him that he looked like an FBI agent now, just like Roman. He'd shake his head in disdain but be laughing while he did it. "Each highlighted river represents a place where at least one body was found since they started finding women. The most recent women were wearing red gowns."

"So, the bodies found in the rivers while The Madame was in operation weren't in red?" she asked.

"Not according to Mina. It was only when the recent bodies were discovered that they were wearing red gowns. A news reporter dubbed him The Red River Slayer, and it stuck." The moniker might be accurate, but something about it set his teeth on edge.

"If you think about it, I could have been one of those women."

Mack sucked in air through his nose. "I try not to think about that, okay?"

"I think about it all the time." She stared at the wall rather than make eye contact with him. "When they found the first woman, I was new to the Red Rye House. When other women I lived with started disappearing, I thought they left of their own free will. But I was naive enough back then to believe we could leave."

"But you didn't know if the women who disappeared were the women they found."

Her shrug gave him the answer. "How could I? It wasn't like we were allowed to watch or listen to the news. We were very sheltered in Red Rye."

"Nothing?" Mack asked in surprise with a lifted brow.

"Nothing. We had no cable or news channels on the television, and all we could do was stream movies. We also didn't have a radio. I heard about them finding the women on the radio when I was on a *date*," which she put in quotation marks, "but they said they hadn't identified them yet. Not that they *couldn't* identify them. I didn't find that out until I left The Miss and came here."

"And now we've found another woman from The Miss."

"Layla." She said the name with reverence. As though saying it that way gave her an identity. "When she disappeared, I figured The Miss sold or killed her. She wasn't bringing any money in, and The Miss didn't put up with that for long."

"And she disappeared eighteen months ago?" Mack asked again.

"I thought about it, and the timeline is correct within a few months. I've already been at Secure One for six months, and she disappeared about a year before I surrendered."

"This is the first time we've had a timeline. You're the reason we have it, even if you did disobey orders. We'll have to talk about your propensity to do that."

"Last time I checked, Cal's my boss, not you." She looked him up and down in a way that brought a smile to his lips.

"Noted, but when you're here with me, I'm the boss regarding quick decisions as the situation warrants."

"Accepted, but I will protect Ella no matter the cost. You may as well know that."

"I do," he promised, tracing his thumb over her jaw, the bump smaller after a night of rest and ice. "But I don't have to like it. Have you always been this brave, Char?"

Her blue eyes held his, and he watched her wrap her arms around herself in a hug. "No. I used to live in fear every second of the day. I was afraid of my foster parents and siblings when I was a kid. When I hit the streets, I was afraid of the dark and the things it held, so I painted at night. It was safer to be awake and see them coming. When I started working for The Madame, I was afraid of the men she made me date. When I started working for The Miss, I was afraid of everything."

"What changed?"

"Me." Her answer was simple, but he knew the explanation was far more complicated. "When I looked back on my life, fear was the common thread running through it. I could keep being afraid and keep being taken advantage of, or I could snip the thread of fear and see what happened."

Mack nodded, the explanation making sense to him. "I understand." Her snort was sarcastic and pithy. He turned her chin to meet his gaze. "I know you don't think so, but I do. My dad and I were in a car accident when I was a toddler. I lived. He didn't. My mother struggled the rest of her life with the fear of losing me. She didn't let me do anything out of fear that I'd get hurt and die too. I grew up thinking every new experience was scary and should be avoided. Our experiences were different, there is no doubt, but I understand what you mean by a thread of fear. I had to cut mine too."

"When you went into the service?"

"No, when my mother got cancer when I was a teenager, I realized she wasn't going to make it. Suddenly, I had to figure out how to live unafraid."

"I'm still afraid a lot of the time, but I tell myself that when I do something even while I'm afraid, the next thing I have to do will be a little easier."

A smile lifted his lips, and he nodded. "You're right, and it's working. I remember the woman who surrendered to us six months ago, and she's not the same woman standing before me today."

This time, it was her smile that beamed back at him. "I'm glad someone noticed. I've worked hard in therapy to accept that a lot of what's happened to me was done to me and not something I did to myself."

"That's important to remember," Mack agreed. It was true for her, but not for him. What happened to him was something he had done to himself. He only had to look at his boots to be reminded of that.

"I argued that I did make a lot of bad choices, and the therapist agreed, but she also pointed out that I never had any good choices to start with."

"She makes a point."

Charlotte tipped her head in agreement and crossed her arms over her chest. "After I thought about it, I decided that I could continue to make bad choices or start from scratch and make better ones. Go to therapy. Work a job. Be part of a team instead of going it alone."

"The changes you've made the last six months haven't been overlooked. I hope you know that. We're all incredibly proud of you."

Mack noted the pink creep up her cheeks at his compliment. That was something else she needed to learn how to accept—how integral she was to the team.

"Thank you," she said, glancing down at the floor.

He tipped her chin up again and held her gaze. "Hold your head high, Charlotte. You've got grit and proved it, including when you fought off someone twice your size to protect a young girl. That takes guts. How is your head?"

"Okay," she said with a shy smile. "I'm being careful and following Selina's orders so I don't make anything worse. It's been fun hanging out and being with Ella today, but I'm ready to work now."

"Eric is here to protect Ella."

"Understood, but I can help in other ways. Let me help you figure this out." She motioned at the map and took a step closer. "Some of these rivers run through more than one state. How do we know what location he put them in the river?"

"We don't," Mack answered with frustration. "That's part of the problem. Obviously, everything floats downstream, and some rivers run through several states. For instance, the Mississippi flows through seven states. It's nearly impossible to know where the body was dumped."

"Which means he gets away with it longer because these rivers run all over the country. Well, except for Layla."

Mack's attention shifted from the map to the woman who always, despite her ordeal, had a ready smile. Her long blond hair was wavy, and she wore it tied behind her head with a band. Her blue eyes were luminous in the light from the projector, even with a black eye, and her lips were pursed as she finished the last word.

"Except for Layla?"

"Think about it, Mack," she said, stepping in front of him to point at the map. Her body slid across his in a whisper of material that sent a burning need straight through him.

"She was found outside St. Paul, right?" He nodded, and she raised her hand to point at the top of the map. "And we know the Mississippi originates at Lake Itasca. That's what, about three hours north of where she was found?"

How had he not thought of that? She was right. The Mississippi headwaters were only an hour from Secure One, the way the crow flies.

"We should have thought of that," he said, snapping the projector off and leaving the lights low. "Thank you for pointing it out. I can't believe we missed something so obvious."

Her tiny hand waved his words away. "The difference is that you have too much information about all the other women. Since I don't know anything about those cases, my mind tracked the possibilities for just Layla. Do you think that means the killer is from Minnesota?"

Mack didn't cut himself any slack despite her insistence. He should have been concentrating on one woman's journey at a time instead of as a group. That was exactly what he would do tomorrow. He'd focus solely on each woman and see if a pattern developed rather than as a whole, where the pattern seemed willy-nilly.

"There's no way to know that, but my gut says no. The women have been found in rivers all over the country. In the beginning, the bodies were found randomly, then we had a period of inactivity, and now, they're finding a woman every six weeks."

"Which means we only have about five weeks until another woman like Layla is found," Charlotte said, and Mack noticed a shiver go up her spine.

He didn't stop himself from reaching over to tenderly rub the base of her back. "I'm sorry. You shouldn't have to keep witnessing women you know dying in this way."

"Those women didn't do anything to deserve this. They

were looking for a better life than one on the streets, just like I was, so as long as I'm still breathing, I'll fight for them."

"I know," Mack assured her, pulling her into him and wrapping his arm around her shoulder. "We know the women were innocent victims. The FBI has known that for years, but when the perp was killing women with no identities, they had nothing to go on."

"They never convinced The Madame or her husband to tell them who the women were?"

Mack wished he could hide his anger when he shook his head, but he knew she could see the way his jaw pulsed at the idea of how badly the FBI had botched the investigation. "Of course not. If they admitted they knew who the women were, it would implicate them in their murders. I'm sure their lawyers told them to remain silent."

"True," she agreed. "Do you have a list of the victims along with when and where they were found?"

"Yes."

"Good, then we take it one step further and mark the exact location where a body was found on the map."

"That still doesn't tell us where the body was dumped."

He felt her shrug under his hand before she spoke. "Just trying to help."

Mack swore internally for shooting her down. "I'm sorry," he said, turning her to face him. "I'm frustrated with this case. It's hard when I know that every time the sun comes up, another woman is one day closer to death. I may no longer be in the army, but I'll always be someone who wades into battle to save the innocents. This," he said with frustration as he flicked his hand at the projector, "has to stop."

Char braced her delicate hand on his chest, and her warmth spread through him like wildfire. It calmed and centered him. She made such a difference in his life just by being in it, and she grounded him when he was ready to pop off into the atmosphere from frustration. She was also the calming touch he needed when he wanted to rage against the world, and he wasn't sure how he felt about that. He could never be with this woman, so having that kind of reaction to her was problematic.

"If anyone can find this guy, Secure One can. You work together to save the people you care about, and that's what makes the team successful. Maybe a pattern will naturally develop if you plot out the places where the women were found."

Mack ran a hand down his face as he stared at the map. "You're right. I'll have Mina do it tomorrow since she has the kind of mind that will see the pattern developing as she goes."

"She'll also be rested, and you're not, Mack. You need to sleep, or you won't be any good to anyone."

He shut off the computer and walked with her to the door. "I'll try to sleep, but I'll end up staring at the ceiling until the sun comes up."

Her laughter was genuine when it reached his ears. "Some nights, I'd rather stare at the ceiling than deal with the nightmares."

"Those are the nights I find you in the kitchen," Mack pointed out as he shut the lights off.

"There's something comforting about a quiet kitchen at two a.m. with the scent of bread baking in the oven. I'd rather be tired and busy than tired and idle."

"It leaves too much time to think," they said in unison.

She glanced at him for a moment with a look of consideration, sympathy and understanding in her blue eyes before she waved and turned away from him. He stood rooted in place until she disappeared. As he walked to his room, the memories of his time with Char filled him. She was far more intuitive than she understood, which made him wonder why she was the way she was. Life on the street hardened a person, but something happened to her before she found herself on the street. What was it? That was the question. Mack was sure the answer would be no more forthcoming than his answer to the question she'd asked one night in the kitchen.

What happened out there in that giant sandbox no one wants to play in, Mack?

There were things he wouldn't discuss with anyone, and that included Charlotte. One of those things was the sandbox that held nothing but pain and regret. Charlotte had enough of those two things in her short life.

Chapter Eight

Charlotte didn't want to wait for Mina to plot the rivers that once held women in their watery grip. She didn't work well with computer-generated models, so she'd drawn her own map of the United States and marked the rivers in their full routes through each state, including their tributaries. Now all she needed were the locations of the bodies. That was easy enough to find. She brought up Google and typed in *The Red River Slayer victims*; within three seconds, she had the list she needed. She plotted the city or town closest to where the victim was brought ashore. That would only help them if they needed information from local authorities.

There was a knock on the office door, and Charlotte glanced up, expecting Mack or Eric, but Ella stood there instead. "Hey," she said to the girl. "Did you need something?"

"Not really. I'm bored, and Eric is hovering. He can go grab some food if I'm in here with you."

Charlotte motioned her in and then closed the office door and locked it. Eric and Mack had a key, but no one else did. "I can't say I'm not boring, but you're welcome to hang out here."

"What are you working on?" Ella asked, taking in the map. "This is huge. How did you find paper big enough for a map?"

"It's parchment paper from the kitchen."

"Really?" She was surprised when she ran her hand over it and realized it was true. "I never thought about drawing on it."

"I like it for certain projects, especially when heavy markers are involved because it doesn't bleed through the back."

Ella's finger followed the rivers on the map with her head cocked. "Rivers? What are the numbers and the towns?" Charlotte didn't have a chance to say anything before Ella let out a shocked breath. "The women from The Red River Slayer?"

"You shouldn't see this," Charlotte said, starting to roll it up, but Ella slapped her hand down on it.

"Please, I'm practically an adult, and it's not like any of this is a huge secret. The last woman was found just steps outside this door."

"I just don't want to get in trouble with the senator. I'm supposed to guard you, not get you involved in a murder case."

Ella brushed her words away with her hand. "He's not here, and trust me when I say he has no idea what I'm doing most of the time." She fell silent and tapped her chin, repeatedly pointing at the rivers as though she were counting. She opened her phone, grabbed the blue marker, and made lines in several states. After more pecking on her phone, she grabbed a red one and made similar lines in others.

"What are you doing?"

"He's hit the Mississippi, Kansas, Arkansas, Red, Rio Grande, Chattahoochee, Missouri, Platte, Snake, Colorado, Canadian and Tennessee rivers, which run through both predominately blue and red states."

"You're talking about politics?" Charlotte asked, and Ella nodded. "I don't follow politics."

"I was thinking about it when they found the woman

here. My dad is running for reelection, so I wondered if politics were the reason for the murders. If you look at the map, the blue or red line means a senator from that party is running for reelection this year. The color of the line indicates a democrat or republican."

"Seriously?"

"I mean, yeah, I know this stuff because of my dad."

"Are these all the senators running for reelection?"

"Oh, no, there are more. We'd have to make the map a little more detailed, but then I could tell you who was running in what state."

Charlotte grabbed the black marker and finished drawing the state lines until she had a complete map of the forty-eight states. She stepped aside and let Ella finish marking the map with senators running for reelection. When they finished, they stared at the map while Charlotte did some fast math in her head. "There are a lot of states that still haven't been touched."

"For sure," Ella agreed. "Every two years, a third of the Senate is up for reelection. This year there are thirty-three."

Charlotte tipped her head to the side. "But wait. Some of these murders occurred more than two years ago." She put an *X* next to the ones found when the murders started. There were six of those women.

Ella shrugged as though she'd grown bored with the whole thing. "I'm probably wrong, but at least you have the information on the map now." Her phone rang, and she looked at the caller ID before she hit the decline button. "That was my grandma. I'm going to go up to my room and call her back. She wants to FaceTime to prove I'm still alive." Her eye roll was heavy, as was her sigh.

Charlotte grabbed a walkie off the table. "Secure two, Charlotte."

"Secure one, Echo," Eric replied, which he wouldn't do

if he were being forced, and then the key slid into the lock and the door opened.

"Ella is ready to return to her room," Charlotte said, patting her shoulder. "Thanks, Eric."

"No problem. The place is quiet. I'll take her up and stay with her. Mack is grabbing a bite, and then he'll be in."

Charlotte nodded and waved as Ella left. Her mind should be on the case, but instead, she was busy picturing the dark brown eyes of the man in the kitchen. The man who starred in her dreams, both day and night. It was becoming a problem, and she didn't know how to fix it.

WHEN MACK WALKED into the office, Charlotte was pacing and muttering to herself. He stood by the door and watched her for longer than he should, but he was taken by her strength and determination to be part of this team. She could do her job and go back to her room, but she didn't do that. She jumped in with both feet and worked the problem with them until it was resolved. Usually, her role was to bring them dinner in the boardroom or command center because they couldn't leave the monitors, but she always stayed. She stayed and offered suggestions from a different perspective they didn't have. That of a woman who had been attacked more times than Mack cared to think about and as a woman kept as property somewhere that looked completely normal. Charlotte always added to the conversation, which was why he wasn't surprised she was trying to work the problem now.

"Charlotte?" he asked from the doorway, and she jumped, spinning to stare at him with her hand on her chest.

"You scared me."

"Sorry," he said, pushing off the door and walking to her. He rubbed her arms gently and waited for her to settle again. "You were so lost in thought you didn't notice me come in. What has you so worked up?" Her gaze darted to the side, and that was when he noticed the map on the table.

His hands fell from her arms, and he walked over to the table to take in the map. "What's this?"

"It's nothing," she said quickly, attempting to roll it up. Mack held it down.

"It's obviously something. These are rivers in the United States. What are the other symbols?"

Charlotte brought him up to speed on the plotted areas and the colored markings. His mouth was hanging open by the time she finished. She must have noticed because she held up her hand to him as though he shouldn't speak.

"I can't make it work either. There was a two-year pause on the murders, but his original victims were before this election cycle."

That break from the murders would haunt them and keep them from solving this case. Mack was sure of it.

Two years.

"Senators run for reelection every two years," Mack said, thinking out loud.

"Yes," Charlotte agreed. "Ella said that every two years, a third of the Senate is up for reelection."

"Okay, so six women died three years ago, which would have been during the previous reelection cycle. You might be onto something here," Mack said in disbelief. "I need to call Mina." He sat and fired up their connection to Secure One. Once they were hooked up, he pulled the tablet from its moorings and walked around the table. He wanted to show Mina the extensive map Charlotte had drawn.

"Secure two, Whiskey." Mina's voice was heard over the tablet, but there was no video.

"Secure one, Mike," Mack answered, and Mina's face popped up on the screen.

"Miss me already?"

Mack noted the smile on Charlotte's face from the corner of his eye before speaking. "I always miss you, Mina, but this time I have a question."

"What do you mean, this time? You always have a question."

Charlotte snorted while trying to hold in her laughter, and Mack chuckled. "Fair point. This one is about our perp. First, I want you to check out this map."

Mack held the tablet out and scanned the extensive map while he filled her in on their theory that the killings may be politically driven.

"That's an interesting theory," Mina said, her head tipped. "What is your question?"

"You were around when the original women were found, correct?"

"Yes," she answered immediately. "Well, for some of them. Others were found while I was on the run, but since it made national news, I was aware of them."

"Then my question is do the early murders mirror our current ones?"

Mina blinked several times before she spoke. "Do you mean in their cause of death?"

"Cause of death and the way they're dressed. That kind of thing."

"Oh, no," she said immediately.

"The new murders differ from the original murders two years ago?" Charlotte asked with surprise.

"Well, the cause of death has been consistent. Always strangulation. From what I read in the FBI documents, the first six women had obvious strangulation marks on their necks. Those were the bodies found during The Madame's time in Red Rye."

"The new victims do not," Mack pointed out immediately.

"No, they don't, but they had broken hyoid bones, which only happens when someone is strangulated."

"What's a hyoid bone?" Charlotte asked.

Mack glanced at her and noted her deep concentration. She wanted to understand, so he nodded at Mina to answer.

"Your hyoid bone looks like a horseshoe, and it's under your chin here," Mina said, lifting her head to point at the spot at the top of her trachea. "Essentially, it connects the tongue and voice box and supports the airway. When it breaks—"

"The airway collapses, and you can't breathe," Charlotte finished.

Mina pointed at her. "Smart girl, and that's correct. Of course, if the bone is fractured in a different setting, the person often survives after seeking treatment. However, in strangulation cases, normally, the bone isn't just fractured but obliterated. Therefore, the victim dies from lack of airway."

Charlotte ran her hand under her chin near her neck. "Isn't strangulation usually lower though? Like here?" She motioned at her mid-trachea while Mina nodded.

"That is where the six original women had strangulation marks."

"What about the presentation of the victims?"

"Negative," Mina replied. "The first six women were dumped. Some were naked. Others were just in their underclothes."

"Are we dealing with two different perps?" Mack asked with frustration.

"Not necessarily. It's not uncommon for serial killers to perfect their game. At the FBI, we called it developing a method. They often start killing helter-skelter—"

"Coined by another serial killer," Mack said grimly.

"The difference is Charles Manson was a psychopath

who never killed anyone. He convinced other people to do it for him. That's not the case with our perp."

"You're saying that maybe during the period he wasn't killing women, he was learning and improving his technique?"

"We can't say he didn't kill women during that time. We just didn't find any."

"Fair point," Mack agreed. "Assuming it's the same guy, he's figured out how to strangle without leaving marks and decides to present the women rather than just toss them?"

"Strangulation is generally a crime of passion. Where the hyoid bone sits, the victim would have to be lying down for him to break it without leaving ligature marks."

"Like during sex."

"That's exactly right. Or, at the very least, he must be the one with leverage and power."

Mack briefly slid his eyes to Charlotte and then back to the tablet. "That was helpful, thanks. Should we proceed with the assumption that this is the same guy?"

"That or it's a copycat with better techniques."

"What is your gut telling you, Mina?" Mack asked her point-blank because he needed to know if he should pivot on this investigation.

"My gut says it's the same guy. He craves power. He may have a job where he has no power or he may have a job where he has all the power. That's not exactly helpful, unless you consider that he keeps these women for long periods and drives around the country to dump them in different rivers."

"That would lead a person to believe he has a job with power and money," Charlotte said from behind him.

Mina pointed at her from the camera. "Exactly. Our perp likely has a powerful job but one that doesn't fulfill him the way controlling a woman does. Having power over a woman he can force to bend to his every whim turns him on. Strangulation is always a crime of passion in this kind of setting. It's possible he has certain kinks that lend themselves to strangulation or he could kill them accidentally when he loses control. I suspect the first few times that was the case. He killed them by accident, so he dumped the bodies just to get rid of them. The next few times were intentional, but he still hadn't perfected his technique. What happened over the next two years, I don't know, but I still believe it's the same person killing these women now. I'm not sold on it being politically driven though."

"It's just a working theory," Charlotte jumped in. "I thought it was a good train of thought to follow for now."

"Agreed—"

The walkie-talkie buzzed to life, and Charlotte grabbed it. "Secure One? This is the estate security guard at the gate. I need assistance."

Charlotte pushed the button so Mack could speak. "Assistance? Is there a threat?"

"I don't think she's a threat, but she's demanding to talk to someone from Secure One. The person who killed The Miss is what she said."

"The Miss?" Charlotte asked, her gaze traveling to Mina's, who sat frozen on the screen while she listened to the exchange.

She released the button, and another voice filled the room. "Charlotte! Oh, my God, Charlotte, is that you?"

Within one second, Mack noticed Mina's and Charlotte's eyes widen when they heard the voice. Charlotte did nothing but hold the walkie with her mouth hanging open, so Mack grabbed it and depressed the button. "We'll be right down."

"I know that voice, so I'll inform the team that the game

just changed," Mina said, her voice tight. "Call me back as soon as you have a handle on this."

"Ten-four. Mike, out."

Chapter Nine

"Charlotte." Mack was in front of her, taking hold of her shaking hands. "Charlotte, you need to breathe. Breathe in and then out," he said, demonstrating until she did the same thing. His warm hand grasped her chin. "You look like you've seen a ghost."

"I heard one," she whispered, shaking her head to clear it. "I think that was Bethany."

"Bethany?"

Her exaggerated nod continued until he gently grasped her chin to stop it. "She was one of the women who disappeared when she challenged The Miss."

The light came on in his eyes, and he took a small breath. "Bethany and Emelia."

"It's been almost two years. I thought for sure they were dead."

He grabbed her hand and started pulling her behind him. "Let's head to the gate and check this out. I need to let Eric know to stay put."

He brought the walkie to his lips to contact Eric, but Charlotte's mind was on the woman at the gate. If she had been alive all this time, where had she been? Why didn't she come back when she learned The Miss was dead? Was she alone, or was Emelia with her? Lost in thought, she didn't notice Mack stop until she ran up against him, her body plastered against the length of his back. He was hot in every way a man could be, and her skin tingled from the contact she worked so hard to avoid.

She was still daydreaming about how warm he was when he held her out by the shoulder. "Charlotte, where's your head?"

"My head?"

"We can't go out there if your head is not in the game. This could be a trick. They could be trying to lure us out to leave Eric vulnerable or take us out. I want you to stay behind me at all times."

"But Bethany," she whispered, her voice breaking on the name.

"If Bethany is out there and alone, we'll make a new plan. We have to proceed with caution until we know otherwise. Okay?"

After taking a breath in and letting it out, Charlotte nodded. "I'm good. It threw me to hear her voice again, but you're right, it could be a trick." She patted the gun at the small of her back. The one they insisted she carry after the last kidnapping attempt on Ella. "I still have my gun from when I was alone with Ella earlier."

"Good, be ready to use it. Just make sure none of us are in the line of fire."

They had a short walk to the front door, but the walk to the front gate was a couple of hundred feet. The cabin was gated, but that didn't mean someone couldn't approach by water and sneak onto the property from the river with no one the wiser. They both pulled their guns, and started their walk, their heads on a swivel. They made it to the gate without difficulty. The night guardsman stood inside the booth while a blond woman sat on a stool across from him.

"Oh, my God, it's her," she whispered to Mack. They

waited until the guard opened the gate for them to approach the booth. "Bethany?"

The woman glanced up, and instantly, her face crumpled. "Charlotte! It is you. I heard your voice, but I couldn't believe it." She never said another word, just cried silent tears, her body spasming from the emotion.

"Is she alone?" Mack asked Lucas, the guard.

"As far as I can tell."

"Is this a trick, Bethany?" Charlotte asked the woman. She had lost weight and was paler than anyone she'd ever seen before.

"No, not a trick," the woman answered. "I need help. I heard on the news that another woman was found by the people who killed The Miss. I didn't know where else to go. I'm—I'm in danger." Her last sentence was whispered with so much fear that Charlotte's gut clenched from reflex. She knew that kind of fear.

Charlotte glanced at Mack and waited for him to make a decision. He lifted a brow and then tipped his head before he spoke. "We'll take her from here, Lucas," he told the guard. "Be on high alert just in case this is an attack we don't see coming."

"It's not," Bethany said in a choked whisper. "I've been on a bus and came straight here. I haven't spoken to anyone and no one knows who I am. I swear."

Mack made a hand signal that Charlotte recognized as the two and one formation. She was to walk with Bethany into the house while he brought up the rear. It was her job to police their approach. Her hand was shaking when she switched her gun to her right hand and motioned Bethany out of the security hut. The woman ran to her and threw her arms around Charlotte, nearly knocking them both to the ground if it hadn't been for Mack grabbing her belt loop at the back of her pants. His warmth there helped ground her as the woman in her arms sobbed incoherently.

"We have to move," Mack said in her ear, sending a shiver down her spine both from desire and fear.

After a nod, she convinced Bethany to walk to the house, but she couldn't help but think Mina was correct and the game had changed. Her biggest fear was that The Miss hadn't stayed buried after all.

WHEN MACK WALKED back into the office, Charlotte was hunched over her pad, the swish of her charcoal pencil the only sound in the room. He wasn't sure if she was breathing as she concentrated on the pad.

"Is Bethany settled?"

The jolt of her body told him she hadn't known he was there. Her pencil fell to the desk, and she quickly closed the sketch pad and rested her elbow on it.

"Sorry, I didn't hear you come in. She's resting in the room next to Ella. I helped her shower, and she had something to eat. Now we wait."

"Do you think she needs more medical care than Selina can provide?"

Cal, Selina, Roman and Mina were in the chopper, and they'd arrive within the hour. Charlotte was glad because they needed more help than they had, but understandably, Cal didn't want to involve the police just yet.

"She's thin, but overall, physically healthy. I think she will need a lot of mental health care after what happened. I don't even know where she's been the last two years, but it was nowhere good."

"I agree, which is why I'm glad Cal is coming in. We need to ask the right questions, and Mina is excellent at that. Once Bethany can give us some answers, we'll let Selina decide what kind of care she needs and where."

"I want to know where Emelia is, Mack. Those two were inseparable."

"She may not know, so don't get too hung up on the need for one answer, Char. This could be as simple as she was hiding from The Miss and didn't know she was dead until now."

Charlotte raised her brow at him slowly. "If she had been hiding out, she would have heard The Miss was dead, Mack. I suspect wherever she was living, it wasn't by choice. My guess would be she's been a captive woman the last two years."

Mack's jaw set and pulsed once as an answer. "The tentacles of those two women always seem to work themselves back into our lives. One's in prison, and one's dead, but we still aren't free of them."

"And never will be, Mack," she whispered, staring at her feet. "Ever."

He pulled her into his arms just as a shudder went through her. He cursed himself for not thinking before he spoke. "I'm sorry, that was insensitive," he whispered. "I'm frustrated, but I often forget those women ruined your life, not mine."

"Not true," she countered, stepping out of his arms. "You carry the burden of killing The Miss."

"I carry no burden about her death, Char. Sometimes the right choice is to take a life if it prevents them from hurting others. I learned that first hand in the army."

He walked toward her. Her blue globes filled with fear, and he paused, holding his next step. Was she afraid of him? "You don't need to be afraid of me, Charlotte."

"I—I'm not," she stuttered before she pushed the pad behind her from where she rested on the edge of the desk.

"I see the look in your eyes when I move toward you too quickly. I try to give you your space because I know that feeling inside your chest when terror grips your heart," he whispered, holding his hand near his chest. "It's all you can do to stop yourself from running."

"I'm not afraid of you, Mack. I just know it's smart to keep you at arm's length. I don't trust easily, but I trust you. That scares me more than anything."

Mack cocked his head. "Because trusting me means I could hurt you?" Her head barely tipped in acknowledgment. "I wouldn't do that, Charlotte. I've been where you're at." He held up his hand to stem her words. "I mean that I've been traumatized, hurt and let down by the people who were supposed to look out for me. The feeling of betrayal is so powerful you can taste it. That's when you realize the only person you can trust is yourself. Am I close?"

"Spot on," she agreed in a whispered tone. "Looking back, I can see that has been true since day one. It took me too long to see it, and the one time I tried to take care of myself, I ended up a pawn in someone else's game. I don't want to be that again."

"You aren't." Mack took another step until he was right in front of her, staring down into her tired blue eyes. He expected her to cower at an entire foot taller than her, but she didn't. She held her ground and lifted her chin. "At Secure One, you're an equal team member."

"I'm the cook. I don't think that's equal to anyone, Mack. That's the hired help."

He laid his finger against her lips. "Wrong. That's not how Cal runs Secure One, and you know it. Everyone contributes to the success of the business. As the cook, you're one of the most important people on the team. We're a group of big guys with healthy appetites, but we can't tell a saucepan from a broiler. You fuel us, which is one less thing we have to worry about when we're busy. It may feel like you're in the background, but you're not. Never doubt that."

Her nod was quick as his gaze traveled to the pad behind her. "You've also contributed to the team with your art. Cal took your suggestions to the client and secured the job as their security company because of your work. He'll square up with you for your contributions. Talent is talent, Charlotte, regardless of our pasts, abilities or disabilities. We aren't one-dimensional."

"I know," she said, sliding her hand up his chest to rest there.

It was as though she knew the secrets that he held but couldn't say.

He allowed himself the pleasure of grasping her tiny hand in his for a moment before he pulled her into a hug when her eyes said yes. With one arm, he held her, and with the other, he flipped the lid open on her sketch pad. When she hid what she was working on, he knew it was important to her. He took in the image on the pad and froze. The next breath wouldn't come as he stared at himself dressed in army fatigues. He was looking over his shoulder with sheer terror on his face. His gaze traveled down the pad to see his pants in tattered, jagged edges at the knees. He wore no boots or socks but had open wounds and blood pooling around his feet that congealed into a broken heart. It was the blood falling from the wounds on the left that broke him.

Has been. Useless. Inadequate. Failure.

The right leg told a different story.

Hope. Victory. Skill. Knowledge. New life.

When his lungs finally released a breath, it sounded like a grunt of pain. He stumbled backward until he hit the wall. "How did you know?"

Charlotte glanced at him in confusion and then at the pad. Her grimace was noticeable when she turned back to him. "I didn't want you to see that."

"Then why did you draw it?"

"I draw what I see, Mack. I'm an artist. It's how I express emotion."

"I don't understand how you knew about my legs."

"I see more than you think," she answered. "I noticed when you were changing your boots and socks that night in the mobile command unit, but I also saw the metal bars across your boots and how your gait is slightly different than the other guys. I asked Roman about it, and all he would say was you were injured in a mission gone wrong. He said the injury was the reason why you left the army."

A mission gone wrong. More like a mission that blew up in his face. Literally.

Chapter Ten

Mack rubbed his hands over his face while he paced the room. She was silent, but he worried it was in judgment rather than patience. "I don't talk about this with anyone, Charlotte."

"I'm not asking you to, Mack. My drawings are for me. They help me process the emotions that are too big to hold inside. I don't know how you were hurt or why. Chances are, what I drew is all wrong, but that's what I see."

The nod of his head was barely there, and she fell silent, staring at her hands rather than meeting his gaze. "We were moving a diplomat and his family to a safe house."

"You don't have to tell me, Mack," she said, halting his words. "That's not why I drew it."

He lifted his chin to hold her gaze. Her blue eyes didn't hold pity as he'd expected. They were open and clear, their depths holding some of the same pain and experiences in his. They'd both fought battles that hadn't ended up in the win column.

"Maybe I don't have to tell you," he said, not breaking eye contact, "but that drawing…" He shook his head and dropped his gaze to the floor. "It brought everything back. Without knowing it, you captured my emotions, from my expression to the words that bled from my soul. Maybe I have to tell someone, so I can finally be free of the shame."

"You have nothing to be ashamed of, Mack."

"You don't know that," he whispered. "The truth is I ran the wrong way. I protected the wrong team."

"I don't believe that." Her refusal was punctuated with her arms crossing over her chest in defiance.

"My job was to protect the diplomat, and I failed to do that, Charlotte. The caravan made it to the safe house without attracting any attention from the insurgents. I was driving the diplomat and his family while my team sandwiched us. The front half of the team was securing the area for me. I told the diplomat, his family and the traveling security team to wait while I reconned with Cal. I climbed from the car and walked toward him when I heard the back door of the car squeak open. That was the last sound I heard before an explosion rocked the air. I glanced behind me to see the fireball from the diplomat's car. I didn't run back, Charlotte. I ran toward Cal and the team like a coward!"

"Mack, no," she said, her tone soft and nonjudgmental. "What made you run for the team?"

He tossed his hand up, the smell of fire and fuel stuck in his head as he relived those moments. "The car was nothing more than a burning shell instantly, but we're trained to render aid, and I didn't."

"If nothing was left but a burning shell, is it safe to say that you knew with just one look that everyone in that car was already gone?"

"Without a doubt." The breath he let out was heavy and filled with disappointment. Disappointment in himself. "I still should have gone back. Instead, I ran toward my team, worried they'd been hit by flying debris."

"When the truth was, you had been."

His nod was immediate and short. "I was screaming for

them to get down and find cover, but they ran toward me. Cal and Roman caught me as I fell, dragged me into a vehicle and took off. I don't remember anything else until I woke up in the hospital."

"And what did you learn when you woke up?"

He stood and paced to the window, pulling the curtain back a hair to stare into the darkness. "They think the bomb was set to detonate when the back door opened. I'm sure whoever rigged it never thought we'd get past loading them into the vehicle. It was just chance that we loaded the family through the opposite door."

"No one had inspected the car for a bomb?"

"They did. That doesn't mean anything in the game of warfare though. For all we know, someone on the security team could have planted it after the inspection. It was a typical device to blow up the gas tank and cause an inferno. The bomb wasn't complicated and didn't require much explosive to get the job done."

"What else did you learn at the hospital, Mack?" she asked as she swiveled her body to face him again.

The curtain fell to obscure the moon, and he leaned against the wall. "I learned that I wasn't the only one hurt. Cal and Eric were also in the hospital. Both of my lower legs were damaged by shrapnel. The nerves in my legs that control my feet were severed or damaged. It took too long to get me into surgery and the ischemia set in. They tried transferring the nerve, but it was too scarred down and didn't take. My time in the army was over."

"I still can't figure out what part of that makes you a coward, Mack. You did your job and paid a high price for something someone else did."

"I didn't go back for them, Charlotte. Right or wrong, I should have gone back."

"You should have gone back to a burning car to do what?

Watch the fire? Get burned? What could you do when one glance told you they were dead?"

"They weren't just dead. The fire was so hot they had evaporated. I knew it. I'd seen it before. I still should have gone back."

"Here's the thing, Mack," she whispered, planting her hands on her hips. "Could have. Should have. Would have. Those are dangerous statements. They're all past tense. There's no rewind and replay in life. There's only did and did not."

"I did not do my job. There's your truth."

"Wrong. You did not die. That's the real truth here, Mack. Those people did, and you did not. This isn't about the decisions you made after the explosion. As humans, when we're faced with situations like those, trained or untrained, we can't predict what we will do. In a split second, you knew those people were gone, but your team was in danger. You didn't even know you were hurt in those first few seconds, did you?" He shook his head but kept his lips pursed, so he didn't argue with her about how wrong she was. "Adrenaline and fear are highly motivating to the human mind, Mack. Toss in the shock of a sudden injury, and the rule book goes out the window. Let me ask you a question?" He nodded, and she stood, walking over to him and standing directly in front of him. "What did the rest of your team do?"

"I told you. My team grabbed me and dragged me out of there. Eric picked us up in his truck and raced us to a waiting chopper."

"Did any of them run toward the burning car, Mack?"

He paused, holding her gaze as his mind returned to the heat and the noise that day. "Cal and Roman were in the front vehicle alone. They were out of their truck and securing the area. Eric and a second team were in a vehicle behind us when the explosion happened. I remember Eric drove around the car and picked us all up."

"Then, from what I'm hearing, you had a full team in two different vehicles, but none of them approached the car either?"

"Not that I remember. In the report, Eric said the fire was so hot they could feel the heat inside their truck as they passed it."

"Did the report say if Eric stopped to check on the occupants?"

"He didn't. He followed Cal's directive to abandon the mission."

"So why, in light of all that, do you feel like a coward? Were you the mission leader?" He shook his head, his jaw pulsing with anger and fear. The terror from that day filled him again, and he clenched his hands into fists to stop them from trembling. "Have you ever considered that no matter what choices you made that day, you couldn't have saved those people? Have you ever considered that it was beyond your pay grade and your control? Has anyone told you that it wasn't your fault? I'm telling you now. It wasn't your fault, Mack. You did your job, and the scars you carry are proof of that. You can't control the way that day changed your body or your mind. I understand that more than anyone, but the guilt is too heavy when it's not yours to carry."

Mack sucked air in through his nostrils and stared her down. "I guess I could say the same to you, Charlotte, but I suspect you'd tell me our situations were different, and you can't compare them. You'd be right. No one died because you didn't do your job. People died because I didn't do mine."

Before she could say anything, he pushed past her and walked out the door. He'd do well to remember that before Charlotte joined Secure One, his singular focus had been to help people in bad situations or protect them from bad people. He'd lost sight of that momentarily when Charlotte came into his life, but it was time he focused on that again. Doing anything else made him think he had a chance at a different life. He knew the truth. Being alone was his path in life. He had to make her understand that before she too became a casualty of his war.

MACK STARED OUT the cabin's window at the tumultuous water of the Mississippi, hoping it would help him sort out the noise in his head. What did Charlotte know about war? Nothing. She knew nothing. At least nothing about the kind of war he fought, right?

Mack walked over to Eric, who had been watching him pace. "Hey," he said, but Eric held his fingers in front of him, wagged them for a second, then punched around on his phone.

That was the sign for *hang on*, which Eric used when his hearing aids weren't connected properly. His hearing had been damaged in the same botched transport that injured Mack's legs. Without his hearing aids, he was legally deaf. Thankfully, he had the best of the best in aids to help him hear.

"Sorry, I had to disconnect the phone's Bluetooth from my hearing aids. What's up?"

"Checking in. Who were you talking to?"

"Cal," he said, holding up the phone before he pocketed it. "They're landing soon."

"Good, with any luck, we can try to make sense of this newest development. How is she?" Mack motioned at the door where Bethany slept.

"Charlotte stayed with her until she fell asleep. I'm supposed to tell her if Bethany wakes up, but she's out."

Mack grunted, frustration evident in the sound. Something had to break soon, or another woman was going to die. Frustration was all he felt tonight, both with the case and Charlotte.

"What crawled up your pants leg?" Eric asked, turning to him.

"Nothing. I'm frustrated with how nothing makes sense in this case."

"No, you're frustrated with how long it's taking to move on it."

"I'd like to figure it out before another woman dies, Eric."

"So would I, but in the end, we have one hand tied trying to work around the authorities. It will take more time when we don't have access to all the evidence."

Swiping his hand through his hair, Mack buried his fingers and left them there, his elbow swinging in the air. "I know, but I don't have to like it."

"Can't say that I do either."

"What do you remember about that day that ended our service career?" Mack asked out of the blue, his trained eye noticing Eric's shoulders stiffen.

"You're asking what haunts me about it, right?" Eric asked, and Mack gave half a nod. "I vividly remember the back door cracking open and a little leg coming out right before the car exploded."

Mack glanced at him sharply. "You could see who opened the door?"

"I don't know if the boy opened it, but he would be the first one out. He probably was the one to open it. He was enamored with you, remember? He may not have understood the stay-in-the-car order."

"I never knew that," Mack said with a shudder. "I don't think it makes me feel better about it either."

"I didn't think it would, which is why I never told you. I also remember seeing you walk toward Cal, and then you just disappeared. I thought you dropped when the car exploded."

"I did, just not by choice."

"It wasn't until I got the truck around the burning car that I realized you were hurt."

"So were you."

"I didn't know that at the time. Getting you to a helo was our priority."

Mack shook his head with frustration. "Cal, me, you, all injured for nothing. I failed to do my job, and people were maimed and killed. Such a waste."

"You didn't fail to do your job."

Mack's snort was loud and sarcastic. "You and Charlotte."

"Charlotte doesn't know the first thing about war."

"Civilized warfare is still warfare, and the streets aren't always civilized, Eric." Mack's tone was defensive, and Eric noticed.

"You're saying she knows a lot about war, just not your war."

With a finger pointed at his friend, Mack nodded. "When she was on the streets, she was an army of one. She was the only one who needed to walk away alive and unhurt. I had an entire team I let down when that mission went sideways."

"I never could figure out why you took that blame when there was never any blame to be had. You followed protocol by exiting the vehicle and taking your position before security inside the car led the family from the vehicle. We'd done it a dozen times the same way. It was unfortunate circumstances that weren't your fault. You didn't put that bomb in the car."

His chest was heavy when he let out a breath. Unfortunate circumstances that weren't his fault. Maybe that was true. Even if he couldn't control them, he still carried the scars from them.

"Listen, Mack, none of us escaped that mission without guilt. I think about that little foot sticking out every night when I go to bed. I have to remind myself that they were never getting out alive regardless of what we did. More of us would be dead if you opened that door at the airport rather than the other side. Stop feeling guilty. Nothing you did would have saved that family, but you did save many other people from dying. I know it will never fade away, just like all the other carnage we saw and participated in, but it's been too many years for you to let it control your life. I know that's easier said than done, but it's time to try."

"I've tried for years, Eric. I'm exhausted from trying."

Eric turned and crossed his arms over his chest, facing Mack with determination in his stance. "No, you haven't. You find it easier to deal with your disability by pretending it's your fault, but it's not. It's time you try to find some happiness in life, Mack. You don't even have to look for it. Happiness is waiting downstairs, but you're too dense to see it. It might be easier to let your past fade if you had someone to share your future with."

"Charlotte?" Eric's head tipped to the left slightly. "It's not like that, man. I'm part of her life to teach her how to trust again. That's it. That's all it can be."

"What a shame," Eric said, dropping his arms to his sides. "She smooths out your rough edges. I'll go prepare the rest of the security team for Cal's arrival. You're on bodyguard duty until I get back."

The treads of his boots made a hiss on the wood floor as he walked away, leaving Mack to stare at the wall. Eric's words echoed in his ears.

She smooths out your rough edges.

She absolutely did, but he'd never ask a woman like Charlotte to tie herself to a guy like him. His demons took up too much space and left no room for love.

Chapter Eleven

"Charlotte?"

Surprised by the intrusion, she spun around to see Mina standing in the doorway. She wore her Secure One uniform with a gun on her hip and her running blade prosthesis strapped inside a tennis shoe. Mina had several prostheses, but when working a job, she always wore the one that made her the fastest.

"Mina!" Before she could say another word, she was wrapped in a warm hug from her friend. "I'm so glad you're here."

"I was the first one on the helicopter. I heard Bethany's voice, and it sent a shiver down my spine. How is she?"

"She's sleeping after she had something to eat. Eric and Mack are taking turns on guard duty. Bethany is beyond exhausted. She'll need a lot of help if she's going to have a life after what she's been through."

"There are resources out there for women like her. We'll get the information we need from her and then, depending on what she tells us, protect her or find her someplace with the services she needs. Until I hear her story, I won't know which one comes first."

Charlotte nodded after ending the hug. "The only thing she told me before she fell asleep was that she escaped someone who had been holding her hostage. She ran, stole a truck and rode a bus to get here."

"But how did she know about here?" Cal asked, walking through the open door with Roman.

"Hey, guys," Charlotte said, her gaze flicking to Mina for a moment, who nodded for her to answer. "She escaped the night we found Layla on the shore. She had the radio on and heard them talking about Secure One finding the body. They also mentioned we'd been involved in the death of The Miss. Since she had no other choice, she made her way here by bus and on foot, hoping she could find us."

"She sounds like a real spitfire," Cal said, bouncing up on his toes. "I know a couple of other women like her too. I can't wait to meet her."

"She's precarious, Cal," Charlotte warned him.

"Meaning?"

"Meaning she's been through hell, and we need to ask questions that don't push her over the razor-thin edge she's on."

"We understand that," Roman said. "Selina and Marlise are upstairs with her right now. Selina is going to check her over in case she needs a hospital. Marlise is there as a familiar face."

"I could have gone up. You didn't need to drag Marlise here," Charlotte said defensively.

Cal held out his hand to hush her. "I need you here to walk me through what we have before they bring Bethany down. You're in the thick of this case, and I need your insight."

Mack strode into the room then and didn't stop until he stood behind her. His hands went to her shoulders as though he noticed her tension. "Everything okay?"

"Fine," Cal assured him. "We were just talking about Bethany and the case. Charlotte is upset, which is completely understandable. This case gets more and more disturbing every day."

Mack rubbed her shoulders up and down as he spoke. "Agreed, and we don't even know if Bethany's situation is tied to The Red River Slayer."

"That's why we're here," Mina said, setting her bag up on the desk. "We can work remotely, and we will, but first, I wanted to talk to everyone in person. That way, I can start a more focused dive into our evidence when I get back to Secure One."

"You mean so you can hack the right agency to get more information," Mack said, tongue in cheek.

"You say potato," Mina answered with a grin.

She unloaded her pack and set up her computer while Cal and Roman taped Charlotte's map to the office wall.

Mack leaned into her ear and whispered, "We'll talk later about earlier."

His breath blew across her skin and raised goose bumps along her neck that she couldn't hide or deny. Why did his simple words and actions raise such a response in her? She was trying hard not to like him, but he wasn't making it easy. What he was doing was making it easy to fall into his arms and let him protect her. She couldn't let that happen though. If she was going to take back her life and find success, it would be because she worked hard. If she let someone else save her every time, that didn't teach her how to take care of herself.

What if he doesn't want to save you as much as he wants to love you?

Absolutely not. Charlotte shut that voice down without hesitation. There was no way she was falling for Mack. Her gaze flicked to Cal at the board, and she wondered how he made it work with Marlise. They lived and worked together all day, every day, but their relationship felt seamless. Her wayward gaze drifted to Mack, who had stepped back to the door to guard it as everyone prepared for the meeting. He was a giant. As much in kindness, empathy and understanding as he was in size. An unfamiliar heat flickered through her. She suspected it was the flame she would carry for this man forever. She'd never been with a man who didn't want something from her. Every man she'd encountered had an ulterior motive behind taking care of her, being with her, dating her or taking advantage of her. There had never been anyone in her life like Mack.

Safe.

Part of her believed that word, but the rest knew he wasn't safe. At least to her heart. He made it feel things it shouldn't, and that made him dangerous. Her therapist told her it was okay to want that kind of life, but she wasn't sure she deserved it. She had done things—illegal things—that harmed others. The drugs she ferried for The Madame probably killed people. She was the kind of person Mack actively worked to put behind bars. Maybe she hadn't done those things willingly, but she'd still done them.

"This is a mess," Cal said where he stood by the map. "The case, I mean. It's not even our case, but we're still in the middle of it."

Eric walked in at that moment and stood at the back by Mack. Charlotte could see that he was tired, they all were, but until this case was solved, no one was getting much sleep.

"All we can do is work the evidence, Cal," Mina said from behind her computer. "That's the only way out of this mess."

"We keep saying that, but it never happens," Roman pointed out, leaning on the desk next to his wife. "It feels like that game *Whac-A-Mole*. We knock one bad girl down, and another one pops up."

"Or, in this case, a bad boy," Mack said from the doorway while motioning at the map on the wall.

"Could still be a bad girl," Roman said with a shrug.

"You think this is tied to Red Rye?" Eric asked. Charlotte could hear the skepticism in his voice, but she had none in her mind.

"I don't know if it's tied directly to Red Rye, but it could be tied to the business The Madame had going at the time."

"The first bodies were found while you were all at Red Rye." Cal pointed at the six rivers where the original women were found. "That's a little suspect if you ask me."

"Especially when you consider what SAC Moore told me the night he kidnapped me," Mina said, glancing at Roman.

"What did he tell you?" Cal asked.

"That Liam Albrecht had some serious kinks, and The Miss had to do cleanup on more than one occasion."

Cal took a step toward the desk. "You could have mentioned that sooner."

Mina shrugged. "It just crossed my mind again when you said the first bodies were all from Red Rye. Maybe The Miss cleaned those women up by passing them off to someone else to do the deed rather than do it herself. We know it wasn't Liam killing the women because he's dead, and we're still finding them."

"But, of the recent women found, only one didn't have an identity, and that was the last one," Mack said, walking to the front of the room.

"Layla," Charlotte said through gritted teeth. "Her name was Layla, and she was just a scared young woman who didn't deserve to die that way."

Mina held up her hand. "The FBI knows her identity. They just haven't released her name yet."

Mack kept his hand on the small of her back to calm her.

"Okay, so now we know all the women from this killing spree were identified."

"Which makes sense," Cal said. "There aren't many washed women left from The Madame's empire."

"No, but he's still taking throwaway women," Mina said from behind her computer. "Our perp chooses victims from the street because homeless people always move around. Even if she had friends on the street, they wouldn't think anything of her going missing."

"And even if they did, the police aren't going to spend time looking for her," Charlotte added. Her voice was thin, tired and exhausted from life, which made her appreciate Mack's strong but caring touch on her back even more. "We know he's not impulsive. He's taking the time to pick the right women and not just grabbing random ones."

"He might even get off on the hunt," Eric said as he walked to the front of the room to sit. "He probably watched each victim for days. Learned their routine. Decided if anyone would notice that her things were there, but she wasn't. He may even watch her long enough to know what things are important to her and makes sure he grabs her when she has those items. That makes it look to her friends like she just took off."

"Or he just grabs the first street woman he sees. We have twelve bodies, but that doesn't mean that all the victims have been found," Cal reminded everyone. "There could be more victims who never floated to shore."

"All true," Mina agreed, typing away on her computer. "I've had my ear to the ground for bodies of drowning victims found anywhere during the two years between Red Rye and now."

"Nothing, right?" Eric asked, but Mina stuck her head around the computer and shook it.

"Actually, no. Two more women were found, but they

didn't fare well in the water. A gator probably attacked one, and one was caught in a dam for some time. No ability to run facial recognition and no recognizable marks to tell a family if it was their missing child. The police couldn't say it was The Red River Slayer, so they didn't."

"They weren't strangled?" Mack asked from next to her. A shiver ran through Charlotte, and he rubbed it away with his hand on her back.

"No way to know. Their heads were either gone or damaged in a way that could have caused the trauma. DNA identification will take a significant amount of time."

"Do you know what rivers?" Cal asked, walking to the giant map Charlotte had drawn.

Mina held up a finger and typed more on the computer before answering. "The Savannah River, which explains the gator attack, and the Colorado River."

"We have a victim in the Colorado already," Cal said, putting his finger on the *X* Charlotte had made on the map.

"We do," Charlotte agreed, moving to the front of the room. She took the marker from Cal, "but that doesn't mean anything. The Colorado runs through like, what?" She paused and counted on the map. "Seven states. The first victim in that river was found in the state of Colorado. Mina, what state was this woman found in?"

"Arizona," she answered. "They think she was caught in the Glen Canyon Dam."

"That's not too far from where we found The Miss," Mack pointed out.

"And we're back to whether this is tied to The Madame," Cal said with frustration.

"I can say it's always in the back of my mind," Mack said. "It's possible someone was killing The Madame's women, and that was why bodies were being found during that time. Then The Madame was on trial, and rather than draw unwanted attention to himself, he stuck a pin in the business until things quieted down."

"The only tie we have is that some of the women killed worked for her. That could be a coincidence."

"Could be," Cal agreed, "but it's not. The Red River Slayer could have started as a client or a fan of what The Madame was doing, but he quickly became a psychopathic serial killer. Regardless of whether he or she was mixed up with the Red Rye fiasco, we need to move that to the back burner while we try to find him."

"Agreed," Eric said from his seat, "but we don't know how to find him."

"Or why someone tried to kidnap Ella the other night," Charlotte added.

"The more I think about it, the more I don't think it's connected," Mack said. "I think the kidnapping had more to do with who her father is, and the attempted kidnapper thought the chaos of that night was a good way to grab the girl without notice."

"And do what with her?" Charlotte asked. "Hold her hostage?"

"Ransom," Mina said from the computer. "Dorian would pay anything to get his daughter back."

"Which brings us back to whether the river slayings are politically driven. I'll need to plot the other bodies in what state and town they were found. Based on Ella's theory that killings have to do with senators seeking reelection, we have to ask ourselves two questions. First, did the killer take a break during those two years because the elections were over? Second, did he take a break for a different reason?"

"Or if he was practicing his technique and we just haven't found the bodies. He may have been preparing for when this election cycle came around." Mina stood and motioned at the map. "A sixteen-year-old girl came up with it as soon as it was laid out on paper. We should have."

"We're not in the business of politics or solving murders, Mina. Ella is immersed in politics, so to her, it was obvious. *If* that's the motivating factor," Cal reminded her.

"When will the police release Layla's sketch to the public?" Charlotte asked. "It's been radio silence for days."

"They're not going to," Cal answered. "They know who she is already, and their theory is every time they release information about the river slayings, they're giving the killer airtime, which is what he wants."

"But she deserves justice!" Charlotte exclaimed in anger.

Mina peeked around the computer again. "Layla didn't have a family, right?" Charlotte shook her head. "The police aren't hurting anything by keeping this under their hat then. From the perspective of a law enforcement agent, I understand what they're doing. As a woman, it angers me that they're stealing her justice."

"My fear is, not giving the guy airtime will result in another woman dying," Cal said with a sigh.

"We can't let that happen," Eric said, standing and grabbing a marker. "List off the senators up for reelection. I'm going to write them in their corresponding state."

Charlotte hadn't turned away from Mack. She was lost in the way his gaze calmed her pounding heart. She wanted to run from the room and the nightmare of this investigation, but he wouldn't let her. He would help her face her past to move on to a better future. That was all she wanted, but it couldn't be with him. Not to be cliché, but he deserved better, and she knew it. Her entire life went against his code of ethics. She was what he was trying to stop by fighting for this country.

"Ron Dorian, Minnesota. Pete Fuller, South Carolina.

Greg Weiss, Maine," Roman was reading off the computer when Mina stood up with a gasp.

"Greg Weiss?" She lowered herself to the chair again and looked at the other computer that Roman was on.

"Do you know him?" Mack asked.

She stood but shook her head with confusion. "He was friends with the two guys The Madame killed in the warehouse the night she kidnapped me. I found his name several times tied to Red Rye. I assumed he knew Liam Albrecht, the city manager for Red Rye, because they were all involved in politics."

"Was there evidence that he was involved with any women in the Red Rye house?"

"None," Mina said. "He knew Albrecht, but that doesn't mean anything in the world of politics. It's all a game. He could have been working them for money for his campaign, or they were friends through an organization. I was never able to sort out their exact relationship."

"Another point in the Red Rye column," Mack said. "Is that all of them, Roman?"

"Yes, for the current cycle. A third of the senate is re-elected every two years—this year, there are thirty-three. If we remove the eight women found, including the two who they aren't sure about, from the last election cycle, only six of the thirty-three states have a dead body." Eric put a check next to the senators from each state that already had a victim. "I'm afraid many more women will be killed if this is politically motivated."

Selina walked in the door at that moment, and everyone turned to her. "Sorry to interrupt, but I can't put Bethany through anything more tonight with good conscience. Her body and mind aren't even working together anymore since she's so exhausted. I can barely rouse her long enough to do her vitals."

Everyone looked at each other and waited for Cal to speak. When he did, it was no surprise what he said. "Then we give her until morning. It's already midnight, so a few more hours won't break the bank. We're rested and will take over security duty so Eric, Mack and Charlotte can get some rest. Selina, you and Marlise stay with Bethany. Roman, you and I will pull guard duty. Mina, can you keep working on this?"

He got a thumbs-up from behind her computer, but she barely broke stride in her typing long enough to give it.

"We'll reconvene here at seven a.m. unless something arises beforehand. We will have to talk to Bethany at that point," Cal said to Selina. "When most of the team is here, the rest of the team at Secure One is in a bind."

"Understood," Selina said. "I think a good stretch of sleep will be enough to help her mind put everything in order. This poor woman was held hostage for nearly two years. Everyone needs to understand that she may or may not have answers, but once we're done talking to her, I have to check her into a facility that can take care of her mental and emotional wounds besides her physical ones."

"That is heard and understood," Cal said. "She came to us, which means she wanted to tell us something. That's the only reason I'm staying here other than to give the team a break. Honestly, I need more help than I have right now. We're stretched too thin."

"I know a guy," Mina said, popping up.

"You know a guy?" Mack asked with a chuckle. "Is he trustworthy?"

"He's an amp friend. He did a tour for the army in the sandbox and lost his left leg but earned a purple heart and a medal of honor for saving two guys even as he was bleeding out. Rehabbed and returned for a tour in the mountains, this time as private security since the government said no to a second tour."

"Private security meaning mercenary," Mack muttered.

"Call him whatever you want. He won't care. He's stateside now and working private security as a bodyguard."

"A bodyguard who's an amp?" Eric asked with a raised brow.

"He can do more on one leg than you can do with both of your own. He can overtake you in seconds when he puts on his running blade. He runs marathons for fun on the weekend. I wouldn't hesitate to let him protect me."

"Does he have a name?" Cal asked, his tone holding interest.

"Efren."

"Sounds like he'd fit in well here. Give him a call. See if he's available. Run our standard background on him. I know you know him, but he has to align with our clearances for our clients."

"On it," she said, sitting again.

"The rest of you find an empty room and get some sleep. It might be your only chance for a few more days."

Charlotte feared he was right, so she headed to the room where she'd left her bag. She was going to grab a shower and some shut-eye. She made sure not to make eye contact with Mack when she left the room. He may want to talk about what happened earlier, but she did not. She planned to be asleep before he ever found her.

Chapter Twelve

Mack's hand rested on the doorknob, and he took a deep breath. It was time to clear the air with Charlotte. He turned the knob and pushed the door open just a crack. He put his lips to the opening to speak. "Char, it's Mack. I'm coming in."

He stood by the door and waited for a response that didn't come. Charlotte was fooling herself if she thought he'd go away if she pretended to be asleep. He stepped into the room and turned the light on next to the bed, expecting to see her there. She wasn't. Fear lanced his chest. Where was she? Had someone gotten to her?

A sound came from the bathroom, and he let out a sigh. His heart was pounding as he lowered himself to the bed and braced his hands on his knees. This case was getting to him, and so was this woman. He was about to do something he'd never done before, and the mere idea of being that open with someone scared him.

The bathroom door opened, and he lifted his head to come face-to-face with Char wrapped in a towel and nothing else. Her long hair was damp around the edges but hung free without a tie.

"Mack? Wha—what are you doing in here?" He noticed

her hands pull the towel a little tighter around herself, but it was too late. He was already imagining her without it.

"We need to talk, Char."

"Not tonight, Mack. We're both tired, and Cal is giving us a chance to get some sleep."

"This won't take long," he promised, standing and taking the robe off the bathroom door. He held it out for Charlotte to slip her arms in, and she stared him down for a solid minute before she turned her back and slid one arm into the robe. She grasped the towel with that hand and slipped her other one in, tying it around her before letting the towel fall.

She may be good at keeping herself hidden, but he saw her and liked all of her. She was wrong if she thought he didn't notice her beautiful skin that glowed in the light of the lamp or the swell of her breasts from under the towel. He noticed all of her, the good and what she thought was bad, but he knew he wanted all of her. He was positive convincing Char of that would be more difficult than it should be.

He hung the towel on the bathroom doorknob and motioned for her to sit on the bed. "What do you want, Mack?" she asked, her fingers toying with the bathrobe's belt.

"I want to talk. You said could have, should have and would have are dangerous because they're past tense."

Char lifted her gaze to his. "So?"

"I talked to Eric, and he said some things that surprised me about the mission that day."

"Things like it wasn't your fault, and you did nothing wrong?"

"That and how others could have died, including me, had I opened the other door to load the family for the transport."

"I suppose he's not wrong," she agreed. "I hadn't thought of that."

"Surprisingly, during all these years, neither had I. There

were so many situations in that sandbox that should have killed me. Do you know about Hannah?"

"Cal's girlfriend in the army?" she asked, and he nodded. "Marlise told me she was killed, and Cal was shot."

"I was there. I killed the insurgent who was firing those bullets at my friends. Cal recovered and returned to the team, but he was never the same. Then the transport happened, and we all left for good."

"And started Secure One. There were worse things you could have done, Mack."

"Cal started Secure One," he clarified. "First, he worked as a mercenary and weapons expert for a few years while I wallowed."

"You wallowed?"

"In self-pity," he said, leaning down and loosening the laces on his boots. He lifted his pant leg, loosened the Velcro strap around his calf, and pulled his foot out. Immediately, his toes pointed to the floor while he pulled the sock off. He did the same on the other side until both feet were sock free and resting on the floor. "I went from running miles daily to barely walking to the bathroom with a walker, Char. The self-pity was strong, but the self-hatred was stronger. It was Cal and Eric who finally forced me to face the truth. This was my life now." He motioned at his feet, then lifted them up again. They hung down, his big toes touching the floor. "No amount of working out will make my feet move again. No matter how long I stare at them, I'll never be able to raise my toes off the floor the way you do. Willpower won't make the muscles, nerves and tendons all work together again. I had to face the truth, accept it and move forward with the hand I'd been dealt. Or in this case, foot."

She turned to face him. "You're trying to say I need to accept my past so I can find a new life."

"No, not at all," he said with a shake of his head. "I'm

trying to say it's okay to want a new life. For the longest time, I thought these scars held me back from life. Then I turned the scars around and used them for good."

"They reminded you that there are bad people in the world who need to be stopped." He nodded, and she couldn't hide her grimace. "That's the problem, Mack. I'm one of those bad people you've worked to stop."

He tipped her chin up with his finger until she was forced to hold his gaze. "That's not true, Char. You're not a bad person."

"I've done a lot of bad things. Things that go against who you are and what you believe, Mack. I've run drugs, been an escort and even had to, you know."

Her gaze hit the floor again, and he rested his forehead against hers. "I do know, but the difference is you didn't do any of those things because you wanted to. You did those things because you had to. I understand the difference, Char. The fact that you're here tonight tells me that you're inherently a good person. You want to help others and rid the world of people like The Madame who prey on innocent people."

"I do, but I still did those other things, Mack. Being with someone like me goes against everything you believe in."

He was silent, simply gazing into her eyes from where he rested against her forehead. "Did you want to do those things?"

"Of course not!" she exclaimed, jumping up and falling into the bathroom door. Mack steadied her, but she ripped her elbow from his grip to walk to the chair in the corner. "I did what I had to do to survive."

He moved his boots aside and stood, readying himself for something he'd never done before. He was about to be vulnerable with someone he only wanted to be strong for. He took an exaggerated step, lifting his thigh high to clear the floor of his toes that hung down. His foot made a "thwap" as it landed back on the hardwood floor. The same happened with the other leg, back and forth, until he stood before her.

"That's all any of us can do, Char. I don't believe in killing people, but I still had to do it in the army. I'm technically a murderer. Does that mean I'm a bad person?"

"No," she whispered, staring at her lap. "You were protecting innocent people and us at home, Mack. Nothing you did in the service can be considered bad if you followed orders."

"Then I say we level the playing field when it comes to you and me." He sat on the ottoman in front of her and took her hands.

"How?" she asked, lifting her head to gaze into his eyes. He got so lost in the depths of her blue ones that he fought to answer her.

"We consider ourselves equals."

"But we're not!" she exclaimed. "You're so much more than I am, Mack. You deserve so much more than I can offer you in this life. You need to leave, please."

She hung her head again, but he didn't leave. He leaned forward and did what he'd wanted to do since he first laid eyes on her. He kissed her. Her lips were soft, and she tasted of stolen innocence. She went stock still the moment their lips connected. He waited, his lips on hers, to see if she would find a way past her fear to enjoy the kiss. He worried she would force herself to kiss him because that was what she thought she had to do. He wanted the first, but if the second happened, he'd stop the kiss until she learned the difference.

Instead, she pulled away and brought her hands to her lips. "What are you doing?"

"Kissing you," he answered. The truth was simple. It was the acceptance that was hard.

"Why?"

"I want to, Char. I've wanted to kiss you since the day I met you."

"You're just saying that to get me to kiss you back."

His sigh was heavy when he shook his head. "No, I'm not, but I understand why you feel that way. It's hard to be vulnerable." He held up his pants legs to show her the scars, pitting and missing flesh from his calves. "But being vulnerable also requires bravery and courage. I didn't want to take my boots off and show you these scars. I'm as vulnerable as I can get when my legs are bare. It's hard to trust someone with the parts of you that you're ashamed of, but sometimes, the right person teaches you how to accept them and lose the shame."

He stood and walked to the bed, his high steppage gait leaving a slapping sound on the floor with every footfall. He bent, picked up his boots in one hand and grabbed the bedpost to steady himself.

"Where are you going?"

"To my room to get some sleep, you should too."

Mack took two steps and stopped when she moved in front of the door. "You aren't going to try to kiss me again?"

"No, Char. The next time I kiss you, it will be because you asked me to."

She was silent, and they faced off. Mack could see the turmoil in her eyes. For a moment, he felt terrible for putting it there. Then that emotion disappeared, and a new one replaced it. Pride. He had given her something to think about—she could change her life if she found a way to be vulnerable again. It wouldn't be easy for her after what she'd been through, but she would be better because of it.

"Aren't you going to put your boots on? You never let anyone see you without them."

Mack glanced down at the boots and then back to her.

"No. I'm no longer ashamed of my legs, Char. Your drawing was the reason I could be vulnerable here tonight. When I saw the expression you'd drawn, it was how I feel inside every day. That's the fear I have of someone thinking I'm less because of these. The words you wrote about my legs were validation about something I couldn't change. If I couldn't change it, I shouldn't feel ashamed." He walked to the door and turned the knob when she stepped out of the way. "Thank you for giving me that little piece of myself back. I'd love to have the drawing when and if you're ready to part with it. Get some sleep, Char. Tomorrow will be another long day."

He bent down and kissed her cheek before he left her room and walked down the hallway, waiting to hear her shut the door. She never did.

She gave her friend a shoulder shrug as she leaned on the deck railing.

"Listen, let me give you a little piece of advice. It's time to take your power back, Charlotte. If you don't, you'll find yourself standing in this same place year after year, wondering why life isn't working out for you."

"How do I take my power back when I never had any to begin with?" Charlotte was angry, and she balled her hands into fists at her sides.

"You're wrong. You are the only one with the power when it comes to yourself. That's the first thing you do to take power back. You stop blaming everyone else for where you are in life."

"But it's their fault!"

Mina held up her hand to calm her. "I know it's their fault. Everyone in your life did you wrong. There's no question. But blame is like poison. The longer you swallow it, the more toxic it becomes and the weaker you get. Letting go of the blame and starting fresh from where you are today gives you back all the power they took from you."

Charlotte stared at Mina for a long moment and then tipped her head. "I guess that kind of makes sense."

"It makes a lot of sense and will be easier to say than do. I get that. You have to trust yourself. Just the way you did the other night when you didn't hesitate to defend Ella. Confidence in who you are as a person helps you let the blame go."

"I don't have a lot of confidence. I never have."

"That's the whole idea of reclaiming your power, Charlotte. You picture yourself as the beautiful, strong, courageous and brave woman we all see rather than what all the toxic people in your life said you were. Once you do that consistently, you have all the control again. Do the things that make you feel powerful, even if that means you take those things back from the toxic people too."

"Like art?" Charlotte leaned against the railing and wiped her face one more time of a wayward tear that refused to stay behind her lid.

"Yes, like art. I'm not going to tell you to go out and start tagging buildings again," Mina said with a lip tilt that made Charlotte laugh. "But you can use your art to do good the same as you have been with Secure One. The map you drew for Mack to help him visualize the rivers across the country was so intricate and defined that it blew my computer-based model out of the water. See what I did there?"

A smile tilted Charlotte's lips up, and she nodded. "Well done. I'm glad I can use my only talent to help others."

"Wrong," Mina said instantly. "You have so many more talents than art. You just made my point. You're listening to the toxic people from your past rather than trusting in what you know about yourself."

After sharing a moment of silence, Charlotte could see her point. "You're right. Why do I do that? I'm free now. I should be celebrating that and moving forward rather than keeping myself locked in that past." Mina nodded and gave her a playful punch on the arm. Charlotte groaned and let her head fall backward. "I screwed up tonight."

"With Mack?"

"How did you know?"

"Woman's intuition," she answered with a wink. Then she hooked Charlotte's arm in hers, and they walked back toward the house. "You can fix it."

"You don't know what happened."

"I don't need to know," she promised, her head swiveling as they walked across the grass toward the house. "I can see the emotion that flows between you when you're together. There will be fits and starts to any relationship, especially with your complicated past, but if you're honest with him, things will smooth out."

Mina held the door open, and Charlotte walked back to her room in a daze. Did she want a relationship with Mack? When she picked up her drawing pad and opened it, the truth was there in black and white.

AFTER A SHOWER and coffee, Mack was still tired. Try as he might, sleep hadn't come easily. He knew he'd done the right thing with Charlotte, even if it hadn't been the easy thing. Now he had to get his head in the game and work this case before another woman died—a woman just like Charlotte.

Wrong. A woman like Charlotte used to be.

The voice was right. Charlotte wasn't a helpless woman caught in dire circumstances anymore. She was an essential part of the team and didn't hesitate to jump into the fray for the good of others. He had to remember that. She didn't need to be saved.

"Everything quiet?" Mack asked Eric as he walked by Ella's room.

"There was a bit of a disturbance, but Mina took care of it." Mack cocked his head, and Eric's gaze drifted to the windows for a moment. "Charlotte went for a walk without telling anyone. Mina saw her on the cameras and pulled her back in."

A curse word fell from Mack's lips. "She knows better than to go out alone."

Eric held up his hands. "Take it up with her. They're in command central. Selina is preparing Bethany to bring her down."

"Are you coming down too?"

A shake of his head said that was a negative. "No one to put on Ella. We're too short-staffed."

"Bring her down."

"To command central?"

Mack shrugged. "Why not? Let's face it. She's already

knee-deep in this sludge. Maybe listening to us will spark something she remembers about her dad and his campaign. If nothing else, she can be there for Bethany. We need you down there so you know what's going on."

"Ten-four. I'll prepare her and be down shortly."

Mack gave him a salute and jogged down the stairs toward the office. They needed a break on this case soon. He already knew what the police were doing, and the answer to that was nothing. Every day they wasted was another day closer to a woman's death. He doubted Bethany had anything to add as far as the river killings went, but she may be able to tie up The Madame's loose strings, including where the other three Misses had gone when they escaped the raids.

Voices drifted out of the control room, and Mack stopped next to the door and leaned on the frame, watching Charlotte at the whiteboard. She had a marker and was making lists next to her paper map. One was in blue, and one was in red. Mack recognized a few of the names on each list. They were the senators up for reelection.

"Good morning," Mack said, walking in the door as though he hadn't been standing there, watching her. "Everything quiet?"

"For now," Mina answered, her gaze flicking to Charlotte. "Just waiting on the rest of the team."

"I told Eric to bring Ella down with him. He needs to be in the loop, and she's up to her waist in this disaster anyway."

Mina stood and stretched. "I agree. Dorian may not, but we just won't tell him." Mack and Charlotte both laughed, but Mack let his die off just to hear Charlotte's. When she laughed, it felt like hope to him. "I'm going to get some coffee. Do you guys want anything?"

"I'd have a cup," Charlotte said. "Let me come with you."

Mina brushed her away with her hand and walked to the door. "I can handle two cups of coffee. I'll be back before everyone gets here."

The room was silent as Mack walked up to the board where Charlotte stood. "How did you sleep?" He brushed a piece of hair off her face and behind her ear.

"I didn't. How about you?"

"Equally as well. I heard you took a walk. You shouldn't do that right now."

To his surprise, she didn't drop her gaze or look away. She held him in her atmosphere as her spine stiffened, and she lifted her chin a hair. "I decide what I do, not you. I was perfectly safe, considering this place is a fortress."

Mack lifted a brow but bit back the need to point out that while they were there, Cal was in charge and gave the orders. He didn't say it because he liked her spunk. She was holding onto the power she'd found within herself here, and he wasn't going to be the one to clip her wings.

Rather than say anything more, he motioned at the boards. "What's this?"

Charlotte smiled as though she were thankful for the subject change. "I was making a list of the senators running for reelection listed by the party. It's hard when they're all over the map. I thought it might help us recognize patterns or common denominators."

"Has it?"

"Not yet, but I just finished the list." She was laughing, and Mack ate up the sound. She didn't laugh freely that often, so when she did, he wanted to be there to hear it. "About last night," she whispered, staring over his shoulder. "I'm sorry for treating you the way I did. I was scared and didn't know how to react."

"I understood that," Mack promised, giving her a gentle hug. "Never apologize for standing up for yourself. You weren't ready, and you let me know that. I wasn't upset. I respect your boundaries, Char."

She sank into him as though those were the exact words she needed to hear.

Chapter Fourteen

"Charlotte?"

Mack and Charlotte jumped apart to see Bethany in the doorway with Marlise on one side and Selina on the other.

"Bethany." Charlotte walked to her and took her hand. "How are you doing?"

"I'm okay," she said with a smile. "Selina and Marlise have been taking good care of me. I'm sorry to scare you the way I did. I didn't know what else to do."

"Don't apologize," Charlotte said, giving her a gentle squeeze. "I wasn't scared as much as I was in shock that you were here. I worried so much about you and Emelia. To hear your voice was a shock."

"You worried about us? Even after what we did?"

Marlise and Selina led Bethany to a chair where she sat. Charlotte sat next to her and offered her a smile.

"You did what you thought you had to do to be free. I would never judge you for that, even if you saw overthrowing The Miss as your only option."

"That wasn't what we wanted to do!" she exclaimed. "We wanted to overthrow her, so we could let all the women go!"

"It's okay," Charlotte said, trying to calm her. "I believe you. There was no way for you to know that her father was running drugs into the states and funding her operation.

Take a deep breath and try to stay calm. We want to hear your story, but we want everyone here, so let's wait for Cal and the rest of the team to arrive."

"Her father was supplying the drugs we had to move?"

"Yes," Charlotte said, squeezing her hand gently. "You never had a chance of overthrowing her. Her death was the only way to be free."

"And she's dead?" she asked, glancing between everyone, but Mack answered.

"She is. Unfortunately, I had to protect my team, and she was the casualty."

"Nothing unfortunate about that woman being dead." Her tone was firm and left no question regarding how she felt about the matter. "The Madame is in jail?"

"For a good long time," Charlotte assured her. "We don't have to worry about her anymore."

Mina walked in with a carafe of coffee while Cal and the rest of the team filtered in. After Mina handed out cups of coffee, everyone sat comfortably in a semicircle to hear what Bethany had to say. The discussion was being recorded in case there was information for the police. Mack was sure that would be their next step, but they'd listen to what she had to say since Bethany came to them first.

"Tell us what you remember about the last time you saw The Miss," Charlotte said. Cal had asked her to take the lead on questioning because the last thing they wanted to do was scare Bethany or make things harder for her. She had a story to tell. That was why she was here, but allowing her to tell it would be the trickiest part.

"After we talked to The Miss about our plan, it was late. She told us she'd think about making us more pivotal members of the team. Satisfied, we went to bed in our pod. When I woke up, I was in a basement bedroom. That's all I remember. I don't know how many days I was out or how

I got there. I know it was a basement because the window was at the top of the room and I could see the ground at the window level. Before I had time to figure out what had happened, he walked in."

"He?" Charlotte asked. "Did he have a name?"

Bethany nodded but then shook her head. She finally shrugged as though she didn't know the answer. "He told me my new name was Angel and forced me to call him Little Daddy."

"Little Daddy? That's different. Usually, they just want to be called daddy," Charlotte said, taking Bethany's hand.

"Right?" she asked, trying to lighten the mood with girl banter, but it didn't hit the same way when you'd been held hostage for years by someone using the name Little Daddy. "But the thing is, there's a Big Daddy somewhere," she whispered, her words falling on each other out of fear. "When Little Daddy thinks you're ready, he sends you to Big Daddy."

"Did you ever meet Big Daddy?" Charlotte asked, and Bethany immediately began shaking her head.

She leaned in to whisper to Charlotte. "The night I escaped, Little Daddy told me I was ready for Big Daddy. That's when I knew I had to run."

"Running was the right thing to do, Bethany. Were you the only woman there? What happened to Emelia?"

"I don't know," she said as her voice broke. "When I woke up in the basement, she wasn't with me."

Mina glanced at Mack, and he knew what she was thinking. Was Emelia one of those unidentified women from two years ago? At this point, he'd believe anything was possible.

"You woke up almost eighteen months ago and were alone in the house?" Charlotte asked to clarify.

"In the beginning, another woman was there with me, but she didn't last very long before he took her to Big Daddy.

He never brought another woman home that I heard after that. There could have been more that I couldn't hear if they were upstairs or in a different room. I didn't stop to check when I locked him in my room that night. I should have checked! What if I left Emelia behind?"

"Shh," Selina said, glancing over her head at Cal for a moment. "You did the right thing getting out of there. Do you remember where the house was located?"

Mack knew Selina was trying to redirect Bethany before she had a meltdown and couldn't answer more questions. He'd seen it happen with Marlise and Charlotte and didn't want to see it again. The fear was paralyzing for these women after they escaped. Fear that they'd done something wrong. Fear someone was coming after them. Fear that they didn't do enough. That was the hardest part for him to swallow. Watching them so filled with fear that they couldn't even move.

"It was in the woods. Deep in the woods. I ran along the river, and when I came out of the woods, I found a little gas station. I managed to hot-wire an old truck, and on my way out of town, I passed a sign that said Sugarville, Pennsylvania. I made it to a bigger city before I ran out of gas, so I asked The Salvation Army for help. They got me a bus ticket to here."

"Because you heard that Secure One had killed The Miss?" Charlotte asked, and Bethany nodded her head immediately.

"I heard that Secure One was here when another body was found. I didn't know if you'd still be here, but I didn't know how else to find you."

"That was quick thinking," Mack encouraged the woman. "Why did you want to find us specifically?"

Bethany turned to look at him, and he saw all the fear in her eyes. There was so much that he worried she would drown in it before she finished her story. "If you killed The Miss, then you had to be good people. I needed help and knew I couldn't go to the police."

"Why not?" Charlotte asked with her head tipped in confusion. "The Miss was already dead and The Madame in prison. There was no one left to hurt you."

"But the police might not believe me when I told them my story. I left Little Daddy in that room, and I don't know if he's dead." A shiver ran through her. "If he's not dead, he might find me. If he is dead, the police might be looking for me."

"I can understand that thinking," Charlotte agreed. "How did you get the better of Little Daddy that night?"

"I don't want to talk about that," she whispered so low that Mack almost didn't make out what she said.

"That's okay," Charlotte promised. "You don't have to talk about it, but I need to know if you escaped the same night the body was found here?"

"I think so," Bethany answered. "I ran the first night, was on the bus the second night and here last night."

Bethany was sinking fast, but there was still so much to ask her. Mack was about to ask a question when Charlotte did. "Bethany, you said you were in Pennsylvania when you found the truck, right?"

"Yes, that's what the license plate said. I hope he finds the truck. I don't want to get into trouble for stealing it, but I was so tired and had to get away."

"You won't get in trouble," Cal assured her. "They were extenuating circumstances that the police will understand. Besides, you left it for them to find."

"Do you know how long you ran on foot?" Charlotte asked to complete her question.

"Maybe two hours? I know it was after ten when I left the room and way after midnight when I found the truck."

Mack was making notes on the whiteboard, so he added that to the list. Maybe Mina could do some calculations and get close to the town where Bethany was held hostage.

"You were there a long time, Bethany. I'm impressed that you were strong enough to run that far."

Bethany straightened as though Charlotte's words sparked her determination. "I knew from the beginning that he was going to move me. I spent a couple of months in a stupor but then decided if I was going to try to run when I had the chance, I needed to be strong. He brought me healthy food, and I did a lot of exercise in my room to stay in shape. That was how I overtook him that night. He thought I was asleep, so he dozed off and I took advantage of it."

Cal leaned forward and clasped his hands together casually. "Did you talk to the other women in the house, Bethany?"

"I shared one wall of my bedroom with another room. When I first got there, a woman named Andrea was in that room. Then she left and was replaced by another woman shortly after that. That woman mostly just cried the whole time she was there."

Mack glanced at Charlotte, whose eyes were wide when she looked up at him. He nodded and motioned with his eyes to ask Bethany the next question.

"Did she tell you her name or where she was from?"

"Andrea went to Big Daddy before me. I think I was supposed to be next, and Layla was supposed to be training to go after me."

"Wait, did you say Layla?" Charlotte asked, leaning forward on her chair.

"I think that's what she said her name was, but it was hard to understand because she was always crying, and we had to talk through the wall. I was surprised when Little

Daddy said he would take her to Big Daddy before me. He said only he could train her to do what had to be done."

"What had to be done?" Mack asked, shelving the information about Layla for a moment.

"We were being trained to take care of Big Daddy. We had to be ready to do anything he needed from writing a letter to, you know, in bed."

"They had you perform sexual favors? Did you ever see his face?" Cal asked, but Bethany shook her head.

"No. Little Daddy wore a leather mask over his face. I never saw more than his lips and his eyes."

"Do you think you could describe him for me, and I could draw him?" Charlotte asked the woman, whose eyes widened. "If you can't, we all understand."

"I can try," she whispered. "I feel like I failed by running. I didn't get the right information to help you."

"No," Cal said before she finished her sentence. "You didn't fail. You got out alive, and that's miraculous after being there for that long. You survived, Bethany. That's all that matters. Any information you can give us will help, but you did the right thing by running and not looking back."

Bethany nodded as she stared at her hands. "I wish I could have helped the other women, but once you went to Big Daddy, you never came back."

"You've been a huge help to us this morning," Charlotte said, squeezing her hand. "I'm so proud of you for getting out and finding us. We're going to help you now, okay?"

Bethany's face crumpled as she nodded. "I need help. Just like you and Marlise did."

"And we'll get it for you," Selina promised, helping her stand and putting an arm around her.

"We'll take her back to rest," Marlise said to Cal, who nodded. "Then we'll figure out where to go from there for her."

They led the trembling woman from the room, and Mack knew life would never go back to the way it was ten minutes ago.

"Layla was with Big Daddy. Big Daddy has to be The Red River Slayer." Mack heard the fear in Charlotte's voice when she spoke.

"It appears so," said Cal, who sat leaning forward with his hands propped under his chin. "But if Layla had only been dead for three days before we found her, that means Big Daddy kept her for a long time. It's hard to hide a human being for that long."

"Unless they're kept in plain sight," Mack said, lowering the tablet. "Bethany said they had to learn to do everything, including writing a letter. Maybe they're his assistant," he said using quotations, "and they're brainwashed enough not to say otherwise."

"You mean he tells them that they're safe and he will take care of them and give them a job?" Charlotte asked, and Mack nodded. "He had to have convinced Layla she was safe."

"Or that he was on the up and up," Roman agreed.

"You're forgetting that he expects sexual favors," Mina said. "How do you convince someone that is part of an assistant's job?"

Charlotte shrugged and glanced down at her hands. "You give them everything they never had," she whispered. "You buy them nice things, let them get their hair and nails done, tell them you love them. When a woman has never had those things, it's effortless to ply her with them."

Mina started to nod as she spoke and then pointed at her. "She's right. I bet that's how he's doing it. Bethany said they took care of her and brought her healthy food. They wanted the women to be functional when they got to Big Daddy."

"We're still missing a piece of the puzzle," Roman said.

He was frustrated by the partial information that didn't make a whole.

"We're missing a lot of the puzzle, Roman," Mack said, his head shaking.

"But wait." Charlotte stood up and grabbed a marker by the whiteboard. She wrote Andrea, Bethany and Layla. "We'll assume, since we don't know, that one of the last five women was Andrea, right?"

Everyone nodded, but Mina spoke. "I'm searching now to see if I can find that name in the databases, but she could have been one of the two that weren't identified, or she hasn't been found yet."

"All of the what-ifs aside," Charlotte said, putting a red X through Andrea's name. "We have a pattern developing. Bethany was supposed to go to Big Daddy before Layla, but Little Daddy couldn't train Layla, so she jumped ahead in the queue." She made an arrow over Bethany's name and then put a red X through Layla, rewriting Bethany's name on the other side of Layla. "That explains why Bethany was held for so long and why she was being moved to Big Daddy right after we found Layla. However, look what happens when we take Bethany away." She scrubbed out her name with her hand.

"She broke the cycle," Mack said immediately.

Charlotte pointed at him with excitement. "Yes! The woman he was planning to move to the coveted position is gone. So now what? Where does he get his next victim if he has no other women with Little Daddy?"

"And if the cycle is broken, will he stick to his schedule of a death every six weeks, or will he become unpredictable because his perfect order has been broken?" Mack was standing next to Charlotte now by the whiteboard. "Does anyone have an opinion?"

The rest of the team sat open-mouthed as they stared at

them. Charlotte was right, the cycle had been broken, and now Mack feared that their perp would react by killing more women.

"He might go underground and try to regroup. Especially if Little Daddy is dead," Roman said. "Or he might have women in other houses that we don't know about yet."

"That I doubt." Mina stood and walked to her computer. "He has to maintain the house where the women are kept with Little Daddy as well as his own living quarters. Unless he's a millionaire, it would be difficult to run three households."

"Then we need to find the guy before he kills another innocent woman," Cal said, his voice tight. "But how? How do we find a guy so good at hiding in plain sight?"

"Do we have a body in the Susquehanna River yet?" Roman asked Charlotte, who stood by the board.

The Susquehanna River was the main river in Pennsylvania and Charlotte knew what he was thinking immediately. "No, but we already know he's transporting these women a long way to leave them in a river, so we can't assume that's the next river."

"We can if the guy's chain of women was broken," Mack said. "It would be safe to assume that he'll act rashly now. Either he's going to kill a random woman, or he's going to go underground, and it will be another two years before we hear from him again. We don't want that."

"We need to go to Pennsylvania," Roman said.

Cal shook his head. "Impossible. I don't have the staffing for that. We're already stretched too thin."

"I have Efren coming on, but he can't be here until tomorrow," Mina piped up from behind her computer. "Then we have the party security to worry about next."

Mack met Charlotte's gaze across the board and knew

what she was thinking. She was going to figure out a way to get to Pennsylvania and offer herself up for The Red River Slayer to grab. He wasn't going to let that happen.

Chapter Fifteen

Marlise and Selina arrived to fill them in on Bethany's condition. "She needs medical care," Selina said, "but I can't convince her to leave yet. I keep telling her she needs to talk to the police, but she's afraid to do that too. She has been held in captivity for years. She needs a psychiatrist and a therapist to help her."

"We agree," Cal said. "But we can give her one more day before we force anything on her."

Charlotte was trying to follow the conversation and sort out the information in her head and on the board. Thirty-three senators were running for reelection, but so far, only six, possibly eight, bodies had been found.

"There's no way," Charlotte muttered as she stared at the board. "There's just no way."

Mack walked up to her and took her shoulder. "There's no way for what, sweetheart?"

"For this guy to kill the number of women necessary to equal the thirty-three senators running for reelection. Now that we know he keeps them for an extended period, if Bethany's captor is The Red River Slayer, there isn't enough time." Charlotte looked over at Mina. "Did they do autopsies on all the women?" Mina nodded immediately. "Did they get a time of death on all of them?"

"No," Mina said, standing and walking around the computer. "Layla's was the first autopsy that was within that tight of a window. It was impossible to know with the other women."

"You're saying they could have been dead much longer?" Mack asked.

"Whether they took that long to float to shore or he held them after death, there's no way to know. It could be pure coincidence that the women were found at that time interval."

"My science teacher said that rivers don't freeze over like lakes," Ella said from the back of the room. Charlotte had forgotten she was there since she'd had her earphones in and was watching a movie. "But shallow parts of rivers can freeze. If a body floated under the ice and got trapped, it wouldn't move again until spring arrived. He also said that the streamflow of rivers changes by seasons."

"Following that train of thought," Mina said, standing up. "If spring hits and there's more snowmelt in one area of the river, that pushes a big deluge of water through the river at a high rate of speed."

"Which could easily upend a body trapped in sludge," Mack finished.

"If he's trying to make a point, wouldn't he want the bodies to be found immediately? He's taking a chance they won't be found where he wanted them to be or at all."

"Serial killers don't think the same as we do, Mack," Mina said, and Charlotte smiled. Mina was going to school him about the psychology of psychopaths, and she couldn't wait. "They do things that aren't logical to us, but to them, it's completely logical. Sometimes, they don't care if and when their victims are found."

"That would explain the longer period with no bodies," Roman added.

"You're saying we got lucky finding Layla just three days after her death." Mack waited for someone to answer.

"Highly probable," Mina confirmed. "This is spring, and the river is high and swift. He may have misjudged how long it would take her to come ashore this time."

Charlotte glanced over at Ella, who was staring at the list of names on the whiteboard. "Did I forget one?" she asked the teen, who shook her head.

"No. The names are all there. Your comment about there being no way for him to kill that many women started me thinking." She took a marker from the board and put checkmarks next to nine names.

"What do the checkmarks mean?" Charlotte asked.

"Those nine senators are committee members on fisheries, wildlife and water. I know because my dad is on the committee."

Charlotte noticed the surprise on Mack's face even before he spoke. "Would this committee deal with rivers?"

Ella shrugged. "Well, sure. I know there's a big fight about dams and the damage they do to the waterways. Or something like that anyway. My dad talks about it all the time."

Mack grabbed a marker and underlined the nine senators' names on their states. There were three senators' states that had rivers where bodies were found, which included Senator Dorian. "If I'm following this correctly, the three bodies recently found match up to a state with a senator on this list."

"And that means instead of twenty-seven more women, there could be six more before this is over," Charlotte said, her voice filled with fury and fear. "We can't let that happen."

Mack walked over to Mina and leaned on her desk. "Can you see if the previous reelection cycle river deaths match the states of any previous committee members?"

"I'm on it," she said, putting her hands on the keyboard. "Give me thirty minutes."

"If this is some nut trying to bring attention to a cause by killing women, we need to stop him now," Mack said, walking back to Charlotte and putting a protective hand on her back.

Cal stood. "I couldn't agree more. Charlotte, take Ella back to her room, please. Eric, Roman and Mack, you're with me. We'll reconvene here in thirty."

Charlotte put her arm around Ella and walked with her to the kitchen. "Forget going to your room. We're going to have breakfast, and then you'll be there to hear what Mina discovered."

"I don't know if Cal will like that," Ella said, nervously chewing on her lip.

"Too bad. If it weren't for you picking up on that pattern, we'd still be stuck in neutral. A good friend recently told me we must control our power if we want respect. This is us demanding respect."

She winked at the young girl and then led her through the kitchen door for pancakes and juice.

HE LISTENED TO the incessant ringing in his ear as he sat at his desk, the low drone of voices outside his office door reminding him to play it cool. The call went to voice mail again, and he angrily slammed the phone down on his blotter. So much for playing it cool.

"Where the hell is he?" His growl scared the cat, who darted back under the leather sofa against one wall. It was his ex-wife's cat, but she'd decided she hadn't wanted it when she moved to the Bahamas to live with her new boyfriend. He often wondered if they were enjoying their extended time under the blue-green waters.

A smile lifted his lips at the thought. That memory didn't

solve his problem though. He had no idea where his guy was or why he wasn't answering his phone. Maybe he was just busy, but even he couldn't swallow that excuse anymore. If that were the case, he would have called him back after the first ten voice mails, each one increasingly angrier.

He glanced at the clock and sighed. He was going to have to mix business with pleasure. He already regretted what was to come, but his guy had left him no choice. He walked to a side door of his office and opened it. "Miss Andrea, I'd like to see you for a moment."

He waited while the young blond woman joined him in the office. Today she was wearing a pencil skirt that accentuated her bottom and a silk blouse that made her look professional and sex kitten at the same time. He motioned for her to close the door, and she couldn't hide the apprehension on her face as she turned to do it. His desire stirred. She knew what was to come and would obey him no matter what he asked her.

When she turned back, her face changed to that of a contented woman ready to please her protector. "How can I help?"

She asked the question that made his beast roar to life, but he forced it down. This was not the time or the place.

"Have you enjoyed your time with me, Miss Andrea?" He propped his elbows on his sizeable executive desk and steepled his fingers against his lips.

"Very much so," she agreed. She sat in the chair he motioned to and crossed her legs. "I'm quite happy working for you."

His mouth watered at the sight of her tanned skin just waiting for his touch, but he didn't. Touch, that is. "And I'm happy to hear you say that, Andrea. I need a favor, and I can't ask anyone else. No one can know about this."

"I wouldn't tell a soul." She batted her lashes at him the

way he demanded of her, but he wasn't looking to score today…at least not yet.

"Good. Be ready to leave in thirty minutes."

"We're taking a trip? Is it for work or pleasure?"

"A little of both, Miss Andrea. A little of both," he said, allowing his inner beast to come through in the smile he offered her. "Work first with pleasure to follow."

She stood and left his office, his gaze savoring the moment. It would be the last time he'd see that bottom walking out his door.

Chapter Sixteen

"A macabre scene played out on the bank of the Susque-hanna River this morning," the newscaster began, and Charlotte swiveled toward the television in the corner of the room. "There were two bodies discovered by a fisherman in a weed-filled slough this morning. Initially, the police suspected The Red River Slayer had killed again until they discovered the bodies were locked in a lovers' embrace. The man and woman were taken to the local medical examiner's office to await identification. If you think you may have information about this couple, please call—"

Charlotte didn't hear another word as she was already out the door and running to command central. Eric was alone in the room, staring at the whiteboard when she arrived.

"Eric," she said, out of breath enough that she needed to pause before saying anything more. "Two bodies were found in Pennsylvania this morning along the river."

He whirled around before she finished speaking. "Women?"

"That's the weird part," she said, walking into the room. "They said it was a man and a woman locked in a lovers' embrace."

"Did they give any other information?" he asked, grabbing a walkie from the table.

"They were taken to the local medical examiner for identification."

"Secure two, Echo," he said into the black box.

"Secure one, Whiskey," came Mina's voice.

"Mina, can you come to the office? I need some help on the computer."

"Be there in two," she answered, and then the box went silent.

"It has to be a coincidence." Eric was addressing Charlotte this time. "Other than the river, it's too far off the norm for our perp. There would be no reason for him to kill a man."

"Unless it was Little Daddy."

"How does the woman come into play then?"

"I don't know, okay! I'm just telling you what the news report said." Frustrated, Charlotte plopped down in a chair and rubbed her face with her hands. She needed sleep, but she suspected that wasn't happening soon.

Mina jogged into the room, and Eric explained what he needed. She started searching for the early copies of the story to see if one had more information than the other. While she did that, Charlotte paced. She had too much nervous energy. Eric might not believe her, but she had a gut feeling about this guy, and her gut never lied. How the woman came into play, she didn't know yet, but if anyone could figure it out, Mina could. They'd have to tell Cal what they discovered when he landed back at Secure One. He'd taken Roman and Marlise back with him, so the team at headquarters wasn't shorthanded. Mina stayed behind to help with anything computer-based since she could work remotely for Secure One simultaneously. Charlotte was suddenly glad she'd stayed.

"From what I can gather, a fisherman found the couple early this morning. The police reported that it was difficult to disengage the pair, but once they did, they realized the couple had died together."

"Rigor mortis?" Eric asked.

"Seems like it," Mina said from behind the computer.

"If rigor was set, then they had to have died recently. Full rigor only lasts for twenty-four hours after death. If the water was cold though, rigor could last much longer." Eric put his hand on his hip. "Anything else?"

"No, they don't have much to go on right now. The police asked the public to come forward with any information."

"Where did they find the bodies?" Charlotte asked. "Near a town?"

"Every station reported it, so I can't use that as the first identifier. I might have to go through some back doors to find that information."

"They worked hard to keep the location from the news report," Eric said, pacing toward the door. "They didn't say where the bodies were found or what ME has them."

"Let me look into this," Mina said as she typed. "If I can come up with the ME who has the bodies, or a report entered by a police station, I'll know within a few miles where they were found."

Charlotte grabbed a walkie and held it up. "Call me when you know something. I'm going to offer breaks."

Eric waved her off, and she headed for the stairs where Mack was standing guard over the women. Selina had stayed back to take care of Bethany until she could transfer her to a facility, and Ella was doing schoolwork in her room. Charlotte knew Mack didn't need a break, but she wanted to update him.

You want to see him.

With an eye roll, Charlotte shut that voice down. There

was no sense even considering a life with Mack. He might want her at the moment, but there was a lifetime of things he didn't know about her.

And he doesn't care.

The grunt she gave that voice was loud and clear as she stomped up the stairs.

Do the things that make you feel powerful, even if that means you have to take those things back from the toxic people too.

Mina's words ran through her mind as she hit the landing and headed toward the bedrooms. What made her feel powerful? That was the question she had to answer.

STANDING AROUND DOING nothing was making Mack antsy. He needed to move, but there was nowhere to go. His gut told him something was about to go down, and he widened his stance a bit in acknowledgment. When Cal returned to Secure One, he would immediately send in the extra help he'd hired for the campaign party rather than wait. Once Mina's new guy arrived, Mack would hand over the bodyguard duties with gratitude. There was nothing Mack hated more than standing around idle.

He ran a hand over his face and closed his eyes for a moment. Exhaustion hung on him after the night he'd had, but he could only blame himself. Instead of dreaming about Charlotte, he should have reminded himself that he couldn't get involved with her. That reminder had nothing to do with who she was and everything to do with what she'd been through in life. She didn't need his ugly baggage to carry when she had enough of her own—

"Kiss me."

Mack looked down at the woman standing in his path with confusion. "What?"

"I said, kiss me."

"I heard what you said," he whispered, leaning closer. "I'm confused why you said it."

"You said you wouldn't kiss me again until I asked you to. I just asked. Now kiss me."

Mack lifted a brow. He liked her spunk, but this felt like a test he could fail no matter his choice. "I would love to, but there are cameras everywhere. We should save that for a time when we're—"

Finishing the sentence wasn't an option when she grabbed him and planted her lips on his. Hers were warm and tasted of sweet strawberries. His head swam at the sensations she evoked in him until he was left little choice but to grasp her waist and pull her to him. He shouldn't be kissing her, but none of him cared. If Charlotte was initiating a kiss, he would enjoy every moment of it, in case it was the only one he ever got.

Tilting his head, he dug in deeper, still letting her control it, but pushing back enough for her to know he was all in no matter where she took it. He wouldn't force it further than she was comfortable with, but he would need the strength of a god to let her go when she ended it. The little moan that escaped the back of her throat fanned his desire until he was sure their closeness revealed his true feelings for her. Again, not one part of him cared. It wasn't a secret that he desired her, and this kiss made it known that she felt the same, even if the whole situation was complicated beyond measure.

Her tongue traced the closed split in his lips until he parted them and let her roam his mouth, his tongue tangling with hers until neither one could breathe, and they had to fall apart just to suck in air. She stood before him, her chest heaving as she lowered her forehead to his chest.

"I shouldn't have done that. I'm sorry."

Mack tipped her chin up until they made eye contact.

"Do. Not. Apologize. In case you didn't notice, I loved every second of it, so no apology is needed."

"But the cameras—"

"Will show them what they already know," he said with a wink. "I am curious to hear what changed between last night and today."

"Mina told me to do what makes me feel powerful, even if I have to take those things back from my toxic past."

"That's good advice," he agreed, tucking a piece of hair behind her ear as she rested her forehead on his chest. "Being the one to initiate the kiss took back your power from the men who always said they owned you, right?" Her head nodded against his sweater, but she still didn't look up. Rather than push her away and force eye contact that would make her uncomfortable, Mack wrapped his arms around her and squeezed. "I'm proud of you. It's not easy to leave our bad experiences in the past and live in the moment. Thank you for letting me be the one to help you do that."

"I didn't use you, Mack. I wanted to kiss you." She finally lifted her face to his and smiled.

"I know you didn't use me, Char. That wasn't what I was implying. I was genuinely thanking you for trusting me enough to know you could. For the record, I wanted to kiss you too. I think I proved that last night."

Her head bob was enough to tell him he'd gotten through to her, and she understood. Slowly, he loosened his arms so she could step back and collect herself. He figured Mina was in command central doing a fist pump if she'd seen them on camera, and he couldn't stop the smirk that filled his face. Until he remembered Eric was down there too.

Mack wasn't sure what was up with Eric, but something was. He was constantly defensive and pushing back on any order Mack or Cal gave. They'd been friends for a dozen years, so he hoped if Eric had a real problem, he'd come to them and talk openly about it, but so far, that hadn't happened. Mack made a mental note to talk to Cal about it once he was back at Secure One and had a moment to think.

"I also have an update to give you," Charlotte said after straightening her hair. Mack listened while she filled him in on the two bodies found in Pennsylvania.

"That's odd, but not necessarily tied to The Red River Slayer."

Charlotte shrugged when she nodded. "I know, but they were found in the same river as the one Bethany was near when she ran." She held her hand out at the door on his right. "She did say she wasn't sure if she killed the guy."

Mack considered this but then shook his head. "It still doesn't make sense. If she killed him, he wouldn't end up in the river. He would have decayed in the house."

"You're ignoring the obvious, Mack. Big Daddy."

"You think Big Daddy found Little Daddy and threw him in the river? Who's the woman?"

A text alert came in, and Mack grabbed his phone. There was a text from Mina, and all it said was get a room. He couldn't hide the smirk on his face, and Charlotte noticed.

"What? Is it Cal?"

He turned the phone for her to read. Her lips tipped up, and she bit the inside of her cheek to keep from laughing. "I'm not great at stealth mode yet."

Mack's laughter filled the hallway, and he put his arm around her shoulders and brushed his lips across her ear. "I'm not complaining."

Her huff was easy to decipher and only made his smirk grow into a full-blown grin. Char had no idea how special she was to him. "Back to the case," she said in the perfunctory tone of an experienced teacher. "The woman."

"Oh, yes, the woman. It doesn't fit, Char."

Her finger came up into his chest. "Maybe not, but you

were the one who said removing Bethany from the chain may make him do something rash or unexpected."

"Fair point," he agreed. "I did say that, and this would be rash and unexpected. Hopefully, Mina has something for us by the time Cal gets back to Secure One. Then we can set up a conference call with him to discuss it."

"We need to go to Pennsylvania, Mack."

Her statement was so decisive that he paused on his next thought. "We? Whatever for?"

"I don't know, but my gut tells me we'll find pieces of the puzzle out there."

Mack grasped her shoulders and held her gaze. "This isn't our puzzle to solve. If the feds got wind that we were sticking our nose into this case again, they might lock Cal down, and I don't want that to happen."

"Neither do I, but they aren't doing their job!" she exclaimed in frustration. "They should have solved this case already!"

Mack didn't react to her frustration except to squeeze her shoulder as a reminder that he was there. Once she settled, he spoke gently to her. "I understand you're angry about this case, and you've come by that right naturally. I can separate myself from the case more because I didn't live that kind of life. Then I think about you, and I know in my heart that it could have been you if you'd played the wrong card at the wrong time. The feds may not devote time to this case because the victims are women without families. They don't feel as compelled to solve it quickly since no one is prodding them to keep after it."

"Yes," she said, her shoulders loosening in his grasp. "No one understands that part of it. It could have been me, and I don't want it to be another woman I know. I can't let that happen, Mack."

He nodded with her just to give her a moment to own

those feelings of fear and determination. "Okay, let's see what Mina finds, and then we'll talk to Cal about letting us do more boots-on-the-ground work in Pennsylvania. Our turnaround will be quick though, since the party is in ten days, and it all rests on Efren getting here to help out."

"Understood," she agreed with a nod.

Mack couldn't help but wonder if her intuition was correct. If their perp found Little Daddy dead and Bethany gone, would he kill a random woman just to make a point? If Mina's answer to that question was yes, then he wouldn't ask Cal if they could go to Pennsylvania—he'd tell him they were going.

Chapter Seventeen

The two-hour ride was made light by the occasional country road he'd pull over on to be assisted by his assistant. It was a perk none of his colleagues had, but none of them were nearly as brilliant as they thought they were. No one suspected a thing, but he wasn't surprised by that. As someone who studied the human mind, he'd learned that a simple explanation was enough for 99 percent of the population. Thankfully, his interactions with the 1 percent of the population that asked too many questions were few and far between. When he ran across one, he usually had to remove them from the population rather unexpectedly.

He put the car in Park and stared straight ahead. He hated what he was about to do, but there was no choice. It had been four days since he'd had contact with his wingman, and he was worried. Dead was okay. Arrested was not.

"Where are we? There's like, no one out here."

He opened his door and walked around the car to open her door and help her out. He was a gentleman after all. "This is a friend's house," he lied. "I haven't been able to reach him, and I thought someone should check on him."

"The police are closer than a two-hour drive," she pointed out. "They could have done a welfare check."

Shame, he thought. She had been in the 99 percent, but she just landed herself in the 1 percent. Honestly, he was surprised. He had her pegged for the typical bimbo. After all, she'd been doing his bidding without question for months. Today, she decided to question him. It didn't matter, she wasn't coming home with him anyway, but it was a reminder that he would have to make it clearer to his next assistant never to question him.

He unlocked the door and motioned her through before him. "Wow, you have a key to his house. Are you that close to him?"

"You should ask fewer questions," he said as he walked through the empty house.

"Is he moving? There's no furniture in here."

The man's sigh echoed through the cavernous space. Suddenly, she was *Chatty Cathy*. He rolled his eyes and flipped on the light to the basement, waiting for her to meet him there. When she did, he motioned for her to go down the stairs, but a flash of self-preservation struck. If his guy was down there, and she saw him, she might try to run. He couldn't be chasing her through the woods if he had a job to clean up here. Without a second thought, he shoved her from behind, and she sailed through the air and landed with a thud at the bottom.

He strolled down the stairs and smiled down at her. "Don't go anywhere. I'll be right back."

He stepped over her twisted body and noticed the door at the end of the hall was closed. That was either a good thing or a very bad thing. He dug out the key and stuck it in the lock with a sigh. He had a bad feeling about this, but he pushed the door in and flipped on the light. What he saw was too much to comprehend, and his beast broke free and took over. All he could do was stand there and watch.

CHARLOTTE WAS FIXING Mack and Selina lunch when Mina walked into the kitchen. The man she had with her held himself in a manner that said messing with him was bad for your health.

"Everyone, meet Efren Brenna."

Efren shook hands with everyone while wearing an easy smile. "Thanks for the welcome. I know these are unusual circumstances, but Mina and I go way back. You can trust me to get the job done."

"I could have guarded the women," Selina muttered around the last of her sandwich, and Charlotte lifted a brow but didn't say anything.

"You could have, but we need you to care for Bethany, not worry about her and Ella."

"I have a lot of experience guarding VIPs. I'll take care of the senator's daughter," Efren said, offering Selina a calm smile, but stiffness to his shoulders told Charlotte he was on the defense.

"Aren't we lucky then?" Selina said with an even tighter smile. "I better head back up and do vitals on Bethany. Physically, she's fine, but emotionally and mentally, she needs a facility. When will I be able to transfer her and get the hell out of here?"

Charlotte glanced at Mina, who had also picked up on Selina's catty attitude. Something was up because Selina was never contrary, and you could always depend on her.

"Once Efren is upstairs to replace Eric, I have some updates to share with the team. We may have a question or two to ask her, but it will be safe to find her the help she needs after that."

"Any questions go through me," Selina said, poking herself in the chest while she eyed Efren up and down with disdain. "Call me on the walkie, and I'll ask her. I'm not putting her through another Q and A like this morning."

"That would be fine." Mina's tone of voice was calm and accepting, but Charlotte knew she too was wondering what was going on with their friend. Maybe it was just this place. Everyone was walking on eggshells, wondering when the next body would show up.

Selina glared at Efren before she left the room, and they all looked at each other for a few moments before anyone spoke. "What's wrong with her?" Mack asked. "I don't think I've ever heard her speak to anyone that way."

"Same," Mina said, still staring after their friend. "Maybe this case is getting to her. She's the one who keeps patching these women up." Mina turned to Charlotte. "No offense meant."

"None taken, you're correct. It's got to be hard on Selina. We need this to end. Do you have updates on the last two bodies found?"

"Yes!" Mina said, clapping her hands together. "Let me take Efren up to meet Eric and take over guarding Ella. Then we can all meet to discuss the new information."

"We'll meet you in the office in five minutes," Mack said, carrying his plate to the sink. "Glad to have you on the team, Efren, despite the lack of welcome from some of our members."

"No offense taken," Efren assured them. "I know what it's like to walk into an established team. You have to find your place on it and then earn your stripes. I've done it before, and I can do it again if this assignment is long-term. For now, I'll take care of Ella and help with the party."

He shook Mack's hand again and then left the kitchen behind Mina. Charlotte was about to start cleaning up the dishes, but Mack grasped her elbow to stop her. "Leave them. We have a few minutes, and we need to discuss something."

"Mack, I won't demand that you kiss me again if that's what you're worrie—"

Before she could finish, his lips crashed down on hers and stole her breath away. She could feel the tremble of desire go through him when she opened her mouth and let him in. She planted her hands on his chest to push him away, but with his strong muscles rippling under her hands and his tongue in her mouth, she didn't want to push him away. The thought made her body tingle with heat and desire in a way it never had before. The therapist had tried to help her understand that there was a difference between being with a man she wanted to be with versus being with a man she was forced to be with, but she struggled to understand it until this very moment. Suddenly, she understood that a man who cared would kiss her differently than a man who wanted to take advantage of her.

Charlotte leaned into his chest and sighed. She felt safe with Mack. After all the men she'd had to deal with working for The Madame and The Miss, she never thought she'd feel safe with a man. Especially a man the size and strength of Mack Holbock, but somehow, he had worked himself around her defenses to show her the difference. With the other men, her heart pounded with fear and dread. With Mack, it pounded with want and maybe a little hope that she wasn't too damaged to love someone else.

The kiss ended, but Mack returned twice more for a quick kiss of her lips before he released her for good. "To be clear," he said, with his breath heavy in his chest. "You never have to demand anything from me. I give it to you freely. Understood?"

"You're as clear as water," she whispered, her fingers going to her lips to check if they were still there. The man could kiss, and the heat kicked up fast and furious when he took over her lips. "If that wasn't what you wanted to talk about, what was it?"

Mack motioned for her to sit and leaned in close to her

ear. "Are we a team, Char?" Her nod was immediate. "Are you ready to prove it?" He gazed at her with a brow up and waited for her answer. She nodded once, and he grinned as he took her hand. "Then let's go prove it."

AFTER THEY MET with Mina and the rest of the team at lunch, they'd immediately hopped on a flight from Minneapolis to Chicago and from there to Harrisburg, Pennsylvania. Charlotte hadn't asked how Mina managed to get them on flights so quickly because she suspected it wasn't the same way others did. Once they landed in Harrisburg, she had a rental car waiting for them too. Mina was good at her job, but now they had to step up and do the rest.

Mack put the rental car into Park and pulled out his phone. "Mina got us the only room she could find this far out in the sticks. As she put it," he added, glancing at her. They'd been traveling for well over six hours, and she was ready to stretch her legs.

"As long as there's a shower, I don't even care if it's the Bates Motel," she said, bringing a smile to his face.

He chuckled and motioned for her to wait while he grabbed their bags from the back seat and helped her out of the car. They walked toward the small motel to check in, and Charlotte couldn't help but hesitate.

"Everything's okay," Mack promised, putting a protective arm around her waist. "No one is going to hurt you."

"It's not that. It's just the last time I was at one of these motels, it was rent-by-the-hour." She paused and then shook her head. "Never mind."

Mack cocked his head, but before he could say anything, they were at the small check-in area of the motel. There was an empty chair but a light in the room behind it. "Hello? Anyone around?"

A man popped his head out and held up his finger. When

he finally came out, he was wearing nothing but a pair of shorts and a tank top. "Sorry about that. You woke me from my beauty sleep. What can I do for you?"

"I'm Mack Holbock. There should be a reservation for us."

"Oh, yes, I only have one room left though. The woman who called didn't think you'd mind."

"No problem at all. We won't be here long."

Charlotte bit her lip to keep from groaning at his choice of words. As though things weren't awkward enough between them, now the man thought she and Mack were getting a room for their secret tryst.

After they had the keys and found the room, Mack opened the door and motioned her in. When he flipped on the light, she was glad he couldn't see the grimace on her face. There was one queen bed in the middle of the room and nothing else. Mack would fill most of that bed by himself. She couldn't imagine having to be that close to him all night and not touch him.

"I'll take the chair. You can have the bed," Mack whispered as he moved around her to set their bags down.

She eyed the chair, and there was no way he would fit in it, much less sleep in it. "We're adults, Mack. We can share the bed."

"Fine with me if it's fine with you," he said so casually that it felt wrong. "Do you want to shower first, or should I?"

"I'll go." She grabbed her bag and disappeared behind the bathroom door to escape the awkward situation. The shower was hot, but she finished quickly so there was enough hot water left for him. After dressing in her pants and T-shirt, she left the bathroom. "Next."

He gave her a tight smile as he walked around her and disappeared behind the door. She set her bag down on the floor and eyed the small desk he'd already covered with technical equipment from Secure One. She hoped he didn't plan to have another virtual meeting with the team tonight. She wasn't sure she would stay awake for it.

When they'd all met in the office after lunch, Mina had a plethora of information. The couple was found on the riverbank near Southwood, Pennsylvania. When they put that into their map and asked for directions to Sugarville, the town Bethany had stopped at, it was less than an hour's drive away. It made sense that Bethany was probably held somewhere in the same area where the bodies were found. It was sloppy on the part of the killer if that were the case, but if he had bodies to clean up, he might not have had a choice.

It wasn't until they discovered that Senator Tanner from Pennsylvania was not only up for reelection but also on the subcommittee that Cal agreed they needed boots on the ground. If this was The Red River Slayer, he was coming unglued, and the possibility of finding another body in the area was high. He still hadn't hit five other committee members' home states, but they were all on the East Coast. However, Cal didn't think he would stick with his original plan. If the killer felt threatened, he'd go underground just like he had last time. He'd have had to get rid of the two bodies, assuming the man was Little Daddy, but he would likely be highly cautious for some time now.

All they needed was a little time and a break to lead them to the house where Bethany was kept. Charlotte didn't know for sure, but her gut told her the man found in the river today was Little Daddy. They didn't know the identities of either person, but Mina was going to keep them abreast of any updates as they came in. In the meantime, she and Mack would use a grid-like search of the area to find the house. It was a long shot, and they didn't have much time, but they couldn't sit around and do nothing.

Cal was afraid Bethany wouldn't be safe until The Red

River Slayer was found. It was a thought that hadn't entered her mind, but he was right. Since they didn't know who he was, they couldn't protect her if she wasn't with them. Selina wasn't happy about the delay in transferring her care and made it known, which was highly unusual. It was a rare occasion when someone questioned Cal's authority, but Selina kept pushing the yard line until he agreed to bring a therapist in to meet with Bethany. Selina still left the meeting with a huff, and Charlotte was worried there was something more going on with her.

For right now though, she didn't have time to worry about anything but locating The Red River Slayer. Women everywhere were in danger and weren't even aware of it. They could be snatched off the street by this sicko and never be seen again until they floated to shore. Charlotte wouldn't let that happen. She was here with Mack not only to prove herself to Cal and the team but to herself. Cal wanted to send Eric instead of her, but Mack insisted he needed a woman with him to soften their questioning. When Cal finally agreed, she was sure Eric gave her a death glare. Something was up with the Secure One team, and she hoped they'd be able to pull off the senator's campaign party without showing dissent in the ranks. If anything happened at that party to endanger a sitting senator or their family, there would be hell to pay, and it would be Cal's head on the chopping block. She and Mack were needed in Minnesota, so time was of the essence. She just hoped when they returned to the state, it wasn't in a body bag.

Chapter Eighteen

The shifting of the woman on top of him was torture. Mack had to figure out a way to slide her back down onto the bed and off his chest before she woke up from the hard rod poking her in the belly. He'd seen the look on her face when she saw the one bed in the room, and it was easy to imagine what she was thinking. He never wanted Char to feel like he didn't respect her or her body. He did, and he'd bend over backward to prove it, even if that meant standing in the corner to sleep. At least the corner gave him better odds of getting shut-eye than being in bed with her on top of him. Her soft, sweet body warmed his skin, and he wanted to let his hands roam over her back and waist to cup her tight backside. He'd dreamed about touching her that way for months, but he wouldn't. She wasn't ready for that kind of relationship yet.

She's not ready, or you're not ready?

Mack tried not to groan at the voice just as she murmured his name.

"Why are you sleeping with a gun?"

He grunted with unabashed amusement. "Sweetheart, that's not my gun. I'm just happy to see you."

The warmth he'd cherished disappeared when she sat up in bed to rub her face.

"In my defense, you were on top of me when I woke up. I wanted to move you but didn't want to wake you."

"What time is it?"

"Only three a.m. Go back to sleep."

"As though that's going to happen," she muttered. She scooted closer to the edge of the bed. "I'm sorry for," she waved her hand over his groin, "that. It wasn't intentional."

"I know," he promised. He patiently rubbed Char's back while she gathered her thoughts. "You were scared and needed someone, which is why I climbed into bed and didn't sleep in the chair."

"I'm not scared of you, Mack," she said, crossing her arms over her chest, but he noticed she didn't ask him to remove his hand.

"I didn't say of me, but I saw the look on your face when we approached the building tonight. You were scared."

"The last time I was in a place like this, I was forced to do things to *earn my keep*, as The Miss used to say. Those men saw me as nothing more than a way to scratch an itch or to have control over someone smaller than them."

He paused. "I bet Mina didn't think about it when she booked the room. I'm sorry. We should have been more considerate."

Her blond hair swayed across her back when she shook her head and it brushed over his already hyperaware skin. "Don't worry about it. There wasn't much choice if we wanted to sleep for the night. Not that we're getting much sleep."

"Hey," Mack said, sitting up and wrapping his arm around her side to pull her into him. "Take a moment to feel your feelings, okay? I know you're trying to take your power back, but sometimes you have to acknowledge the past and how it shaped you. Some experiences in life leave scars on our minds. When that happens, we'll always struggle in that situation. It's understandable, and I accept you no matter what, Char."

Slowly, her head lowered to his shoulder, and she sighed. "You're talking about PTSD."

"I suppose I am. I don't know many who have fought battles in war who don't have it in one form or another."

"Maybe for soldiers, but I wasn't a soldier."

"Oh, darling, you absolutely were," he whispered, resting his cheek on her head. "You lived through those battles, but just like mine, they left scars. My battles were more straight-forward. I knew my enemy, and I had a lethal weapon to defend myself. You had neither of those things. All you had were your wits and a prayer."

"My wits kept me alive, but the prayers didn't work," she murmured, burrowing her head into his chest.

"You'll never have to use your wits with me. I'll never tell you to let it go or get over it. I'm a safe zone for you to feel what you need to feel, Char."

When she laughed, there was no humor behind it. "But you aren't safe, Mack," she whispered. "When we're to-gether, the things I feel are confusing. When you kiss me, there's so much emotion in my chest that I don't know what to do with it."

"Confusing good or confusing bad?"

"Good, but also bad. I like how you make me feel, and I like being with you, but I also know you deserve someone who hasn't fought battles while unarmed and outmanned."

Mack kissed the top of her head. He wanted to connect with her again, if only briefly. "Life doesn't work that way, Char. I will live with my disability for the rest of my life. What if I said you deserve better than being with someone who can't walk without strapping on braces every morn-ing? Would you agree and walk away?"

"Of course not." Her eyes sparked with anger as she sat

up to glare at him. "The scars on your legs don't make you less than anyone else. They're just part of you."

"More proof that life doesn't work that way. When we connect with another soul, that's all that matters."

Char was silent for so long he thought she'd fallen asleep as he rubbed her back. "Do you think our souls have connected?" she whispered. "Like, do you think soulmates exist?"

"Do soulmates exist? Yes. I only have to look at Cal and Marlise. Did our souls connect?" he asked, running a finger down her cheek. "The moment I took you in my arms."

"Mack, will you show me what you mean? I learn better that way."

When he gazed into her eyes, the truth was obvious. She wanted him to show her the connection. He scooted backward on the bed until he could lean against the headboard and then pulled her onto his lap to straddle him. "If you get uncomfortable or scared, tell me to stop."

Her only response was to capture his lips and press herself against his chest. She wrapped her arms around his neck and buried her fingers in his hair. He held her around the waist, her warmth a balm to his injured soul while he searched for a foothold on this slippery slope. He was afraid he'd fall over the edge and do something he shouldn't. But her kisses and caresses made him want more. They made him want to be more for her even when she didn't ask. He still wanted to give her everything.

The need for air overtook his desire to keep caressing her tongue. He let his lips fall away from hers to trail down her neck to her collarbone. He suckled gently, raising goose bumps on her flesh as he made love to her with his lips. He tugged her T-shirt lower to kiss the tender skin at the base of her neck. Her pulse raced beneath his lips because of him. For him. With him.

"Mack," she moaned, the sound of his name airy on her lips. "I want more." To make her point, she rubbed her hips against his desire, dragging a moan from him.

He didn't want to hurt her. He also didn't know if he could make love to her and walk away when the inevitable happened. The old saying about it better to have loved and lost came back to him, and he suckled hard on her chest, leaving his mark where only she would see.

While she was lost in the sensation of his lips, he slid his hand under her shirt. His fingertips skirted across her ribs to the edge of her breast. She stilled, so he did too, waiting for her to decide what she wanted.

"I want you, Mack, but I don't know if I can do it. I want to, but I can't promise—"

With his finger to her lips, he hushed her. "I understand, sweetheart. You don't have to do anything. That's not why we're here tonight. I'm safe. I won't take more than you can give. You're in control of everything."

It was as though she needed to hear him validate her fears and desire in a way that put her in control. He saw the shift in her when she remembered that she could trust him to stop if she said stop. And he would, even if it killed him to hold her until she fell asleep and nothing else. He would. He would protect her, whether on the job or in his bed.

Before he could clear his head of the thoughts running through it, Charlotte lowered her lips again and drank from his, her desire no longer capped by fear but fanned by trust. *Trust.*

The word hit him in the gut as she leaned back and stripped her T-shirt off, revealing her perfectly taut nipples waiting for his attention. He took a few moments to appreciate her beauty and learn her curves, picturing the path his tongue would take from her nipple to her navel and then if she was ready, lower still. "You are gorgeous," he whispered, his finger trailing down her ribs. "I want all of you, Char."

"Even the broken parts?" she asked in a whisper that made his chest clench from an emotion he didn't want to acknowledge.

"Especially the broken parts."

Then her lips were back on his, and he knew, given enough time and trust, they'd heal each other.

"SECURE TWO, WHISKEY." Mina's voice filled the room, and Mack scrambled to answer before she hung up.

"Secure one, Mike."

The tablet came to life, and Mina's face filled the screen. "Good morning, early birds," she said, her trained eye taking in Charlotte on the bed as she tied on her shoes. It was the reason she insisted on making the bed rather than leaving the bedclothes rumpled.

"Good morning, Mina. Do you have an update?" Mack asked. "We were just making a plan of attack."

"Glad I caught you then," she said, typing on her computer as she spoke. Charlotte was always in awe of how she could do both and not lose track of either. "I have an identity on the man found in the river yesterday."

"Seriously?" Charlotte stood up and walked closer to the tablet. "That was fast."

"Fast, but not helpful. His name is Chip Winston."

"Did you run specs on him?" Mack asked, strapping on his gun belt and vest.

"I did, but lo and behold, he doesn't exist except on paper."

"Washed?" Charlotte asked with surprise. "How is that possible?"

"I don't know, but I'm still digging. Someone washed

him, but I don't believe he was CIA or FBI. I can't say for sure though."

"What about the woman?"

"Police haven't had any hits on her, and I'm still waiting to pilfer the autopsy photos so I can run facial recognition. But if Winston is washed, I don't have high hopes."

"None of this makes sense," Mack said, his fist bouncing against his leg as he paced. "I don't buy that it's unrelated, but he's never dumped a male body before."

"He's never dumped two locked together before either," Mina pointed out. "It makes me wonder if he had to get rid of the body and wanted to throw the cops off so they wouldn't link the two victims to him."

"Possible," Mack said with a head tilt and then paused in his pacing.

"Likely if the man is Little Daddy," Charlotte said, still incredibly aware of Mack's maleness every time he got near her. "If he came up with no past, I'm inclined to believe it's him."

"Me too," Mina agreed. "I'm trying to get an autopsy photo of him to show to Bethany."

"Is that smart?" Mack asked before Charlotte could say anything. "She said she never saw his face."

"The eyes don't lie," Charlotte whispered, and Mina pointed at her through the camera.

"The eyes don't lie. A woman will always recognize the eyes of the person who hurt her."

Mack glanced at Charlotte. She knew what he was thinking, so she smiled. He hadn't hurt her last night. If anything, he healed another little piece of her.

"In the meantime, I found six properties within twenty miles of where the bodies were found that are owned by holding companies. I will send the addresses to your GPS unit."

"Are they rented or empty?" Charlotte asked, grabbing her gun belt from the bed and strapping it on. Mack was insistent that they both be armed, so she had no choice but to wear it today. She still didn't like carrying a gun, but she'd come to realize that sometimes they were necessary to protect those you cared about—and she cared about Mack.

"I'm still trying to get a bead on all of that. For now, approach with caution."

"Affirmative," Mack said, holstering his gun.

"You're not going to approach the houses dressed like that, are you?" Mina asked, her head shaking. "You'll get shot."

"If that's the case, at least we'll know we found the right house." Mack's statement was tongue-in-cheek but didn't make Charlotte feel better. He glanced between the two women and rolled his eyes. "I was kidding. When people see someone dressed in all black with a flak jacket, security logo and a gun, they automatically see you as an authority figure. It might help us get information from neighbors who surround these places."

"Sounds like you have your work cut out for you. I'll stay in touch via your phone. If I call, answer it, no matter what. It could mean life or death depending on what comes through in the next few hours."

"Ten-four. Mike out."

Mina gave a beauty queen wave, and then the screen went black, plunging them into silence. They had to get going if they were going to check out all six houses today. Charlotte grabbed her things and followed Mack to their rental.

"Ready?" Mack asked, straightening her vest. "Remember, head on a swivel and stay behind me until we know the house is empty."

"I got it, Mack," she promised, offering him a smile. Less than two hours ago, they were exploring each other's bodies.

He'd been a gentle and patient lover, but she still couldn't give him what he wanted, what he needed. Not in a seedy motel. Her time in places like this one had left scars too deep to overcome last night. She'd helped him reach a satisfying conclusion, but she knew it wasn't how he'd hoped.

"Stop," he whispered, leaning into her ear to kiss it. "What did we talk about this morning?"

"That you have no expectations, and I have the control over any relationship we have."

"And do you believe that, or are you just repeating it back to me?"

She paused for a minute to gaze into his chocolate eyes. "I believe it." He raised a brow. "I believe it." The words were firm and loud. "I believe in you, Mack, and I trust you."

He pulled her to him by her vest and took her lips in a too-short kiss. "Now I believe you. We're in this together, Char. Let's find this killer and return to our lives at Secure One."

"Ten-four, Char out," she said with a wink as she climbed into the car and prepared for battle.

Chapter Nineteen

The first three houses had been a waste of time. There were two without basements, and the third one was rented by a lovely family who was scared to see the "police" arrive. Charlotte had quickly assured them they had done nothing wrong, but after chatting with them, it was easy to see they knew nothing. Mack was frustrated but determined to find the rest of the properties even if it was a waste of time. They'd managed to avoid the actual police, and he was glad the place wasn't crawling with FBI agents. If he had to guess, he'd say the police hadn't tied the two victims to The Red River Slayer, so they hadn't called in the feds. He was starting to think this was a wild goose chase.

A glance at the passenger seat reminded him to trust his gut. Char was, so he'd follow her lead. The couple had gone into the river relatively close to where they were found, considering the time of death. Earlier, they'd parked off the beaten path and used high-powered binoculars to scope out the crime scene. Mack noticed a reedy area that could have trapped the bodies if he'd dumped them in just a little farther upstream. He hoped Mina would get them more information before they had to return for Dorian's party. They had one more night here, two at best, before they'd have to leave for Minnesota.

He slid his gaze to Char for a moment before focusing back on the road. Last night had been special. In his mind, they had made love. Maybe not in the traditional sense, but she had learned to trust him with her body. He always knew baby steps would be required when teaching her about intimacy, and he was okay with that. They were a team, no matter what.

He couldn't help but think how gorgeous she was in the light of the noon sun, but he knew he could never be with her once she healed. Despite the things he told her about healing and hope, none of it applied to him. He would live the rest of his life knowing what he did, but he couldn't ask someone else to live it too. He didn't deserve a family. Not when one died because of his mistakes.

Mack waited for his gut to clench at the thought of that day as it usually did. He waited for another mile but still nothing. He tried to drag the memory up front and center, but all he could see was her curves in the moonlight, and all he could hear was the sound of her moans in his ear.

"You broke the rules." His voice was harsh and needy inside the car, and he cleared his throat. "I told you to stay behind me."

Char rolled her eyes, but he pretended not to notice. "We were approaching a house with a woman and two little kids outside. I didn't want her calling the cops before we could talk to them. Sometimes, you have to know when to lead and when to follow, Mack."

Her sentence was pointed, and then she fell silent. Maybe she could sense the anxiety rolling off him about the case and what happened last night. Would last night change their working relationship once they returned to Secure One? He'd like to say no, but he knew better. He could pretend it didn't affect him, but every time he saw her, he'd know he could never have her. He slammed his palm down on the steering wheel with disgust.

"Everything okay?" Her question was meek and worried, so he forced himself to relax. He didn't want to scare her.

"I'm just frustrated," he said with resignation. "This guy is out there killing people, and we're running all over creation on a wild goose chase."

"We don't know that it's a wild goose chase, and besides, at least we're doing something. That's more than we can say for the authorities. Did they ever get anything out of the guy who tried to kidnap Ella?"

Before he could stop himself, his thumb came up to trace the bruise across the bottom of her chin. The bruising on her face had turned to a sickly yellow as it started to fade, but it never detracted from her beauty.

"No. The guy took his right to remain silent and has done so, but Mina is looking into his background. She has to be careful since Secure One is also wrapped up in that situation."

"Secure One is wrapped up in many situations, it seems."

"We're a security company," he said with a shrug. "It's bound to happen when you have high-profile clients. This won't be the last tangle we have with law enforcement, but we earn our stripes with them by cooperating and working together."

"I thought the feds didn't want us involved in this."

"I'm not talking about the feds. They're entirely different animals as far as cooperation and working together. They don't and won't."

Mack noticed the smirk on Char's face before she spoke. "I wonder if they know one of their former agents is the one who gets us the information."

"I'm sure they often look the other way regarding what

Mina does. Roman figures that they don't come down on her because they can't prove she's hacking their system."

"Mina thinks they feel guilty for what happened with her boss and The Madame."

"That could be too," Mack said on a shrug. "They owe that woman more than they can ever repay her. Besides, they know if anyone can figure out what's going on, it's Mina Jacobs."

"True story," Char said with a smile. "Are we almost to the next place?"

"About two miles out. We have two on this side of Sugarville and one a few miles outside of town. After we stop at these two, we'll look around Sugarville for something to eat and a little information."

"Lunch with a side of snooping. I'm in," she said, throwing him a wink that sank low in his belly and reminded him just how empty his life would be without her.

CHARLOTTE CLIMBED FROM the car and stretched. She'd taken the flak jacket and gun belt off after the last house was nothing more than rubble. She'd put it back on after lunch, but if they wanted to blend in and get information about Bethany or the people in the river, they couldn't look like cops. She eyed Mack as he pumped gas. That was going to be harder for him than for her. Maybe she should take the lead and do the talking.

When they'd pulled into Sugarville, Mack had pointed out the service station as the one Bethany had used the night she ran away. He'd even smiled for the first time all day when he saw the truck parked next to the station. He said Bethany would be pleased to know they got it back. Bethany would be pleased, but Charlotte wasn't. Since they'd climbed out of bed this morning, Mack had been distant and gruff. She tried to tell herself he was just frustrated by the case, but part of her knew that was a lie. Before the sun rose, he had already pulled away from her and climbed back inside his armor.

A warmth slid through her at the thought of their night together. She never intended to fall into bed with him, but their connection was too strong to ignore when they were alone. How he touched, kissed and cared about her spoke volumes about him. Mack wanted to pretend he was hardened by war and unwilling or unable to care about someone now, but that was all it was. Pretending. She knew the war had changed him. Shaped him. Hurt him. But all of that made him more empathetic and in touch with people's emotions. He'd have to come to that realization by himself though.

They walked into the tiny gas station to pay for their fuel. With any luck, they'd learn a bit of information from the attendant as well. A man turned from the back counter when they walked in.

"Welcome to Sugarville Service Center. Find everything you need, folks?"

"Sure did," Mack said with an easy smile. Charlotte noticed he did that whenever they wanted information. She could picture soldier Mack doing the same thing. She'd tell him anything he wanted to know if he flashed that smile at her. "I noticed the old truck by the station. Is that a '61 Ford?"

A grin lit the man's face as he took Mack's money to cash him out. "Sure is. It's been a workhorse all these years. It was stolen, and I nearly cried when I discovered it was gone. I was never more surprised than when the sheriff from two towns over drove it back to me. It wasn't even damaged."

"Sounds like some kids took it for a joyride."

"Could be. The police said people near where it was abandoned saw a woman get out of it and take off on foot. I tell myself she was in trouble, and the truck got her to safety. That way, I don't get too mad about her stealing it."

Mack dipped his head in agreement, but his gaze slid to Charlotte's for a moment. "I'm glad you got it back." He took his change from the man and motioned outside. "We're looking at some property and heard there was a house for sale up the way here. I'm having difficulty finding it on my GPS though."

The man shook his head for a moment before he spoke. "No houses for sale that I know of unless they're selling the old Hennessy place. Last I heard, it was in probation. No, what's the word?"

"Probate?"

He pointed at Mack. "That's it. Probate. Old man Hennessy died years ago, and nothing has happened with it since. Maybe it is for sale now, but I'm usually the first to know if a place goes up. I wouldn't buy it though."

"Bad water or foundation?" Mack asked, stepping closer as though he were ready for some hot tea to spill.

"Bad juju," he said, looking over Mack's shoulder to the door. "We call it the murder house around here. Someone should have torn it down long ago. Nothing good is going to come from that place. Years ago, a young couple rented the place. Their lives ended in a murder-suicide with a young baby in the house. By the time they found the couple way out there in the woods, the youngster was nearly dead from lack of food and water. It was an ugly scene, but the landlord, old man Hennessy, wouldn't part with the place. He kept saying one day he'd clean it up and sell it. He may have cleaned it up, but he never sold it. He just let it sit empty. I'm still hoping they tear it down. Nothing good comes from land tainted with that kind of violence."

A shiver ran through Charlotte. *Nothing good comes from land tainted with that kind of violence.* Something told her he was right.

THE ALLURE OF a hot meal lured them into the small café. Mack's stomach grumbled from hunger, and he was ready to dive into a plate of whatever the server set in front of him. He wasn't picky. The army had cured him of that. MREs were no joke, and you learned quickly that the hot sauce was there for a reason. Besides, when you're hungry and hunkered down, trying not to get shot, you don't care what you put in your mouth as long as it keeps you alive long enough to escape.

"What did Mina say?" Charlotte asked when they slid into a booth.

"She's looking into it. She said the house is now owned by a holding company, which contradicts what the service station guy said."

"I didn't get too far in school, so I don't know what a holding company does."

The look on her face told him she was embarrassed to admit that, but he was proud of her for asking questions rather than wondering what things meant.

Stop it. You cannot be proud of this woman. She is not yours.

After a firm reminder to himself, he answered her. "A holding company is a business that owns, holds, sells or leases real estate. They get paid multiple different ways depending on the property. If a holding company owns the property in question, there were likely no heirs to leave it to, or the heirs didn't want to deal with the property, so they sold it to a holding company."

"Is it a way to hide properties you don't want people to know you own?"

Mack made the so-so hand. "It takes longer to find the owner, but the information is still there. On the surface, yes, if you don't dig any deeper."

"But Mina will dig to the bottom."

He tossed her a wink as the server approached them to

take their order. After ordering a burger and fries with a cold pop, they waited for the server to return with their drinks. Mack had his phone on the bench, awaiting Mina's call or text. He had a bad feeling about this place, and the last thing he wanted was to put Char in the middle of an ambush. He forced his mind to slow and remember that the house was probably crumbling like all the others.

The server brought their drinks and set them down. "Can I get you anything else?"

Mack promptly picked up his glass and took a long swallow, giving Char the chance to jump in. "Actually," she said, holding up her finger. "Do you know anything about the murder house?"

Mack cringed, but rather than shut her down or try to smooth it over, he decided to wait her out. Sometimes shock value was the best value.

"You shouldn't be asking after that place now," the server said in an accent that made Mack smile. "Nothing good gonna come by talking about it."

Charlotte smiled the smile he'd seen before when she was summoning patience from within herself. "We are here to represent the property owners and just wanted to get a feel from the locals before we went out there."

This time Mack opened his mouth to jump in because the last thing he wanted was to have the actual holding company find out someone was impersonating them. He snapped his jaw shut when the server started to speak. After all, they wouldn't be here long enough for anyone to know who they were anyway.

"Oh, I see, ya," she said, putting her hands on her hips. "Well, that place has been empty so long that it should be torn down. Who'd want to live there anyway? Devil worship and rituals, sex rings and murders. I'm glad it's hidden in the woods, so we don't have to look at it."

Mack raised a brow at Charlotte as if to say, *Next question*. She didn't disappoint him.

"Devil worship and sex rings? We knew about the deaths and the poor baby inside the house, but devil worship? You don't say?"

"The seventies were wild times," she said with a shake of her head. "The locals say the pentagram is still on the wooden floor in the living room. Before the owner put up a gate, kids used to go out there huntin' ghosts. The new generation doesn't bother it now, but the stories will be campfire legends forever."

"I see," Charlotte said with a smile. "Thank you for your candidness."

"No problem. Your food will be up in a few minutes."

The waitress turned away, and Mack waited until she had disappeared behind the counter before he leaned in and spoke to Char. "Excellent interrogation. Just be careful about misrepresenting us. We don't want that to roll back on Secure One."

She sipped from her pop, her perfectly pink lips wrapped around the straw, and his groin tightened at the thought of them being wrapped around him. Working with her but not having her was going to be the greatest torture he'd ever been through, and he knew torture.

"We won't be here long enough for anyone to know the truth," she said with a shrug. "A little white lie was warranted. I took a chance."

Mack leaned back in the booth but couldn't wipe the smirk off his face. He was so damn proud of this woman, and no matter how much he told himself not to be, he couldn't help it.

"So now we know there's a gate," she said, pulling him from his thoughts. "How do we plan to get around that?"

"Go in from the backside." His answer was simple, but

the execution would be more difficult. "I'm not pulling a rental car up the driveway and hopping a fence. We don't know if they have cameras on the place or a security system. It won't be an easy walk through the woods, but it will give us the advantage of checking out the property before we step foot on it."

"I'm ready," she assured him. "Or I will be after I down that burger and fries. Breakfast left me unsatisfied, but I guess that was my fault. I'll make sure you get a raincheck." She threw in a wink that said she was serious.

Mack groaned, partly at the memory of her body under his hands and partly because he wanted that raincheck more than anything else in this world. He was already on a slippery slope, and making love to her would have him tumbling right into love with her. That couldn't happen.

Chapter Twenty

Charlotte followed Mack through the woods, and the sun filtered down through the heavy overhang of leaves this time of year. Under her feet, the earth was spongy, and with every step, she sank deeper and deeper into the history of this house. If even some of the stories about this house were true, it should be torn down. No one should live in a place with that kind of violence. She stumbled, nearly face-planting on a fallen tree, until Mack grabbed her vest and stopped her fall.

"Careful, sweetheart," he whispered, his voice husky instead of gruff. "I don't want to carry you out of here on a stretcher."

She looked up at him and smiled with a nod before they started moving again. According to his GPS, they should be getting close to the property line. Charlotte could see nothing but trees, leaves and shadows of light and dark. She couldn't deny that she was creeped out being encased in the woods on their way to a murder house. Who wouldn't be?

Mack held up his hand, so she held her position, waiting for him to tell her what to do. He pointed to his right and then motioned to a fallen log. They walked to it and sat, using the log as back support. He pulled out his phone and flipped open the top. It might look like an old-fashioned flip phone, but it was as high-tech as they came. It was text, call and GPS sensors and trackers.

"Has Mina sent more information yet?"

"That's why I stopped. The property is just through those trees, but before we approach, I want to know if there's a security fence."

He opened the text app and read silently for a moment, a heavy sigh escaping as he hit two buttons and then snapped the phone shut.

"Bad news?" she asked, his posture now soldier-straight.

"More like Mina was able to confirm what the waitress said. All of it. The house has been abandoned, and the holding company plans to take it down and sell the land. The couple who lived there were known to be devil worshippers, and the townspeople weren't happy about it. Especially when they found out the couple held rituals on the land and near the river. The police suspect the murder-suicide was staged, but they could never prove it."

"Staged? As in someone else killed them both?"

"Exactly," he said, grasping his lower lip as a shiver went down her spine. "The townsfolk may have had enough and taken them out, shifting the blame to the guy as the shooter."

"It wouldn't be hard to do that, I suppose," Charlotte said. "Disgusting and wrong, but not hard."

"And with a baby in the house," he said, his teeth clenched. He had seen atrocities done to families and children while in the service. Sometimes, the human race angered him beyond words.

"They may not have known the baby was there if it was sleeping," she mused. "Regardless of all of that, what about a security system?"

"None that Mina could find. There's the gate to stop interlopers and a fence that fell years ago, but no one bothered to repair it. We'll approach with our eyes open and look for signs of recent use before we go in. If I say fall back, you do it. Do not question it. Agreed?"

"Agreed," she said as they stood and stepped over the log, heading for the small knoll that would let them look down on the property before they tried to walk in.

Driving in and parking the car in the driveway would be much simpler but too obvious. Secure One preferred ghost status. If they could get in and out with the information for the team without leaving a trace, it would be worth the long walk through the woods. When they got to the knoll, they rested on their bellies while Mack surveyed the property with his binoculars. They couldn't see a car, but the property was too overrun with vines and leaves to look for tracks from this far away.

"Hey," Charlotte said when he put away the binoculars. "What happened to the kid?"

"Mina hit a dead end with that one. The baby was taken to the hospital, nursed back to health and then adopted. The adoption was closed due to the crime and stigma, so no one knows where the baby ended up." Mack reached for his pants at that moment. "Just got a text." He pulled out the phone and checked it, his brow going up this time while he read. "They identified the woman. Her name is May Rosenburg. She's from Philly. She lived on the streets and had a sheet for minors like theft and prostitution. She was reported missing by a friend about two years ago, but no one has seen her since."

"That means he held her about the same amount of time as Bethany," Charlotte said, her heart in her throat. "Maybe she was the woman who went to Big Daddy when Bethany first arrived. She may have been told by Little Daddy to use a different name, just like Bethany."

"Feels like it. Bethany never saw her face, so it won't help to ask her. The problem is the couple's cause of death."

"They weren't strangled?" she asked, and Mack shook his head.

"No. May had a broken neck and what looked like recent trauma to her body. Chip died of cerebral edema and a head wound."

"If it is The Red River Slayer, something happened that threw him off, and he just had to get rid of the bodies."

"Little Daddy," Mack said with conviction. "I bet he found Little Daddy locked in the room where Bethany left him. Why May would have a broken neck, I can't say."

"If this is him, he's coming apart at the seams, that's why," Charlotte muttered. "Can we go check this place out so we can leave? I don't like the air here."

"Me either." He helped her up so they could start down the hill. "It reminds me of this one time in the sandbox when we were guarding a village. There was a rumor among the locals that a witch put a spell on the town that required bloodshed every twelve and a half days. You felt the blood on the ground under your feet and tasted the copper on your tongue. The evil seeped into your soul. That's what this place reminds me of."

As they approached the house from behind, a cold shiver of dread worked its way down her spine. The place may be empty of souls, but the evil remained. He motioned for her to follow him to the back of the house, where he plastered himself along the door. After looking through the window, he stepped around her, and she followed as he walked to the edge of the house.

"I've seen no cameras, and the kitchen was empty," he whispered as they walked around the side. He paused to peer in every window and ran a hand across his neck before he went to the next one. At the edge of the building, he searched for cameras on the eaves or near the front door. "No cameras on the front of the house. No tire tracks. There's a concrete walkway, so there is no way to check for footprints. Stay tight to the house, and we'll check windows."

She nodded, and they slid around the corner. Mack ducked his head around the edge of the first window and gave her another hand gesture. He pointed for her to stop by the concrete steps leading to the front door. He climbed them quietly and looked through the sheer curtain that hung over the window. He gave her a headshake and a gesture to come around the steps and meet him on the other side. She followed him around the house as he looked in the windows until they got to the back of the house again.

"The house is old and empty. There's a basement, but didn't Bethany say she went out a door in the basement and ran?"

"That's what she said. Is there an old-fashioned cellar door in the yard?" she whispered, afraid to speak at full volume in case they weren't alone.

"I didn't see one, but that doesn't mean it isn't there. We're here. I say we go in."

"Is that smart without backup?" Charlotte asked, her stomach tossing the hamburger and fries around like a blender. Her nerves were taut, and she didn't like the feel of the place.

"No one is around, and Mina is monitoring us on the GPS link. We'll take a quick peek and then head that direction to the river." He pointed straight ahead through the trees from the back of the house. "It can't be far."

"I don't hear the water though."

"It's a slough, so you wouldn't." He pulled out a kit from his vest, but she stopped his hand before he could pick open the door.

"Shouldn't one of us stand guard?"

"In and out. I'll check the basement while you aim your

gun at the top of the stairs. Shoot anyone who shows their face because it will be no one good. Got it?"

"Understood," she said and waited while he picked open the door. She understood it, but she didn't like it.

THEY SHOULDN'T BE HERE. The hair on the back of Mack's neck stood up as they crept through the house. It was empty, of that he had no doubt, but the evil permeated the air like a black fog. Mack held up until Charlotte bumped into him. They were walking back-to-back, keeping both exits covered, just in case.

"We're running on the assumption that the basement is clear, but you know what they say about assuming. Can you walk down backward, or do you want me to?"

"I can," she whispered, and he noticed her avert her eyes from the faded pentagram on the floor.

He twisted the knob on the basement and swung his gun down the stairs, the filtered lights from the windows illuminating the floor below. It was finished with worn '70s carpet and smelled of mildew and pine cleaner. It appeared empty. His mind's eye was still stuck on that pentagram as he started the slow and careful trek down the stairs. He swung his gun in both directions of the open stairway, being slow and cautious to ensure Char could keep up with him.

You shouldn't be here.

The warning was louder in his mind this time, and he shook his head, forcing his heart to slow and stop pounding so loudly he couldn't hear his own thoughts. His boots hit the carpet, and he paused, waiting for Char to take her position with her gun aimed at the stairs. He looked right and left, noticing a utility room with a washer, dryer, hot plate and old fridge in avocado-green. It had been new fifty years ago. His trained eye took in the washer and dryer, and he swallowed around the nervousness in his chest. The doors hung open on the machines, and a bottle of laundry soap sat atop one. They had been used recently.

He motioned to Char that he was going down the hallway to the right, and she nodded her agreement but kept her concentration on the stairs. They hadn't found a second set of stairs or a door to the outside, which meant this probably wasn't the house Bethany had been held hostage in, but he wasn't taking any chances until he knew that for sure.

His gun braced on his flashlight, he turned the beam on and aimed it waist height, swinging it left and right to glance in the open doors as he walked down the hallway. The first door was a small room with a bed and nothing else. The carpet was newer, but the bedding was brand new.

He walked to the next room and swung his flashlight inside. It was a bathroom. There was a toilet, shower and vanity. The floral print shower curtain hung open, and he could smell the fancy soaps from the door. He ducked into the room and took a deep breath before he opened the sink cabinet. Feminine supplies were stacked on the bottom, and a nearly silent grunt left his lips. The garbage can was empty, and the shower was dry. No one had been here recently.

Mack swung out the door, and the flashlight beam flashed off a doorknob at the end of the hallway. It wasn't open like the rest of the doors in the basement, which meant it could be a closet or a door leading out of the basement. There was a doormat on the carpet below the door. Not a closet. With his gun pointed ahead, he glanced backward at Char, still braced to shoot with total concentration. Once he checked the last room, he'd see if the other door led to a set of stairs. If it did, he'd grab Char, and they'd follow them to see where they went.

The third room in the hallway was bigger. Mack stepped in and swept his light in an arc. The room was in shambles.

Shattered dishes were strewn across the floor, a broken table and a bed with sheets and blankets sliding onto the floor. He could see that the bedding and dishes were modern, which meant they'd been bought long after the appliances.

It's time to leave.

The voice was right, but not before he got solid proof that this house was where Bethany had been held. He walked to the bed and lifted the bedsheets to see lines of four scratches slashed out by a fifth, repeating across the wood in a macabre pattern of desperation. He stood and lowered his flashlight to the floor long enough to get his phone. He'd take a picture, and then they were heading straight to the authorities with what they knew.

He checked the door and then knelt to take the picture, the low light making it difficult, so he set his gun down on the bed and picked up his flashlight. Something tickled his nose, and he sniffed. There was a soft swish of fabric, and he turned, expecting Char. Instead, a crack of pain was followed by encroaching blackness around his head. He fell to the floor and slumped over as the door to the room slammed shut and the lock engaged.

I told you we shouldn't be here.

THE GASOLINE MADE a satisfying sound as it spilled onto the ground around the house. It was time to burn this place down the way it should have been years ago. Was he taking a chance that the rest of the town would go up with it? Sure, but that'd be fine too. Let everyone in this town burn for the sins of their parents. Things were getting a little hot for him here anyway. He chuckled at his joke as he stood in the middle of the yard with the can. He'd allow himself the joy of staging a dramatic scene for the townspeople first. *This would be the most fitting tribute of all though*, he thought as he poured the gasoline, following the lines in his mind to draw the pentagram. It always came back to the blackness in his soul. He couldn't get rid of it. He'd been born with it, and no matter how hard his parents tried, they couldn't cast it out of him. And they'd tried so many times. He had flashbacks to the priest tossing the holy water on him repeatedly until he was dripping wet. He was never saved because he was owned by the darkness, and he would remain there until he died.

He proved that when he killed his parents in broad daylight and tossed them in the river the day he turned eighteen. They were never found, which didn't surprise him, considering where he'd dumped them. The hardest part had been playing the woeful son who didn't know why his parents hadn't returned from vacation. They'd never found their car, and after thirty years, they never would.

The match flared to life, and he tossed it into the middle of the design, the beast inside roaring as the design came to life in flames of beauty. The heat seared his skin, and he took several steps back, watching as it licked and burned until it ran out of fuel to stay alive. He took the can back to the garage and slipped inside, stowing it in the front of the garage where it would only add to the inferno once he touched a match to this piece of his history. People thought him to be so normal and morally upstanding, but they had never seen the beast that lived within him. They had, but they didn't know those women in the river were offerings from the beast himself.

One final walk down these steps, and he'd say goodbye to the piece of his childhood that had shaped him as a man. This house had nearly killed him, but in the end, it had offered him so much life. He would miss it, but he had to go underground for a bit until he knew where that woman ended up. A shame. He had just gotten into a rhythm too.

A beam of light flashed under the door, and he froze on

the third stair from the bottom. It flicked across the door two more times before it disappeared. He wasn't alone. The game had just changed, but no matter who waited on the other side, they'd perish in a fire hotter than the bowels of hell.

CHARLOTTE CONCENTRATED ON the stairs, but it wasn't without difficulty. Mack had disappeared down the hallway what felt like an eternity ago. It probably hadn't been more than a few minutes, but she slid a glance to her right without moving her gun. She caught his vest as he disappeared into the final room at the end of the hall. They had to get out of here. She could feel it in her bones. The scent of laundry detergent and cleaner filled her head, telling her someone had been here recently.

A door slammed, and she swung her arm in an arc toward the sound. "Mack?"

The response was a guttural roar as a figure ran at her from the end of the hallway. It wasn't Mack. The man's face was twisted into a mask of horror, his hands out, ready to grasp her neck and take her down. The gun went off, the bullet striking him in the shoulder, but it barely slowed him down. Three more shots rang out in the basement, the sound echoing around the cement until she was sure she would never hear anything again. The man stumbled and then fell to his knees at her feet.

Charlotte gasped when he gazed up at her. With the mask gone, she knew the man sitting before her. He was a United States senator. He fell to his side, one hand gripping his chest as blood poured from his wounds.

She kept her gun aimed at him while she screamed Mack's name. When she got no response, she gazed at the man before her. "What did you do to him?"

He gasped, and blood bubbled up around his lips. "Help

me," he muttered, gripping his belly where more blood oozed over his fingers.

Charlotte grabbed her cuffs and attached one of his ankles to the stair railing. He wasn't going anywhere in his condition, and she had to help Mack. She jumped over his writhing body and ran to the room at the end of the hallway, but the door was locked when she tried to turn the knob. "Mack!" she screamed, throwing her shoulder into the door without it budging. She ran back to the man on the floor. "Where's the key?"

Greg Weiss smiled at her, his teeth stained pink from the blood bubbling out of his lips. He spat at her. "Go to hell."

"I've already been there because of men like you," she growled, placing her foot on his gut and pressing until he howled in pain the way her soul had wanted to for years. She dug in his pockets until she found a key ring and gave him one solid kick to remember her by before she ran back to the closed door, her boot leaving a blood print on the carpet every other step.

Her fingers weren't cooperating, and she fumbled with the keys while Weiss howled. The sound had changed. It was no longer pain. It was anger and the fading light of a man who had taken souls that were now driving him down into hell where he belonged. The key went into the lock, and she flipped it, the door opening to reveal the man she loved. The thought nearly sent her to her knees, but she couldn't take the time to stop. She had to help him.

"Mack!" she screamed again, running to him and sliding to a stop next to where he lay crumpled on the carpet. "Mack," she cried, checking for a pulse. It was strong and steady, but that gave her only a modicum of relief. He was alive but unconscious, and they needed to get out of the house. Charlotte lifted his head onto her lap and noticed a spot on his head that was matted and bloody. "Come on, Mack," she cried, slapping his face gently to wake him.

The man in the other room had quieted other than an occasional moan and stream of cuss words sent her way. Charlotte hoped he lived so everyone could see the monster he was.

"Mack," she whispered, kissing his soft warm lips. "Please, Mack, wake up. I need your help. I don't know what to do." She begged him to wake up, kissing him over and over until she left her lips on his, and tears ran down her cheeks. "I love you, Mack Holbock. You can't do this to me." Her tears fell silently until a hand came up to hold her waist. She started but realized it was Mack's warm hand holding her hip.

"Char," he whispered until she met his pained gaze. "Slayer."

Weiss took that moment to cuss her out again, and Mack's lips tipped up in a smile. "He's been neutralized," she promised, rubbing his cheek.

"Who is it?" he managed to ask, putting his hand to the side of his head by the wet spot.

"You won't believe me, but it's Senator Greg Weiss."

"Call Mina. Now."

Charlotte grinned and lifted the phone from his pants pocket. "No need to rush. He's got four of my bullets in him, and they all had a woman's name on them. He's not going anywhere other than hell."

She flipped the phone open and hit the call button while Mack grinned. "Sweetheart, I love you too."

His eyelid went down in a wink as she heard, "Secure two, Whiskey."

That was when she knew they were finally safe.

Epilogue

Charlotte closed the sketchbook with a sigh. It had been a week since they had unknowingly ended the reign of terror The Red River Slayer had had over the country. When the news broke that Senator Greg Weiss was fighting for his life in surgery as the suspected slayer, the media converged on the little town of Sugarville like the vultures they were. Charlotte didn't care. She was already in Cal's plane after Mack was treated and released from a hospital for his head laceration.

Weiss had used a weapon of convenience and hit Mack with a piece of the broken table he had killed Little Daddy with just a few days before. According to his confession, Weiss had pushed May down the stairs, which resulted in a broken neck and her death. To throw the authorities off, he wrapped May in Little Daddy's arms and tossed them in the river as a red herring. If the authorities were busy concentrating on a new twist to the case, he had time to disappear.

First, Weiss had to destroy the evidence. He planned to burn down the old house, but Char and Mack had beat him to the property. Had they been thirty minutes later, the house and the evidence would have been gone.

As it turned out, Little Daddy was one of the senator's "staffers." The only thing he staffed was the senator's deranged house of horrors. He trained the women to be the senator's "assistant."

The fact that no one on Capitol Hill questioned his turnover of assistants or his story of where the last one went was concerning, but that was above her pay grade. It was good that Bethany had never been transferred up as his assistant because she wouldn't have kept his secret the way the other women had. They believed that he would take care of them forever and be their sugar daddy if they did his bidding. Bethany knew better.

Greg survived his surgery, but one of her bullets had hit his spine, and he would never walk another day in his life. When the police deposed him with a list of his suspected crimes and the threat of life in prison without parole looming over his head, he asked for a deal. He knew he would never survive in the general population in a wheelchair, so there was little choice. He sang like a canary, documenting his killings on a timeline that shocked even the seasoned FBI agents. It started, he said, when he found out that his birth parents had been killed by Christian conservatives in their house and left him there to die. He swore that he sold his soul to the devil for the chance to avenge their deaths. Adopted by a loving family in Maine, he had a charmed life on the surface, but underneath simmered a monster so evil that Charlotte wasn't convinced anyone was safe until he was dead, no matter how many doors they locked him behind.

And then he died.

The nurses walked in one morning to find him dead in bed. An autopsy revealed he threw a clot, and it went to his heart. Good riddance was Charlotte's first thought. Her second thought was she was the one to bring closure and justice to the families of his victims. Sure, some of his victims had no family, but that didn't mean they didn't deserve justice.

Before he died, he'd signed the confession and accepted the title of The Red River Slayer.

A shudder went through her, and warm hands came up to grasp her shoulders. "Hey, you okay?" Mack asked from near her ear.

"Fine," she promised, shaking off the evil of a man who no longer walked the earth. "I was just finishing a sketch. How are things in the control room? I know I caused Cal a huge headache."

"No, you saved my life and the lives of countless other people by killing that monster. A little time and money are nothing in the scheme of things. You can always make more money but you can't bring people back to life."

Her sigh was heavy, and she nodded, not making eye contact with him. They hadn't discussed their adrenaline-driven declaration of love since it happened, and she wasn't sure they ever would. She promised herself she would wait for him to bring it up again, but so far, he'd remained mum. "Do you have a minute? I was wondering if I could give you something."

Mack walked around the table and perched on a stool. "Sure, what's up?"

With her heart pounding, she opened her sketch pad and pulled out the loose sheet waiting there. She slid it across the table and waited while he gazed at it.

"The real-me sketch," he whispered, running his finger across her signature at the bottom. "That's what I call it in my head," he explained, lifting his gaze to make eye contact with her.

"You said you'd like to have it when and if I was ready to give it to you. Is that still the case?"

"Absolutely," he said, drawing it nearer as though she may take it back. "I love that you signed it Hope."

"That's what you've given me, Mack. You gave me hope

back that first night I was here, and you've continued to offer it over and over until I was strong enough to believe that I deserve it."

"You do deserve it, Char. You became my hope the moment you walked onto this property."

"Do I deserve your heart too, or is that not on the table?" she asked, fear making the words shake. "I'm sorry for asking, but I have to know—"

His finger stopped her words, and he stood in front of her, his forehead touching hers. "My heart is yours if you think you can also accept my ghosts."

"I'll carry yours if you carry mine. Sharing will make them lighter."

He didn't wait. He kissed her with the love of a man who finally had what he needed in life. "I'm so thankful for you, Char," he whispered when the kiss ended. "I didn't know how to come to you and ask, so I prayed you'd come to me. Mina called me a chicken and a coward. In fairness, I agreed with her."

Her laughter was soft, but there were tears of pain, fear, acceptance and hope in the sound. "Mina is never afraid to call it as she sees it."

"And I always will," Mina said from behind them. "I'm glad you two finally figured yourselves out before we formed a Secure One intervention."

Mack grabbed Charlotte when she tried to pull away and kissed her neck. "You're ruining our moment, Whiskey."

"Sorry, but you'll have to save that moment for later when you're alone. We've been summoned to the conference room. There are updates to the case."

Charlotte had to admit that she was curious, so she followed Mack to the conference room where the team had gathered. Cal was at the front and motioned for Charlotte and Mack to sit in the empty seats. Eric, Selina, Roman and Efren had rounded out the table.

"Efren," Charlotte said with a smile. "Good to see you again."

"You'll be seeing more of him," Cal said. "He's agreed to sign on as another security member for Secure One. We're growing, and we need the help." Selina rolled her eyes with a huff but said nothing else. Cal handed Efren a security badge. "Everyone, welcome Tango to the team."

"Tango. Because I have two left feet?" he asked with a raised brow.

"The way I hear it, you have at least four, but you have to admit, it's the perfect call sign for you," Mina said with a wink.

"I'll accept it, as long as dancing isn't required."

"I can't promise that," Cal said. "As a bodyguard, you may have to take one for the team if your subject has to attend a ball, but we'll try to keep it to a minimum."

The team offered him some good-natured ribbing, minus Selina, who sat mute, her arms crossed over her chest. The moment she'd heard that The Red River Slayer had been taken down, Selina transferred Bethany to a hospital. She was undergoing treatment for her physical conditions as well as her mental health. Bethany had a long road ahead of her, but Charlotte had every intention of being there to help her. Maybe Cal would offer to let her finish her recovery at Secure One when she was released from the treatment facility. Something about the land and the people here healed broken hearts and minds.

After a few moments, Cal brought the room to attention. "As you know," he began, "Weiss confessed before his death, and I was able to obtain a copy of the confession."

He glanced at Mina, who was smirking but said nothing. "Mina, would you like to take over?"

She stood and leaned on the table as she stared down Marlise and Charlotte. "Before The Madame set up shop in Red Rye, Greg was killing people sporadically and weighing them down in lakes and rivers where the chance they'd be found again was slim. He killed his adoptive parents and anyone else who got in his way. Then his childhood summer camp friend, Liam Albrecht, called him from Red Rye to tell him about a new escort service in town. Since Liam was on the *special practice date committee—*" which she put in quotation marks "—he funneled women that The Miss wasn't happy with to Weiss. He kept them in the house and used them, but that was when he came up with the idea of dropping them in rivers to make it look like the serial killer was targeting politicians. What he was doing was satisfying his sick fantasies."

"The early women were from The Madame's house in Red Rye?" Marlise asked, and Mina nodded.

"Hard to confirm, but since their identities were washed, we know they were women from within The Madame's empire, no matter what house they lived in."

"And he went underground when The Madame was arrested?" Charlotte asked.

"He never stopped killing. He just didn't showcase the bodies. We know now that the woman in Arizona stuck in the dam was Emilia. According to the confession, he joined the committee for the waterways in order to throw the cops off his tracks by making the killings look political. That's why he made sure the bodies of those he killed during the two-year break weren't found immediately."

"So he purposely drove to other states with women to dump them in rivers?" Mack asked.

"According to his confession, he transported the women

to the river, killed them while they were underwater to make the police think they drowned and then dressed them before their final journey downstream. He claimed in the confession that Layla was a sacrificial lamb, his words," she said, holding her hands up. "May, the woman found with Little Daddy, was a good assistant, and since Layla was untrainable, he killed her specifically to coincide with Ella's party. He was a sick, sick man, and the twenty-page typed confession will take a long time to get through. The point is there was no doubt he was the man behind the slayings."

A shiver settled down Charlotte's spine at the thought, and it was as though Mack knew because his warm hand rubbed it away. "I'm sorry for the trouble my part in this caused you, Cal."

"No," Cal said firmly. "You were the hero that day, Charlotte. Scum like that should eat the bullet of a person they wronged, in my opinion. He may not have held you hostage, but he was responsible for the deaths of so many women in your same situation."

"We couldn't agree more," a voice said from the back of the room. Everyone turned, and Senator Dorian and Ella stood in the doorway.

"Ella!" Charlotte exclaimed, grabbing the young woman as she ran to her for a hug. "I'm sorry I didn't get back to the house after everything."

"I missed you, but I'm so glad you're okay," Ella said, hugging her tightly.

They'd had to postpone the senator's reelection party when he was called back to Washington to deal with the fallout from Weiss's arrest. The party had been rescheduled for next weekend, and Charlotte was looking forward to spending more time with Ella.

She joined her father at the side of the table and squeezed Charlotte's hand. "I just wanted to thank the woman who saved my daughter from a murderer. When Weiss died, the man in custody admitted that Weiss had hired him to kidnap my daughter and take her to the murder house. If you hadn't been there to stop him that night…" He waved his hand around in the air. "I don't even allow myself to think about it. I just know I owe you a debt of gratitude."

"I'm glad she's safe," Charlotte said, embarrassed by the attention. She preferred to stay in the background. "I still intend to give you those drawing lessons, Ella."

"Maybe you can get a few in later this year when you fly to DC to accept an award for your exemplary bravery and service to your country," Dorian said, putting his arm around his daughter.

"What now?" Charlotte asked as everyone else around the table smirked. "DC? Award? Not necessary."

"I will pass your opinion on to the president, but I'm certain he will not feel the same."

"The—the president?" Charlotte stuttered, and Ella was the one to laugh.

"He's the guy who sits in that oval room and runs the country."

Charlotte snorted and put her hand on her hip. "Please, no. That's… No. I was doing my job."

"Technically, you weren't," Cal said from the front of the room. "Your job is to cook, but you were a soldier that day. You didn't hesitate to protect your fellow soldier, even if that protection was driven by love rather than brotherhood."

Charlotte's face heated as Cal handed her a box. She lifted the lid off, and inside was a badge like the one she wore in the Secure One control room. This one didn't say Charlotte though. It said *Public Liaison, Secure One, Hotel.* She glanced up at Cal. "No. I can't take Hotel. My name starts with *C*." Mack rested his hand on her shoulder, which calmed her instantly.

"You can, and you will," Cal said with a smile. "I'm Charlie, so we had to pick a different call name for you. Mack told me that you went by Hope on the streets. In my opinion, Hotel is fitting, and I know Hannah would approve. I hold wonderful memories of her in my heart, but I'm with my soulmate now," he said, winking at Marlise. "Hannah would be proud to share her call name with a woman of your caliber."

Charlotte nodded, tears pricking her eyes as she looped the badge around her neck. "I'll wear the name proudly then. I don't know anything about being a public liaison though. Also, you guys realize I was terrified, and my knees shook the whole time I was in that basement. I think you might be taking things a bit far."

Mack chuckled from behind her as Cal shook his head. "I've never gone into battle and not been terrified with my knees shaking. I don't think anyone around this table has either." Heads shook to the negative until Cal spoke again. "Regardless, you did what had to be done. That's what makes you a soldier and a hero. As for the new job title, we'll talk about that tomorrow."

"Now," Dorian said, motioning toward the door. "There's a whole host of goodies waiting for us in the dining room, and I'm starving!"

Everyone offered congratulations, hugs and laughter before slowly working their way out of the conference room. Charlotte was at the door when an arm looped around her waist and held her back.

"Hold up, Hotel," Mack whispered in her ear. "I need a moment."

Charlotte swung around and draped her arms around his neck. "You can have a moment anytime, Mike."

"Good, because I'm low on hope and need a refill."

"I'm not sure I know how to refill your hope," she quipped, her brow dipping. "Maybe you better give me directions."

"Now that I can do," he promised before he dropped his lips to hers.

* * * * *

COLTON'S SECRET STALKER

KIMBERLY VAN METER

Chapter One

Frannie Colton had a sixth sense about things. She wouldn't go so far as to call it a genuine psychic gift—but she had a feeling in her gut when a bad wind was blowing.

Today seemed to be one of those days.

A shiver tickled her spine as if the July sun wasn't doing its best to break seasonal records in Idaho. She hustled into her bookstore, Book Mark It, thankful for the air-conditioning that hit her face and cooled her skin.

Usually, Idaho had mild summers but brutal winters. However, this year, Mother Nature seemed interested in pushing boundaries. Today, the temperatures were pushing 90 degrees, which was practically like setting the state on fire.

She waved at her friend Darla, who'd held down the fort so she could make a quick run to the post office, and helped herself to an iced tea from the attached café.

Finally able to breathe, she joined Darla behind the counter. "Thanks for covering the store for me. I had to get those certified documents mailed before the end of the day."

"No problem. It's not every day something that beautiful wanders into the veritable bore factory known as Owl Creek."

Puzzled, she looked to Darla, who then covertly gestured

to the man sitting in one of the comfy high-back chairs, sipping a mocha while thumbing through a table book on ancient Greek architecture.

Frannie chuckled. He was definitely worth a second glance, but he wasn't new to the shop. In fact, he'd been in a few times, but Darla must've missed him.

"His name is Dante Sinclair and he's really nice. Don't go scaring him off," Frannie warned playfully, reminding Darla, "Also, you're about to be married. Keep your eyes in your head."

Not for nothing though, Dante was the kind of man you'd have to be blind to miss. He was tall enough to make the oversize chair appear modest, and his short, cropped hair and the beginnings of a beard were flecked with gray. She didn't know much about him, just that he was polite and courteous and enjoyed a quiet moment with a new book. He definitely wasn't from around these parts. Whether that was a good thing or not remained to be seen.

Darla pouted as if suddenly remembering her fiancé, Tom, was still in the picture. "Fine, but if I can't, you have to promise me you'll try to flirt with that incredible specimen. I'm serious, that right there, is an import. That's no corn-fed farm boy. He looks…dare I say… European?"

"Flirt? That's unprofessional," Frannie scoffed, "Just because he's not wearing mud-caked work boots doesn't mean he's from Europe. And what's wrong with a corn-fed farm boy? Honest work builds strong character."

"Mmm-hmm. Tell that to the Higgins boys. All raised on a dairy farm and all criminals at some point or another."

"The Higgins family has issues. That's not a fair comparison." She sipped her tea while surreptitiously stealing another peek at the stranger. Okay, he wasn't hard on the eyes, and there was a certain air about him that seemed more distinguished, more polished than the local men who called Owl Creek home, but he was probably married, and Frannie wasn't looking for drama.

Besides, men that handsome were trouble—they couldn't help themselves.

"He's probably just on vacation."

"Who in their right mind would vacation here?" Darla quipped.

"Why are you hating on Owl Creek?" she teased. "Blackbird Lake is a popular destination for boaters."

"Does he look like he spends a lot of time on a fishing boat?"

"I try not to judge a book by its cover," Frannie replied with a saucy grin. Darla rolled her eyes, and Frannie pointed finger guns at her playfully, adding, "See? There's a benefit to being a bookworm. Makes you delightfully witty."

"Don't quit your day job, kid." Darla popped from the stool and grabbed her purse. "If you don't need me for anything else, I need to run. I'm supposed to meet Tom at The Tides to go over the wedding details, sign contracts, pay our deposit…you know, all that fun stuff."

"It'll be beautiful," Frannie assured Darla. "And you'll be the most gorgeous bride this town has ever seen."

"We'll see about that. I'm starting to wonder if we should've eloped. I'm over all this wedding crap. What a huge headache. But Tom insists on doing it up big, so here we are. I mean, honestly, who are we trying to impress? Let's just head to the courthouse, sign documents and then spend all that wedding money on an epic honeymoon."

"Stop being a sourpuss and enjoy the moment," she told her best friend. She shooed her out the door, smiling as Darla drove away. Bless Tom for being a saint. Although she loved Darla with everything in her heart, the woman was difficult on her best days.

But she was also intensely loyal and would chew anyone

to pieces if they dared to hurt someone she loved. Frannie found that level of commitment reassuring. Not that she wanted Darla to commit a felony in her honor or anything, but…it was nice to know that Darla had her back.

Her gaze strayed to the handsome newcomer. What would it hurt to be friendly and say hello again? Not flirting, of course.

Being neighborly was good business.

But she held back even as she contemplated walking up to the man and interrupting his quiet time. He probably didn't want to be disturbed. Being interrupted while reading was one of her biggest pet peeves, second only to people calling mayonnaise MAN-naise. She always argued, "You don't say, 'Hold the MAN-O,' you say, 'Hold the MAY-O.'"

Darla said Frannie needed to let that peeve die because it made her sound like a card-carrying member of the grammar police.

So be it. Words—and their proper pronunciation—mattered. Hence, her love of books.

But the man was intriguing, sitting in a small-town bookstore in the middle of the day as if he had nothing but time on his hands. He was older than her, she thought. If the gray flecks in his beard weren't enough, the subtle weathering of his skin gave him a rugged, if not sophisticated, look that she found appealing.

Frannie sipped her tea, contemplating the handsome stranger's back story as if he were a character in a novel.

People-watching was one of her favorite pastimes, mostly because she enjoyed creating narratives for her amusement.

He was safely engrossed in his reading, which gave her the perfect opportunity to watch without being weirdly off-putting.

Maybe Darla was right. He did have a vibe that wasn't quite American.

International spy? James Bond–type right here in Owl Creek? What were the odds? Highly unlikely but not impossible.

It seemed everyone had secrets these days. A sour note threatened to ruin her good mood. The thing about painful breakups was that the pain popped up at unexpected times, even if you've convinced yourself that you're over the cheating jerk-face.

Three months was plenty enough time to move on from a bad boyfriend.

Except…there remained an emotional bruise beneath the skin that hurt like a sonofabitch when she poked at it.

Solution? Don't poke at it.

Instead, enjoy the imported eye candy and remember that books would always be better than boyfriends.

As the thought zipped through her head, the handsome stranger swiveled his gaze straight to hers and smiled.

BEING SHARP AND observant was his bread and butter at work. The minute the cute young woman entered the shop, her cheeks flushed from the heat, her blond hair damp at the hairline, he'd been aware of her every move.

He unintentionally caught a whiff of her skin—a blend of coconut butter and citrus—and his senses prickled with interest.

He'd been coming to the bookstore for a while, but today seemed to be the first day the woman had taken more than a cursory notice of him.

He liked the quaint bookstore and café. For one, books had a calming effect on his nerves, and two, the mocha blend with cream was nearly as good as the one at his favorite café back home in Italy.

Owl Creek was suitable for his needs—small enough to be unremarkable and big enough for him to blend into the scene without drawing too much attention. But he'd abandoned all hope of finding a coffee shop capable of making anything remotely palatable.

And then he'd stumbled on Book Mark It.

That first tentative sip had flooded his mouth with joy. He missed Italy, but not enough to go back. Not that he could.

And the woman had stunning hazel eyes that sparkled with curiosity and intelligence.

Collecting the book, he rose and approached the counter. "If I haven't said it already, you have a lovely shop," he said, pushing the book toward her. "And I'd like to purchase this."

"Oh! Yes, thank you." Was it the heat, or had he caused that fluster? She quickly rang up the purchase. "So... I have to ask, are you on vacation or something?"

He ignored her question yet extended his hand. "I'm not sure if I've formally introduced myself... I'm Dante Sinclair."

"Frannie Colton. Likewise."

Her hand had calluses on the palm like she was accustomed to working with her hands. Was she the handy sort? Lugging hardware and hammering nuts and bolts for her business? Didn't she have a man to do that for her? He had to remind himself that American men weren't like Italian men, and women here were far more independent. "Is this your shop?"

"Yep. Every nook and cranny. My love affair with books is an obsession that will never end. I figured I ought to try and monetize it so I can at least use my book purchases as a tax write-off."

He chuckled. "We share a similar love. Whenever I travel, I always seek out the bookstores first."

"Me too! I thought I was the only person to do this anymore. It seems everyone's nose is so stuck in their phones most days that reading an actual book is a foreign concept.

My friend Darla, the woman who just left, she's always saying that I was born in the wrong generation, though I don't think I would do very well in a corset with these sturdy hips."

Her self-deprecating humor made him chuckle. Although he didn't see anything wrong with her build. He liked what he saw. *Careful. You're not here to make connections.* He straightened, collecting his book with a short smile. "It was a pleasure to meet you."

"Same to you. You didn't say whether you're here on business or pleasure…"

"A little of both," he answered. "Colton…any relation to the Colton hardware store I saw earlier?"

Frannie's little bashful laugh was adorable. "Um, yeah, my family's been here for generations. There are plenty of Coltons running around this place. You can hardly walk down the street without bumping into one. Made it difficult to get away with anything when we were kids."

"I can only imagine. Probably makes it hard to date, too."

"Oh, yeah, forget about dating," she agreed, chuckling, though there seemed a strained quality to her humor. "Especially with three older brothers who think their baby sister should be kept behind glass. They were a little overprotective."

"Brothers are good for protecting sisters." He paused before asking, "Any older sisters?"

"Yep, two of those. We have a big family. You?"

"No, I'm an only child," he answered without elaborating. Talk of his family was a bad idea. Especially if he wanted to glide under the radar. He supposed no matter where he landed in the heartland of America, he was bound to draw some attention, but he'd needed a place where his family wouldn't think to look.

"So, I hope it's not offensive or anything, but my friend

said you have this look about you that's... I don't know how to say...not from around here, which I think is a good thing! Don't get me wrong, you're like a breath of fresh air but was she totally off-base to guess you're from...?"

She was fishing. He ought to lie. But it seemed harmless enough to share a small truth. "Italy."

"Oh damn, she was right. She said you were European."

He smiled, reluctantly charmed, though a frisson of alarm followed. "Is it that obvious?"

"Um, well, a little bit, but I like it. We don't get many international visitors around here." Her cell chirped to life, and she grabbed it quickly, apologizing as she glanced at the message, a frown gathering on her face. "Sorry... I... have to make a call. It was nice to meet you," she said hastily before disappearing into her office.

The door was thin, but her voice was muffled enough only to catch a word or two, and it didn't seem like good news.

He was inclined to wait and see if she returned, but whatever was happening wasn't his business.

He had his own troubles, and he didn't need to add the cute bookstore owner's woes to his plate.

Dante exited the bookstore and hoped whatever had stolen Frannie's smile worked itself out eventually.

Lord only knew he held on to no such hope for himself.

Chapter Two

"I don't understand," Frannie said, still trying to wrap her brain around what her oldest sister, Ruby, was saying. "Aunt Jessie is saying *what*?"

Ruby's voice on the other line was strained as she repeated, "She's saying that…well, that she and Dad had a secret affair for decades and…that she has kids that are owed consideration in his will."

Frannie's mind was spinning. It was hard to decide which bomb to prioritize first. "Okay, give me a minute to process, this is wild. I mean, I know Mom has a twin sister, but we've never heard from or seen Aunt Jessie for pretty much our entire lives. And now she pops up out of nowhere to lay claim to Dad's assets? What does Mom say about all of this? Oh my God, she's probably devastated. Has anyone checked on her yet?"

"I thought we could go see her tonight, maybe bring her dinner or something? I don't know, Mom is so private… even if she did know about this alleged affair, I doubt she would've shared."

"Yeah, it's not like that's something you'd want to shout from the rooftops," Frannie quipped with a rare burst of understanding for her mom. She and Jenny Colton had never been terribly close, but Jenny had been reserved with most of her children. "I shouldn't even find this shocking… It's not like she and Dad had a stellar relationship."

"Well, they got along well enough to have six kids," Ruby pointed out dryly.

The thought of her parents getting biblical ruined Frannie's appetite for the foreseeable future, but Ruby had a solid point. "All I learned from our parents' relationship is that marriages are complicated." She drew a deep breath and peered out of her office to the bookstore, disappointed to see the handsome Italian had left. She returned to her conversation with Ruby. "Okay, I'll pick up a brisket family meal from Back Forty Barbecue. Mom always said food helped bad news go down easier, though I rarely find myself interested in eating when I'm already choking down something terrible."

"Can you rally the troops? I'm swamped with patients today and my break is almost over."

"Sure," Frannie agreed but secretly she didn't want that job. Her siblings were ridiculously hard to wrangle, and she didn't like chasing them down. The easiest to get to agree would be her brother Fletcher because he frequently popped into the shop to say hi, and they were fairly close. The hardest would be her oldest brother, Chase, who was now running Dad's property business. And to be honest, sometimes Chase didn't want to carve out time for family stuff because everything else under the sun was more important.

Maybe that wasn't nice or kind to say, but the truth often stung.

Family dynamics were complicated. Just like marriages.

"So, how did you hear about this?" Frannie asked.

"Dad's attorney called to let me know Aunt Jessie had marched into his office demanding a copy of Dad's will. When questioned, she dropped her little scandal bomb." Ruby groaned. "God, I hope she didn't do this in front of people we know. I can only imagine how quickly that little nugget would roll around town."

"Small towns love gossip," Frannie agreed, wincing. "Well, I guess we'll cross that bridge when we come to it. See you around six?"

"Yeah, thanks for picking up the food. I'll call Mom and make sure she's home tonight."

"Sounds good."

They clicked off, and Frannie took a minute to breathe through the chaos swirling in her head. Was it possible Aunt Jessie was lying? Maybe she and her kids were trying some desperate money grab? No one knew the woman's financial situation. Maybe there was nothing to Aunt Jessie's claims, and all of this would go away once she realized no one was buying her story. But it sure was a whopper of a tale to tell without proof.

A DNA test would immediately prove whether or not her kids were owed something from Robert Colton's assets.

Eww. Just saying that in her head made her want to vomit.

And how old were these supposed half siblings? Younger than her? It would be unsettling to discover her place as the baby of the family had been usurped by these mystery kids.

She groaned. Two more siblings? *Our family is big enough as it is.*

Frannie rubbed her rumbling belly. Her stomach had always been sensitive to drama. The conflict made her stomach yowl in protest. Imagine being the youngest in a loud, boisterous family, the only one who preferred peace and quiet with a book somewhere far away from the shenanigans of her siblings.

Her bookstore was not only her happy place but a reminder of how books had always been her safe place growing up.

Chase had teased her mercilessly whenever he'd found

her nose in a book, and Wade, desperate to impress his big brother, had almost always chimed in. Fletcher, on the other hand, had always defended her. It was probably why they'd remained close and why Fletcher continued to be so protective. When Fletcher had discovered how dirty her boyfriend had done her, it'd taken a reminder that he wasn't cut out for prison that'd saved Bobby Newfield's worthless hide.

But Lord knew Frannie loved him for it.

Releasing a deep breath, she sent a quick group text to the gang:

Important meeting at Mom and Dad's @ 6 p.m. Aunt Jessie blew into town with a potential scandal. I'm bringing a brisket meal. Feel free to bring a dessert or drinks.
Frannie

Texting was better than a phone call, anyway. It wasn't like anyone liked to answer the phone anymore.

As expected, Chase's response was cut, dry and impersonal.

Sorry, out of town, but I'm already aware. Handling it.

He probably didn't mean to sound that way, but he did. And, wait a minute, if he already knew, why did Ruby have to find out through Dad's lawyer? *Damn you, Chase, always acting like the gatekeeper. So annoying.*

Hannah quickly apologized.

Sorry, Lucy's got that bug going around, so I'm going to stay home with her. Let me know what's happening after you talk to Mom. Love ya, Han.

Wade didn't respond at all. *Typical.*

Fletcher's response made her smile.

I'm around the corner. Be there in five.

He knew how to make her smile and, somehow, feel less agitated.

Thankfully, it was almost closing time. She started her closing routine, and Fletcher walked in moments later, just as he'd promised.

The look on his face pulled at her heart. "What the hell is going on?" he asked, hands anchored above his law enforcement utility belt. "Is this for real? Aunt Jessie? What kind of scandal are we talking? Has a crime been committed? Is this something that should be reported?"

Frannie sent Fletcher an exasperated look, glancing meaningfully at the last straggling customers left in the store, and Fletcher caught her drift, reluctantly waiting as Frannie closed and locked the door and flipped her sign. "Sorry, your text got me all riled up," he apologized. "But what the hell? I need more details than that."

"Honestly, I don't have much to go on. Ruby said Dad's lawyer called to say that Aunt Jessie showed up in his office demanding a copy of the will. When he asked who she was and why she was entitled to the documents, she said that she and Dad had been together for decades and that she had two of his children, who, by law, are entitled to a portion of Dad's assets."

"What?" Fletcher exploded. "That's some bullshit if I ever heard any."

"Well, maybe? I guess a DNA test will clear up that mystery real quick, but what if she's telling the truth? I can only imagine how hurt Mom will be by this news. I mean, her own sister? Her *twin*? That's cold by any flick of the channel."

Fletcher softened at the mention of their mother. "Yeah, that's a crap sandwich if it's true…but do you really think Dad would—hell, I don't even like to think he was capable of being that big of an ass."

They'd long suspected their dad wasn't faithful to their mom, but no one liked to talk about the elephant in the room.

However, to cheat with Mom's sister? Frannie pushed down the wave of disappointment. Everyone thought Frannie had been their father's favorite, but Robert Colton hadn't exactly been involved in any of his kids' lives. He'd been a solid provider, but as far as emotional support went, he'd been sorely lacking.

Even so, Frannie and her dad had shared some commonalities that had created a bit of a bond, which made the current news sit uncomfortably.

"Is it bad to hope that Aunt Jessie is mentally unstable or lying through her teeth?" Frannie asked.

Fletcher sighed, shaking his head. "Hell, I don't know but I feel the same. Guess we'll find out."

"Yeah, I guess so. Do you think I should pick up a bottle of wine or something? Feels like alcohol might help settle the nerves."

"For you or for Mom?"

Frannie laughed. "Maybe just for me."

Fletcher chuckled. "All right. I've got to finish my shift. I'll see you in a bit."

Frannie nodded and followed Fletcher, pausing to lock up the shop and head to the barbecue joint.

It might've been a misplaced attempt at distracting herself from current events, but as she placed her order, Frannie thought of Dante, the Italian stranger. As Darla pointed out, Owl Creek wasn't a huge draw for international travelers. Sure, it was quaint, and it had its charm, but it was hardly a mecca of touristy attractions, no matter what the Chamber of Commerce tried to assert with their splashy local commercials.

So why would a man like Dante, who was sophisticated, well-spoken and sticking out like a sore thumb, pick a place like Owl Creek to hang out?

Maybe she'd read too many true-crime novels because she was already formulating less-than-legal reasons why.

This was one of the downsides to being a voracious book-worm—the what-ifs were endless.

"Lord knows, Francesca, your imagination is enough to fuel an entire literary career," her mother had once said to her in a moment of exasperation. And she'd used her *given* name, which always made her cringe. Not that *Frannie* was much better, but she had to deal with the hand and the name she'd been dealt.

"Order for Frannie C," a voice rang out, and Frannie snapped out of her random thoughts to scoop up the order with a brief smile.

As she climbed into her car, the aroma of fresh barbecue filling the cab, she thought ruefully that at least the food wouldn't disappoint.

But she had a feeling tonight was going to be rough.

DANTE STOOD ON the porch of his rustic rented cabin and listened to the wind whistle through the trees. The warm air caressed his cheek and ruffled his hair. The temperate summer was similar enough to his native country, but that was where the similarities ended.

There was a comforting simplicity to the ebb and flow of Owl Creek. He'd been here almost two weeks and had begun to get a feel for the vibe. The countryside was breathtaking, and the rental was fitting for the area. The A-frame log cabin was built to withstand bitter winters with plenty of snowfall, but he didn't know where he'd be come winter.

He wasn't accustomed to the quiet.

Dante breathed in the clean air, closing his eyes as birds twittered from the branches while unseen forest floor creatures rustled from beneath the ground cover, but something was soothing about the fact that out here, nature ruled supreme.

Not his family.

Being part of the Santoro family—one of the most powerful and dangerous in Italy—was a double-edged sword. It was only a matter of time before you got cut somewhere.

It would be disingenuous to say the money and prestige didn't have its perks: the fine clothing, expensive cars and the privilege that came with the association. But nothing came without a cost.

And he was done chipping off pieces of his soul to pay the toll.

Dante straightened, rubbing his arms as an errant chill popped goose bumps along his skin. The paranoia never left him. No matter how random Owl Creek seemed on a map or how remote this cabin was, he couldn't shake the tension that eyes were on him.

His uncle Lorenzo wasn't the kind of man to let any perceived slight go unanswered.

Not even when it was family committing the offense.

His only insurance policy until he could figure out a better solution?

Something his uncle would kill to have returned.

For now, it was locked away in a safety-deposit box under a fake name.

But sometimes, he worried not even that would keep him safe from his uncle's reach.

Dante pushed away from the railing and went inside, locking the door behind him.

Chapter Three

Jenny, always calm during any crisis, was no different when faced with the possibility that her husband had fathered two children with her twin sister. Just saying the words in her head made Frannie want to sink into the floor.

Damn you, Dad.

If he wasn't already dead…

"Frannie, can you please get the plates out," Jenny said, moving on autopilot as she unpacked the brisket meal Frannie had brought. Of course, Frannie was there before any of her siblings showed up because even when she tried to drag her feet, her need to be on time took the reins.

"Mom, we don't need to use the real plates. Paper plates should be fine."

"Not for brisket, dear," Jenny replied without missing a beat. "Also, did you manage to talk to Mrs. Gershwin from the Garden Club about those dead azaleas in the planter berm in front of your store? It's such an eyesore and takes away from all the lovely work you've done for your little shop."

Dead azaleas were the least of Frannie's concerns at the moment. "Mom, I know what you're doing. It's okay to admit that you're upset. We're all here for you. What Dad did—"

"We don't know anything yet," Jenny cut in, her soft voice with the slightest reproachful edge, as if Frannie were the one acting out of pocket for even mentioning it. "I don't believe in building bridges for rivers we don't need to cross just yet."

"But that's just it, Mom, we do have to cross that bridge, the river is here and it's about to wipe out the aforementioned bridge. We have to face this head-on."

"What's to face? If it's true..." Jenny paused, revealing a minute crack in her reserve before pushing forward "... then we deal with it. It is what it is."

Frannie hated that saying. Not only did that phrase feel like a cop-out, it also felt like defeat. "Do you think your sister could be lying?"

"I haven't seen or spoken to Jessie in decades. I haven't a clue what she might be capable of at this point in her life."

"Yeah, but you knew her as a kid. What was she like?"

Jenny blinked as if Frannie had viciously poked a bruise to see if it still hurt. It took a minute, but Jenny recovered, saying, "It was a long time ago. I hardly remember. Besides, no one is the same person they were as a child. I know I'm certainly not. Life changes people. Circumstances, choices, all those variables go into the mix, and you pop out a different version of yourself when it's all said and done. It happens to everyone. It's just the way of things, Frannie."

Frannie heard the hidden pain in that statement. As a mother, Jenny had been competent, solid and appropriately present. Even as a full-time nurse, Jenny had been the one to oversee her children's schooling, sports and home needs, though Frannie had never felt that Jenny loved being a mom. It felt contradictory to admit that truth when the woman had given birth to six kids. But Frannie always wondered if that had been some attempt to keep Robert interested in staying, not so much an interest in being a mother to a large brood.

It always hurt to stare hard truths in the eye.

But it also made her sad for her mother. "Mom…did you and Dad ever actually love each other?"

Jenny stilled, her back to Frannie. "In the beginning, very much." She slowly turned, exhaling a long breath as she admitted, "Well, at least for me, anyway. I've spent a lifetime trying to make something better than it was for the sake of my children. The truth of the matter was, Robert and I… well, maybe we were never a good fit at all."

Jenny's revelation stunned Frannie. Intensely private by nature, her mother would rather lick a dirty sidewalk than share the depth of her feelings on any particular subject. The fact that Jenny was sharing even a smidge of her business with anyone was jarring.

And Frannie didn't know how to respond.

Jenny seemed to understand and returned to unpacking the brisket meal.

But Frannie had to say something. "Mom…if it turns out to be true… I'm really sorry. You deserved better than what Dad gave you."

Jenny accepted Frannie's sentiment, sniffing back what may have been a tear or two, and then excused herself to the bathroom with a reminder that the sturdier napkins were in the pantry.

Sighing, Frannie sank into the chair at the kitchen island and mentally prodded her siblings to hurry up and get their happy asses to the house. She wasn't sure how much more she could absorb on her own. She needed the buffer of her brother and sister, or she'd end up stress-eating everything in sight.

Her gaze wandered around the home she'd grown up in, seeing memories in a different light. It was funny how kids could be incredibly intuitive yet miss obvious clues staring them in the face.

Their home was aesthetically beautiful. Jenny had refined tastes that she used to shape Robert's rough, masculine edges into something strong yet elegant. Frannie had never known the sharp pangs of hunger or gone without anything she needed. Between Jenny and Robert, their six kids had enjoyed the privilege of an upper-middle-class upbringing. Christmas had been a favorite holiday, with the smells of holiday baking permeating the house and plenty of gifts beneath the tree.

As a kid, she remembered her dad sitting in his chair, watching the chaos with a small, satisfied smile, like the proud papa enjoying the fruits of his labor. And she remembered the hushed arguments behind closed doors and the strained smile of her mother as unspoken words between them created an invisible tension.

But even on Christmas Day, Robert only hung around for a short time, always with an excuse or reason to cut out. Now it made her wonder, had he been rushing off to spend time with his other family?

Frannie groaned, hating every syllable of that question. Even worse, had her mother known the reason he was leaving? The thought of her mother suffering such emotional agony in silence was more than she could bear.

Fresh anger at her father washed over her in a wave, and tears stung her eyes.

The front door opened, and Frannie muttered, "Thank God." She quickly wiped at her eyes, relieved that the troops had finally arrived.

Ruby lifted a brown paper bag, announcing, "I brought the wine," and Fletcher, right behind her, said, "And I brought peach pie and beer, because I don't drink wine and peach pie is good for any occasion."

"Mom's freshening up," Frannie said, motioning to Ruby. "I'll take a glass, if you don't mind."

Ruby's eyebrow rose as she reached for the wine glasses. "Already? What'd I miss?"

Frannie didn't have the words. "Just pour the wine."

"That means I'll start with the beer," Fletcher quipped with dark humor, but they all felt the heaviness in the air. How could they not? As if their dad collapsing from a stroke hadn't been a big enough shock to the family. Now this? Well, if this situation had taught Frannie anything, it was... sometimes the secrets of the dead didn't stay in the grave.

IT WAS A dream and a memory morphing into one another to create a hellish movie that Dante couldn't escape.

"I'm not doing this anymore," Dante shouted at his uncle Lorenzo. "I'm done being the club you wield to ruin lives. I'm out."

"Who do you think you are?" Lorenzo's thick Italian accent deepened with florid anger. "I made you—I will end you. I decide when you're finished, and that time is not now."

The Santoro trust had paid for Dante's law degree, but Lorenzo acted as if the check came from his personal account. As the executor, Lorenzo knew he held a certain power over the entire Santoro family, and he wasn't shy about reminding anyone who stepped out of line.

But Dante wasn't afraid of his uncle. Maybe he should be, but Lorenzo had exhausted Dante's endurance, and if he didn't get out now, his soul would never recover. "You've gone too far. I won't be a party to this level of corruption. You'll have to find a new attorney to represent the family."

"For a smart man, you make stupid moves," Lorenzo said. "I've destroyed men for less than what you dare right now. I'll allow this one moment of insanity because I have a softness for you, nephew, but don't press your luck. My patience only stretches so far."

Dante held his uncle's stare without flinching. "I'm out."

And he left Lorenzo's office, his uncle's shouting still ringing in his ears.

One truth about Lorenzo, and perhaps why the family was obscenely wealthy—his ruthlessness was exacted with purpose.

The scene shifted, and he was at Belinda's apartment, waiting for her shift to end at the hospital. A pediatric surgeon, Belinda was at the top of her field. Hospitals worldwide courted her services, but she loved her home country and refused to relocate, no matter the offer.

Belinda made Dante realize he couldn't keep doing what he was doing at his uncle's command if he wanted a life with a woman like her. She was kind and generous and believed in the inherent goodness of people. If he married her and inevitably dragged her into his world, it would ruin everything he loved about Belinda.

And he couldn't do that to her.

Besides, he could start fresh. He didn't need the Santoro money to make his way. He'd have to start small, but he could build something he could be proud of from scratch.

Something his father would've approved of. There'd been a reason his father had moved away from his brother and the entire Santoro legacy.

If he hadn't died…maybe life would've been much different for him and his mother.

May she rest in peace.

The loud ticking of the clock reverberated in his head. Belinda was late.

The scene shifted again.

Belinda, broken and bleeding, beaten within an inch of her life, barely alive after the attack.

But the brutal destruction of her fingers made Dante realize with horror that someone had specifically targeted the very thing that made Belinda special in her field.

The tendons in her right hand had been severed, the bones in her left, crushed. The reality that she may never operate again struck his core, lodging a permanent stone in his stomach.

And then the note, delivered with a brilliant spray of flowers to Dante while he spent every hour at Belinda's beside, praying desperately for a miracle that chilled his blood.

The Family is here for you and Belinda. Arrangements are already prepared for Belinda's care when you return.

His guts twisted in agony. Lorenzo had done this. *That sick bastard.* He'd crushed an innocent woman to get Dante to return as a warning to get back in line, or else the consequences would be severe.

Dante had foolishly believed he could handle whatever Lorenzo threw at him.

He'd never imagined Belinda might be the one to pay the price for his actions.

His hands curled, shaking with impotent violence.

How could he prove it? He couldn't.

Lorenzo's strength was his ability to protect himself from legal ramifications. Dante had spent his legal career doing that for the Santoro family—enabling them to ruin people from behind the safety of legal might.

And Lorenzo had just ruined Belinda.

Belinda's eyes popped open, bloodshot, and rimmed with tears. "You did this to me!" she screeched, holding up her gnarled and broken fingers, the unnatural bend of her digits like something from a horror film. "This is all your fault, and I will never forgive you until you die!"

With Belinda's scream ringing in his mind, Dante shot up, his heart racing, staring blindly into the dark of his bedroom. *Where am I?* Sweat dampened his body and made the sheets tangled around his legs feel like cling wrap. *Idaho.* Not Italy.

Just a nightmare. No, not just a nightmare, a terrible memory. Six months later and the same nightmare chased him wherever he went.

Kicking off the sheets, he rose on unsteady feet to splash water on his face. Pale moonlight bathed the rustic bathroom, creating unsettling shadows where anyone could lurk. His heart was still beating hard against his chest.

A million apologies would never fix what Lorenzo had taken from Belinda.

What Lorenzo had taken from Dante.

And if Dante was right…that tally was far bigger than he could've imagined.

Pushing away from the sink, he returned to the bedroom and quickly dressed.

It didn't matter that it was only three in the morning. There'd be no more sleep for him tonight.

Chapter Four

Frannie would need all the coffee to keep her eyes open today at work. She tried to get Darla to come by the shop to help her do inventory, but wedding details had her busy all day. Frannie's request probably wasn't entirely based on her need for help but rather on someone to talk to about her current family situation, someone she knew she could trust.

It wasn't like she wanted to share her family's embarrassment all over town. But the news was likely circulating in hushed whispers, because the gossip hotline in Owl Creek was second to none.

The usual customers milled about, enjoying their lattes and browsing, or sitting in the big, comfy chairs while reading, which gave Frannie a chance to decompress from last night's meeting.

She supposed it went well enough, but only because Jenny Colton wasn't the type of woman to weep and wail, no matter her tragedy. If there was one thing her mother excelled at, it was internalizing emotional trauma. Marrying Robert had given her plenty of practice, if the rumors were true.

"Mom, we just want you to know we're here for you," Ruby had assured their mother, trying to get their mom to open up. But Jenny, as always, had kept her emotions in check and smiled at her daughter, suggesting that Ruby get a trim because her split ends were starting to show.

Frannie had shared a look with Ruby, feeling her sister's frustration but appreciating her restraint when she just accepted their mother's mild reproach with a tight-lipped nod. Even if she were bleeding out in the street, their mother would never admit to needing help. Maybe that was why she'd never talked about why she and her sister stopped speaking to each other. The emotional pain was private, and no one needed to know. Frannie was fairly sure her mom saved her tears for the privacy of the shower. She could recall one instance when she thought she'd heard her mom crying in the bathroom, but when Jenny emerged an hour later—dressed and ready to start the day—it was like Frannie had imagined it.

What kind of life was that?

Frannie winced as her gut cramped. She pushed away the half-eaten croissant and blew on her coffee before sipping. What she wanted to say to her dad if he were still alive to listen would make her childhood Girl Scout leader gasp.

"Frannie…a good woman minds her business," Robert had once told her when she'd dared to ask why he never bought his wife flowers on any occasion despite knowing that Jenny loved flowers of any kind.

"But Dad…"

"Your mother gets what she needs."

Even at a young age, Frannie didn't believe that. A sadness pulled on her mother, even though Jenny did a bang-up job hiding it beneath a veneer of efficiency and practicality.

But Robert Colton never made mistakes and therefore hadn't felt the need to entertain the opinions of others on the subject. Even those of his "favorite" daughter.

God, her dad had been such a prick.

And then there was her Aunt Jessie, too. What kind of

woman not only slept with her twin sister's husband but then carried on a decades-long affair with the man? That was almost sociopathic.

There were also her supposed half siblings to think about, which caused an involuntary shudder.

She didn't want to be salty to innocent people—Jessie's kids didn't ask to be part of this drama—but it was hard not to feel some standoffishness when it felt like interlopers were trying to cram their way into her family.

If her Aunt Jessie was telling the truth, that meant these new cousins were her siblings—the thought gave her an instant headache. Never in a million years had she ever thought her family might have scandal lurid enough to land a guest spot on some tell-all TV show.

The front door opened, and the handsome Italian walked in. Even though she wasn't much in the mood to smile, the urge tugged at the corners of her mouth. Her heart did a little jig when he walked straight to the counter instead of perusing the shelves.

"Good morning," he said with a brief smile before going straight to business. "I'm going to be in town for a little while longer and I wondered if you'd be able to order some books for me?"

Frannie stood a little straighter. "Oh! Yes, of course. I'd be happy to. What did you have in mind?"

"Well, a combination of legal works and fiction." He slid a prepared list toward her, including his cell number. "Just call me when they come in, and I'll come and pick them up right away. I'm also happy to pay in advance."

"You don't have to do that. I trust you," she said, the words popping from her mouth before she realized she had nothing to base her assumption on. Was this her problem? Always assuming people were inherently good? Look where that had gotten her. For all she knew, he could be an incredibly attractive swindler. She hastily replied, "But if you'd feel more comfortable paying in advance, that works, too."

"I'll just go ahead and pay now," he said, smiling as if somehow privy to her mental conversation. He pulled cash from his wallet as she rang up his purchase. Hadn't she read somewhere that someone carrying a lot of cash was a red flag nowadays? Or was her overactive imagination running away with her?

"Is everything okay? I couldn't help but notice you got an upsetting call yesterday," he said.

Surprised but inordinately touched that he noticed, she answered with a smile. "Just family stuff. You know how that goes."

"Of course."

Dante had ordered legal tomes, different from the usual purchase for the average reader. Was it possible he was an attorney? She might not want to share her family drama, but Dante might have some tips on handling the situation with her Aunt Jessie. *Ten seconds ago, you questioned his moral integrity, and now you're considering asking him for legal advice?* Fair point, but what were the *actual* odds that he was a bad person? She was going to risk it. "I'm sorry if this is none of my business, but I wondered, might you be an attorney?"

He hesitated for the barest moment before confirming, "I am. Why?"

"Oh, no reason. I mean, the books you ordered suggested you might be connected to law in some way, and I could really use someone to talk to who has some understanding of certain legal things."

"Are you in trouble?" he asked with a concerned frown.

"Me? Um, no, not exactly, but my family might be."

"Do you mind sharing?"

She hesitated. Was it wise to talk to Dante about this

stuff, or was she tripping headlong into a muddy puddle by asking him for advice? There was no way to explain it logically, but she felt she could trust him and needed someone to talk to.

"I should warn you, it's very 'Maury Povich' level."

His expression deepened in question. "What is… Maury Povich?"

"Sorry, it's a saying when something is scandalous and geared toward 'revealing taboo secrets.' From a daytime talk show host. Anyway, it's embarrassingly scandalous." Was that a slight smile? He must be like most people who thought nothing bad happened in small towns. *You sweet summer child.* Frannie was about to ruin his illusions. She chuckled ruefully, "No, trust me, it's next-level embarrassing. Shocking, even."

"Now you have to tell me. To leave me hanging would be cruel."

Frannie glanced around her shop. The nearest customer had left, and the only other was deep in the Self-Help aisle farthest from them. She felt safe enough to share. "I might as well just rip off the bandage. My dad died of a stroke a few months ago—it was a shock, but then again, not so much. He didn't do much to safeguard his health, so it was either going to be a heart attack or a stroke, and in the end, it was the stroke that took him out."

"I'm sorry for your loss," he murmured appropriately.

"Thank you. It's been hard but we'd started to adjust to life without Dad. Until my aunt Jessie—my mom's twin sister whom I've never met, by the way—showed up demanding a piece of my dad's assets for her children because, surprise, she and my dad were having a decades-long affair beneath my mom's nose."

Dante absorbed the information without reacting, which lawyers were trained to do, but she appreciated the mature response. It was hard enough to get the words out without having to navigate big reactions, too.

"Does this Aunt Jessie have proof of her children's paternity?"

"Not yet but that's the first thing I suggested. In this day and age, if you're going to make a claim like that, you'd better have proof."

"Yes, indeed. Your family has legal representation?"

"Um, well, we have my dad's attorney who facilitated the will and stuff like that."

"But you haven't retained him for this specific purpose?"

"No, not that I'm aware but I didn't think to ask my mom about that specifically. For all I know, maybe she already has that handled. It's hard to know the appropriate way to deal with something like this," she admitted forlornly. "Honestly, it feels like an out-of-body experience just hearing the words come out of my mouth."

Dante was kind but firm, saying, "You need to find out if you have an attorney safeguarding your father's assets. It'll be important in the future. The burden of proof is on your aunt to prove paternity. That's the first hurdle. If she fails to produce evidence that your father is in fact her children's father, then she has no case. But a good attorney will be able to smother that spark before it has a chance to cause any damage."

She didn't know if her father's attorney was good, but her brother Chase might have a good attorney on the job. Chase might be distant and preoccupied, but he wasn't stupid. He'd do whatever it took to protect the family's assets. "I appreciate the insight," she said. "My brother is probably already handling all the business side, but I can't help but worry this will unravel my family. I'm more worried about the emotional shrapnel."

"The consequence of infidelity is often destructive,"

he agreed with empathy. "Have you met these alleged half siblings?"

"No, my aunt and mother had some kind of falling out before we were even born. I've never met my aunt or her kids. I don't know if that's a blessing or not. I don't know how I'd feel if I found out cousins I'd known my entire life turned out to be half siblings. Blech, the whole thing is gross."

He chuckled, then apologized. "It's not funny, but I've never heard anyone characterize a family trauma as 'gross' before. I suppose you're right, though. If it's true, very gross, indeed."

I like him. Frannie smiled, biting her lip. Was she flirting? *Well, that's inappropriate as hell.* She let the smile fade, shaking off the warmth Dante's attention created. "Anyway, I don't mean to bore you with all this stuff. I'm sure it'll work out in the end, somehow."

"You're an optimist."

"Yeah, I guess so. You're not?"

"I'm a realist."

"Sounds depressing," she said with a laugh. "Reality often sucks, which is why I prefer books."

"Fair enough. Maybe that's why I prefer books, too," he agreed, flashing that million-dollar smile again. Did all Italian men have that subtle twinkle in their eye? Like a flash of banked mischief just waiting for the right opportunity to flare up?

"So, subject change, have you read the books I'm ordering for you?"

"Yes. When I left Italy, I didn't have room in my luggage, so I planned to buy new copies when I landed."

"Not that I want to talk you out of a purchase, but you know you can just download these onto your phone?"

"I prefer to hold a book in my hand. Helps me to absorb

the information," he said, shrugging. "It's more of a comfort as well."

"I'm the same way," she said, tickled that they shared the same preference. She loved all access to literature but truly loved settling into a cozy chair with a printed book in her hand. Reading was more than absorbing information—it was an experience. "Well, I'll let you know when they arrive."

"Thank you," he said. If it seemed he was looking for a reason to stick around, it passed, and with a small wave, he left the shop.

Frannie wasn't looking for a date, but if she were... Dante would be at the top of a very short list.

YOU'RE PLAYING A *dangerous game*, a voice warned Dante as he climbed into his car. Frannie was a sweet young woman—and he wouldn't put her in harm's way just because he found her sharp mind intriguing.

That's not the only reason you can't stop thinking about her, the voice added.

All right, there was a wholesome sweetness about Frannie that he found alluring, but that was precisely the reason he had to keep his distance.

Even though he took precautions to remain under his uncle's radar—he paid cash wherever he went and maintained a low profile—the second his diligence started to slip, he only had to remember Belinda's gnarled hands, and he snapped back to reality.

He couldn't risk Frannie falling into Lorenzo's sights.

Besides, what did he think could happen between him and Frannie Colton? If she thought the potential of her father stepping out on her mother and creating another family was scandalous, the crimes of his own family would put her into a coma.

Financial extortion, intimidation, hostile corporate take-downs…all skirting the letter of the law, but the lives ruined at the expense of his uncle's greed was nothing short of emotional bankruptcy.

What one can convince another to do with manipulative persuasion is amazing.

In the beginning, his uncle had greased the wheels with praise, pride, and familial attachments. Then it had progressed to outright bullying whenever someone pushed back.

The movies helped perpetuate the myth of the Italian mob family, but you didn't have to be toting guns and blowing up cars to intimidate people into doing your bidding.

Lorenzo wasn't a mobster, but he'd done things that should've been criminal.

And Dante had helped him.

God save my soul. It was bad enough that Dante felt he'd never be free of the stain on his soul, but after Belinda's attack, he suffered the sickening realization that maybe his uncle's crimes went farther than white-collar financial greed.

And he had to know.

Speaking of…

His cell rang with the number of the private investigator he planned to hire. The man had a reputation for having a sharp mind, discreet tactics and international contacts. Dante needed a ninja who wasn't afraid of the Santoro name.

"Dante," he answered.

"This is Nicholas Gladney, but you can call me Nick. You left a message."

"I did. I want to hire you."

"What would Dante Santoro need a private investigator for?"

The man had already done his homework. *Good.* It would

be the first time verbalizing his suspicion, but after what happened to Belinda, he was done speculating.

Cutting straight to the point, he replied bluntly, "I suspect my uncle had something to do with my mother's death—and if it's true, I need proof."

Chapter Five

Frannie felt as if she were doing something wrong. She didn't know why she'd agreed to this meeting with her estranged aunt Jessie. Morbid curiosity, perhaps? Maybe she was a glutton for punishment? Who knew.

Purposefully asking for a table in the back, she chewed her cheek while waiting for the woman trying to rip her family apart. She wondered if she still had time to bail before her aunt arrived.

This was ridiculous. At the very least, she should've asked Ruby or Fletcher to come with her—safety in numbers. Not that she thought her aunt would jump over the table and stab her with a dinner fork, but she didn't know this woman from Adam. Who knew what she was capable of?

Just when Frannie's anxiety was about to hit the roof, a woman rounded the corner, and Frannie instantly knew it was her aunt Jessie.

She was the same height as her mom, but her hair was a brittle blond as opposed to her mother's dark blond with streaks of gray, and Jessie's sharpness almost seemed hawkish.

Frannie knew her mother and sister had been known around town as great beauties. Small towns loved to cling to the memory of someone's past. Whereas Jenny had aged gracefully, allowing time to soften the edges and claim its due, her sister seemed determined to cling to her youth with almost palpable desperation.

"Darling, sweet Frannie," Jessie cooed, coming straight at Frannie to fold her into a hug. The woman was so thin that Frannie could nearly count the bones in her spine. "Goodness gracious, you've grown into such a beauty."

As Frannie had never met Jessie, she didn't know how her aunt would know anything about her. Unless her mother had contacted her sister unbeknownst to anyone else, but that didn't seem likely.

Especially when Jenny had maintained that she hadn't seen or spoken to her sister since Aunt Jessie divorced Uncle Buck.

What was the etiquette for this kind of situation? She took her seat and waited for Jessie to take the lead. After all, Jessie had asked to meet.

Jessie signaled for the waitress and ordered an iced tea without sugar or lemon, which, as far as Frannie was concerned, was just bitter dark water, but that seemed appropriate given the circumstances.

"My dear, I can only imagine how confused you must be—how confused you all must be—and I want to assure you, I never wanted things to happen the way they did."

Which part? The part where she had an affair with her sister's husband or demanded some of Robert Colton's assets after he died? Frannie didn't want to be sharp but found Jessie's comment disingenuous. Frannie chose her words carefully. "Aunt Jessie... I don't want to be rude, but I can't make head or tail of anything that's happened recently. I have so many questions but don't even know where to start."

"Of course," Jessie said, flicking her napkin and placing it on her lap. "I understand. I always wanted to tell the family, but for obvious reasons, your father had adamantly opposed my ardent desire to be honest with Jenny. It was one of our more frequent disagreements."

Frannie was grateful they hadn't ordered any food. She doubted her stomach would allow for anything beyond a breadstick. "I'm not a fan of placing all the blame on a woman when infidelity is involved but I gotta say, you're coming off as real cold to do what you did with your sister's husband. You knew he was married. How could you do that?"

Jessie's smile froze, and her gaze frosted. "It's easy to stand in judgment, darling, when you're not involved."

"But I am involved, aren't I? You're my aunt, he's my dad…kinda involved by default. And now my cousins are my half siblings? It's all very Jerry Springer, you know what I mean?"

"I told your father it was best to be honest," Jessie returned, narrowing her gaze. "But your father wasn't a man who listened to any opinion above his own."

That much was true. "I'm sorry," Frannie murmured because it felt like she should, but it was hard to feel compassion for a woman who'd purposely had another life with a married man on the sly. "So what happens now?"

"Well, as distasteful as my request may seem, the ugly truth remains—Robert and I may not have been married but I was his wife in all things except on paper. My children deserve their fair share of their father's assets…as do I."

"You?"

"Yes."

"How so?"

"As I said, I was his wife as much as Jenny. The only difference—"

"The big difference was that he was *actually* married to my mother. Legally," Frannie pointed out, her temper rising at her aunt's audacity. "I fail to see how you can think that you're owed anything when you knew what you were doing was wrong."

"When is loving someone wrong?" Jessie countered. She seemed to be trying to appeal to Frannie's sense of romanticism.

"When the other person is already married to someone else," Frannie answered flatly.

"Yes, I suppose that may be true but what's done is done. Your father isn't here to bear your judgment, so that leaves only me. Whether you agree or not, legally, I'm assured I have a solid case." It didn't look like Jessie was going to go quietly.

Frannie stilled. "You have an attorney?"

"I wouldn't have stirred the pot without ample assurances that doing so would be worth the trouble."

Worth the trouble of blowing up my family's life. A blithe statement for such a terrible action.

Frannie swallowed the sudden lump in her throat. "Did you think of your sister at all? How this might hurt her? You're twins…surely you must've cared for her at some point in your life."

"I loved your father, and he loved me. It may be hard to hear but your father never truly loved Jenny."

Maybe it was the subtle shrug or the feeling that Jessie didn't actually give two figs for her sister, but Frannie saw red. "You're a piece of work. How dare you. Who do you think you are? You were my father's *mistress*, not some great love—and I hate to break it to you, but I doubt you were the only one."

Jessie's cold smile matched the chill in her eyes. "Darling, I knew your father better than anyone. Fidelity was never his strength, but he always returned to me."

"No, actually, he always returned to my mother."

Something flashed in Jessie's eyes—rage, perhaps?—

and Frannie sensed this entire meeting had been a ruse to try to feel out the family's disposition about her claim. As if they were going to hand over a portion of Robert's assets with a smile and an apology for her trouble. "Your loyalty is admirable, but the law is on my side."

"And what do your kids say about all of this?" Frannie fired back, wondering if her half siblings/cousins were cut from the same cloth as their mother. "Are they okay with what you did?"

"I wouldn't dream of speaking for my children."

"Yeah, well, I can't help but wonder if they're anything like you."

Jessie drew a measured breath though the strained smile never faltered. "So full of fire and brimstone, just like my Robert."

That was a purposeful dig. Frannie rose stiffly. "I think we're done here. Please don't contact me again. I have nothing to say to you."

"No worries, dear. I'm sure the lawyers will sort the details soon enough."

With nothing left to say, Frannie left the restaurant beyond thankful she hadn't ordered anything. Sharing a meal with that woman would be enough to turn the strongest stomach.

DANTE INTENDED TO keep a professional distance from Frannie, but fate seemed to have other plans.

He seemed to sense the minute Frannie entered the brewery, his pint half raised to his lips when his gaze zeroed in on the blonde woman. In an instant, the bustling chaos of a popular place faded to a low hum.

But even as he watched, privately soaking up everything about her—the way her hair lightly dusted her shoulders, the stubborn tilt of her chin—he could tell something was bothering her.

A heavy weight dampened her usually sunny disposition. Likely more of the family troubles she'd been telling him about earlier. Even though their family issues were apples to oranges, he understood the stress of familial drama.

Just mind your business, a voice inside his head warned.

And yet, he was drawn to say hello at the very least. Nothing wrong with being friendly, he argued with himself.

Making eye contact, he waved to Frannie, letting fate decide the direction. If she waved and kept on her way, that was the way of it, but if she came over to say hi, then he'd enjoy the friendly company.

Warmth spread across his chest and excitement followed when she brightened and headed his way.

"Mind if I join you?" she asked, hopping beside him at the bar.

"Not at all." He motioned for the bartender. "What'll you have?"

"I'll take a pale ale," she said, reaching for her purse, but he waved away the need. She raised a brow with an uncertain but appreciative, "Are you sure?"

For a man raised in Italy with staunchly Italian roots, it was a foreign concept for a woman to pay for her drinks in a man's company. "I'm happy to pay for your drink," he assured her.

Her smile widened, and his mouth curved in response. She had this infectious way about her that was hard to ignore. After everything he'd been through last year, he craved the sunshiny warmth Frannie radiated effortlessly. She probably didn't even realize how she lit up a room.

The bartender set down her ale, and she gratefully took a drink, instantly relieved. "God, I needed this. It's been a day."

"Everything okay?" he asked, not wanting to overstep but genuinely curious.

She drew a deep breath, shaking her head. "Honestly, I don't even know. I don't want to bore you with my family stuff, though."

"I don't mind listening," he said.

"Really?"

He gestured with a generous smile. "Please, I'm all ears."

Frannie chuckled. "Okay, well, just remember you offered."

"Go for it."

"Against my better judgment I met up with Aunt Jessie a bit ago and as you might imagine it was about as enjoyable as a poke in the eye. For one, she's a horrible human being and doesn't seem to understand that having a decades-long affair with a married man is a bad look. Two, she doesn't acknowledge how hurtful her actions were to my mom, her own sister. I was flabbergasted at how blatantly selfish she was, and I guess I was hoping that maybe there was some kind of explanation that would make sense but there's nothing that could excuse what she did. And yes, I realize it takes two to tango, but I can't help but judge her more for being such a horrible person to her sister."

"I'm curious...why did you agree to meet with her?"

"Excellent question—one I kept asking myself when it all went to crap. I'm not sure what I'd hoped for or what I thought might happen, but it surely didn't end happily. Let's just say, the word *lawyer* was used instead of a friendly goodbye."

"Always a sign that negotiations have reached a stalemate," he agreed.

She nodded. "The thing is, she seems pretty confident that she's got a legitimate claim. I get that the kids would be entitled to something if it turns out they are my dad's, but can she claim anything? They weren't married."

He didn't want to worry Frannie, but there could be grounds for compensation for the aunt if Frannie's father had been the woman's sole source of support for more than ten years. He didn't want to insert himself where it wasn't appropriate, but he hated to see her weighed down by the situation. "People can make claims. Doesn't mean they'll win in court," he said. "However, if possible, it might benefit the estate to offer a lump-sum settlement to encourage the problem to go away without dragging the family through the courts."

"I can't imagine giving that woman a dime," Frannie said with a shudder. "I don't want to be mean but she's the one who made the choice to carry on with a married man. I don't have a lot of sympathy."

"It's not so much about sympathy as it is efficiency. Settlements make problems go away."

Frannie's subtle frown as she considered his advice reminded him that they came from different worlds. She had relatively normal problems, even if they were emotionally distressing. The crises he dealt with as Lorenzo's right-hand legal muscle would turn your hair white. As if summoned by his memory, the hairs on the back of his neck prickled, making him quickly look around the brewery out of habit.

It was Frannie's turn to ask, "Everything okay?"

He forced a chuckle, shaking off the paranoia. "A goose must've walked over my grave."

"Oh, I hate when that happens," Frannie commiserated with a shudder. "Every time my grandma said that, I got the heebie-jeebies."

"The *heebie*-what?" he asked with an incredulous laugh.

"Heebie-jeebies," Frannie repeated with a grin. "You know, the creeps."

"That might be my new favorite word."

Frannie's laugh could chase away any lingering fears. It didn't feel right to enjoy this time with her, but he was selfishly unwilling to cut the night short.

He needed a mental break from the constant stress of looking over his shoulder.

And Frannie was precisely what he needed tonight.

Chapter Six

It felt good to laugh. After her disastrous meeting with Aunt Jessie, she didn't think anything could lighten her sour mood. But seeing Dante across the crowded brewery had instantly chased away the clouds.

There was something about Dante that calmed and soothed her nerves. People tended to make her fidgety, which was probably why she preferred the quiet company of books to actual people. She had a tight-knit group of friends but often kept to herself.

However, with Dante, she didn't feel fidgety or out of place.

His eyes, sharp yet compassionate, held her stare without being off-putting, and he listened when she rambled, which in her experience was rare.

Frannie often felt set apart from her peers and family, even though no one was mean. Well, her brothers used to tease that she was "weird," but that was only because she'd preferred her nose in a book than anywhere else when given a choice.

But there was something about Dante she couldn't quite put her finger on—a wariness to get too close, perhaps?—that probably should've put her off but instead intrigued her more.

Had he been hurt in the past? A harsh breakup, maybe? If so, she could relate. Also, why did he pay cash for every purchase? He walked around with a clip of money, which in this day and age seemed unusual, but to ask why felt too personal. Of course, it wasn't any of her business why he paid cash for everything, but her curious, okay, nosy mind pressed for more details.

"So, you're from Italy, and you mentioned being here for business and pleasure… What drew you to Owl Creek?" She hesitated to mention that he didn't seem the type to spend all day on a boat like most tourists who flocked to the area during the summer, but she also didn't know much about him, so it was possible he loved boating.

"I spent ten years in the States before relocating to Italy with my family. There's something wholesome about American small towns and I needed a break from my usual scene."

Frannie snorted. "Wholesome? That's a stereotype that needs to die a grisly death. We have our share of terrible stuff. I mean, I hate to be the bearer of bad news but drug use in small towns is on the rise. For some reason, the Chamber of Commerce is reluctant to put that on the brochure, though."

He grinned. "Seems like a lost opportunity."

"Absolutely." She laughed, sharing, "Oh, here's something else—last year Blackbird Lake had a red algae bloom that killed tons of fish and sections of the lake had to be cordoned off to keep people from getting sick. But no one mentioned that."

"Are you always this passionate about your lake health?"

She shrugged. "I'm not obsessed with it, but I do feel not enough attention is being put on the right things. It's a beautiful place but too many people on the water with their boats and garbage pollutes the natural ecosystem. You can't deny that there have been so many ecological disasters that have been directly attributed to human interference."

"No argument from me. Keeping the balance between the carbon footprint and nature is a constant battle that we often lose," he admitted. "Italy faces similar issues with pollution as the rest of the world. There are always going to be people who champion the environment and those who fight any change that threatens inconvenience."

"Do you practice environmental law?"

If only. His predatory uncle was his own kind of human pollution. "No, sadly, not my area of practice but I appreciate anyone who goes into that field. It's a tough one to chase. Too much collective greed to truly affect demonstrable change. But we need warriors out there fighting the good fight."

She met his gaze, her insides warming, tingling with awareness. He had the most expressive eyes. How was he single? She wanted to ask, but it seemed so personal, and she didn't want to ruin the moment, but her mouth had other plans. "Why don't you have a girlfriend or a wife?" she blurted out.

Her abrupt question threw him off-guard—*shocker*—and he waited a minute before answering with a short yet restrained smile. "Uh, too busy, I guess. Up until recently, I was a workaholic. Never seemed to have enough time to do both."

Relief flooded her. That made sense to her. For a moment, she was secretly afraid that he had some dark secret he was protecting. Reading too many crime novels had warped her brain. "I understand," she said. "There's a comfort in the routine of work. I love my little shop, but my best friend, Darla, keeps reminding me that there's more to life than work. She's actually getting married in a few months."

"Your friend is a smart woman."

"Yeah, probably smarter than me for sure, but there's another thing about living in a small town that no one talks about…"

"Which is?"

"The dating pool is excruciatingly small." When he chuckled, she explained with a laugh, "No, seriously! I've known everyone in this town my whole life. It's hard to see guys I went to kindergarten with in a romantic light. I know too many things about them." She glanced around the brewery, spying on someone she knew. She gestured discreetly. "See that guy over there with the ball cap talking a mad game with his buddies like he's some kind of baseball stud? That's Johnny Rogan. He peed his pants in the third grade, and when I see him acting all macho, that's all I remember."

Dante regarded Johnny. "He seems a good-looking enough adult. Has he ever asked you out?"

"Multiple times. I can't think of more creative ways to turn him down at this point. He's nice, I guess, but I literally feel nothing for him in that way. Besides, he isn't a big reader and I can't see myself tied to someone who thinks books are a waste of time."

"So a man interested in taking you out for a date…should share your love of books?"

"It's a great start," Frannie said, holding his gaze, adding, "and I wouldn't mind a foreign accent, either…"

It was bold of her—and entirely out of character—but she wanted to kiss him, and she sensed that he wouldn't make a move without her obvious interest.

Besides, being coy? Never her strength. She was either clueless or awkward, and sometimes both, when it came to approaching guys she was interested in, and that wasn't likely to change anytime soon.

SHUT HER DOWN, *don't encourage that kind of involvement*, that infernal voice urged again, but Dante felt caught in a whirlpool dragging him ever closer to Frannie. He knew why he ought to politely set her straight, to tell her that he wasn't interested in her romantically, but it would be a lie.

He wanted her.

He thought of Frannie in ways that crossed the line, even if he knew he shouldn't. He wanted to taste her lips, touch her skin and feel her beneath him.

The smart—responsible—play would be to make some excuse, pay the tab and end the evening, but the idea of walking away was physically painful.

And he couldn't do it.

But his hesitation cost him.

"Oh, I'm sorry, I just made it weird, didn't I?" Frannie said, her cheeks flaring with pink. "I... Oh, man, this is awkward. Forget I said anything. Actually, I think I should probably go. I've taken up enough of your time whining about my problems. I'm sure you have plenty of your own, you don't need to listen to mine." And before he could say anything, she jumped from the stool and practically ran from the brewery.

Damn it. He tossed down a wad of cash and hurried after her. He couldn't stomach the thought of Frannie feeling rejected when it was a lie.

Even as he ran after her, that voice in his head countered that this was a blessing, but he couldn't let her go like that.

"Frannie! Wait!" he called after her, catching her seconds before she climbed into her car for a quick getaway.

He skidded to a stop, breathing hard. The woman could run like a track star, getting a surprising distance before he caught her. "Jesus, you're a good runner," he said, sucking in a big breath. "It's been awhile since I hit the treadmill. You reminded me that I need to return to my exercise routine."

"Sorry, I ran track in high school and the habit kinda stuck," she said, unsure of why he'd chased after her. "Are you okay?"

He wiped at the bead of sweat on his brow, admitting, "Aside from feeling a little sheepish, yes. However, I couldn't let you go with this misunderstanding between us."

"No, it's my fault, I shouldn't have made such a forward comment. We barely know each other."

"Frannie, I like you but—"

"Oh, God, the dreaded 'I like you, but.' Thanks but I think I know where this is going and it's totally okay. We can just pretend that I never said anything, okay?"

This was going from bad to worse. "Frannie, that's not what I was going to say."

She frowned. "What were you going to say?"

"I like you, a lot. More than I should. But you deserve complete honesty. I'm not in a position to start anything real or meaningful and I respect you too much to suggest something casual, if you catch what I mean."

"You mean, sex?"

"Well, yes."

She surprised him with a chuckle. "Dante, I think you're getting ahead of yourself. I'm not looking for anything super serious either. My life is a mess right now. But we're both adults and I like you. Is that so bad?"

Frannie was giving him the green light for something casual between them. Did he want that? Was it possible to entertain a casual arrangement while he was in Owl Creek? It wasn't exactly his style, but if he couldn't offer much more, he liked the idea of spending more time with Frannie.

But was it safe?

Perhaps if they were careful…even then, it was taking a risk. He didn't know if Lorenzo had spies looking for him, but it would likely happen sooner or later. Dante had something Lorenzo wanted back. That much wouldn't change, which could put Frannie on Lorenzo's radar.

And how much should he share with Frannie about his circumstances? He wanted to be honest but couldn't see that conversation going well. If he wasn't a red flag, he didn't know what was.

He'd underestimated his uncle's reach in the past, and he swore he wouldn't do that again. Yet, here he was, his brain clouded with desire for a woman he had no business wanting.

It was so damn selfish of him to want more with Frannie knowing that getting too close to him would put her in danger.

And yet, he still reached for her.

Was he really that much of a selfish bastard?

The answer was immediate and humbling.

Dante pulled Frannie into the cove of his arms. She nestled against him, gazing into his eyes with a shy smile. "Does this mean you're down for some casual adulting?"

"I think it does," he murmured, brushing his lips across hers, his tongue darting to taste hers. She sank against him with a sigh, and he knew he'd made a mistake immediately, but it was too late to turn back now.

She felt like a dream he didn't have any business enjoying. There was a sweetness to Frannie that felt like stolen treasure in his hands. But as before, when the voice warned him to keep his distance, he ignored every bit of good sense and tightened his hold around her waist.

"My place or yours?" she murmured against his mouth, her lips curving in a flirty smile.

"Mine," he answered, pulling away to slide his hand into hers but not before giving the parking lot a glance to check for anything that shouldn't be there.

Frannie grinned, unlocking her car. "I'll follow you."

And Dante knew there was no turning back from this decision.

He'd sealed his fate—and hers.

Chapter Seven

Frannie's heart thundered in her chest as she followed Dante out to his place. Who was she? What was she doing? Listening to herself boldly offering a casual relationship with the sexy Italian when she was a serial monogamist was a surreal experience.

Darla always said she needed to put herself out there more, but this felt so far afield that she didn't know how to navigate the unfamiliar terrain.

But this was exactly what she needed. Another thing about small towns—if you weren't careful, they would keep you thinking small.

Frannie didn't want to fall into that trap.

Also, something about Dante set her blood on fire in a way she'd never experienced.

And she wanted more.

She pulled up behind Dante and exited the car, immediately recognizing the rental property. "This place used to belong to Gavin Pritchard's family. They moved away a few years ago." Frannie smiled at Dante's amusement, adding with a shrug, "Another one of those pro/con arguments for living in a small town."

"Did you and this Gavin date back in the day?" Dante asked as he unlocked the front door and waited for her to

pass through before closing the door and locking it behind them.

"No," she answered, tickled by his chivalry and sense
of protection. "My mom and Gavin's mom used to sell
Tupperware together and would host Tupperware parties."
Of course, he had a higher chance of being surprised by
a bear in his kitchen than a burglar, but she liked that he
cared about her safety and watched as he quickly checked
doors and windows.

Satisfied they were secured, Dante asked, "Can I get you
something to drink? Wine or...juice? I don't think I have
beer stocked."

"Water is fine with me," she answered, taking in the
surroundings. It looked different from when the Pritchard
family had lived there, but she remembered the house's
general layout.

Dante returned with two bottled waters, cracking hers
open before handing it to her.

She smiled: there was that chivalrous nature again.
"Are all Italian men as considerate as you?" Then, when
he seemed puzzled, she pointed to the bottled water, adding, "And the opening of the door. It was very old-school
and charming but not what I'm used to."

"Do men not open doors here?"

"In my generation? Not really. I mean, some do, but it's
not common. I can't remember the last time a guy opened
the door for me, much less opened my water for me."

"Would you prefer I not?" he asked, furrowing his brow.

"Oh, gosh, no, please don't stop. I like it. I'm just not
used to it, that's all."

"If that's the case, American men have lost the art of appreciating women."

"It could just be here. Other states might have different
traditions. All I know is Owl Creek, Idaho, though."

Dante smiled, reaching for her hand. She accepted, allowing him to pull her gently toward the bedroom. Her heart rate immediately picked up as anticipation wiped away all thoughts of anything but what was happening between them.

Dante clicked on the small bedside lamp, illuminating the room in a soft glow.

A large, rustic bed framed in rough-hewn oak and covered with a Midwestern-style comforter dominated the room. The faint aroma of Dante's cologne clung to the space—a spicy masculine scent that was both sophisticated and brawny—and Frannie immediately felt at home. But there was still the awkwardness of being in a relative stranger's bedroom after only sharing a kiss in the parking lot of the Tap Out brewery.

"Can we sit and talk for a few minutes?" she asked, hoping he didn't mind.

"Of course," Dante said, following her lead with grace. She sat gingerly on the bed, and he sat beside her. "If you've changed your mind—"

"I haven't," she assured him quickly. "I just need a few minutes to get my bearings. It's probably not very cool of me in the hookup era but I'm not in a habit of going home with someone like this. Usually, my sexual relationships happen within the framework of an actual relationship, so this is new territory for me. But I definitely haven't changed my mind."

"If it makes you feel any better, I'm not accustomed to this sort of thing either."

It did make her feel better. She smiled. "Can you tell me about your last relationship? What was she like?"

A curtain closed behind his eyes, and Frannie knew in an instant that question was probably off-limits. She knew the signs of a painful breakup when she saw one and felt like an idiot for dragging him into the deep end of the pool before finding out if he could swim.

"Actually, that's way too personal, I'm sorry," she hastened to add, letting him off the hook with a rueful chuckle to share, "One thing about me? I have a tendency to ask all the wrong things at the absolute worst time. Either you'll find it endearing or terribly off-putting. Just let me know where you land on that score, and I'll try to adjust accordingly."

"I find you...enchanting," he admitted, gently pushing an errant strand of hair behind her ear with such tenderness she almost melted. "However, my last relationship is one I'd rather not talk about, if you don't mind."

"Of course, I understand," Frannie said quickly, her breath hitching as he leaned forward to brush his lips across hers. "We could...stop talking all together...if you like..."

"I'd like that very much," he murmured, deepening their kiss.

In an instant, Frannie forgot everything—potentially even her own name—as her senses exploded.

Beneath Dante's masterful touch, Frannie's anxiety drifted away, leaving her free to sink into the pleasure of discovering one another.

DANTE PUSHED AWAY all thoughts of anything before Frannie. He didn't want to contaminate the moment by allowing memories of the past to color the present.

Frannie's skin was like silk against his fingertips. Her soft moans ignited his desire like embers alighting on tinder.

She was beautiful and unfettered by an ugly past. He didn't deserve her trust or sweetness, but his bitter soul needed it.

Dante pressed soft kisses along the column of her neck,

drinking in her subtle shivers as she gave him complete access to her body.

When he came to Owl Creek, he'd never imagined meeting someone like Frannie. She was the variable he couldn't have planned for, which would probably end up being his Achilles' heel. But he couldn't stop what was happening between them.

The second he felt her body against his, something inside him shifted, and that need to protect her at all costs made the idea of something casual between them laughable.

But keeping a safe emotional distance between them was for Frannie's protection.

Even if all he wanted to do was hold her close.

"You're an incredible woman," he said, rolling onto his back, trying to catch his breath.

Frannie grinned, wiping away the sweat as she rolled to her side to regard him playfully. "No complaints on this end either."

He chuckled, grabbing his water bottle for a long swig. The pale moonlight bathed her form, giving her the glow of a reclining goddess, like something from a Renaissance painting.

Dante returned to the bed, lying on his side, facing her. He didn't have a lot of experience with "casual." He had a feeling snuggling afterward wasn't the general way of things, but he liked the idea of Frannie curling into his arms and falling asleep together.

Frannie must've had the same thoughts as she reluctantly rose and dressed. "Well, this was fun," she said, sliding on her jeans and buttoning them up quickly. "I should probably get going. Tomorrow is inventory day. I have a big shipment of books coming in— Oh! And the books I ordered for you might be in that shipment, too."

"You don't have to leave," he said, going against the advice in his head. "You could stay."

"The night?"

"Yeah."

She paused as if thinking over his offer but ultimately declined because at least one of them was thinking straight. "The thing is, I'd really enjoy sleeping over, but I'm sure that's how lines get blurred, and if we're trying to keep it casual, we probably shouldn't push boundaries at the very start."

"Of course, you're right," he agreed through his disappointment. "As long as you feel okay about our arrangement."

"I mean, I don't love the idea of calling this an 'arrangement'...but yeah, it's better if we don't get too comfortable with each other's personal space."

Solid advice. Why did it feel wrong? Maybe he wasn't cut out for this kind of situation. Or maybe he should've followed his good sense and buried things in the "casual acquaintance" zone.

But now he knew the sound of her breathy moans and had learned how her body responded to his touch. The taste of her skin was stamped on his memory, and her throaty laughter made his insides hum.

Yes, helluva way to keep things light and easy between them.

Maybe it wasn't ideal, but it was necessary, he reminded himself as he walked her to the door.

"A kiss for the road?" she asked, gazing up at him with a playfulness in her smile that immediately made him want to scoop her up and carry her back to the bedroom.

But he obliged her request, ending the kiss when his resolve weakened.

"You are the best kisser, and I'm not just saying that

to butter up your ego. Honestly, it would be better if you weren't so good," she said against his mouth, giggling at her assessment. "Would make it easier to leave if you slobbered like an enthusiastic puppy."

He laughed at her odd humor and finished with one last kiss before sending her on her way. "Drive carefully. As everyone has been fond of telling me since coming here, 'Watch for deer—and if you see one, there's more.'"

Frannie saluted with a "Will do!" and climbed into her car. He watched her drive away until he no longer saw her headlights and then returned inside the house, locking the front door as was his new habit.

Back home, he hadn't been as diligent about his safety, feeling insulated against harm because of his name and stature. Now he knew that feeling of safety had been an illusion.

And danger could lurk around any darkened corner.

Had he made a major mistake in allowing Frannie into his life, even peripherally?

His satiated body tricked his mind into thinking it might be okay. He was thousands of miles away from Lorenzo, and his trail was well covered as far as he could tell.

Maybe it was possible to enjoy his time with Frannie, even if it felt like borrowed time.

Chapter Eight

Frannie had spent the day humming lightly beneath her breath, replaying her night with Dante in her head ad nauseam. It was her current favorite memory. She'd just finished her inventory toward the end of the day when Darla walked in, looking harried and the opposite of the blushing bride.

"Tell me I'm doing the right thing by marrying that man," she said as she huffed in the chair opposite Frannie. "I swear, if he lives to breathe another day, it'll be a miracle."

"What's poor Tom done now? Aside from the audacity of not wanting to elope," Frannie said with a small grin at Darla's pique.

"As my best friend and maid of honor you're obligated to be on my side," Darla warned with a glower. "And don't give me that look. Tom has crossed the line this time."

"How so?"

"He's insisting on a half chocolate cake when I specifically told the baker we would have vanilla and strawberry. It's ridiculous to have three flavors in one cake. Everyone knows that!"

Frannie shrugged. "Who doesn't like chocolate?"

"If we have a third flavor tier, people are going to get all picky about the slices and the next thing you know, we'll have a lopsided amount of leftovers and that's just wasteful. Strawberry and vanilla, people choose one or the other and that's it."

Frannie knew she ought to commiserate with Darla, but she could only giggle at how ridiculous it was. She was in too good a mood to see anything but the lighter side. However, Darla was unamused and suspicious. "Why are you in such a good mood? Isn't it inventory day? Usually, you're stressed out and grumpy on inventory day."

"No, I'm not," Frannie disagreed, wondering if that was true. She loved inventory day—*new books, what's not to love?*—but it could be a little stressful logging everything in while still running the front desk. She was a one-woman army, after all.

But before Frannie could adequately defend herself, Darla gasped, "Oh my God, I know that look!"

"What look?"

"The look that says someone got lucky last night!"

Frannie's cheeks flared with immediate heat, and she shushed Darla. "Oh my God, keep your voice down," she said, embarrassed. "And what makes you say that?"

"Because I'm your best friend and I've known you our entire lives. Since your breakup with that douche monkey, you've been depressingly celibate for reasons I can't even fathom. But you have the look of a woman who has been deliciously taken care of, if you know what I mean."

Good Lord, nothing got past Darla. "Okay, fine, yes, I had a date last night," she said, gesturing for Darla to keep it on the down-low, "but it's nothing serious. Just casual."

"You? Casual? Do you know how to do that?"

"Of course I do," Frannie lied, hating that Darla knew her that well. "I mean, I can learn. Besides, I'm not ready for anything more serious anyway."

"Okay, with *whom* did you knock boots last night?" Darla asked, needing to know all the details.

Frannie almost didn't want to say, but there was no way Darla would be satisfied with anything but the truth, and she'd get it out of Frannie at some point anyway. "You have to promise to keep this to yourself," she warned. When Darla motioned to zip her lips, Frannie shared. "Last night I ran into Dante at Tap Out. One thing led to another and the next, I was at his place."

"The hunky, mysterious Italian?" Darla exclaimed. "Oh my God, please, I need to know…was he…"

"Darla!" Frannie glared. "I'm not about to kiss and tell those kinds of details. Suffice it to say we had a nice evening."

"Nice?"

"Okay, it was amazing," Frannie corrected with a tiny swoon at the memory. "But please, we agreed to keep it casual and it's not a thing, like we're not dating or anything like that."

"And why is that?" Darla was immediately suspicious. "Is he married or something?"

"No, he's just…well, he doesn't plan on staying in Owl Creek. He's here for a short while and it doesn't make sense to start something serious when we both know he's not staying."

"Are you sure he's not married?"

"I didn't ask Fletcher to run a background check if that's what you're asking."

"Not a terrible idea, though," Darla said, believing the idea had merit. "First of all, he's not local and he could be making up any sort of story and how would you know any different?"

Frannie frowned at her best friend. "When did you become so suspicious of everyone?"

"You need to be more suspicious of people," Darla countered. "You're so accepting of everyone's motives, and I love that about you. But I worry that you're a perfect target for people who have bad intentions."

Remembering her meeting with her aunt Jessie, Frannie scowled. "Speaking of people with bad intentions... I went against my better judgment and agreed to meet with my aunt Jessie yesterday."

Darla's eyes bugged. "And why did you do that?"

"I don't know, I was hoping that maybe she was going to call the whole thing off and admit that she'd made it all up as a poor attempt at connecting with her estranged family."

Darla grimaced. "Yeah, if that were a bet in Vegas, I wouldn't take those odds."

"Yeah," she sighed, "it went about as well as you could expect."

"What did she want to talk about?" Darla asked, ignoring Dante for a moment.

"I think she was fishing for information. She's doubling down on her claim, and I have this bad feeling that she's actually telling the truth. If that's the case, I have two more siblings and I don't know how I feel about that."

Darla's expression softened. "I'm sorry, Fran. What your dad did...it's just not right. How's your mom holding up?"

"Mom is Mom. She's acting like she's fine but there are cracks in her veneer. Sadly, even if she's brokenhearted, she won't let us in. Too many years pretending like everything is fine to let the gates down now. I don't know how to help her."

"Your mom is the sweetest person I know. She doesn't deserve this."

The funny thing about Jenny Colton...to everyone else, she seemed sweet as pie, always with a smile, generous and compassionate to everyone in need. And she was that person—but there was more to the woman than met the eye.

And that was something only her children knew.

Jenny Colton was intensely private and guarded her secrets well. It was as if she prided herself on hiding her cuts and bruises from the world, no matter how she might be bleeding inside.

And Frannie could only imagine how many cuts and bruises she carried after being married to Robert for all those years.

"I do wonder if my mom knew about her sister and my dad all along but chose to ignore it because he always came home to her at some point?"

"Like the mentality of a stereotypical fifties-era housewife?" Darla suggested, pursing her lips in thought. "That generation was definitely cut from a different cloth. If I found out Tom was carrying on with another family, I'd end up in an orange jumpsuit for the rest of my life."

Frannie chuckled. "See? If you're willing to go to prison over the idea of Tom cheating, it's definitely love. Let the man have his chocolate cake," she said.

Darla huffed a short breath. "Fine. But don't say I didn't call it when I end up with an entire uneaten tier of vanilla cake."

After a beat of reflective silence, Frannie noted it was closing time. "I think I'd better go see my mom tonight. She might not want to open up to any of us, but it might be a good idea to let her know we're here for her all the same."

Darla smiled, nodding. "I think so. She needs her family, whether she wants to admit it or not." Then, as she rose, slinging her purse over her shoulder, she added, "Also, not a terrible idea for Fletcher to run lover boy's name through the system. You'd hate to find out too late that your hot, international stud muffin is a cheating bastard."

"I will do no such thing." Frannie rolled her eyes, gesturing, "Go on, get out of here."

But as she went through her closing routine, Darla's advice stuck in her brain. If Dante had nothing to hide, nothing would pop up.

There was no harm in peeking, right?

Maybe she'd talk to Fletcher about it tomorrow.

In the meantime, time to do her daughterly duty and check on her mom.

WITH PERMISSION FROM the property management, Dante spent some time installing video cameras on the front and back of the house, though it'd been a hard sell.

"Mr. Sinclair, Owl Creek is very safe," the plump lady behind the desk had assured him, regarding Dante with faint confusion at his request. "We've never had any complaints from renters in the past. Did something happen to cause concern?"

He couldn't exactly share that he needed to ensure his uncle wasn't sending henchmen to break his fingers in the dead of night, but he also couldn't set off alarm bells with the property manager.

The fat stack of cash he'd put down for the deposit when he rented the property was the only reason she was even considering his request.

"It'll be at my expense, and I can either take them down when I leave or donate them to the property, whatever the owner prefers. But I would feel more at ease if I knew there was proper surveillance around the house."

"I…that's very considerate of you, but I still don't understand the reason. Was there something that made you feel unsafe at the property?"

Yes, the fact that his unscrupulous uncle would stop at nothing to reclaim what Dante had stolen.

"In my line of work, I require a higher level of security," he'd explained with a slight, apologetic smile. "I'm truly happy with the property and I don't want to have to move but the security must be upgraded while I'm renting out the space. I'm sure you understand, and I hope my request can be accommodated."

"Oh, yes, of course." She stopped short of asking what he did for a living, but he could see the question on the tip of her tongue. When she sensed he wouldn't budge, she'd said, "I'll ask the property owners how they feel about it and let you know."

"I appreciate your attention to the matter," he'd said, adding, "The sooner the better."

Thankfully, the owners had been amenable to a free surveillance system, and within a day, Dante had purchased the system and installed it himself, not willing to trust anyone he couldn't vet with his current location.

Satisfied, he returned to the house in time to hear his cell phone ringing. Only two people had this number: Frannie and his private investigator. He would be lying if he didn't hope it was Frannie calling, but it was his private investigator.

"Hello?"

"Nick Gladney. I have some more information you might find of interest, and it's about your father."

"Go on."

"It wasn't easy, but I had a friend pull the records from your father's accident. Not a lot to go on—pretty cut-and-dried from the report—and not a big incentive to dig any deeper, if you know what I mean."

"How so?"

"You said you were a kid when your dad died, right?"

"Yes, around ten."

"Well, do you remember your dad being a drinker or anything like that?"

"My father never drank," he answered, wondering where this was going. "Why?"

"According to the records, your dad had a blood alcohol level way over the legal limit. If the report is to be believed, your dad was drunk as a skunk when his car crashed into that tree."

"That's bullshit. My father hated the smell of alcohol. Neither of my parents drank." Which made his mother's subsequent death by a drunk driver cruelly ironic. "The report has to be wrong."

"Well, through official channels, the report says your dad was drinking the night he died. I mean, you were a kid, maybe your memory is distorted of who your dad was. It happens. Kids want to believe the best of their parents."

"No—" Dante cut in sharply. "Believe me when I say, I know my father wasn't a drinker. Dig deeper. Go beyond the official channels. Find out who signed off on that report. Find out if they suddenly came into a large sum of money. Someone lied about how my father died and I want to know who."

The information nagged at his brain, deepening his suspicion of his uncle. Lorenzo had always been willing to go to great lengths to get whatever he wanted—even if it meant removing a brother who threatened his position within the family.

Dante remembered bits and pieces of conversation between his parents behind closed doors, hushed voices always coated with a sense of urgency. His father, Matteo, kept them on the move, always hyperalert and ready to hit the ground running for reasons he never shared. His sweet mother, Georgia, always tried to hide the worry in her heart by covering it with a sunny smile and pretending they were on a grand adventure.

But Dante remembered details from his childhood that most would've happily forgotten.

And he knew with certainty that his father wasn't drunk that night.

Chapter Nine

Fletcher surprised Franny when he walked into the bookstore the following day.

"Aren't you supposed to be working?" Franny teased, though she was always happy to see her brother.

Fletcher smiled and kissed her on the cheek. "That's a funny way of saying, 'Hey, bro, always a pleasure to see you.'"

"I'm not saying I don't love when you drop in, I'm just saying that I'm not sure Owl Creek PD is getting their money's worth if you're constantly popping in here for a latte. Because I know that's what you're here for."

Franny and Fletcher had always enjoyed the kind of relationship where they teased one another mercilessly, but it was their closeness that enabled them to poke at each other without injury. Unlike Chase, with whom she didn't feel close enough to even enjoy small talk about the weather.

"Actually, I'm kind of glad you're here, because I need to talk to you about something."

Fletcher was intrigued. "I'm happy to listen while you whip me up that aforementioned latte. I mean, since you mentioned it."

Franny winked as she walked over to the café side of the shop. She made a quick latte, just how he liked it and handed the frothy drink to him. "Although I think it's kind of bizarre that you can drink something so hot when it's warm outside. When will you let me talk you into trying a nice herbal iced tea? They're quite good if you give them a chance."

Fletcher grimaced. "That sounds disgusting, no thank you. So, what did you want to talk to me about?"

Franny straightened, remembering. "Yeah, about that… so last night I went to drop in on Mom and see how she's doing and when I got there, Uncle Buck was there, too."

Fletcher shrugged. "And?"

"I don't know, they just seemed…there was something odd about the way they were talking to each other. I might be imagining things, but it seemed like they were *close*. I don't know how to say this without it being more than it is, but it seemed like there was a vibe between them."

"A vibe? As in a romantic vibe?"

Franny understood Fletcher's confusion because that was exactly how she'd felt when she saw it. She nodded with a grimace. "And I'm reluctant even to mention this because what if I'm wrong, but they took like two steps away from each other when they saw me walk in like they got caught or something, which seemed weird."

Fletcher seemed to mull over the information before ultimately rejecting the speculation. "Here's the thing. Uncle Buck and Mom have been close for years, but I think it's more of a brotherly/sisterly thing because Mom helped Uncle Buck when Aunt Jessie left him high and dry with the kids. We've spent how many summers out at the ranch? He's family, there's nothing more going on there."

Franny wanted to believe that, and if it weren't for the fact Aunt Jessie was currently in town telling anybody who would listen that she was Robert Colton's long-term lover, it would be easier to swallow. But the reality was that her aunt had maintained an inappropriate relationship with Robert Colton, so was it out of the question to wonder if Jenny Colton had decided to do the same with her sister's husband? *Yuck*, the whole thing made Franny want to vomit. Still, she saw what she saw. "I'm the last person who wants to think about this stuff, but I'm telling you, there was a vibe."

. Fletcher grimaced at the idea as well. "They're both adults. I guess we don't really have room to say anything to them if it's true. Dad's gone, so it's not like Mom would be cheating on him. Even if it were true, it kind of feels like, maybe, payback? I don't know, the whole thing sucks to think about, and I'd rather just push it out of my brain."

"Hopefully, I'm way off base and I'm imagining things because I don't think I can take any more family surprises."

"Amen to that." Fletcher said with happiness as he sipped his latte. "You make the best lattes hands down."

Franny smiled. "Thanks, bro."

"Was there anything else you wanted to talk about? Because as much as you tease me, I do have a job to get back to."

"Actually, yes. My second reason for wanting to talk to you is a little more complicated."

"How so?"

"There's a new guy in town. His name is Dante Sinclair, and I was wondering if you would be willing to take a peek into his background."

Fletcher's demeanor changed, morphing into that of a protective brother. "Is there something I should know about this guy? Has he hurt you?"

"Good grief, no. He seems like a really great person but Darla mentioned that maybe I should ask some questions because he's not from around here. Honestly, even saying it out loud feels like I'm overreacting and makes me cringe."

"I can't run a background check on someone for no reason. That's illegal."

Franny's hopes fell. "Oh, I'm sorry I didn't know that. I wouldn't want you to do anything that compromises your job."

"I said I couldn't do it for no reason," he clarified. "Maybe this guy gave you a weird feeling? Or maybe he was asking for you to order some materials that felt a little suspect?"

Franny wanted to laugh at her brother's suggestions because they were all ludicrous. Dante seemed like the straightest arrow she'd ever met, but she also didn't want Fletcher to do anything that would get him in trouble.

She supposed a small white lie wouldn't hurt in this instance. "Maybe you could run his license because he went over the speed limit or something like that."

"What does he drive?"

"A Toyota sedan, a Camry I think? A rental."

"Color?"

"White."

"What else can you tell me about him?"

"Um, well, he's from Italy."

Fletcher's brow rose. "Italy? What's he doing here?"

"I don't know. He said it was a combination of business and pleasure."

"And you didn't ask any more questions?"

Exasperation colored her voice. "Fletcher, it was none of my business. I wasn't going to grill the poor guy when I just met him."

Guilt pinched at Franny. Why did it feel like she was selling Dante out somehow? "I don't want to make a big deal about this, okay? Just a peek. Don't go getting the FBI involved, okay?" At the mention of the FBI, Fletcher perked up, and immediately Frannie shot that idea down. "Don't you dare go bothering Max over this. He's doesn't need us pestering him with something as frivolous as this."

"No promises, sis. It all depends on what my little peek turns up. Besides, Max wouldn't mind. Hey, how about while I'm doing my little peek, you keep your distance until I can give you the all clear? Just to be on the safe side?"

She didn't like the idea of involving her cousin who worked for the FBI at all. In fact, she was looking forward to seeing Dante tonight. "I think you're going a little overboard. I'm sure Dante has no big, dark secrets. I was just curious because he's not from around here. I don't want you to get freaked out over nothing. I probably shouldn't have said anything."

"Look, not that I would ever want to find myself agreeing with Darla, of all people, but I think she's right. It's best to err on the side of caution nowadays. What is he even doing here? It's not like Owl Creek is a haven for international travelers."

Franny had had the same questions but framed in a far less suspicious manner. "You're going to feel real bad for thinking so poorly of the man when you find out Dante is a normal, friendly person."

"We'll see." Fletcher smiled, scooped up his latte and waved as he walked out the door.

Brothers.

She wasn't worried. Dante was exactly who he said he was.

At least, she hoped he was. Or else Franny would never hear the end of it.

DANTE OPENED THE front door, smiling when he saw Frannie, who was holding the books she'd ordered for him, looking like a sugary confection in a white sundress with pink accents. "Special delivery," she said, smiling up at him. "They were in the shipment that arrived this morning. I thought you wouldn't mind me bringing them to you personally."

He should mind—but he couldn't bring himself to care.

"I don't mind at all," he said, accepting the books and stepping aside so she could come in. "That's some top-tier service. Does everyone get this level of customer service or is it just me?"

Frannie's flirty smile as she shrugged nearly stole his breath. Goddamn, the woman was beautiful. "Can I get you a glass of wine or something?" he offered, trying to get his bearing before he threw her down on the sofa and devoured every inch of that smooth, succulent skin.

"I'm not much of a wine drinker but if you have something on the sweet side, I'll give it a go."

"Americans and their sweet palate," he teased, placing the books on the table before heading to the kitchen. "But I think I have something you'll enjoy. Make yourself comfortable. I'll be right back."

Dante pulled a chilled Riesling from the fridge and quickly poured two glasses. It wasn't a Moscato, but it was the sweetest wine he had to offer. He'd planned to spend a quiet evening researching, but Frannie's unexpected visit kicked those plans to the curb. He shouldn't encourage her popping in unannounced, but he'd be lying if he said he wasn't happy to see her.

She accepted the wineglass, took a delicate sniff, pretending to be a connoisseur, then sipped the wine, nodding with approval before giggling, admitting, "I have no idea if this is a good wine but it's yummy."

"That's all that matters," he said, amused at her playful nature. Frannie was unlike anyone he'd ever met. Somehow, she'd retained that sense of whimsy and wonder that most adults lost as they grew up. The part of him that needed goodness in his life soaked up her energy like a dying man.

Clearing his throat, he shared, "I'll let you in on a little secret—wine snobs like to go on about a wine's properties, but at the end of the day, people like what they like, and that's what's important."

"Works with people, too," Frannie murmured, catching his gaze with a mischievous look that immediately made him forget about the wine. "I mean, from what I see…what's not to like?"

"Miss Colton, I get the impression you did not come here just to be neighborly and deliver my books."

"You might be right," she admitted, setting her glass down and climbing into his lap, straddling Dante with a boldness that ignited a fiery need between them. Her strong legs bracketed his hips, and the soft swell of her breasts caused his eyes to glaze over as he struggled to remember his name. "The thing is, I like you, Dante. I like you a lot, and I know we're doing the casual thing, but there's something about you that I can't get enough of. So, in the spirit of keeping it casual…would you like to 'casually' get naked?"

He grinned. "Right now?"

She nodded. "Right now."

He surged against her hot center. "I don't have a problem with that request," he said before she sealed her mouth to his. She tasted of sweet wine and heavenly temptation. That internal voice of reason faded to a whisper as his hands cupped her behind, drawing her close.

Their tongues tangled, and he anchored her hips against him as she ground against the hardened ridge beneath his jeans. Her little moan pushed him over the edge, and he lifted her up and onto her back, rising above her. She curled her hand around his neck, drawing his mouth back to hers.

He would lose control right then and there if he didn't slow down, but Frannie decimated his self-control in ways that should've been a red flag.

There were many good reasons to keep a healthy distance between them, but his thoughts were hazed, and all he could focus on was the exquisite torture of Frannie writhing beneath him.

Dimly, he heard his cell phone going off. It took a minute to realize the call had to be coming from his private investigator because Frannie was the only person with the number. He hesitated, torn, but when the phone rang again, the urgency of a double call made him stop and grab his phone with a muttered apology before disappearing into his bedroom and closing the door.

He answered on the last ring before it transferred to voice mail. "Hey, Nick, this isn't a good time," he said in a low voice. "What have you got?"

"I knew you'd want to hear this right away. It's pretty significant. After you shared that your father wasn't a drinker, I did some poking around and got lucky. The investigating officer of your father's accident has since passed away, but I managed to talk to his widow. I don't have an amount, but she remembers her husband coming into a lump sum of money around twenty years ago when he still worked on the force. He bought a boat, a source of contention between him and the wife because she said it was too expensive."

"Did she say where the money came from?"

"It was hard to get specific details without coming off as suspicious for asking. I made up some story about a financial audit. She's old and trusting, so she bought it, but I couldn't dig too deep without producing some kind of documentation proving the audit."

"A boat..." he repeated, thinking over the information. "That all she said?"

"Taking into account that she was frail and nervous, she seemed real keen on protecting her old man's name. Talking about what a decorated officer he was on the force and how much pride he took in protecting his community."

"Sounds like a woman trying really hard to make sure her husband didn't sound like the kind of man to take a bribe," Dante murmured.

"Yeah, I think it's safe to assume that that boat wasn't purchased on his small-town cop salary."

When Dante's father died, they lived in a tiny town in Wisconsin. They'd only been there for two months when the accident happened. He remembered his mother's screams when the officer came to deliver the news.

Then, he remembered his mother receiving a phone call late at night, and the following morning, they were packed and on a plane for Italy. He knew Uncle Lorenzo was on the other end of that call.

His life had changed forever with that phone call.

Lorenzo had seemed the knight in shining armor at the time, swooping in at his mother's time of need, placing them under his protection, and taking Dante under his wing.

It wasn't until later that he learned nothing came without a cost.

And now? He had reason to believe someone had killed his father, making it look like an accident.

Had the same thing happened to his mother two years ago?

Was it possible his uncle had been the one behind their deaths?

Before Belinda, he never would've imagined Lorenzo to be so cruel…but now…

He couldn't deny the possibility.

Chapter Ten

Frannie didn't know what to think when Dante disappeared into his bedroom. Whatever needed to be said was clearly private, but it felt wrong to stay when he didn't return.

The moment went from sensual to awkward. Now Franny wasn't sure if she should stay or go.

She could hear the muffled conversation, a low, urgent hum that felt ominous even though she couldn't exactly make out what was being said—not that she was trying.

Frannie attempted to occupy herself to avoid accidentally eavesdropping, but she couldn't do much but fidget and wait.

After another five minutes, Frannie collected her purse, preparing to quietly leave, when Dante emerged from his bedroom with an apologetic expression. But there was something about his demeanor that was far different than before.

"I'm sorry about that, a business call that couldn't wait."

"Of course, I understand," she said, feeling awkward. "Actually, it was insensitive of me to drop in on you without checking to see if you had plans for the evening. I should probably go."

She had hoped that he would ease her concerns, but her feelings were hurt when he accepted her offer.

"I think tonight I might not be the best of company. I

have a lot of work that I need to finish and we should probably just call it a night."

"Right, sure, no problem," she said, feeling foolish. "I'll
just see you around, I guess."

Was this what a casual sexual relationship felt like? She
had no idea. She'd never been in one before. But she didn't
like this feeling, and if this was how casual was supposed
to work, maybe she wasn't cut out for it.

Dante walked her to the front door, polite and considerate
as always, but she could tell he was a million miles away.

The urge to ask if he was okay overrode her bruised feelings. "I know I'm probably breaking all the rules, but I can
tell whatever was said on that phone call upset you. Do you
want talk about it? I can be a good listener."

Dante paused as if torn between wanting to share and
keeping her at arm's length. She held her breath as hope
kindled in her heart, but when he ultimately shook his head,
she knew that he was determined to keep private whatever
was eating at him.

"I appreciate the offer. It's very kind of you, but I think
I need to handle this on my own. You needn't worry. It's
business and I don't want to bore you with details that aren't
necessary for our relationship."

Ouch. If that wasn't a brush-off, then she didn't know
what was. How could they go from nearly tearing each
other's clothes off to a wall of ice suddenly going up between them?

She faked a bright smile. "I guess I'll see you whenever
it's convenient. I don't know how this works but whatever.
I'll see you around."

Frannie didn't mean for that to come out as sharp as it
had, but Dante seemed to realize that she was wounded
and tried to make amends. He reached for her hand. "I've
offended you. It's not my intention to hurt your feelings. I

probably should've sent you home when you first showed up, but I was really happy to see you. You aren't intruding. Due to the nature of my business, it's probably a good idea to give me a heads-up the next time you want to come out. That way, I'm fully prepared to give you all of my attention."

It was reasonable, and yet his request stung. Just one more example of how whatever was happening between them was superficial at best. He had never promised anything more, so why was she disappointed?

"Yep. Sounds good," she said, eager to get out of there before embarrassing herself further. "I will see you around. Bye."

"Frannie—"

But listening to Dante dance around the obvious would only further her excruciating humiliation for practically throwing herself at him, and that was where she drew the line.

She left so fast that she probably looked like she was running to her car. But she had to get out of there because if she had stayed a minute longer, she would've started crying, ruining the appearance of being fine with the situation.

Because she wasn't. God, she really wasn't.

See? She didn't do casual because she was terrible at it. She wasn't the kind of woman who slept around and engaged in hookups. She was the kind of girl who got invested, cared about her partner and liked feeling part of a team.

What was happening? She had to get her head back on straight and her feelings in line with the reality of the situation. Dante wasn't her forever guy. He was a man passing through town who'd been honest about his situation. So why was she hurt that he was putting up boundaries?

Because she really, *really* liked him. Damn it. That'd happened fast.

Whatever this was, it was bound to end badly—for her.

DANTE SWORE UNDER his breath for handling the situation like a jackass.

Frannie's feelings were plain as the nose on her face. He'd wounded her by sending her away. If the situation were different, he would've loved to spend the evening together, but that wasn't the situation he was in. The phone call from Nick had only reminded him.

Reality checks were rarely kind.

He never should've encouraged anything with Frannie because she was bound to get hurt at some point.

Like tonight.

She might think he'd rejected her, but he was trying to protect her. He'd never forgive himself if anything happened to Frannie because of him.

Still, hurting her didn't feel right.

If he left the situation as it was, Frannie would probably ghost him, which would be a blessing in disguise. Then, at least, he'd know she was safe from him. But even as his brain offered the solution, he violently rejected it.

He had to make amends.

Letting Frannie think that he wasn't interested in her, to let her marinate in that kind of emotional rejection, was more than he could stomach.

Hell, he knew the right thing to do would be to let that door close, but he couldn't bring himself to do it.

That's a problem for tomorrow.

His thoughts were a maelstrom as he processed the new information about his father's death.

He needed more information. Sitting on his hands and waiting patiently wasn't in his nature. Even though he'd hired the private investigator to do the heavy lifting, he wanted to do his own digging around. It wasn't wise, but he couldn't escape the feeling that he could be doing more.

The answers were out there—he just needed to ask the right questions.

The memory of his father's death was crystallized in his brain. Emotional trauma had a way of imprinting like no other.

Of course, experts said memories were a shaky foundation to build a case on, but sometimes a memory was a good springboard.

He remembered the bitter cold of that night. A terrible storm had blown through the state, dropping temperatures to thirty below. Weather forecasters had warned residents to prepare for dangerous conditions. Stay home, bring in your livestock and avoid the roads if possible. Of all the places they'd lived, Dante hated Wisconsin the most because of the extreme cold.

After that night, he'd had another reason to hate the place.

His cell phone chirped for an email received. His private investigator had sent a file. He opened the file to find a scanned copy of the police report.

Matteo Santoro, 32, DOA, from blunt force trauma sustained from a motor vehicle accident on Greger Road at 2200 hours. Testing revealed a Blood Alcohol Content of .30. Impaired driving and poor road conditions led Mr. Santoro to lose control of his vehicle and collide with a sugar maple tree. Mr. Santoro was ejected through the windshield and died on impact.

Report: Ulysses Weisel, Detective, Hawthorne Police Department.

In all the years since his father's death, Dante had never thought to get a copy of the police report. No one had ever told him that his father's accident had been attributed to drunk driving. Ice on the roads had been blamed, which had seemed plausible because that storm had been a doozy.

Now, as he read someone's lie in an official document that his father had been drunk, rage percolated through his veins. Why the lie? Someone had gone to great lengths to ensure that no questions were asked, that Matteo's death was written off as an unfortunate consequence of some poor sap making a bad choice.

But his father never drank. Surely his mom had to have known that was a lie? Why would she go along with something she knew to be false?

Looking back on his memory, he was willing to bet his uncle Lorenzo had somehow persuaded his mother to let him care for them. She would've been vulnerable, lost, and grieving—a perfect target for Lorenzo.

Only now did Dante realize how his mother might've been lured into a trap. She was never able to escape, which made him feel complicit in keeping her in a golden cage, unknowingly participating in what had kept her silent and cowed.

In truth, when they first arrived in Italy, his uncle had seemed a kind blessing after a lifetime of struggle and confusing instability for a young Dante.

Lorenzo had spent time cultivating a bond with him, nurturing a place in his young heart that his father should've filled.

But even in life, Matteo had seemed too preoccupied to spend time with his son. There'd been no tossing the ball back and forth in the backyard for the Santoros. At the time, Dante had resented his father's distractions, but now, he saw things differently.

Maybe Matteo had been doing his best to keep his family safe from a threat that only he understood.

Dante had only known the struggle of surviving as they'd

hopped from one place to another, his dad unable to hold down a job for too long, and his mother trying to make ends meet with barely enough resources to keep them alive.

He couldn't imagine being so terrified of his brother that he kept his family far enough away to avoid all contact— walking away from a veritable fortune because of a rift that couldn't be mended.

But he now understood his father's motivation better, and it shamed him that he'd never thought to dig deeper until it personally affected him.

Even as disgrace and guilt ate at him, there was grief in the mix, too.

For all his faults, Lorenzo had become his father figure, and for a long time, Dante had trusted him implicitly.

Lorenzo had put Dante through school, seen to his needs, and put a roof over his and his mother's heads when they needed it most.

There was a time when Dante had thought the world of his uncle.

But the thing about misplaced hero worship was that the facade eventually crumbled, leaving nothing to hide the rot lurking beneath the shell.

Now he understood why his father had been adamant that his family would have nothing to do with the Santoro name or legacy.

What had Lorenzo told his mother to convince her to leave everything behind and accept the family's help?

Had she been coerced? Or had she been tired of hiding? Struggling and too lost in a sea of grief to see the shark's shadow closing in?

Either way, it was too late now. Both his parents were gone. Lorenzo was determined to bring him back into the fold by any means necessary, and the only thing keeping Lorenzo at bay was locked in a safe-deposit box.

An old piece of paper might seem a flimsy protection against the Santoro might, but that little slip of paper had the power to go off like a bomb in his family—and Lorenzo would do anything to keep that from happening.

However, that didn't mean Lorenzo would quit. He'd get sneakier in his efforts.

Because that was Lorenzo's superpower—getting what he wanted without getting his hands dirty.

Chapter Eleven

Frannie tried to put the fiasco at Dante's house in a locked box and forget about it, but the feeling of being rejected remained with her, lodged in her brain like a poky sticker burrowing into her sock.

The shop door opened, and one of her favorite people, Della Winslow, walked in with her black Lab, Charlie. It was an instant mood saver.

"I need the biggest, strongest cup of sweet tea you can manage before I fall over," Della said, flopping down in the nearest chair and wiping her brow. "I cannot handle this heat wave. We're not built for this kind of torture. Give me snow and ice any day, not Satan's armpit." She gestured to her dog, who was panting. "Look at poor Charlie, he's practically hyperventilating."

Frannie laughed, setting down a bowl of water in front of the parched dog before making Della's tea. "It's not that bad. I kind of like it. I can pretend I'm living somewhere beachy and warm. Like California."

"That's a myth about California. I spent the summer with an aunt who lived in a town called Planada. Definitely no beach. Just a lonely strip of highway, some mountains off in the distance, and a 'saloon' that offered twenty-five-cent root beers. That part actually was kind of nice but other than that…zero stars, do not recommend."

"And to think you gave up a promising travel guide career for that of a dog trainer," Frannie quipped with a teasing smile.

"Um, not just any dog trainer. Charlie is one of the best cadaver dogs in the state. It's not like his factory settings defaulted with that skill."

"My apologies," Frannie said, winking. "No, you're right, Charlie is pretty amazing and you're an incredible resource to our little town. Honestly, I know you can probably get hired someplace else and make a lot more money but I'm glad you're here with us."

Della appreciated the compliment, reaching down to rub Charlie's dark head. "So, I heard a rumor yesterday—"

"If it's about my dad and my aunt…as much as I'd love for it to be trash talk, it very well could be true," Frannie said, knowing that dancing around the issue would only delay the inevitable. People were already talking. The only way to kill a fire was to deny it oxygen. "We're going to ask for a DNA test proving paternity, but I'm not holding my breath that she's lying. If it's true, we'll deal with it like adults. I mean, what choice is there?"

Della pursed her lips in commiseration, admitting, "I guess that's the only way to handle it. Still, it sucks for your family."

"Yeah, it's a crap sandwich. But clearly, Jessie isn't going away anytime soon." She paused, curious, "Where did you hear about this?"

Della exhaled a breath, embarrassed. "I overheard a conversation that I probably shouldn't have been listening to, but to be fair, the woman was being very loud."

Frannie rubbed her forehead. "Yeah, it appears my aunt Jessie has a flair for the dramatic."

"I think she was talking to her attorney, or I don't know, he was dressed nice but there was something smarmy about him. Like a used car salesman vibe. I didn't recognize him, though. I don't think he's from around here. Anyway, she was going off on how much money your dad had, and she was entitled to a piece of it. Then, she said something that was really out of line—"

"Yeah?"

"She said that she deserved more than your mom because she was his *real* wife, no matter what a piece of paper said. That's when I'd heard enough, and I left the restaurant."

Frannie tried to keep her temper in check. The amount of sheer audacity flowing through that woman's veins was nothing short of narcissistic. "She can run her mouth all she wants, doesn't change the fact that my mother deserves every penny she inherited from my dad's estate. My dad wasn't an easy man to live with and she put up with more than her share of bullshit."

An impotent well of frustration sloshed in the pit of her stomach for her father's actions, but he was dead, and even if he weren't, it wasn't as if he would've allowed himself any accountability.

"The worst part? It doesn't surprise me that Dad had a mistress—it's that he chose to carry on with his own sister-in-law. That feels particularly low."

"Were you close with your dad?" Della asked with a subtle grimace, as if she were apologizing preemptively for the question and Frannie's answer.

Frannie sighed. "For a time, yes. We got along the best, I suppose. But as I got older and started having opinions of my own, we were less close. By the time he died, we barely saw each other, and I didn't miss his company. Sounds sad to say that, though. Like, I should've felt worse when he passed. A part of me was…relieved. Just saying that out loud…makes me feel like a terrible person."

"Feelings are complicated. Sometimes they don't make sense and we have to leave it at that."

"How is that you're younger than me and so much wiser?" Frannie teased, wiping away the sudden gathering of moisture at the corner of her eyes. "Look what you've done. I'm leaking."

Della chuckled softly. "I didn't know your dad well but sometimes we have to make a mental agreement with ourselves that when it comes to family, we're going to accept them as they are, good and bad."

"That's a tall order," Frannie said, thinking of Aunt Jessie. "Some family aren't worth claiming."

Della nodded, knowing exactly whom Frannie was referencing. "My personal opinion? I think it's in really bad taste that your aunt would come into our town and start mouthing off like that for anyone to hear. It's personal business and it should stay that way."

Frannie appreciated Della's stance even though she knew plenty of people were probably eating up the fresh gossip about her family. With a family as big as hers and as connected in the town, there were bound to be people who didn't like them. Frannie tried not to dwell on the people who were eager to see the Coltons fall.

The front door opened, and Dante walked in. Before she could temper her expression, her eyes widened in surprise, and her breath caught. He was so damn handsome, and it immediately irked her how her heart rate seemed to jump a beat the minute he appeared. Why was he here? After last night, she assumed their little "casual" adventure was over.

Charlie sensed the tension and cocked his head, licking his lips as he looked to Della for direction.

Apparently, Della could feel the same energy in the room

as Charlie and took that as her cue to leave. She rose from the chair, patting Charlie's head for reassurance. "Thanks for the tea and the water for Charlie. I better get going. I'll talk to you later."

"Sure thing." Frannie waved, and Della and Charlie left. Now it was just Frannie and Dante, and the awkwardness was epic. Maybe she should tackle and be done with the elephant in the room. "Dante…"

He surprised her by going first. "No, I want to apologize for last night," he said, shaking his head firmly. "I was caught off guard by the phone call and I needed to deal with a few things. I wouldn't have been good company and I didn't want you to see me like that. But I should've handled it better."

Frannie softened. "Oh…" Well, that felt different than what she had been imagining. "I'm sorry for whatever you're going through. Sounds serious. Do you…want to talk about it?" she asked.

"It's complicated and I wouldn't want to bore you. Suffice it to say I would much rather have spent the evening with you than think about what was said in that phone call."

That was cryptic. *Red flag, much?* True, but it wasn't like Dante was a criminal or anything like that. *Cue the nervous internal laughter.* Frannie didn't know what to think. All she knew was that Dante apologizing for his abrupt change in demeanor made her feel less standoffish and more willing to try again.

Was that a bad idea?

DANTE HAD HAD his out, but he didn't take it. Sure, walking away without further entanglements was wise, but he couldn't bring himself to do it.

And he was about to go deeper into the realm of bad decisions.

"I'd like to make it up to you. Are you busy tonight?" he asked.

She hesitated, and he didn't blame her after last night. He was surprised she was still willing to talk to him. "What did you have in mind?"

"A nice dinner with my favorite person in Owl Creek."

"Well, that's not a great endorsement. You don't know many people."

He chuckled. "You're right. I can do better than that. How about dinner with the most *beautiful* woman in Owl Creek?"

She grinned in spite of herself. "You're definitely getting closer to success. And what would we do after dinner?"

"I would leave that up to you. But I would definitely like to take you back to my place and really make up for my poor behavior last night."

Franny's smile brightened. "Now, that sounds like a plan. How about you pick me up at my place around six?"

This time it was Dante who hesitated. He wanted to keep Frannie as safe as possible. Even though he was technically putting her in danger just by spending so much time with her, he didn't like to think that any eyes on him would follow Frannie. But he also didn't want her to think he was hesitating for the wrong reason. He finally answered, "I would be happy to pick you up," with a warm smile to chase away doubt.

"Careful, Dante, this almost sounds like a real date," she teased.

"I suppose it is," he said, fighting against the knowledge that he had no business encouraging her affection. "Text me your address and I will be there promptly at six."

"Promptly?" Her grin deepened. "A man after my own heart. I was raised to believe on time is already late, so that gives you a glimpse into my secret quirks."

It was silly, but somehow knowing that Frannie prized punctuality the same as he did only made him desire her more.

His hands itched to touch her, to wrap her in his arms

and make up for all the kissing they didn't get to do last night, but he restrained the impulse. He didn't know who might be watching.

"Aren't you going to kiss me goodbye?" she asked coyly, striking with unerring accuracy at his secret desire.

"Tonight, you'll get all the kisses you can handle and then some," he promised, going to the door. "Gives us something to look forward to."

"Tease," she laughed as he left the shop to run errands.

He hadn't planned to stop at Frannie's bookstore, but he couldn't regret his choice even though it was all wrong. He couldn't deny his mood felt considerably happier than when he left the house, and he was selfish enough to enjoy it.

But now he had things to get done, such as paying the biweekly rent, which he did in cash.

Dante stepped into the property management office, expecting a quick transaction, but the property manager was feeling chatty.

"How are things with the rental?" she asked with a wide smile. "How's the heat treating you? It's not always this warm here but we're getting a real sizzler this year."

"The heat doesn't bother me, and the fans work well enough to keep the temperature down," he answered, being polite. "How about you?"

She fanned her face for emphasis. "Oh, I can't hardly handle this heat. I feel like I'm about to melt. But I'm glad to hear that you're still enjoying our little town. Do you know how much longer you'll be staying with us?"

Dante was purposefully vague. "It's hard to say. I appreciate the biweekly payments. My work is unpredictable. However, just to show I appreciate how accommodating you've been, I'll pay for the month even if I end up leaving."

"Oh, that's real considerate of you. It's not very often that we get long-term rentals like you popping into town."

"Like me? What do you mean?"

"Honey, you're practically a celebrity in this town. Seems everyone's talking about two things. The handsome Italian with the sexy accent and, of course, that terrible gossip that's going around about Robert Colton and his supposed lover who just happens to be his sister-in-law. Sordid business, that."

So, both he and Frannie's family drama were the talk of the town. Not a great combo for either of them. "I suppose all places have their secrets," he murmured, trying to downplay it for Frannie's sake.

"I feel so bad for Jenny. She doesn't deserve what her sister's done to her. Let me tell you, Jessie Robards has always been nothing but trouble all her days. It doesn't surprise me at all that she's come back just to stir up trouble."

Dante didn't like the feeling that he was participating in gossip about Frannie's business and felt mildly protective. "I'm sure it will all work out in the end. These things usually get sorted out somehow."

"I suppose so," the property manager conceded, but she looked dubious. "All I know is that if Jessie is back in town that bodes real bad for Jenny."

"How so?"

"Oh, that woman has always wanted anything that was her sister's. It doesn't surprise me none that she went after Jenny's husband. That woman has no shame. It's hard to believe Jenny and Jessie are twins. They are night and day. Good and evil, if you ask me."

He felt terrible for Frannie. He knew something about toxic family members. "I hope it all turns out okay," he said, signaling the end to the conversation with a polite reason to leave.

Toxic people were like cancer. Sometimes it took a while to realize the insidious destruction they were doing behind the scenes. He didn't know this Jessie woman, but her intentions could hardly be good.

Stay out of Frannie's business, the voice warned. The last thing he needed was to draw unnecessary attention to himself. Engaging with a greedy woman was likely to do that.

Besides, Franny seemed capable of handling her aunt and whatever she had up her sleeve.

He might be unable to solve Frannie's family issue, but he could show her a good night.

For now, that would have to be enough.

Chapter Twelve

Frannie was humming under her breath the following morning as she tidied up her shelves, still thinking about last night with Dante. Dinner at The Tides—*exquisite*—followed by quality sexy time at his place—*addictive*—and she couldn't stop the giddy smile that kept curving her lips.

The man was everything she'd never realized she wanted.

Kind, considerate, funny, thoughtful—oh, and so handsome she could stare at him until the day she died. But she knew nothing about him, which was starting to bug her.

She'd begun to notice that he was skilled at dodging personal questions, but he did it so well that it wasn't until much later that she realized he never really answered anything of substance about himself.

She didn't like to create problems where there weren't any, but she also couldn't help but wonder if she was overlooking a major red flag.

People who didn't like sharing details about themselves usually had something to hide.

Like a wife or a girlfriend.

Or worse.

No, she told herself sternly, Dante was a good man who was just a little private. Clearly, he'd suffered a terrible breakup and was still healing from the emotional trauma.

That much she'd surmised when he'd admitted he didn't want to talk about his past.

Wasn't he entitled to his privacy? Of course he was.

Besides, their relationship was created within certain boundaries, which didn't encourage deeper connections, so Dante's reluctance to share details seemed to fit within those parameters.

Ugh. That level of circular justification had just made her dizzy.

Frannie already wanted to break the rules of their "relationship."

She wanted more.

It felt strange to allow someone access to her body yet receive so little of the person.

Her intrusive thoughts threatened to kill the sweet high she'd ridden all morning as the questions and insecurities started to pile up.

Grabbing her phone, she texted Fletcher.

Any luck finding anything of interest on Dante?

Even sending the text made her feel guilty, like she was doing something wrong and sneaky, but she rationalized that once Fletcher came back empty-handed, she could relax knowing that Dante was exactly who he said he was, and he wasn't hiding anything.

And if Fletcher discovered Dante was lying about something?

What then?

She pushed that thought aside. *Don't build bridges for rivers you don't have to cross yet.*

Frannie hoisted a box of books and started to walk toward the display table when the front door opened, and a deliveryman with a massive spray of flowers walked in.

"Frannie Colton?" he asked hopefully.

"Yes?"

"Delivery for you."

Frannie accepted the beautiful bouquet, flabbergasted and tickled at the same time. "Thank you!" she called out after the man as he left the shop. Dante must have some kind of telepathy. How else would he have known she was fighting her thoughts about their connection? She smiled, placing the flowers on the counter to find the card, but there was none.

"You sly dog, playing secret admirer," she murmured, gazing at the expensive blooms, approving of his choices. "This is gorgeous."

She grabbed her phone and quickly sent a text to Dante.

They're beautiful, thank you!

Her phone dinged almost immediately in response.

What is?

She giggled at the game. Sure, he had no idea what she was talking about. She liked this playful side of Dante. Frannie texted back.

How did you know I love white lilies?

Dante ditched the text and called seconds later. "Frannie, I didn't send you flowers," he said, his tone nothing like the loving and sensual man she'd spent last night with. "Whoever sent you flowers, it wasn't me."

His denial splashed water on her happiness. Then, straightening with confusion, she pressed him. "What do you mean you didn't send them? Are you being serious? You truly didn't send them?"

"No, I did not," Dante said, his tone clipped. "Who else might've sent them?"

Was he jealous? If he knew her, he'd understand how ridiculous he was being. Frannie wasn't the type to date multiple people at once. She was very much a monogamous person. She tried not to take offense, but it hurt. "I have no idea who might've sent them. I'm not seeing anyone but you."

That should've put him at ease, but if anything, he seemed more tense. "Perhaps family? A friend?"

She shook her head, baffled by his reaction and the subtle urgency in his tone. "Dante, maybe it was a mistake. There wasn't a card attached. Maybe the flowers were meant for someone else."

"Who delivered the flowers?"

"A random delivery person. I didn't pay attention."

"A local florist company?"

She paused to think. "Maybe? Like I said, I wasn't paying attention. I was so tickled by the flowers I didn't notice anything else because I thought they were from you."

Admitting this private truth felt more revealing than standing naked in the town square. She wasn't supposed to have feelings so quickly for a man who was only meant to be casual fun.

Damn it, she'd told Darla she was terrible at this stuff.

"Forget it, it's probably a mistake. I'll call the local florist and find out who the flowers actually belong to and then we can move past this awkward phone call."

The silence on the other end was unnerving. Why was he freaking out over a flower delivery likely meant for someone else? And why was she hurt that the flowers weren't from him?

"Yes, please let me know as soon as you have more information," he said as if they were discussing a business transaction that went awry.

"Yeah, sure." She blinked back stupid tears. She wasn't going to cry over this. Wiping at her eyes, she lied. "Okay, well, I have customers, so I better go," she said, hanging up so she could get off the phone and be pitiful in private.

Why did it bother her so much that Dante hadn't been the one to send her flowers? Last night had been perfect—romantic, fun, sensual—and she'd floated home on a cloud. She knew she wasn't supposed to be thinking of Dante as her boyfriend, but it was hard not to daydream about a life with him.

Too soon! Red flag! Except she was the red flag in this instance. She had no business fantasizing about a man who'd been up-front and honest about not being available for anything more than casual.

She was starting to hate that word.

Sighing, she blotted her eyes with a tissue and grabbed her phone to call the florist. The lilies were lovely, even if they weren't meant for her. Someone out there had a secret admirer with discerning tastes.

If only it had been her.

DANTE STARED AT the phone after Frannie clicked off, his thoughts racing.

His knee-jerk reaction had been a flare of jealousy, but he could hear the sincerity in her voice when she claimed he was the only one she was dating.

Under normal circumstances, that would've been enough to calm his nerves, but more was happening behind the scenes than he could share.

If she wasn't dating anyone else, and he hadn't sent the flowers, who had?

An unexpected gift could be an ominous portent, depending on its origins.

It could be a message to Dante that no one in his life was safe—anyone could be reached.

Intimidation and manipulation were his uncle's bread and butter.

With luck, the flowers were inadvertently delivered to the wrong address.

But the warning tingle in his gut told him that the flowers weren't an innocent mix-up.

Dante started to pace while he waited for Frannie's call. It was hard not to jump in the car and start asking questions himself, but that would only make him look like a jealous jackass or a paranoid fool, and he wasn't keen to embrace either look.

Especially not with Frannie.

He knew it was too soon, but he had feelings for her. The way she laughed, her quirky sense of humor, her sense of compassion, and her levelheaded demeanor—everything about Frannie lit up his insides like a carnival.

Which was why he had to know where those damn flowers came from.

He'd never forgive himself if he'd selfishly put Frannie in danger.

He'd made the mistake of underestimating his uncle's ruthlessness once, and he couldn't afford to do it again.

Not with Frannie's life.

Maybe he ought to level with her, share with her why he was in Owl Creek, hiding from the man who'd essentially raised him after his father died.

The man he was afraid had something to do with both his parents' deaths, years apart.

He shoved shaking hands through his hair, willing the

phone to ring with good news, but staring at the phone only ramped up his anxiety as silence followed.

Finally, Frannie called back.

"Hi, it's me." She sounded standoffish, but she went on to say, "So, I'm officially confused. I haven't a clue who might've sent these flowers. The florist said they were commissioned through one of those internet companies and don't have access to any booking information. The order just shows up on the computer with proof of payment. Then, the florist fulfills the order. The only information provided on the order was my name and the shop's address."

Dante felt a cold chill dance on his spine. An internet commission could come from anywhere—even another country. "You should close up early today."

"Why?" Frannie asked, confused.

"Because your location is compromised."

"Compromised?" She forced a chuckle as if he were being ludicrous. "You sound like a spy or something. I'm sure there's a logical explanation for this, and I won't get worked up over a flower delivery. Besides, they're quite pretty and dress up the shop nicely."

Dante wanted Frannie to throw them in the trash, but he knew asking her would only create more questions and an even bigger gap between them.

"I'm sorry…maybe you're right," he conceded, forcing himself to sound less anxious than he felt. "I apologize if my reaction was inappropriate."

"Well, it hurt my feelings," she admitted. "But maybe that's the cultural differences between us. I keep forgetting you're from another country."

"Yes, perhaps."

"So…were you a teensy bit jealous?" she asked.

It was easier to admit to jealousy than to admit he had a

murderous uncle on his tail who could be targeting anyone Dante got close to. "Yes, it's possible."

"I mean, that's not so bad to be jealous… Sometimes it means you really care for someone."

"I do care about you," he said without hesitation. *More than I should.*

"I care about you, too."

He couldn't let his suspicions go, though. "There's no one that you can think of who might've sent them? Not even your ex? Perhaps he is trying to win back your affections."

"No. My ex didn't believe in sending flowers or doing anything remotely romantic. He once told me flowers were only for men who craved validation from the women in their lives. Just saying that out loud makes me embarrassed I ever thought he was The One. He was an insensitive ass-hole with zero emotional intelligence. So, no, I don't think he sent them."

"Yes, but manipulative men often use methods that previously would've been uncharacteristic of them, to seem changed."

She paused before admitting, "Well, that might be true, but I know he didn't send them. He's engaged to someone else and it's unlikely that he gives me a second thought."

Dante heard the quiet hurt in Frannie's voice. It was irrational, but he felt the urge to punch this ex in the face for stupidly losing an incredible woman, even though the only reason Dante had the opportunity to know her was because of this jackass's actions.

"He's an idiot," he assured Frannie. "His loss is my gain."

"Dante…when you say things like that, it's hard to remember that we're keeping things simple between us."

She was right. He was sending mixed signals. "I know. I'm sorry."

"It's okay. Just wanted to point it out."

But without solid proof that there was no dangerous intent behind that mysterious flower delivery, there was no way he'd let Frannie out of sight now.

He'd made the mistake of assuming his uncle would never stoop so low to get what he wanted—he couldn't afford to make that mistake again.

Not with Frannie.

"How about I cook you some authentic Italian tonight?" he offered.

"Are you sure that's a good idea? Somehow dinner always ends with us naked in bed."

"I'm not complaining."

She chuckled. "I'm not either, but maybe we need to put the brakes on what we're doing for a while."

Absolutely not. "Do you prefer Tagliatelle al Ragù or Rigatoni alla Carbonara?"

"I don't know what either of those are, but it sounds like pasta, and if that's the case, I love all pasta. I'm lactose intolerant, though, so nothing with dairy."

"Trofie al Pesto it is then. Bring a beverage of your choice."

She laughed in spite of the seriousness between them. "I haven't said I'll come."

"You will always come with me, that's a promise," he said in a sultry tone.

Frannie's breathy "I'll bring the wine" was all the confirmation he needed. At least when Frannie was with him, he felt secure in his ability to protect her.

If anything happened to Frannie—he'd tear his uncle apart.

And that was a different kind of promise.

Chapter Thirteen

Frannie planned to meet with her mom for lunch at a small park within walking distance from one of Jenny Colton's private nursing clients. Despite having enough of a nest egg to retire comfortably, Jenny preferred to work part-time to keep her mind sharp and her body in shape.

Frannie thought her mom kept working because the idea of being stuck in the house with the ghosts of the past was too much to bear. But on the more practical side, Jenny prided herself on being helpful and needed, and nursing fit the bill.

She waved as her mom walked toward her. After that disastrous meeting with her aunt Jessie, Frannie couldn't help but compare the two women.

Jessie was thinner but brittle, as if she punished herself by restricting her calorie intake, whereas her mom was thin but fit. Jenny Colton didn't have a problem indulging in a slice of cake or a glass of wine, but she also stayed active at the local gym, enjoying her water aerobics and yoga classes.

"Hi, Mom," she said, kissing Jenny's cheek in welcome. "I brought sandwiches from the brewery. I hope that's okay."

Jenny approved, "I love a good sandwich." She slid onto the picnic bench opposite Frannie. "This is nice. What's the occasion?"

"Do I need a special occasion to spend time with my mom?" Frannie teased, although there was some truth to Jenny's inquiry, and that stung a bit. The recent passing of her dad was a stark reminder that her parents weren't getting any younger, and sometimes past squabbles needed to be put to rest to enjoy what time you had left.

Of course, easier said than done when the past showed up barking about wanting a piece of your inheritance.

"I love the garlic aioli they put on their sandwiches," Jenny said with an ecstatic appreciation of her bite. "I tell you, the main chef at the brewery can put a five-star restaurant to shame. It's like a little pocket of high-end cuisine hiding in an unassuming brewery."

Frannie agreed. They just enjoyed their sandwiches for a moment, soaking up the sunshine and scenery. The park was mostly empty today, which was nice because sometimes the youth soccer teams used the grassy fields for practice. Frannie had made plenty of memories in this park, some of which would remain private. She smothered a small smile and took another bite.

Jenny broke the silence first. "I heard your aunt Jessie is creating a stir in town."

Frannie was grateful her mom had brought up the topic first, but it still made her cringe. Going straight to it, Frannie nodded. "Yes, she's saying all sorts of things, and I wish she'd just shut her trap."

Jenny chuckled ruefully. "One thing Jessie does not do is silence herself for the sake of others' convenience or comfort. I used to be envious of her ability to do and say whatever she wanted regardless of how others felt. Now it seems less of a positive quality."

"Yeah, especially with what she's saying about our family."

Jenny sighed, wiping her mouth with a paper napkin. The

sadness in her mother's eyes made Frannie want to march up to her aunt and punch her in the mouth, or at the very least give her a scathing piece of her mind.

"Are you okay?" Frannie ventured, hating the position her mother was in. "It would be totally understandable if you weren't."

"Oh, I'm fine," Jenny answered with a quick smile that seemed rehearsed. "It's one of those things that you just have to accept and move on. No sense in crying about spilled milk."

She disagreed. "No, Mom, this isn't something you have to accept, and you don't have to pretend to be okay with it. How could your sister do this to you? I hate to put too fine of a point on it but aren't twins supposed to be ultra close?"

"I'm sure she had her reasons."

Frannie couldn't stop the aggravation from creeping into her voice, even though she tried to be compassionate. "Mom, please stop being so accommodating. She stole your husband and now she's trying to steal our money. It's not like Dad was an oil tycoon. Sure, he did pretty well for himself with investments and whatnot but he wasn't a billionaire. The piece of the pie is already being split seven ways, and now we have to figure out how to include three more people? It's not fair."

Jenny tried to use logic instead of emotion. "According to Chase, nothing will change until the DNA tests on the two adult children are completed. As far as Jessie is concerned—" she lifted her hands, unsure "—it's a bit more complicated, legally."

"Yeah, I heard. I will puke if she's awarded one red cent."

Jenny's small laugh reminded Frannie of when she was a kid, and she'd said something outlandish.

Frannie didn't want to laugh, but a reluctant chuckle escaped. "It would be awesome if I could manage to time that so it landed right in her greedy lap."

"Jessie can't stand bodily fluids, so that would be a perfect way to ruin her day," Jenny shared. "She couldn't even handle her own. Once she threw up when she got a bloody nose. That was a mess."

It was hard to imagine that brittle woman as anything other than the hard woman trying to ruin their family. "What was she like as a kid? I mean, what happened between you two? Weren't you ever close?"

Jenny swallowed as if pushing down a sudden lump in her throat. "Yes, we were close at one time. And I don't know what happened," she answered sadly. "Or maybe, I do know and I don't want to say because I would never want you to feel differently about your father. For all his faults, he was a good father."

Eh, that's being generous. "Mom, I love how you want to create a positive memory out of something that was crap, but he doesn't deserve that kindness right now. I loved my dad, but I'm not sure how I can forgive him for this."

Jenny accepted Frannie's frank admission and didn't try to change her perspective. How could she? The facts were hard to rearrange. "In high school your dad was quite the catch. Very popular, charming, and an incredible athlete. When you ask what happened between me and Jessie? Well, the answer is your dad. We were close until we both fell for Robert—and we both dated him."

"Ew. Gross." Frannie made a face. "I definitely feel sick to my stomach. Hadn't you two ever heard of the term 'sloppy seconds'?"

"Francesca," Jenny admonished with a grimace. "Should I continue or stop?"

"No, go ahead. Might as well hear the whole sordid

story so at least I'll know the backstory of this reality TV episode."

Jenny exhaled a short breath as if praying for patience, then continued. "Yes, he dated us both but at the time, I never really thought Jessie was in love with Robert. We'd always been competitive with each other, but never maliciously, until after Robert. In the end, he chose me, and it created a deep rift between my sister and me. Your father and I got married shortly after graduation, and soon after, Jessie married Buck and I thought we'd moved past the hurts from high school. But our relationship was never the same, strained at best. Then, when Jessie divorced Buck, she took off, leaving the kids for Buck to raise alone."

Jenny's kids were close to Uncle Buck's, having spent countless summers at the Colton ranch, but Jessie had bailed on her first family while Frannie was still a baby, so she had no memory of her aunt until that horrid meeting the other day.

Speaking of, might as well share that information, too.

"I need to tell you something… The other day, against my better judgment, I agreed to meet with Aunt Jessie."

"Why on earth would you do that?" Jenny asked with a mild frown.

"Because…morbid curiosity, perhaps?" Frannie admitted, cringing. "I'm sorry. I shouldn't have met up with her. It was stupid and all she did was make me mad. Now she's running her mouth all over town saying how she deserves a portion of Dad's estate because she was more of a wife to him than you and I'm just about at my limit of patience with her. I mean, I guess there's nothing we can do about it if her kids turn out to be Dad's, but I'll be damned if that piranha should get any of Dad's estate."

"Well, we'll just have to put our faith in our lawyer's expertise," Jenny said, gathering their trash just like she would at home, as if on autopilot. "The sandwiches were delicious, darling. Really hit the spot, but I need to get going. I have a hair appointment in an hour."

Frannie nodded, mildly disappointed. Her mom was intensely private, and that wasn't likely to change, but for once, she wanted her mom to feel safe enough to be open and vulnerable with her kids. Even if she were devastated by the revelation about her sister, she wouldn't dare show the true depth of her pain.

Not even to her grown children.

ONE OF THE worst parts about being a nomad in a strange land was the lack of creature comforts, and the lack of creature comforts inevitably led to too much downtime with nothing but the thoughts in his head to keep him company.

And that was a scary place to be.

With the troubling mystery of the recent flower delivery, the tension in his body was enough to break bone. He couldn't seem overly anxious without seeming off to Frannie, who was already ready to dismiss the mystery, but he also couldn't let it ride, knowing the real threat out there.

After Belinda's attack, Dante had moved quickly to get her to safety. Once she could travel, he had arranged for Belinda to be transported to a private rehab facility in Switzerland. He didn't want Lorenzo to have easy access to Belinda in any way as she recovered, but moving her out of the country had been the only way to keep her profile low.

It hadn't been easy.

But he'd convinced her of the danger she would be in if she remained in Italy, and she'd agreed to go.

She'd left behind everything she'd built for an unknown future in another country. That kind of bravery made him feel weak in comparison, but it also pushed him to be stronger.

In his nightmares, Belinda blamed him for her injuries,

but in real life, her kind heart had never placed the weight on his shoulders.

But she should have—he was to blame.

His hubris, his smug belief that Lorenzo couldn't leverage his compliance, had cost Belinda her future in surgery.

And yet, she never blamed Dante.

Dante carried a different kind of guilt; sometimes, he didn't think he'd ever be free of its weight.

He'd decided that his penance would be to hear her voice when he checked on her progress until the day she managed to recover her hands like before.

But the doctors had been honest about the slim chance of that happening, which meant his reprieve would likely never be granted.

Grabbing his cell, he dialed the secret number, knowing it would be close to bedtime in Switzerland.

Belinda picked up on the second ring. "Dante?"

Her voice, soft and soothing, remained the same, despite her situation. "I'm sorry to call so late. I wanted to check in before time got away from me. How are you feeling? How's your therapy?"

"I'm fine, therapy is progressing. You needn't worry. I'm safe."

He didn't know that. He would never make that assumption again. "Do you need anything?"

"My needs are well cared for," she assured him. "How are you? Are you sleeping?"

Always thinking of others...some things didn't change. It was now six months since the attack. "How do the doctors feel about your progress?"

"Dante, you need to stop blaming yourself," she admonished gently. "I will be fine. And even if I never operate again, there are plenty more things I can do with my expertise. I am safe and that's what matters—because of you."

No, he was why her life was unrecognizable from before the attack. "If I could go back in time—"

"Stop. Thoughts like that are a useless expenditure of energy. You cannot change what happened, only what happens as we go forward. I refuse to look at my life as cut short. It's simply going to be different. You need to get to that place as well."

"He won't stop until I return to the fold, and I refuse to do that."

"You will find a way to beat him at his game and when you do, you must promise me that you'll get on with your life."

Her belief in him only stung more. Their romantic relationship had died in the attack, but he would never forget what they'd once had.

Still, even at their happiest, Dante had never felt with Belinda the way he felt with Frannie, which only deepened his fear of losing her.

"I've met someone," Belinda shared, surprising Dante with her admission. "I think you would like him."

"Who?"

"My physical therapist. His name is Sven. He's kind and compassionate but very funny. I like how he makes me laugh."

Belinda deserved all the laughter in the world, and if this Sven could give it to her, he had Dante's blessing.

"You don't need to call and check up on me anymore," Belinda said warmly. "I'm well cared for. I will be safe. All I need to know is that you're safe, too."

He couldn't make that promise, and he didn't want to burden her with the information he was struggling with.

"I'm happy for you, Bel," he said, his voice thick with emotion, "I really am. You deserve the best life has to offer."

"So do you."

He wished he could believe that.

"Good night," he murmured.

"Good night, *dolcezza.*"

They clicked off, and Dante spent a good minute staring at his phone, wondering how this all ended.

Did it end with him finally free of his uncle's grip, able to live as he chose?

Or did it end with Lorenzo dragging him back into the fold, yoked to the Santoro family until he died?

He didn't have the answer.

He only knew one thing for sure. He'd do anything to keep Frannie safe—even if it meant walking away from her forever.

Chapter Fourteen

Frannie's gaze strayed to the lovely lilies, only a little bothered by the mystery. She liked to believe that sometimes
nice things happened for no reason. Her brother Fletcher
might say that was naive, but she preferred to look at the
world with hope in her heart rather than a sour expectation
that everyone was out to screw each other.

Although her aunt Jessie was challenging that worldview
at the moment.

No, not going to waste the energy on that woman today,
she vowed, drawing a deep breath, determined to shake off
the dark thoughts, but it wasn't easy.

After lunch with her mom, she couldn't stop thinking
about what it must've been like for her, knowing her sister had coveted her husband even before discovering this
level of betrayal.

What happened to the "girl code"? She couldn't imagine
even looking cross-eyed at Darla's soon-to-be husband or,
for that matter, her sister's husband (RIP to that amazing
man). Even thinking of such a thing made her physically ill.

Was Aunt Jessie a sociopath? Was that genetic? Did it run
in families, lurking in the genetic code to pop out when you
least expected it, like daisies in a field?

Maybe she ought to read a few books on sociopathy.

Darla blew in like a tornado, sucking up all the oxygen in the room as usual, her cheeks flushed from the heat and whatever crisis she was running from.

"Please tell me you've started serving liquor from your little café because Lord help me, I need a margarita, heavy pour on the tequila, please!"

It probably wasn't funny, but Darla's theatrics were always amusing. "Sorry, still no liquor license and I don't know that I'll add that to my list of things to do."

"I think you're missing out on an untapped revenue stream. Wine and books always go together. Who doesn't sip on their chardonnay while reading a spicy book at the end of a long day?" Darla quipped as she flopped into a chair with a long-suffering exhalation. She opened her mouth to start again but saw the flowers and stopped, straightening abruptly to gesture at them. "And what the hell is that?"

"Last I checked, flowers," Frannie answered.

"I see that. And from whom? A certain Italian stallion, perhaps?" she asked coyly.

"Um, funny story about that…no. I have no idea who sent them but they sure are pretty. My favorite, too."

Darla's smile faded with confusion. "What do you mean you don't know who sent them? That bouquet looks expensive. People don't just send pricey flowers to strangers out of the goodness of their heart."

Frannie disagreed. "That's not true. I read the other day of someone who received an anonymous donation of $500 to their GoFundMe for medical expenses to help cover cancer treatments."

"That's not apples to apples," Darla said. "Did you post a GoFundMe for flower deliveries to the shop?"

"Of course not," Frannie said with a chuckle. "But someone wanted to do something nice, and I think it's lovely. I mean, maybe it's a condolence for losing my father? Who knows. The universe works in mysterious ways."

"And so do murderers," Darla warned.

"You watch too much true crime."

"So do you, which is why I'm baffled why you aren't freaked out by this. Honestly, it's weird. I think you should throw them away."

Frannie balked. "No way. They're gorgeous and they add a certain something to the lobby. Makes it more inviting."

"Yeah, they're beautiful but honestly, it's kinda creepy if you ask me."

"You worry too much," Frannie said, waving off Darla's paranoia. "So, what's the crisis for today? I'm assuming it's wedding-related?"

Darla scowled, not ready to let it go. "What does Fletcher or Max think about these mystery flowers? Or Dante for that matter?"

"I didn't tell Max or Fletcher. They have busy lives doing their actual jobs. I'm not going to clutter up their headspace with something as silly as this. That'd be like calling 911 because you got a sliver. It's just flowers. No big deal. As for Dante, well, he was a little jealous, actually. It was kinda hot to see him get all riled up but then, once he realized the flowers weren't from another date, he got kinda quiet, maybe even a little protective? It was really sweet."

"Yeah, because he knows it's weird, too."

Frannie shrugged, ready to be finished with this conversation. Why everyone wanted to make a federal case out of a rogue delivery was beyond her. The world had bigger problems."

"So you're really not going to chase this down and figure out who sent them?"

"I tried. It was called in using an internet web service for flower delivery but there was no way to trace who made the purchase unless I wanted to have a forensic accountant come in and request the company's purchase logs. Which, honestly, isn't going to happen with the very little information I have. It's not like there was a threatening note or anything attached to the delivery. It was just the flowers and I love them, whether they were mistakenly sent to me or sent to me by someone who just thought I'd benefit from a little cheer in my life."

At that, Darla softened. "Your family has been served up a terrible hand as of late. I'm sorry. My head's been so full of wedding stuff that I haven't been a great friend when you need it. Is there anything I can do?"

Frannie appreciated Darla's offer, but there was nothing anyone could do but ride out the storm. "No, everything's in the lawyer's hands right now. I talked with my mom yesterday, and that's pretty much her attitude and while it sucks, she's right. My aunt isn't going to suddenly grow a conscience overnight, so we'll have to trust our lawyers know their stuff. Can you believe she's going around town saying she was more of a wife to my dad than my mother, his *wife*?"

Darla grimaced. "She's got a brass set of balls on her, that's for sure. Your mom is practically a saint."

"I wouldn't go that far but compared to my aunt Jessie, yeah, she's definitely leagues ahead on the 'decent person' track." Frannie sighed, hating the entire mess. "But it is what it is, I guess."

"You're a better person than me. I would be tearing every strand of hair from the woman's head before we even stepped foot in court. That reminds me, I ought to make sure Tom knows that if he cheats on me, I'll turn him from a rooster to a hen real quick and then I'll redecorate his prized truck with my keys."

"All of that is illegal," Frannie reminded Darla with barely suppressed laughter, "but I approve."

Darla jumped to her feet, helping herself to a bottled water from the fridge. "Okay, so enough about that, tell me about your man."

"He's not my man," Frannie corrected her with a subtle blush. "We're keeping it casual."

"Ha! You don't do casual."

"Well, I'm trying something new."

"Good luck with that. Well, how's it working out?"

Frannie pursed her lips, admitting, "Confusing."

"Go on."

"Well, I really want to ask him to go to the lake with me, but I don't know if that's overstepping our boundaries in this whole casual setup because when I'm with him, it doesn't feel casual at all."

"What does it feel like?"

Dreamy. Perfect. Exciting. Passionate. "Um, well, it's good."

"Good?"

"Better than good, amazing."

"And he feels the same?"

"I think so?"

Darla frowned. "You don't know?"

"He's hard to read. Sometimes I feel like we're totally on the same page and then the next, I feel he's shutting me out and keeping me at a distance."

"The dreaded hot/cold dance. Hate to break it to you but that's not a good sign."

"What do you mean?"

Darla's expression didn't bode well as she explained, "That's guy code for, 'I'm just not that into you, but you'll do for now.' I should've known he would be a player. He's international, for crying out loud. Too sophisticated, too handsome, too 'not Owl Creek' material, you know what I'm saying?"

Those were precisely the reasons Frannie adored him. "I think he's been hurt in the past. He doesn't like to talk about his past relationship."

"Another red flag."

"Darla, people can have things they aren't comfortable talking about. Doesn't make them red flags."

"You've had sex, right?"

Frannie blushed. "Yeah." *Multiple times—and each time was better than the last.*

"If he's truly not a player, by this point, he should be able to share some intimate details about his life before you. It's not asking too much. If anything, you're not asking enough."

Frannie digested that advice. Was it true? Was she being too accommodating and ignoring her own needs? She wanted to know more about Dante, even if he wasn't interested or available to stick around; she wanted to learn more about him as a person.

"So I should ask him to the lake this weekend?"

"Hell yeah, and his answer will go a long way toward showing you who he is as a man."

What if he turned her down? Was she ready to walk away from Dante if it turned out he was exactly as Darla feared?

Better to know now than later.

Because at this rate? She was going to fall head over heels in love with the man.

If she hadn't already.

FRANNIE WAS COMING over tonight. She'd called about an hour ago, asking if he wouldn't mind some company, and while he should've made some excuse and declined, he couldn't stop his mouth from saying yes.

He rationalized that she was safer in his house with him than anywhere else, but it was a flimsy attempt at justifying his actions.

Just say it, a voice taunted. *You can't stop thinking about her, and you'll take any opportunity to be with her.*

Even if doing so put her in danger.

He growled under his breath, irritated at the useless circular nature of his thoughts. Striding to the kitchen as if he could outrun the guilt on his heels, he turned his attention to putting together a quick dinner.

He enjoyed cooking for Frannie. For one, she was open to trying anything—even though she was lactose intolerant and should avoid dairy—and truly loved his efforts. It was as if everything they did together fit like they were made for each other. He didn't consider himself a great romantic, but since meeting Frannie, he understood why poets created sonnets, even if he'd never have that level of talent.

Plus, there was something sensual about cooking for someone he cared for—the level of intimacy was something he'd never experienced before.

Belinda had been too busy with her work to spend too much time in the kitchen. They'd always eaten separately or ordered in, but at least their kitchen was always immaculate.

Mainly because they were rarely home at the same time.

Looking back, it was easy to see how they'd become affectionate roommates who'd occasionally passed each other in the night, enjoyed a smooch or two, and then went about their routine as usual.

It'd been a comfortable routine but lacking a certain level of passion that he hadn't realized he needed.

Until Frannie.

The attack had irrevocably changed their relationship, but now he realized their romantic life had died long before.

A knock at the front door told him Frannie had arrived. He wiped his hands and put the eggplant lasagna into the oven. He'd even made it with dairy-free cheese, though they'd have to wait and see if it turned out as good as the original recipe.

If it bombed, he had a mini dairy-free charcuterie board waiting in the refrigerator.

When he opened the door, Frannie smiled, holding up a bottle of wine. "I brought the beverage," she announced, lifting on her tiptoes to kiss him as if he were her favorite person.

His chest warmed and his groin tightened, and he was immediately tempted to scoop her into his arms and carry her to the bedroom for a little loving before dinner, but he restrained himself and accepted the wine with an appraising smile. "Ahhh, let's get this chilled so it's ready by dinner."

"You're the chef," Frannie said as she sank into the sofa with a happy sigh. "Have I mentioned how I love this sofa? I'm having sofa envy. It's so much better than the one I have. But to be fair, I did purchase it at a thrift store, and it may have enjoyed a full life in a frat house prior to moving in with me. Not that you would know that because you've never actually been to my house."

"Well, now that you've revealed that your sofa might've been involved in college adventures, I'm not sure that's a glowing endorsement."

"It does kinda smell, too," she grimaced. "But think of the character it has. The stories it could tell."

He grinned. "You're unlike anyone I've ever known."

"You're not the first person to say that," she said with cheek. God, she was beautiful.

He drew in a short breath, feeling as if his chest were being compressed, resisting the urge to tell her everything about his past, his family, and the trouble that was no doubt following him, but he bit down on his tongue and went to the kitchen to chill the wine.

When he returned, she patted the seat beside her. She

didn't need to—it wasn't as if there were any other place he'd rather be. Dante slid in next to her, catching a whiff of her shampoo and the lingering scent of her coconut lotion, and he almost forgot why it was wise to keep things casual between them.

"So, I was thinking…how'd you like to spend a day on the lake with me this weekend? I could pack a picnic and show you some of the secret spots that the locals enjoy. We could rent a canoe and paddle to a secluded beach to each lunch."

A secluded beach? On the surface, the offer sounded terrific, but immediately he thought of all the ways that would make them vulnerable to attack if, by some chance, his uncle's men were watching and waiting for the best moment to strike, and his enthusiasm faded.

Make an excuse, say you already have plans.

It was the smart play, but he saw something in her eyes that told him saying yes was far more important than following his good sense, and he didn't dare risk turning her down.

The stakes felt so much higher than a simple outing together.

As if their future somehow rode on what fell from his mouth at that moment.

"Sounds like a perfect day," he finally answered, unprepared for how she squealed and climbed into his arms as if he'd just agreed to cosign a loan for her. "Whoa! Wild girl," he chuckled, holding her close.

"I'm so glad you said yes," she admitted, sealing her mouth to his. "We're going to have a great day on the lake!"

"Any day with you is already the best," he murmured against her lips.

He just hoped no nasty surprises were waiting for them.

Chapter Fifteen

Frannie's heart was filled with sunshine as they slid the rented canoe into the water at the launch point. The weather was incredible, the skies blue without a cloud in sight, and she was excited to show Dante a piece of her hometown that felt personal.

"Summer days spent on Blackbird Lake were an important part of my childhood growing up in Owl Creek," she shared, hopping into the canoe and dipping her paddle in, encouraging Dante to do the same. "We're going to paddle away from the congested areas and head over to my favorite beach. You're going to love it."

"Are you trying to get me in a private place so you can have your way with me?" he teased.

She tossed him a mischievous look from behind her shoulder. "You should be so lucky."

He laughed at her sass, and they continued paddling. Soon enough, they were away from the tourist-friendly areas and heading down a calm channel where the water was barely waist-deep but crystal clear.

"So, this stretch of the river goes on for about three miles and because of the gentle current, it's great for canoeing or paddle boards. During the summer my mom and Uncle Buck used to rent paddle boards for all of us and we'd spend the entire day on the water. Some of my best memories were made on this lake. Sometimes we even got to see a moose on the shore. Of course, we left the moose alone because we valued our lives but one time my brother Fletcher got the bright idea to try and get closer. Thankfully, Uncle Buck didn't let him follow through with that idea. Otherwise, I might've been less one brother."

Dante chuckled. "Young boys often need someone smarter than them to keep them alive." But he realized she'd mentioned an uncle and not her father. "Your father didn't accompany you on these lake days?"

"My dad was always too busy. I don't think he enjoyed all the ruckus created by the kids. He was happy to let my uncle Buck handle the heavy lifting. Plus, now that I look back on the memories, I think my mom and Uncle Buck got along a lot better. I don't remember them bickering at all."

"They were close?"

"Yeah, they became close after my aunt Jessie bailed on the family and left Uncle Buck with the kids to raise." Frannie frowned. "I don't know my new alleged siblings but I kinda feel bad for them having to grow up with Aunt Jessie. At least with my other cousins, they were raised by Uncle Buck, and they had pretty good childhoods."

"Your aunt Jessie is unkind?"

Frannie lifted her shoulders, admitting, "I don't know her, but first impressions go a long way. She's kinda awful. I mean, maybe I'm biased because of what she's doing to my family right now, but she has this hard, jaded way about her that doesn't seem real conducive to being a loving parent."

"And your father was the same?"

"Um, he wasn't hard, per se, more like, disinterested. He always had other things to occupy his time. My dad was like a stereotypical fifties-era man—he expected his wife to keep the house and children while he made the money.

I don't think I ever saw my father lift a finger to clean the house, ever, and he sure as hell never cooked a meal for us. My mom did all of that and worked a full-time job. God, the more I think about it, she must've been exhausted. I need to cut my mom some slack."

"It's similar in Italy in many ways. Many traditionalists. For the record, I don't feel that way. I don't agree that the work of a household should be so unevenly split. My father and mother often cooked together. It's one of my favorite memories of when he was alive. They cooked with joy and love and perhaps it's in my head, but I always remember it tasting amazing."

"I think that's a beautiful thing to remember," Frannie said. "So, no brothers or sisters for you?"

"No, it was just me. My mother never remarried after my father's death. So it remained she and I."

"I can't even imagine being an only child, although sometimes I think I wished for it when things were total chaos around my house."

"I always wanted a sibling. Being an only child can be lonely."

"Makes sense. *Lonely* was never a word in my vocabulary. *Irritated, annoyed, frustrated*—definitely in the lexicon—but *lonely*? Nope."

His low rumble of laughter felt like sunshine on her soul.

"Oh! Look over there!" Frannie pointed to the shore on their left. "There's a deer. I know it's common, but I still get excited when I see them. My brothers used to make fun of me every time I got excited to see a deer. They said it was like getting excited to see a potato at the grocery store."

He laughed. "Depending on how hungry you are, the sight of a potato would be very exciting," he said.

"Ha! That's true. I wish I'd had the wherewithal to think of that comeback when I was a kid."

"I'm fairly certain I have the cutest tour guide in all of Idaho," he said, earning a blush from Frannie. "I love that you get excited about things that most people would take for granted. That's a gift."

She didn't know about that, but she felt warm whenever Dante complimented her over random stuff that most people never noticed about her. Dante made her feel seen, as if she'd been overlooked by those who should've been paying attention her entire life.

Girl, you're falling in love with him.

Frannie swallowed, knowing it was true. She couldn't seem to help herself. Everything about Dante was addictive. His smile, his touch, his voice—she couldn't picture anyone else as intoxicating.

Stop. You don't know anything about him. He could be an international felon.

That was why this day was so important. Today, she'd get to know more about the man.

And he agreed to come, right? That was a good sign. Besides, she wouldn't let anything ruin their beautiful day, not when it was already so amazing. It was possible Dante was very private and didn't enjoy oversharing. Once he realized his past was safe with her, he'd open up—she just knew it.

She saw her favorite beach coming up and gestured for him to paddle in that direction. Within minutes the bottom of their boat dragged through sand, and they hopped out to pull it further from the water so that the lazy waves didn't send the boat floating downstream. Swimming after a retreating boat was an experience she didn't want to repeat from her childhood.

Dante grabbed the picnic basket Frannie had prepared while she scooped up the blanket and walked up the beach to a shady spot.

"It's not the Italian coast but I think it's pretty damn

spectacular," Frannie said with pride as she carefully laid out the blanket and sat down to kick off her water shoes so her toes could dig in the warm sand. Golden sunlight glistened off the water's surface, glinting as if winking to the sky, and the gentle lap of the waves along the shoreline was a soothing sound that never failed to make her smile. If a happy place existed, it was here.

Dante sat beside her, agreeing heartily. "You do not disappoint. It's stunning."

His joy made her happy. She wished she could bottle up this feeling and moment to enjoy it forever.

A flicker of sadness threatened to dampen her joy as her mother inexplicably popped into her head. Knowing what she knew now about Jenny's past made Frannie wonder if there was ever a moment when Jenny experienced that giddy kind of love.

Somehow, she doubted Jenny and Robert had ever been madly in love. Small towns had a way of pushing people together for whatever reasons, but when those reasons expired or lost their luster, circumstances and reasons less than love kept them together. In some situations, obligation, expectation and habit were iron chains around people's necks.

With a frown, Dante caught her subtle shift and asked, "Is everything okay?"

"Oh, I'm fine." She waved away his concern, a little embarrassed to be a Debbie Downer when everything thus far had been perfect. Opening the picnic basket, she said, "I hope you like ham and turkey because that's what I packed. I even packed a few cheeses for you."

"I like whatever you thought to make."

"Stop being so perfect," she teased, leaning over for a quick kiss.

"I hate to disappoint but I'm far from perfect," he warned with a rueful chuckle.

"Hard to tell from this angle," she said, popping open the basket and pulling out the wrapped sandwiches. "Seriously, I think I'm going to need you to share some of your less desirable traits so I know you're human."

The subtle quirk of a grin was adorable, but it didn't escape her notice that he deliberately shied away from the topic. She tried a little harder. "I mean, you can't be perfect, no one is, but at least tell me something that makes you less intimidating. You're devastatingly handsome, an attentive lover, you can cook like a master chef, and you love books. I've never had self-esteem issues, but when I look at you, suddenly, insecurities start popping up like daisies in a field. Help a girl out."

"You're amazing in every way. You should never question your value, no matter who you're seeing."

"Of course, I'm just…okay, so I guess I'll stop beating around the bush and trying to be clever… I want to know more about you. What I can see is nothing short of amazing, but I need to know more. More than just the surface stuff." She traced her finger along his jaw, gazing into his eyes to ask in a throaty murmur, "Who is Dante Sinclair? Who is the real you?"

Dante froze. The urge to pull away nearly ruined everything good about his day. He wanted to be honest, but he couldn't. She wasn't asking anything out of the ordinary. She had every right to know whom she was sleeping next to, but it was the very thing he couldn't give her.

For her own good.

Swallowing, he forced a smile, gently grasping her hand and pressing a kiss to her palm, prepared to lie through his teeth. "Sweet Frannie, you make me sound more interesting than I really am. I'm just a regular guy who got tired of the same scenery and wanted a change. I didn't want to go to the usual touristy places like New York or California. I wanted something off the beaten path so I could rest and recharge. Owl Creek has been exactly as I hoped it would be—even better, I found you—making the trip unforgettable. What more could I ask for?"

Frannie smiled at the praise, but he could see that she wasn't entirely satisfied. The woman was smart. She sensed he was holding back, and the longer he danced around simple questions about his life, the more suspicious she would become.

He'd have to give her something to chew on, or she'd keep digging—and he couldn't afford her curiosity.

"Okay, you want something material...something personal..." At her small nod, Dante straightened and shared. "Well, the reason I needed a change in scenery is a little cliché. I'm a little embarrassed to admit that my last breakup was a bit intense, and it threw me for a loop. I couldn't function without bumping into memories from the past, and I thought the best way to heal and regroup would be to go on an extended vacation. My work is such that I can telecommute for most of it, so I decided to pack up and go find myself."

The way Frannie melted at his admission made him feel like a toad. He supposed it wasn't entirely a lie—he and Belinda had broken up—but after he'd had to spirit her out of the country for her own safety, they decided it would be best for them to go their separate ways. *Being attacked and left for dead by your boyfriend's uncle tended to destroy the romance in a relationship.*

"I had a bad breakup, too, so I totally understand the desire to pack up and run away. If I hadn't had the shop, I probably would've skipped town, too," Frannie conceded. "In the end, I didn't want him to have the satisfaction of seeing me break, so I toughed it out. But I feel like there's no wrong way to heal from emotional pain. We need to give ourselves permission to do what our minds and bodies need without feeling judged by everyone else."

God love this woman for her kindness and compassion. Even if he didn't deserve it. "Are you healed now?"

"I'm definitely on the right path. Relationships, good or bad, always leave a mark. I think that's what people mean by 'baggage' from previous relationships because we take a little piece of that relationship and bring it with us when we meet someone new."

"Was he a good man, this past boyfriend?" he asked, curious. "He wasn't abusive or anything like that?"

"Bobby? Oh gosh, no, just a cheater. I mean, that's pretty bad but in the grand scheme of things, not something I can't get over. Shortly after it all went down, I read something that helped put things in perspective. It was a book on healing emotional trauma. I read this part that said, 'People's actions say more about themselves than what they say about you,' and I realized Bobby's decision to cheat on me was a defect in his character, not mine."

"Very wise."

"Well, it resonated, and it really did help put things in their proper place."

"I'm sorry he hurt you."

Frannie sighed, remembering. "Yeah, I was heartbroken when I found out. Embarrassed, too. Felt like the whole town knew and was whispering about it behind my back. Small towns are big on gossip and when someone's running around on another person, it's just too juicy to pass up."

"How did you discover he was unfaithful?"

Frannie drew a deep breath, wincing as if it hurt to remember. "I found text messages. And pictures. The evidence was pretty incriminating. He didn't try to deny it, and I was glad. I can't say I wouldn't have punched him in the mouth for lying. Growing up with a big family taught me how to throw a good hook. But, like I said, he didn't deny it. I think he was relieved, actually."

"Relieved?"

"Living a lie takes a lot of energy. Once the cat was out of the bag, he didn't have to pretend anymore."

Dante identified with that statement far more than he would've liked. The burden of a sustained lie was heavier than most people realized. Still, he felt no sympathy for this Bobby character. "He lost you. He got what he deserved."

Frannie smiled, seeming to appreciate his compliment. He'd shower her with sweetness every day if it were up to him because she deserved nothing less. She cozied up to him. "Well, sounds like whoever broke your heart got the worst end of the deal because you're amazing, and I don't like to share."

If only that were true. He'd do anything to go back in time and make a different choice, to believe how dangerous his uncle was instead of blowing off his threats. Belinda had deserved far better than she had received. *You deserve to be happy, too.* Belinda's words echoed in his head, but he couldn't take them to heart, just like when Belinda said them. He shook off the dark thoughts and directed attention to their lunch. "All that paddling worked up an appetite... Let's eat."

"Oh, right!" Frannie laughed, good mood returning. "You'll love this bread. I buy it from the local bakery, and they make it fresh every day. It's my guilty pleasure."

Dante took a bite, appreciating the flavors. "Reminds me of home," he admitted. "In Italy, most everyone buys their bread, fruits and vegetables at the outdoor market for the day. Fresh bread should never be a guilty pleasure, *dolcezza.*"

"*Dolcezza*, what does it mean?"

"It's a term of endearment, such as sweetheart," he explained.

"I like it," she said, leaning toward him. "I like it a lot."

Lunch temporarily forgotten, Dante curled his hand behind her neck and drew her in, sealing their mouths together. She tasted like the promise of a new day with a sweetness no chocolate could ever hope to possess. He didn't deserve any of her love, her compassion or her goodness, but he selfishly craved it.

The kiss deepened, Dante needing to feel Frannie all around him. He didn't care that they were in broad daylight, that anyone could happen upon them and gawk. When he touched Frannie, the world melted away, and it was only the two of them in a tight, safe cocoon.

In those precious moments, he was far from the reality that his uncle would stop at nothing to bring him back to the family. That he held a ticking time bomb in a safe-deposit box and that his uncle would do anything to prevent the ruin of the family.

Nowhere was truly safe. His uncle had the money to chase Dante around the globe, and eventually, he would find him.

But in this stolen moment—it was only he and Frannie.

And he greedily enjoyed every second as if it were his last.

Because it very well could be.

Chapter Sixteen

Frannie was floating on a cloud. The day couldn't have been more perfect if she'd dreamed it up with the power of a fairy godmother. She'd convinced Dante to come to her place for dinner, which was a massive win because he usually talked her into going to his place.

"You have to promise me that you won't judge my collection of knickknacks," she said, unlocking the front door. "I have a thing for collectible plates. I blame my grandmother for the obsession. She bought my first collectible plate when she vacationed in the Netherlands and the tradition stuck."

Dante smiled. "Have you ever been to the Netherlands?"

"Nope. I've never been outside of the United States, but I do have my passport just in case the opportunity presents itself."

Frannie had always wanted to travel, but she was embarrassed to admit that she was intimidated by the idea of traveling too far from home. It was a fear she hoped to conquer at some point in her life, but when she purchased the shop, her opportunities became limited.

Too limited to traipse along the countryside.

So, she purchased plates instead.

Frannie deposited her keys in the ceramic bowl by the door. "Have you been to the Netherlands?" she asked Dante.

"Not yet."

His answer sent shivers tripping down her back like he'd said he would take her to the Netherlands if she wanted to go. It was silly to think that because he hadn't said anything, but she'd felt like he had.

She was overthinking things.

"How about a quick tour?" she asked, shaking off the dizzying thoughts that served no purpose. Her mother had always said she had her head in the clouds most days and lived in a fantasyland. Probably why she loved books. "Again, no comments on the choice. I call it 'boho chic with a touch of French gothic' but my sister Ruby calls it 'thrift store chaos.'"

Afterward, Dante laughed but nodded, saying, "It suits you—and it's perfect."

"I don't know if I should be flattered or insulted," she said as he pulled her into his arms. "But I'll go with flattered for the sake of my ego."

"What's not to love? It's carefree, cozy and inviting—all good things in my book," he said, walking her backward to her bedroom, which was a short walk from the living room because her house was the size of a postage stamp. He brushed a kiss across her lips. "You know what's the best part about your place?"

She gazed up at him. "The antique claw-foot tub?"

"It's nice but no."

"What then? The suspense is killing me."

The back of her legs bumped against her bed. Dante gave her a tiny push, sending her falling back to land on the soft comforter as he followed, towering over her. "It smells like you—and I love the way you smell," he finally answered before descending for another kiss, searing her lips with the passion that bubbled between them.

Frannie wound her arms around his neck, drawing him

closer, loving the way he devoured her from head to toe. When Dante made love, he made her pleasure his sole purpose. She'd never known a man so utterly consumed with his goal, and she was completely addicted.

Dante's weight pressed against her as his big hands cupped her face tenderly as if she were precious to him. *Don't you dare fall in love with him*, the voice warned, but she knew it was a pointless demand because she was falling fast.

Like being dropped from the moon and free-falling to the earth.

What they were doing felt the opposite of casual, but what did she know about being in a "situationship," as her younger cousins called it? Nothing. She was a one-guy kind of girl. And she wanted to be Dante's girl.

Don't ruin the moment, go with the flow.

"Dante…are you hungry?" she asked breathlessly as Dante lifted her shirt up and off, wasting no time nibbling along her shoulder blade, traveling up her neck. "I could… make some…pancakes."

"All I want is you," he said, pulling his shirt off and tossing it to the floor. He started to unbuckle her pants, but his gaze caught on something, and he stopped to stare with a subtle frown.

Frannie, her lips still tingling, propped herself up on her elbows, confused by his sudden change in demeanor. *Was it the mention of pancakes?* "Are you okay? What's wrong?"

He reached past her to pluck a single lily from the opposite pillow. The same type of lily that'd been delivered to her shop.

Frannie startled, staring as she scrambled to sit up, more confused than ever. "Where'd that come from?"

"It was on your pillow. Who put it there?" he asked.

"I don't know," she answered, biting her lip, bewildered. "I…honestly have no clue."

This felt different than a random delivery to her shop. She hated to admit it, but it gave her a creepy vibe. Someone had entered her house while she was gone and deliberately placed that lily on her pillow. She swallowed, feeling very exposed.

"You are positive no one you know could've left this flower for you?" he asked in a quiet yet hard tone.

She swallowed. "Dante, I swear I have no idea where that lily came from."

Dante swung away and scooped up his shirt, dressing quickly as he went to the window to check for signs of entry. Frannie grabbed her shirt, unsure of his reaction. Was this jealousy? Mistrust? Or was he concerned that someone was stalking her? "You're not staying here," he decided, pointing to her closet. "Gather your things. We're leaving."

Frannie needed a minute to think. Her heart was thundering in her chest, but she refused to be chased out of her home over something that might have a logical explanation. "I don't want to sound like the dumb girl in the movie that gets killed, but I don't want to rush to conclusions either. Let's calm down and think for a minute."

"There's nothing to think about. You're not staying."

That authoritative tone reminded her too much of her father, and she bristled. "No, I need a minute to think. I'm sure there's a logical reason… I need to find it."

DANTE WAS ABOUT ready to ignore Frannie's protests, toss her over his shoulder and physically carry her to the car, but he restrained himself, realizing that the harder he pushed, the more she'd dig her heels in.

She didn't know how much danger she could be in, and he couldn't tell her.

How could he convince her to leave when he couldn't be honest about his circumstances?

Sweat beaded his brow. *Okay, think.* Frannie wanted logic. He'd give it to her. Throttling down his fear, he tried a different tactic. "It could be something innocent, but don't you think it's better to err on the side of caution than assuming it's nothing? What if you're wrong? What's one night? How about this…come back to my place for the night, we'll order a pizza, watch some TV, and tomorrow you can run it by your brother to see how he feels about it. If he feels it's nothing to worry about…well, maybe you're right."

"Fletcher is a cop, so maybe that's not a terrible idea, if only to create a paper trail," Frannie conceded, thinking it through. Still, she seemed undecided. "But on the surface, a pretty flower doesn't seem all that threatening. It's not like it was a bloody horse head or anything like that."

Dante wanted to shake her head off her shoulders. Her place felt compromised, and every moment they remained felt like a minute closer to his uncle's hired men showing up for an unpleasant interaction. He tried again, using a different tactic.

"Someone entered your house when you weren't home and left that flower on your pillow. An anonymous person paid for the flowers to be delivered to your shop, which was suspicious enough, but now the flower in your home? You can't see how that's something to be concerned about?"

He was pressing a little harder, desperate to get her to a safe place. Not that he knew his place was any safer, but he doubted Frannie would let him put her on a plane to Switzerland to hang out with his ex-girlfriend, the last victim of his uncle's revenge.

Frannie wavered. "It's weird," she admitted.

"Yes," he agreed, holding his breath with the hope that she was close to seeing his way of things. "If you're wrong, and someone left you this flower as a warning, I can't fathom not doing something about it. Frannie, please. I care about you."

"I know you do, and I appreciate the concern. I'm just worried about making a big deal about nothing. My family has enough to worry about without me crying wolf over strange flower deliveries. Even saying it out loud makes me cringe. Who gets scared over a beautiful flower?"

"If the message, 'I'm going to kill you,' is delivered in calligraphy does it make it any less threatening?"

Frannie blinked at the change in perspective, biting her lip with apprehension. "Oh, that's a good point. I hadn't thought of it that way. When you put it like that, it's very creepy."

Relief flooded him when he sensed he was finally winning the argument. "Can I help you pack?"

Frannie chuckled with discomfort. "It's just overnight, Dante. I'm not moving in."

He smiled, acknowledging her point. "Good. Five minutes? We can pick up the pizza on the way."

He pretended to be switching gears, excited about pizza, but he knew everything would taste like cardboard. His head was swimming with upsetting possibilities, and he felt pressed on all sides by potential danger.

Frannie reappeared with a small overnight bag, and he relieved her of the burden as he walked to the front door. He tossed her bag into the back seat and opened her door, his gaze scanning the surrounding area, looking for anything unusual. Frannie's tiny house wasn't tucked away in the mountains like his place, but the older neighborhood wasn't heavily populated either. A lot of For Sale signs in yards, which he hadn't noticed before. Vacant houses were excellent places to hide for people who didn't want to be seen.

"I didn't realize there were so many empty houses on your street," he said.

She sighed, looking out the window as they drove by. "Yeah, the economy isn't what it used to be and if you're not in the tourist trade, there isn't a lot of opportunity. I wish the city would come up with some kind of incentive to keep locals here, but I suppose their hands are tied, too. The piece of the pie is only so big."

Dante nodded, pretending to be invested in the plight of the local economy, but his mind was elsewhere, moving at the speed of light, processing possibilities, second-guessing every little thing.

God, he wanted to tell Frannie the damn truth!

If he could level with Frannie, she might understand why he was agitated about a seemingly odd but maybe innocent flower mishap.

But c'mon, a flower deliberately placed on her pillow? That screamed malice.

"You know what? I just thought of a wild idea," he said, catching her attention. "What if we got out of town for a few days? Maybe find a cozy cabin near the lake or even head to the city, get dressed up and hit the town? I'd love a chance to pamper the prettiest woman in Owl Creek. Hell, possibly prettiest in the whole state."

"You're laying it on a little thick, but I like it," Frannie teased. But she shook her head, saying, "As much as I love that idea, I can't leave the shop."

"You're the owner, you can make the rules, *dolcezza*," he reminded her.

"Yeah, but not sticking to my own rules…that's how a business fails. I know my dad wasn't great at the whole father gig, but he was a solid businessman. One of the things he shared with me when I opened the shop was not to fall into the trap of thinking I'm above the rules just because I pay the mortgage."

It was solid advice—but Dante didn't care about that. He

wanted Frannie somewhere safe and getting out of town for a few days would give him time to determine if his uncle had people in town. "Sure, that's excellent advice, and I agree. But there's also something to be said for knowing when to enjoy the fruits of your labor. I've seen how hard you work. You deserve a little pampering."

Frannie laughed but otherwise let the offer die, and he took the hint. If he kept pushing, it would cease to be romantic and turn into something weird, which would only backfire.

"All right, I can see you're not on board, I understand," he said with a short smile. "Should we order the pizza to go, or do you want to eat in the restaurant?"

"Oh, to go. I'll go ahead and order so it's ready when we get there," she said, grabbing her cell phone from her purse.

As Dante listened to her order while he drove, sneaking covert looks her way, he could tell she'd already written the flower incident off as weird but harmless, which worried him. He couldn't blame her, though. Before Belinda's attack, he'd been confident he could handle whatever his uncle threw at him, but he'd been wrong.

Fifteen minutes later, they were pulling into the parking lot. "My treat," she told him when he started to exit the vehicle. "I was going to make dinner tonight, remember?"

He grinned, accepting the offer only because it seemed he'd have a moment of privacy while she grabbed the pizza. Frannie smiled and left, giving him a lovely view of her perfect backside that, if he hadn't been riddled with anxiety, he would've appropriately appreciated.

Once she was inside, he picked up his cell phone and dialed his private investigator. When it went straight to voice mail, he left a message. "I have reason to believe my uncle's associates have followed me to Owl Creek. I need you to find out if my location has been compromised. ASAP. No matter the hour, let me know what you find out."

He clicked off just as Frannie reappeared carrying the pizza. He smiled as she climbed into the car. "Smells amazing," he said.

"Tonight, I'm going to splurge," she announced. "I have special lactase enzymes in my purse and I'm going to enjoy a slice or two of this gooey, cheesy pizza. There's only one thing…"

"Which is?"

"Sometimes they make me gassy," she admitted with a short, embarrassed laugh, shrugging as she added, "You know what they say…gorgeous, gorgeous girls have stomach issues."

He laughed, momentarily forgetting about the looming danger. He leaned over to plant a hearty kiss on her perfect lips. "If that's the deal, I think I can handle the terms."

At that, Frannie barked another laugh as if he didn't know what he'd just agreed to, and he realized that she was the kind of woman he'd be lucky to call his.

Except he had no business dreaming of a future with Frannie…or anyone.

Chapter Seventeen

Even as Frannie had been determined to downplay the flower incident, her private thoughts were in turmoil. She didn't want anyone to worry unnecessarily over something that seemed silly, but Dante had planted a seed of doubt that was quickly germinating.

As she lay beside Dante, her head resting on his chest, it should've been easy to push aside anything unpleasant, but tonight her anxiety was determined to needle her brain, making restful sleep—or sleep at all—impossible.

Usually, when she had difficulty sleeping, a little fresh air helped. Careful not to disturb Dante, she rose from the bed, grabbed a bottled water from the kitchen, and quietly stepped outside to the front porch.

Sighing, Frannie sank into one of the two porch chairs and enjoyed the starry sky with the night sounds all around her. Owl Creek might not be a mecca of modern convenience—no fast-food places or chain restaurants—but there was something special about being nestled in the heart of nature.

Drawing a deep breath, she closed her eyes and let the cool night air caress her nude skin. The best part about Dante's place was that no one was around for miles, so only the wildlife saw her naked on the front porch.

Hannah always accused her of being a closet nudist because she'd always been running around the house with as little clothing as possible, and if they all went swimming in the creek in the middle of the night, Frannie was the first to shuck all her clothes and jump in naked as the day she was born.

The memory curved her lips in a smile.

Then, there were her wild college days, of course. But that was what college was for—making a few mistakes, poor judgment calls, and memories.

Well, that and getting an education.

A subtle frown pulled her brows as she recalled a name she hadn't thought of in a long while. *Allen Burns.* He'd had a mad crush on her, but she'd only seen him as a friend. That'd been an awkward conversation when she'd had to set him straight.

She winced at the memory.

Poor Allen. So shy with the girls. Had he ever figured out the social dance steps required to find a partner?

Frannie always found it interesting that even as evolved as humans were, they were still animals and programmed to respond to certain mating rituals.

Allen hadn't been very good at discerning social cues, which made people shy away from him, but that was why Frannie had gone out of her way to befriend him.

Why had Allen popped into her head when she hadn't seen him in years?

The door opened, startling her. When she saw it was Dante, and he was holding a blanket, she smiled. "Sorry, did I wake you?"

"It's not your fault. I'm a light sleeper," he said, draping the blanket around her shoulders. His constant chivalry tickled her, but the fact that he did things out of concern for her comfort struck a chord deep inside. "Are you okay?" he asked.

"When I can't sleep, I like to go outside for some fresh air and the fact that I can come outside naked is a huge plus. I can't exactly do that at my place."

"Yes, even with all of the empty houses, it probably isn't a good idea," he said, amused.

"Thank you for the blanket," she said, patting the seat beside her. "Sit with me a minute?"

"Sure," he said, settling into the chair. "Why can't you sleep? Is there anything I can do?"

The subtle suggestion in his tone made her blush, but she playfully tapped him on the thigh. "Dante, you dirty boy," she admonished with a laugh. "No, I just needed Mother Nature, and you have the best view."

He agreed. "I was lucky to find this place. It's been exactly what I was looking for. It'll be hard to leave."

Frannie fell quiet, hating any mention of Dante leaving, but she supposed it was healthy to acknowledge that he wasn't planning to relocate to Owl Creek soon. "Do you miss home?"

Dante considered her question, finally answering, "Italy is a beautiful place but lately, I've been asking myself if I want to stay there."

Hope dared to flicker in her heart. "You're open to relocating?"

He hesitated, as if realizing he'd stumbled onto a subject he wasn't ready to talk about, but he offered a noncommittal "Well, I suppose anything is possible," before dropping it.

Frannie took the hint, but she'd be a liar if it didn't hurt. She wanted an open and honest conversation about their feelings for each other, but she was afraid of pushing against an established boundary and losing him altogether.

She winced internally—that sounded pathetic even in

the confines of her head. She should be able to be honest. Without honesty, there was nothing. Why shouldn't she be able to come out and say, 'Dante, I have feelings for you. No, actually, I think I'm falling in love with you. And I need to know if you feel the same.'

But she couldn't get the words out of her mouth. Instead, she grabbed her bottled water and took a long swig before sharing, "So, a name popped into my head while I was sitting out here that I haven't thought of in years—a guy who had a crush on me back in college."

"Why'd you think of him?"

"I think because of the flowers."

Dante frowned. "What's the connection?"

"Maybe nothing but I remember he used to work part-time in the horticulture department. I think he was an Ag major. Sometimes he would bring me fresh flower clippings from the greenhouse. A lot of times, they were lilies. It was sweet."

"Did you date?"

"No, just friends. But he did like me a little more than a friend should," she admitted. "However, I set him straight, telling him that I only felt friendship for him. I didn't want to lead him on."

"How'd he take the news?"

"Um, well, he was hurt, of course, but he didn't freak out or anything," she said.

"Does he live here in Owl Creek?"

"No, we met at Boise State. I don't remember where he originally came from, and we didn't keep in touch," Frannie said with a shrug. "I don't even know why he popped into my head. Probably because he was into flowers. Anyway, random stuff goes through my head at three in the morning." A sudden, welcome yawn cracked her jaw, and she said, "See? Mother Nature is better than any sleeping pill. Ready to go back inside?"

Dante nodded and followed her into the house. Climbing back into bed, she cuddled up to Dante, sighing happily until she realized there was no turning back. She was in love with Dante, and she wanted him to stay.

But did he feel the same?

THE FOLLOWING MORNING Dante rose early to make the coffee and prepare bacon and eggs for breakfast. When he'd woken in the middle of the night and found Frannie gone, his heart had nearly stopped.

When he realized she was sitting outside—naked—on the porch, he'd immediately wanted to drag her back inside. A wave of possessiveness washed over him at the thought of anyone else seeing Frannie's beautiful body, and he realized he had to stop thinking of Frannie as his girlfriend.

Even so, he'd brought her the blanket, though she looked like a wild goddess in the moonlight with her hair loose and the pale light kissing her bare skin.

Frannie appeared, wrapped in his robe, and shuffled to the kitchen, her bleary gaze going straight to the coffee. He quickly poured her a cup and pushed the oat milk toward her that he'd purchased specifically for her in deference to her tummy issues with dairy.

For himself, he enjoyed real cream, which he poured liberally into his morning coffee. "Good morning, beautiful," he said, kissing her cheek as she doctored her coffee. "How'd you sleep?"

"Good," she said, sipping her coffee with a pleased smile. "Perfect."

He chuckled, enjoying how expressive she was about everything in life. She made a sip of coffee seem like time had stopped, and nothing else mattered but that sip. He loved that about her. He didn't blame her college friend for falling for her—how could anyone resist Frannie Colton?

But given everything behind the scenes, he'd feel better if he looked into the guy.

"I was thinking, just to be on the safe side, I should look into this college guy and see if there's anything to be concerned about."

Frannie waved off his suggestion. "Oh, goodness, Dante, surely you have better things to do than do background checks on guys I haven't seen in ages? Besides, Allen was harmless."

"You're right, it's probably nothing. But I'd feel better if I confirmed that fact."

She seemed to realize he was serious, and sobered. "Dante, are you really that worried?"

"About your friend? I don't know. But I am worried about someone breaking into your house and leaving flowers that you didn't ask for."

"I didn't want it to get into my head because it's nothing serious, but I'm a little unnerved about it."

"As you should be," he agreed, relieved she finally saw things from his point of view. "Look, I know it might seem an overreaction but it's always better to be safe than sorry. And when it comes to your safety, I don't want to take any chances."

She smiled up at him, a vision of sunshine and light, and his heart threatened to jump from his chest and land in her lap. Did she have any idea of the effect she had on him? Never in his life had he ever felt this way about a woman. He was out of his depth. The best he could do was make sure she was safe.

"If it makes you feel better about it, sure, go ahead and look into him. Although, I could probably just have my brother Fletcher look into it."

"I want to do it," he said, fighting that wave of possessiveness again. He wanted to be the one to keep Frannie safe. Ironic, seeing as he was the one putting her in danger.

"Okay," she said easily, taking another sip of her coffee. "Plans for today?"

He was waiting on word from his private investigator, but he couldn't mention that. Instead, he smiled and kissed her forehead, saying, "I'm playing detective today. Enjoy your coffee. There's a plate of bacon and eggs in the microwave. I'm going to jump in the shower. Feel free to join me if you like."

"That's not a fair choice. You know I love food, but I'd also like to be naked with you in the shower."

He shrugged. "You could always reheat the eggs and bacon after…"

Frannie considered the option, then hurried after him, taking a final sip of her coffee. "Water conservation is far more important than the inconvenience of reheating breakfast," she rationalized.

Dante couldn't say he was disappointed. She shrugged out of his robe, and he scooped her up, carrying her to the bed first.

"Hey! You said shower…" she said, playfully accusatory. "What are you doing?"

"Making a mess of you, darling," he answered with a dark grin as he pressed kisses down her belly. "Might as well make sure we're making proper use of the shower."

Her delightful giggle switched to moans, and Dante knew he could happily drown in the sound of her pleasure for the rest of his life.

He needed to find a solution to this situation with his uncle, or he'd lose out on any chance of happiness with Frannie.

He'd always known running wasn't a permanent solution, but he hadn't figured out how to keep his uncle off his back for good.

What kind of life was he offering Frannie if they took things to the next level?

He wanted her in his bed every night, not just here and there, like some meaningless hookup with a casual stranger.

Casual—that word couldn't possibly describe what he and Frannie shared, but it was what they'd agreed to.

But how could he offer anything else?

He couldn't.

Not yet, anyway.

Maybe never.

All they had was now.

Chapter Eighteen

Frannie closed the shop and headed for the grocery store, still thinking about the exciting new shipment of books that had arrived that morning. Dante was so good about taking care of the food she wanted to show him that she could throw something together that was not only edible but delicious, too.

She wasn't Emeril but could hold her own in the kitchen. Jenny had taught all her children how to find their way around the kitchen, and it was a small point of pride that even though she had a modest menu of dishes she could prepare, she made them well.

The farmers' market was only a short walk from the shop, so she grabbed her canvas shopping bag and headed toward her favorite fruit and vegetable vendor.

"Frannie! There you are! I knew I'd find you here, sniffing mushrooms and talking about how a mushroom could be a good substitute for meat," Darla said, rolling her eyes. "As if that was actually a thing. I know you're not a vegetarian, but you do a pretty good imitation of one, always pushing those vegetables."

"Technically, a mushroom is a fungus," Frannie reminded Darla, to which Darla grimaced. "I'm just saying…if you want to be accurate. But yes, it all depends on how you season and cook it." She held up a beautiful portobello mushroom. "See? Doesn't that look delicious?"

"No, it smells like dirt and looks like something I wouldn't ever put in my mouth. I'll stick with a porterhouse."

Frannie shrugged with a grin as she put the mushroom in a baggie to be weighed. "Each to their own. What are you doing here tonight? You barely cook, and you don't like crowds." She paid for her purchase, and they walked on.

Darla sighed, nodding in agreement with everything Frannie had said, but she gestured across the street, "I blame him," and Frannie saw her fiancé admiring a handmade wind chime. "He loves the farmers' market. He says it makes him feel good to support local artisans. I didn't have the heart to tell him that most of this stuff is purchased from China and passed off as homemade."

"That's not true," Frannie said, laughing at Darla's sour attitude. "I happen to know for a fact that Stacy Spencer makes her tie-dyed T-shirts in her bathtub—and they're really cute. I might just buy one today."

"You hate tie-dye," Darla drawled, calling her bluff. "You once said tie-dye is the clothing trend that refuses to die and has worn out its welcome."

She had said that—but to be fair, she'd been in a bad mood that day. "A woman has the prerogative to change her mind."

The hairs suddenly stood on the back of her neck, and she shuddered, glancing around to see why she felt like someone had been staring a hole into her back.

"You okay?" Darla asked, noticing her sudden shiver. "You look like a goose walked over your grave."

"Yeah, it was weird. It felt like someone was standing right behind me, staring."

"I didn't see anyone," Darla said, scanning the crowd.

"But I hate when that happens. Maybe a ghost was standing right next to you."

Frannie didn't like that thought at all. "Hey, don't be putting those kinds of thoughts in my head. I sleep alone, you know."

"You big fat liar. I know you're not sleeping alone these days."

Frannie blushed, clarifying, "Okay, maybe not but it's not an everyday thing. It's a casual arrangement, not a relationship and..." Her voice trailed. Why was she even trying to lie when Darla knew her like the back of her hand? *Pointless*. She met Darla's knowing smirk and gave it up. "I think I'm falling in love with him, Darla. How did this happen?"

Darla shook her head as if to say, 'You poor summer child,' and put her arm around her shoulders. "First, there are worse men to fall for—he seems pretty top-shelf. Second, would it be so bad if you were falling for him?"

"Um, yeah, we agreed to keep things casual because he's not planning to stay in Owl Creek, and I have no plans to move to Italy...or wherever he's going next. Also, I don't actually know much about him. Each time I try to get a little deeper, he switches things up and deftly changes the subject. It's a little 'red-flaggy.'"

"Yeah, you mentioned something about that. How'd the day on the lake go?"

"Amazing! Best day of my life. The lake was beautiful, I packed a picnic lunch for the beach, and we...well, we made good use of the privacy, let's just put it that way."

"Mmm, I love lake days like that," Darla said with a wistful expression. "And then what happened?"

"Well, we went back to my place and...do you remember those random flowers that showed up at the shop?"

"The lilies?"

Frannie nodded. "Well, Dante and I were messing around

and just as we were about to get serious, Dante saw a single lily—the same kind as the delivery—on my pillow."

Darla's eyes bugged. "Excuse me? On your pillow? How'd it get there?"

"I don't know."

"That's some creepy shit, Fran. Did you report it to Fletcher?"

"No, it seems silly to report something so small."

"Small? No, someone broke into your house and left something there to let you know they'd been there. It's creepy and potentially dangerous. You need to tell Fletcher."

"So, Dante wants to do a little checking on a guy I went to school with at Boise State. Do you remember my friend Allen Burns?"

"The horticulture nerd who always brought you dead weeds?"

"They weren't weeds, they were clippings, and most of the time they were gorgeous lilies."

Darla's gaze widened. "Do you think it was that guy who left the flower?"

"I mean, it seems unlikely, but he popped into my thoughts at three in the morning. It's funny, I hadn't thought of him in years until I couldn't sleep and then, there he was, in my head."

"I remember him being a little on the weird side," Darla said. "Are you sure it wasn't him?"

"He wasn't weird," Frannie protested. "He was just a little on the shy side and maybe awkward but I'm awkward, too, so we got along."

"Frannie, you're quirky, which, paired with your face, is adorable. Pretty privilege goes a long way to smoothing the road for those with unusual personality quirks. If I'm remembering correctly, he didn't have that luxury."

"He wasn't traditionally handsome, but he was very sweet."

"Did you keep in touch after graduation?"

Frannie shook her head, feeling bad about that. "No, we went our separate ways. We really only had a few college experiences to draw us together. After that, our connection wasn't organic but that's the way of college, right? Everyone goes their separate ways after graduation to pursue their careers."

"I'm still not clear why you haven't told Fletcher?"

"Because it seems silly and Dante is looking into it."

"I thought Dante was a lawyer?"

"He is."

"And he moonlights as a private investigator?" Darla's incredulous expression was pretty damning. "Seriously, Fran, props to your guy for wanting to be your knight in shining armor but sometimes we have to leave certain jobs to the professionals. Dante can pitch legal advice about your family situation if he wants to feel useful."

"It's likely nothing and that's why I didn't mind Dante asking around," Frannie said, defending Dante. "Plus, with everything my family is dealing with, I don't want to add some frivolous nonsense to their plate. Whatever this is, I'm sure I can handle it with Dante's help."

"I love your loyalty to a man you barely know. I'm just saying, I wouldn't trust Tom to know what to do in this situation and I'm crazy about the guy."

"You should be," Frannie said. "Clearly Tom hasn't figured out that you're a double shot of irrational and bossy, and for your sake, I hope he doesn't figure it out until after the wedding."

"Ha! You think I don't have the same concern? That's why I wanted to lock that man down sooner rather than later. We could've eloped, and I would've had a ring on my finger by now." They shared a laugh, but Darla saw Tom waving her over, and she had to cut their conversation short, but not before she made Frannie promise to tell Fletcher. "I don't want to find out on the morning news that my best friend—and maid of honor—was abducted in the middle of the night by some stalker that no one took seriously."

Frannie rolled her eyes and waved Darla on her way. "You worry too much. Go catch up with Tom before he buys that wind chime that will definitely keep you up all night with its bing-bonging in the wind."

Darla's expression of horror as she hustled toward her fiancé made Frannie laugh, but a sliver of doubt remained even as her mood had lightened.

Was it possible she'd made a mistake in not telling Fletcher about the flower on her pillow? What were the chances that she had a real stalker? *Here in Owl Creek?* Seemed far-fetched...but not impossible.

She couldn't help another glance over her shoulder as that feeling remained that someone was watching her.

Stop freaking yourself out. You're surrounded by people you know.

No one is watching.

But just the same, she hurried with her shopping and quickly headed home.

HIS CELL RANG as Dante was getting ready to leave his place to go to Frannie's.

Seeing that it was his PI, he clicked over immediately.

"Dante," he answered.

"Hey, it's Nick. I had a contact with the Wisconsin State Coroners Association pull some strings to send me the confidential autopsy report on your father. It was relatively easy to get the information—probably too easy, they need to really improve their security systems—but I found something I thought you'd like to know."

Dante's stomach muscles clenched with tension, but he was ready. "Go ahead."

"So, I already told you there was alcohol in your father's system when he was killed but there was something else wasn't part of the public record that definitely seems suspicious."

"Which is?"

"Fentanyl—enough to kill him. Someone wanted to make sure your father didn't survive that night. My guess is that your father was dead before his car even hit the tree."

Dante took a minute to digest this bombshell. His father had been murdered. Alcohol might've been easy enough to explain, but fentanyl? If he knew his father hadn't been a drinker, he knew beyond a shadow of a doubt he never did drugs of any kind—much less a drug as dangerous as fentanyl.

"Any chance the coroner shared how the fentanyl had gotten into his system?" Dante asked.

"No, it's anyone's guess. The coroner didn't do a real extensive report. He probably assumed your dad was a drunk and a drug addict and his vices finally caught up to him. I'm sorry."

Dante accepted the man's condolences, fighting the lump in his throat. His memories of Matteo were dim and hazy, but it hurt in ways he couldn't describe knowing that it hadn't been a cruel but impartial twist of fate that'd taken his father from him but a deliberate act by another person.

"Damn it," he muttered, rubbing the moisture from his eyes, trying to regroup. "Anything else?"

There was a brief pause, then Nick shared, "The widow of the cop who wrote your father's accident report? She died yesterday."

A frisson of alarm spiked his blood. "Natural causes?"

"It appears that way, but I'll know more in a few days. It

seems real suspicious that days after I spoke to the woman and she told me about the money her husband received around the same time your father was killed, she ends up dying. I was born at night, but it wasn't last night. Could be natural causes—but then, it doesn't take much to silence an old lady either."

Dante felt sick. Had he inadvertently caused that woman's death by asking questions?

"Send me her obituary so I can see if she left donation wishes."

"It's a nice thought but I'd advise against it."

"Why?"

"Because the old lady didn't have any natural ties to you. If you go and offer some pricey donation to this random lady's cause, it could alert your uncle's men as to your whereabouts. Say a prayer in your head and let God decide whether it's enough. For now, my advice to you is to continue to lay low."

It was solid advice. He wasn't thinking straight. Refocusing, he conceded with a low murmur, "You're right. I've got reasonable evidence that my father was murdered but still nothing tying it to my uncle." Not that he'd likely find any, either. Lorenzo wasn't sloppy—he was exact and precise, calculated. He didn't do anything without multiple fail-safes in place in case plan A went awry.

He used to think his uncle was a genius, which he might be, but now Dante saw him for what he truly was—a murderer with a limitless bank account.

"Keep looking for possible ties. In the meantime, I have something else I need you to look into that's unrelated to my family."

"Yeah?"

"I want you to check out a guy named Allen Burns, attended Boise State University in 2019, possibly an agriculture or horticulture major."

"What am I looking for?"

"Anything. If the man so much as sneezed the wrong way I want to know."

"Sure."

Dante clicked off and sat for a long moment, thinking about his past, present and future. How would he feel if he never found his uncle's ties to Matteo's death? Unfulfilled? Unable to let the past go?

He didn't want that—not for himself and not for Frannie.

He knew he loved her. It was foolish to pretend otherwise. She was the light in his life, the laughter in his soul that made everything else fall away and seem less important.

But how could he drag her into his life knowing that ghosts might chase him without a chance of peace?

He didn't have the answers. All he knew was that he had to keep her safe. Right now, that meant finding out who was sending her flowers—and if they meant her harm.

Chapter Nineteen

Frannie was still unsettled by the time she reached home. She'd planned to make a summer salad, but her thoughts were anywhere but with her food prep. Before she realized the time, Dante was at her door with a bottle of wine and that adoring smile she'd come to crave at the end of a long day.

After a sweet kiss, she admitted she was behind in making dinner, but he wouldn't let her carry any burden, much less that of sole dinner prep. "What do you still need done? I'm happy to help. You know how I love being in the kitchen. Especially with you as my sous-chef."

"Sous-chef? No, you're *my* sous-chef, you silly goose." She said it with a playful smile but was glad to have his help. She enjoyed cooking with him. Together, they were a seamless team that made light work of any task they set out to do.

Wasn't that the hallmark of most successful relationships? Embracing the concept of "many hands make for light work," as her grandmother used to preach to her grandchildren, as they groaned at having to haul wood, pick blackberries for summer jam, and peel apples to jar as applesauce for the winter.

He chuckled, seemingly accepting her statement as fact without a single protest. The man was nearly perfect. "I don't want to be casual anymore," she blurted, shocking herself and Dante with her outburst. Her cheeks flared with heat, but she couldn't take it back—not that she wanted to—and it was out there, floating between them like a giant ethereal question mark.

She held her breath, afraid of what he might say, afraid of her feelings getting squashed, but she lifted her chin and stood by her declaration, waiting for his response.

Was that fear? Disappointment? Anger? Or was he embarrassed that the young bookstore owner had gone and done the one thing he'd warned her against, ruining an otherwise great thing between them?

"Please say something."

Dante cleared his throat, apparently realizing his silence was becoming heavier by the moment. He reached for her hand and pulled her close. "You're trembling," he said softly.

"Because I think I might've just ruined what you liked most about us," she admitted in a shaky voice.

"That's not what I like best," he assured her. His throaty voice that never failed to send shivers dancing down her spine.

Was it all about the sex? Granted, the passion between them was out of this world, but she'd be a liar if she didn't say that she wanted it to be about more than something physical.

"Frannie…"

No, she couldn't do this. She couldn't hear him try to let her down gently. Her pride wouldn't suffer such a blow. She tried to pull away, but he held her close. "Dante, you don't have to do this. I get what you're not saying… It's my fault for pushing against the boundary we both set."

"It's not that," he said, furrowing his brow with frustration. "It's…complicated."

"How?"

"I—I don't really want to get into it right now, but I need

you to trust me when I say that it's better to keep things as they are between us," he said, though he looked pained just saying the words, which confused her more.

"Dante, I can't—that's not good enough—I need more from you. I hardly know a thing about you. It was okay in the beginning, before feelings got involved, but now? I crave more than you're willing to give. Maybe it's not fair but I'm honest to a fault, and I can't hide what I'm feeling."

"And I love that about you," he assured her and kissed her passionately, framing her face with both hands. She could feel the love between them, yet he continued to keep her at arm's length emotionally. It was maddening. It was also starting to frustrate her because her feelings were bruised.

"Stop," she said and pulled away, separating them. She wiped at her eyes. "Look, I didn't mean to ruin dinner, but I suppose this was a conversation that was coming eventually. I know you feel something for me, but maybe it's not equal to what I feel for you."

"No, that's not it," he said quietly. "You're not alone in your feelings."

Hope dared to spark in her chest. "I'm not?"

"No."

"Then why do you pull away from me and then say things like, 'It's better this way,' as if you know that we don't have any kind of future together?" she asked, confused and hurt.

"Because I can't give you what you need and deserve," he admitted bitterly. "And I hate that I can't."

"What do you think I deserve? I don't need a fancy house or anything like that. Is it finances? Are you broke or something? I wouldn't care if you were. Finances can be fixed—but not if you walk away."

"I'm not broke," he answered, shocking her. "I—" He

stopped short, leaving his statement unfinished. Shaking his head, he said, "I have more than enough to see to my needs but even if I didn't, I would never allow you to carry the financial burden of my care."

"It's not a burden if you're helping someone get back on their feet," she said, trying to be gentle. She sensed his pride was speaking. Men were so funny about money and where it came from. Her father had always ensured they all knew that no matter how much money Jenny brought in, he still made more.

"Frannie…please. I can't talk about this right now."

She had a choice—let it go and continue their evening as if it had never happened—or hold her ground and expect some answer.

Her heart hurt. For years she'd watched her mother swallow any grievance for peace in the house, and she swore she'd never be like that.

Yet, tears burned behind her eyes at the thought of ending things with Dante over his lack of equal communication. Was it a cultural difference? Or was she making excuses and dancing around the obvious that he was an emotionally unavailable man who'd been content to keep their relationship surface-deep, but he hadn't wanted to hurt her feelings, so he pretended there was more to it.

"Dante… I need more," she said as a tear snaked down her cheek. "And if you can't give that to me, I understand. But I can't allow myself to fall deeper for a man who's ultimately going to break my heart because he never promised me forever."

"What are you saying?" he asked.

"I'm saying, don't ask me to pretend that my needs don't matter because your needs are more important."

There. She'd said it—she'd essentially thrown a gauntlet.

Now, how he responded would reveal the depth of his true character.

Please, don't make me wrong about who I thought you were.

THE TRUTH BURNED his tongue. She deserved nothing less than honesty. How could he spill his guts about everything he was dealing with without putting her in more unnecessary danger?

Just tell her. You're already in the thick of things. More lies will only make it worse.

Dante turned away from her, needing to get his head on straight. He needed a minute to think. The smart decision would be to take the out—a clean break for reasons that would make sense without too much explanation.

He could easily say he was still torn up about his last breakup, and it wouldn't be fair to her to keep pretending otherwise. It would hurt, but she'd get over it. He would wear the "international asshole" badge for her safety.

But then he'd have to find a way to make peace with the knowledge that someone else would claim her heart, warm her bed and share her future—which made him want to smash things.

In a relatively short time, she'd become such an important part of his life, almost as if she were fused to him, and he didn't know how he'd survive without her.

He wasn't the romantic type—he didn't fall in love easily or frivolously—and he took matters of the heart seriously.

He would never pretend to love someone for sex or emotional warmth.

It was Frannie he wanted—even though the woman's gas could kill a moose when she ate too much dairy—because she was everything he never realized he needed in his life.

If it weren't for the threat of his uncle looming over his future, he would've proposed to the woman already.

"Dante?"

It was the tremulous tone that killed him. It was as if it was taking everything in her not to bawl her eyes out, and she was holding it together by a thread to get the answers she needed.

And he was doing this to her.

It was his fault that she was hurting.

He turned to face her. He needed more time. He would be honest with her soon. But not tonight. Tonight, he had to save what they had because he couldn't fathom letting her think he didn't care for her.

"My mother died in a car accident two years ago—a drunk driver—and I inherited a modest sum from her estate. Finances aren't a problem," he said, skirting around the truth. He had inherited money from his mother, but it was nothing compared to what he had inherited from his father's family trust—and what he'd banked as the family's premier attorney.

Lorenzo had secured Dante's inheritance the moment they returned to Italy—yet another reason he'd believed his uncle had been a good man.

Suffice it to say Dante would never have to worry about money.

Only his head.

Frannie blinked, unsure of how to process that information. "You're...rich?"

"Comfortable," he corrected, but he was obscenely wealthy, though he was less proud of how that money had been built. His family's legacy was a patchwork quilt of vice that would turn a holy man's hair white.

"So, why are you so reluctant to take our relationship to the next level?"

"Because it isn't finances that keep me from taking that next step. Emotionally, I'm not ready," he lied. "And you deserve better."

Her expression crumpled, but she nodded. "I understand."

No, you couldn't possibly.

He needed more time to sort things out. "But I want to be in a position to be the man you need," he said. "I just need a little more time to sort things in my head."

"So, you're open to more, you're just asking for more time to get there?" she clarified, wiping at her eyes.

"Yes."

"I suppose that's fair," she said, though clearly that wasn't the answer she hoped for. He hated that she thought he was asking for more time to figure out if he loved her because he already knew the answer. He was head over heels about her. "I mean, I can't fault you for being honest from the start that you weren't ready for more. It's my fault for hoping for that to change."

"No, things happen," he said, unwilling to let her think it was one-sided. "I didn't plan on feeling this way about you either, but anything worth having is worth exploring slowly. There's no need to rush what is already beautiful."

It wasn't the romantic declaration she deserved, but it might keep her safe while he continued to find the answers he needed to move on.

Assuming he could move on.

That was the ugly truth lurking in the background of his thoughts. He was doing all this work, trying to piece together a puzzle, and he had no idea if it would help him. It was possible he'd finish the puzzle, discover how everything came together to create one messed-up picture, and then he'd have to be okay with the knowledge that he was right but couldn't change a damn thing.

Which wouldn't keep him or Frannie safe.

"I accept your offer. But, Dante… I won't wait forever."

Fair enough.

Hopefully, he wouldn't have to make her wait much longer. But he had a terrible feeling he was running out of time to solve anything, much less offer her the future she deserved.

Chapter Twenty

The following day Dante was running errands in town when his cell rang. Believing it was his PI, he answered without checking the caller ID.

"Dante, what are you doing? Running all over the place, making trouble...it's unnecessary. Come home."

Dante's blood chilled. He glanced at the caller ID, but Unknown Caller was all that showed. "Who is this?" He scanned the street, feeling exposed. "Who's calling?"

The caller ignored his question. The voice sounded altered to disguise identity and gender. Whoever it was didn't want to be recognized. "The family is worried. Such division, such pain. It doesn't have to be this way. People poking their noses in family business..." the person on the other line tsked like Dante was the problem child. "It's an ugly thing, unbecoming of a Santoro."

Was this his uncle calling him? No, if it were Lorenzo, he wouldn't waste time altering his voice; he'd want Dante to know that it was him. So, if not Lorenzo, who?

"Either you tell me who this is, or this conversation is over."

"Trust that I don't want to see you hurt," the caller said. "You're testing your uncle's patience. Come home and ask for his forgiveness. He will forgive you. He loves you like a son."

Unwelcome pain squeezed his heart. He didn't want his uncle's forgiveness, just as he didn't want his "love." He didn't have the proof yet, but he knew his uncle had had something to do with his father's death, possibly even his mother's. Lorenzo was willing to kill to keep the family secrets, which didn't make Dante feel safe or "loved."

But at one time, he'd loved Lorenzo like a father—and it was that pain that he didn't want to feel.

"Like he loved his brother?"

The silence on the other end was damning.

Dante's temper flared and took hold. "I know my father was killed and I'm going to find a way to prove that it was Lorenzo's doing. Cops paid off, alcohol *and* fentanyl in my dad's system when the man never drank, much less did drugs? I'm getting closer to the answers I need and when I find them—"

"Stop it," the caller hissed. "You're fighting a game you will lose. Don't risk everything for something in the past that can't be changed. You're acting like a child. Time to grow up, Dante. You're the heir to the Santoro empire. Don't throw that all away chasing ghosts."

Something about the caller reminded him of someone. Everyone in Lorenzo's inner circle was intensely loyal—out of fear or true admiration—but there was only one person near enough to Lorenzo to know his every move, scheduled his appointments and handled all details of his life.

"Pietro?"

Lorenzo's secretary and right-hand man, Pietro Romano, had been around the family for as long as he could remember. He handled Lorenzo's details and was as close as any family member to his uncle, possibly closer because he doubted Lorenzo would ever hire someone to take out Pietro like he had his brother.

"Did he kill my mother, too?" Dante asked point-blank. If anyone knew, it was likely Pietro. "Why?"

"From the beginning, he loved your mother. He would never hurt her."

Dante stilled at the unexpected information. For a moment, his tongue was tied, and the caller took advantage.

"You're angry, hotheaded, and set on what you believe is a righteous path. What if you're wrong? Your uncle is not a storybook villain."

"My father might disagree," he replied coolly.

"A rift between brothers you can never understand—and it's not your place to understand."

If that statement was meant to put Dante in his place, it had the opposite effect.

"I won't be lectured by a man who condones and supports my uncle's actions. You're just as bad."

"Everyone is a villain in someone's story, Dante," the caller reminded him.

He was done being schooled. "I won't stop until I have answers. He'll have to kill me."

"Dante, you're being foolish," the caller said, disappointed. "I thought you were smarter than this."

"And I thought my uncle was a good man. I guess we're both disappointed."

"Your answer is final? You will not come home?"

"No."

"Foolish boy." The heavy sigh on the other end sent a chill down his back. "Stubborn-headed like Matteo. And destined to end up in the same place."

The line clicked off before Dante could respond.

What did that mean? The same place? Did that mean Lorenzo planned to have him killed, too?

He always knew that was a possibility, and he'd been willing to take that risk, but now he had Frannie's safety to worry about, too.

Somehow, he had to convince Frannie it was a good idea to leave Owl Creek for a few days.

A few days? Hell, he'd need to convince her to run away with him forever. Owl Creek was compromised at this point.

A sense of déjà vu washed over him. He was replaying his childhood. His father had scooped up his little family and run from the Santoro influence, never staying long in one place for fear of being found.

And eventually, that was exactly what had happened.

Was that his fate, too?

Would history replay itself with him and Frannie?

What if she got pregnant? Would Lorenzo wipe them out and take his child to start again with a fresh slate?

Lorenzo had never married and never had kids of his own.

But he remembered Lorenzo being solicitous and accommodating to his mother when they arrived in Italy. He'd been too young and grief-stricken to look beyond the surface values of their relationship to wonder why his mother had been so quick to return to Italy when his father had done everything in his power to keep them far away.

What was that bullshit about Lorenzo loving Dante's mother? But something was disturbing about that little nugget of information that he couldn't quite push away.

His mother, Georgia, had never remarried.

His uncle had never been far from her side.

He'd never seen them act inappropriately with each other but over the years, Georgia had become very familiar with Lorenzo, decorating his home as if it were her own, and Lorenzo had always ensured Georgia had whatever she wanted.

A sick feeling lodged in his gut. Had his mother been

having an affair with Lorenzo all those years after his father's death? And had she known that Lorenzo had been responsible for Matteo's death?

No, impossible. His parents had loved each other. But love needed healthy soil to grow, and it was hard to imagine a life such as theirs as anything conducive to nurturing romance.

Perhaps Georgia had grown tired of running, and Lorenzo's offer of protection and wealth had been too much to refuse.

Lorenzo had been kind to Georgia, but was there more than he'd known? A story he hadn't been privy to that started behind locked bedroom doors?

The thought of his mother and uncle being intimate made him irrationally angry on behalf of his dead father. But did ghosts care about what happened after they died?

He pocketed his cell and hustled to his rental. He felt vulnerable out in the open. If Pietro had found him, chances were high that Lorenzo knew where he was, too.

Was he playing with him? A cat and mouse game?

Was Pietro trying to pull on his heartstrings at Lorenzo's bidding, or was it possible that Pietro truly cared and wanted Dante to be safe?

He hated all the mind games. It was one of the many reasons he'd realized being the Santoro attorney wasn't a good fit for him any longer. He loathed manipulating the law to benefit people who were controlling the system for their benefit, no matter who it hurt in the process.

Lorenzo was all about the end game—he didn't care at all about the pawns on the board.

And everyone was a pawn.

Including him.

FRANNIE WAS ABOUT to close the shop when Fletcher called her cell. She picked up, ready with a wisecrack about a fictitious book order, *Men Who Are Emotionally Constipated and the Women Who Love Them*, but Fletcher's news killed her good mood.

"Frannie, there's been an accident."

Immediately, her brothers and sisters jumped to mind, but when Fletcher said it was Dante, she almost couldn't process the information. Shaking her head, she repeated, "Dante? What do you mean?"

"He's okay, but his guardian angel must've been riding shotgun because his car went straight into the lake."

Frannie gasped, horrified. "Oh my God, are you sure he's okay? Where is he?"

"Ambulance took him to Connors to be checked out. He's got a bump on his head and the clinic doesn't have a CT machine. They want to make sure he doesn't have a concussion. But honestly, it's a damn miracle he's alive. I know you're not family or next of kin, but I knew you'd want to know."

Frannie was too stressed to appropriately thank Fletcher for breaking the rules for her, anxious to get to the hospital. "Thanks," she said hastily and hung up. She quickly shut down the store and practically ran to her car to drive forty-five minutes to the nearest hospital.

She might've broken several laws driving to Connors, but she didn't care. All that kept running through her head was how Dante could've been taken from her in a blink of an eye. She swallowed the lump in her throat, too terrified to think straight. She needed to see him, to see for herself that he was okay.

What if he had a concussion? What if his brain was swelling? What if when they did the CT scan, they found a tumor in his head that otherwise would've been lurking in his brain until it took him out on a Tuesday?

Whoa, settle down. A concussion was manageable. Fletcher said Dante was going to be okay. She screeched into a parking spot, not caring that she was parked like a blind monkey had been behind the wheel. Hurrying into the lobby and to the reception desk, she gave Dante's name and lied about her connection to him. "I'm his wife," she answered when the receptionist asked if she were family. It didn't feel weird or uncomfortable to claim either. She'd unpack that later.

She heard Dante's voice from behind the curtain in the emergency room bay, and relief flooded her to tears. Pushing aside the curtain, she smiled at Dante, his head bandaged but otherwise looking as healthy as ever and even a little sexy in his blue polka dot hospital gown.

"Are you okay, honey?" She asked, hoping Dante caught on so she didn't get tossed for being nonfamily.

"I'm fine. Just a little bump on the head," he answered. He introduced Frannie to the doctor. "This is my wife, Frannie."

She pushed away the thrill the tiny lie caused because now was not the time to get all fluttery about the future. "Give it to me straight…is he really okay?" She asked the doctor sternly.

The doctor chuckled, pocketing his pen. "Your husband is correct. The CT scan came back with no damage to the brain, though he might have a headache for a few days while that bump heals. I'd recommend light duty, plenty of rest, and no heavy equipment operating for a week or so. Other than that, he's one lucky guy. A car into the lake? That's a story to tell your grandkids someday."

Frannie chuckled and murmured thanks as the doctor left to start Dante's discharge papers. As soon as the doctor was gone, Dante's easy smile disappeared. He started dressing immediately, shucking the hospital gown and pulling his sodden clothes from the personal bag left with him by paramedics.

Alarmed, Frannie stopped him. "What are you doing? You have to be discharged first. You can't just leave and your clothes are sopping wet. I can run over to Target or something and get you some sweats and a T-shirt to change into now that I know you're not going to die."

"A little wet clothes don't bother me. I'd rather leave now."

"Dante, that's not how the American healthcare system works. You have to finish your paperwork so the hospital knows where to send the bill. I know our healthcare system sucks in comparison to Italy's but it's what we have to work with."

"I'll send cash. We need to go. I didn't need a CT scan and told paramedics that but they insisted because I passed out when they pulled me from the water."

"Well, then it was the right call," Frannie agreed, confused why Dante was so hell-bent on leaving before being officially discharged. "You could've been seriously hurt. What happened?"

"I'll tell you in the car," he said, fully dressed. "Let's go."

Before she could stop him, he pulled her after him, and they slipped out the back door reserved for emergency personnel.

What is going on? "Dante...wait!"

But Dante was like a man being chased by the cops, and he wasn't interested in having a little chat while they sorted things out.

She swallowed, realizing that a giant red flag was flapping in her face, and she could do nothing but hope she was wrong.

Chapter Twenty-One

Dante couldn't afford to stick around for the discharge papers. His fake ID would only hold up to so much scrutiny. He hadn't planned on ending up in the hospital anytime soon. But if they'd tried to run his information, it would've returned as false, tripping authorities to his fake identity. Another reason why he'd tried to refuse a trip to the hospital.

Frannie was understandably confused. "Is there something you're not telling me? I don't understand why you were so freaked out about the hospital. Do you have some bad memories associated with a hospital stay? Does it have something to do with your dad?"

She was grasping at straws, trying to understand, *bless her heart*, but if he told her the truth, he would look like a criminal and ruin any chance of convincing her to leave Owl Creek with him.

As it was, his task was an uphill battle, but the minute his brakes failed and he landed in the lake, he'd known he was no longer safe in Owl Creek.

It also made his anonymous call—he assumed it was Pietro, but he couldn't be sure—seem much more of a last-ditch effort to get him to heel before more permanent measures were taken.

He felt terrible for soaking Frannie's car seats, but he'd

pay for a full detail later. "Yes, hospitals bring up bad memories," he said, stacking another lie on the pile he was racking between them.

"You'll need to call the hospital to make financial arrangements," she warned, trying to make sense of his actions. "I mean, I suppose as long as they get their money, it's fine, but it seems like it would've been a lot easier if you could've waited ten more minutes before running out—and you were literally *running*. I felt like I was being dragged down the hallway like a character in a movie being chased by bad guys."

"Sorry, I didn't mean to frighten you."

"It's okay, I guess, just weird," she admitted with a troubled frown before returning to the subject of the crash. "What happened? How'd you end up in the lake?"

Here was the real test—how much to share without tripping any internal alarm bells. He feigned confusion. "I have no idea. Maybe a faulty brake line? I took the turn and maybe I was going a little too fast, but when I pumped the brakes, nothing happened and I plunged over the side of the hill, crashing into the lake. I think I blacked out on impact."

"How'd anyone know you'd crashed?"

"A boater coming in saw the car go in and he called 911 on his cell."

"That boater is your true guardian angel," she said.

He nodded, but his mind was racing. There was no way that his new car had faulty brakes. He was sure that someone had cut the brake line, but he didn't want to scare Frannie.

"It seems so," he agreed, shifting in his wet jeans, hating how the damp fabric clung to his thighs, but he didn't want to return to his place. "Hey, I think I left some clothes at your place. Let's go straight there."

"I don't mind stopping," she assured him. "I think all you have at my house are a pair of pajama pants and a T-shirt."

"Honestly, I didn't want to admit it, but I do have a headache. I just want to relax for the night so pajama pants sound perfect."

Frannie softened immediately. "Of course. I'm sorry, I can't even imagine the horror of what you've been through tonight. It's one of my worst fears to drive into a lake. If you hadn't had your window open… I don't even like to think of what might've happened."

Yeah, same. "Too close for comfort," he agreed. "I'm grateful for getting through it."

Frannie sobered. "Dante, my heart just about stopped when Fletcher told me. Everything else seemed to fade to the background as unimportant in that moment. I was terrified that you were hurt."

"I'm sorry for worrying you," he said.

"It's not your fault. I'm not telling you to make you feel bad. I already knew how I felt about you, but this just made me realize that I can't fathom life without you. I hope I never have to experience that."

If his life were his own, he'd ask her to marry him right now, but he didn't have that luxury.

"I promise to never drive into a lake again," he said, trying to make her smile. "I confess, it wasn't ever on my bucket list, but I guess I can check it off anyway." Her strained chuckle hurt his heart. He reached over and squeezed her thigh. "They say statistically people are in one bad accident in their lifetime—looks like I just lived through mine. So there's a bright side to losing my rental car."

A tear tracked down her cheek, but she chuckled as she wiped it away. "And who is 'they'? Is that a legal term?"

It was his turn to laugh. "Definitely. I use it in court all the time. Judges love nebulous sources."

"I bet they do," Frannie said, rolling her eyes. They pulled up to Frannie's house, and Dante exited the vehicle so fast his head throbbed, but he ignored it. He couldn't help but scan the street, looking for anything that seemed out of place.

But Frannie noticed. "Are you sure you're okay?"

"Yeah, my head is pounding, though. My plans for the night include you, aspirin and a bed."

"I think I can make that happen," she said, brushing a tender kiss across his lips.

He didn't deserve a woman like Frannie. If he lived through this, he'd make sure she never went a day without knowing how he felt about her.

The only problem? His uncle seemed determined to snuff out his only nephew—and the heir to the Santoro legacy.

FRANNIE TRIED NOT to fret, but there seemed to be a lot of holes in Dante's story and his reaction to being in the hospital. Every time she thought they'd crossed a threshold and reached another level of trust, something made her question everything they shared.

And she hated that she couldn't take his word at face value.

She'd always told herself that she'd never put herself in a position where her partner didn't deserve her trust, because trust was the foundation of a solid relationship. The questions nagged at her brain, whirring in the background, creating noise that kept her grabbing her attention.

Was Dante lying to her?

He didn't seem all that shaken up about landing in the lake.

He hadn't said anything about contacting the rental agency or filing an insurance claim. For that matter, he hadn't said anything about filing a lawsuit against the car manufacturer for the alleged faulty brakes. Nor had he said anything about asking for an investigation into the accident.

It was like he climbed out of the lake with a nasty bump on his head, shook the water from his hair and decided to put it all behind him like a bout of food poisoning from a questionable restaurant.

But he'd landed in a *friggin'* lake!

If it'd been her, she'd still be wrapped in a blanket, shivering and possibly crying over the ordeal.

Wasn't almost drowning considered a traumatic event?

"I can almost hear your thoughts," Dante murmured, half-asleep beside her. "What's keeping you awake?"

She couldn't be honest, not with him recovering from a head injury, so she lied. Badly. "Inventory. I was supposed to get a new shipment and it didn't come, so I will have to check the tracking tomorrow."

"I'm sure it'll show up," he said. "Shipping has been backed up for a while. I think I read something about a strike on the docks or something like that. No one to unload the ships."

"Yeah, probably."

Dante turned to pull her into a snuggle. "You smell like home," he said with a sigh before dropping back off to sleep.

Was it an old wives' tale that you're not supposed to let someone fall asleep with a head injury? She wouldn't know because they'd left before the doctor could give them discharge instructions, including how to care for someone with a head injury.

But Dante was already asleep, dozing as if he hadn't nearly met his maker a few hours ago.

It was wild how people adapted to circumstances in their life, how things became part of their routine, even if it was anything but normal.

For years she'd suspected her dad wasn't faithful, but her mom had been brilliant at hiding any reaction to his infidelity, so as kids, they weren't subjected to screaming fights or relationship drama. Not that it was healthy, but it wasn't in their face.

But then her dad died, her aunt showed up, and all hell broke loose, shattering the illusion that their family was happy, healthy and well-adjusted.

Which made her think of her current situation with Dante. Something wasn't right.

She was ignoring her intuition because she'd fallen in love with him, which wasn't a great endorsement for their future.

If they had a future.

He's hiding something, a voice whispered, and she couldn't look away from the facts staring her in the face.

She had this sense, a tingling in the back of her head, warning her that Dante was lying about something big, which should be all the evidence she needed to walk away and cut her losses.

But she couldn't bring herself to do it, which worried her.

A few years ago, she'd decided to purchase her first brand-new car. She'd been saving all year for the down payment, and she'd been ready to sign on the dotted line. She'd asked her cousin Max to go with her so she didn't get bamboozled by slick car salesmen.

Before they walked into the dealership, Max had imparted the best advice, saying, "Okay, the key to a successful negotiation is to be prepared to walk away at any moment—even if they have the car of your dreams on the lot ready to go, make sure *they* know you can walk away. Desperation makes people sign bad deals and it's their job to make you feel desperate."

Max had been right. She had walked away from one dealership because the deal wasn't to her liking, but the next dealership had met all her terms, and she'd left the place with the car of her dreams—and the best percentage rate for her loan.

Knowing that you were willing to walk away—even if you were in love—was how people saved themselves from staying in a relationship that was bad for them.

A bad deal.

Was Dante a bad deal?

And by staying, was she signing on for something that ultimately was a bad emotional investment?

She didn't know the answer.

And that was the problem.

Chapter Twenty-Two

Dante woke up to find Frannie had already left for the shop. His cleaned clothes were folded neatly on the dresser and there was a note on top that said she had breakfast scheduled with her sister Ruby before the clinic opened and that she'd see him for lunch. He was welcome to use her old pickup until he got a new rental.

Damn it, he must've slept like the dead not to realize Frannie was up and moving around this morning. His brain was still banging from yesterday's event, and it took a minute to shake the cobwebs free. Rising, he groaned against the fresh aches and pains that erupted throughout his body after being tossed about like a rag doll in a washing machine, and went to the shower.

Letting the water sluice down his face, he suffered a moment of panic and anxiety as the situation threatened to overwhelm him.

Too many questions, too many loose threads.

He'd paid cash for the car, stuck a rental agency sticker on it so anyone looking would assume it was a rental like any other, and paid for the cheapest insurance he could find on the internet using his fake identity, but he wasn't concerned about the car. He could get another without breaking a sweat, but it was more about the situation with Frannie.

If it weren't for his feelings for her, he would've bailed on Owl Creek the second he started to feel twitchy, but he couldn't leave her behind, knowing he might've put her in danger.

Attachments were a liability, so he'd been careful not to have any until now.

He hadn't seen it coming. Frannie was the contingency he hadn't been able to foresee.

Losing his phone was inconvenient, but he had another burner back at his place, already preloaded with the important numbers he couldn't lose, including that of his PI.

Dressing quickly, he found the keys to the old truck parked out front and locked up before leaving. He needed to go to his place, pack and figure out how to get Frannie to leave with him.

Desperation had some crazy ideas percolating in his head, but short of kidnapping her, he didn't know how he'd convince Frannie to jump in the car and head into the unknown because it wasn't safe here anymore.

By the time he reached his place, he still didn't have the answers he needed, but he went straight for his hiding spot where he kept a thick stack of cash, his burner phones, and two more fake IDs in case his current identity got burned.

Booting up the phone, he sent a quick message to his PI, letting him know his number had changed.

Almost immediately, Nick called.

"I wondered why you weren't calling me back," he said.

"Yeah, my phone ended up in a lake."

"How's this?"

"It was in the car that also landed in the lake."

Nick whistled low. "Damn. Lucky to be alive. That's some *Final Destination* type stuff."

"Seems my uncle is upping the pressure. What you got for me?"

"Not much on your family yet but I do have some information on that person you asked me to look into."

Frannie's potential stalker. "Go ahead."

"Your guy graduated Boise State with average grades and then moved to Connors, not far from Owl Creek. Maybe about a forty-five-minute drive?"

"Yeah, about that," he confirmed. "What does he do for a living?"

"He's a gig driver for various companies—Uber, Door-Dash, you name it, he does them all."

"So he makes his own schedule."

"Pretty much."

Which would leave him plenty of time to drive to Owl Creek to mess with a former unrequited love. "Anything on his record?"

"Nothing criminal. Just a civil complaint from a neighbor that he failed to bring in his trash cans from the street for a week or so after pickup."

"Was it a recent complaint?"

"About a month ago. Nothing after that, though. Seems harmless."

Didn't feel harmless to Dante. No one right in the head snuck into another person's house to leave flowers uninvited. Especially if they hadn't seen or spoken to one another in years.

"Single? Married?"

"Not married but he might've had a girlfriend at some point. I hacked into his credit card and one of the transactions showed purchases at a lingerie store and a jewelry store a few months back. Nothing since, though."

He didn't like it. Dante had a sense about things. It was one of the reasons he'd been so good at negotiations—he could tell when someone was lying, hiding something, or otherwise off. Except he'd missed all the signs with his uncle until it was too late, and he'd been in waist-deep Santoro muck as his soul started to drown.

"Keep digging. I want to know everything."

But Nick had reservations. "Can I be honest?"

"Of course."

"I think you're barking up the wrong tree. This guy isn't anything but your run-of-the-mill awkward type. He doesn't exactly fit in with the usual social scene but that's not a crime. I think you're hypersensitive because of what you're going through with your family and that's making you see motive where it doesn't exist."

Nick made a solid point. Being chased was enough to make the most levelheaded person paranoid, but someone was messing with Frannie, and he needed to know why. If it wasn't this Allen guy, then who?

Dante grudgingly switched gears. "Right before my car ended up in the lake, I was contacted by someone using a voice disruptor. I think it was my uncle's man, Pietro Romano. He tried to convince me to come home and make peace with my uncle."

"Interesting. Did you get the number?"

"It wasn't a number I recognized but whatever it was, it's now gone because it was on the phone currently at the bottom of Blackbird Lake."

"What made you think it was your uncle's secretary?"

"Something in the way he was trying to get me to come home, to play nice for the sake of family. It reminded me of Pietro. Pietro is rigidly loyal to the family, my uncle in particular, but he was always kind to me. Not everyone attached to my uncle was a bad person."

"But he must've known something was coming because he tried to warn you."

"Yeah, it would seem so."

"What do you have in your possession that is dangerous enough for your uncle to kill to have back?"

"Something that would bring incredible shame to the Santoro name—a secret my uncle will do anything to keep hidden."

FRANNIE WAS STILL thinking about the situation with Dante's car as she shelved books and enjoyed the quiet of the empty store. She hadn't shared her concerns with Ruby at breakfast, but her sister had commented on her pensive mood, mistakenly attributing her uncharacteristic reserve to the family situation.

"It's going to be okay," Ruby assured her, reaching across the diner table to squeeze her hand in solidarity. "No matter what, we'll get through it as a family."

Frannie had smiled, appreciating her big sister's thoughtfulness, but felt guilty that her thoughts had been far from the family drama. Still, she'd said, "I know, it's just a lot to take in."

"Yeah, you're right about that. I talked to Chase yesterday and he said that Aunt Jessie is pushing for *half* of Dad's estate."

"Half? Is she serious?"

"I don't know serious, but greedy and self-centered comes to mind," Ruby said, sipping her coffee. "The nerve of that woman is beyond me. How are Mom and Aunt Jessie even related?"

"She's the evil twin, obviously," Frannie joked.

Ruby chuckled. "Amen, sister. But according to Chase, she has a snowball's chance in hell of getting what she's asking for. If anything, she might qualify for a small settlement, but honestly, I don't think she should get a single cent."

"Me either," Frannie murmured, playing with the handle of her coffee mug. "Mom seems to be handling things well."

"That's Mom in a nutshell," Ruby said dryly. "Allowing anyone to see what's really happening behind the curtain is beyond her capabilities. But then, I guess that was the consequence of living with Dad. He wasn't an easy man to love."

"Do you ever wonder why she didn't leave him?" Frannie asked.

"No. For all his faults, she loved him, and I don't know if that's an endorsement for unconditional love or toxic codependency. All I know is that I wish she could've fallen in love with someone better."

"The heart wants what the heart wants, I guess."

"Yeah, no matter how many red flags are flapping."

Ruby paid for breakfast, and they'd parted ways, but Ruby's last statement still echoed in Frannie's head.

Was she being blinded by love the same as her mom had been with her dad?

"Earth to Frannie, are you listening?"

Frannie was startled as Fletcher's voice abruptly popped into her thoughts. She had no idea Fletcher had even walked into the store, much less was calling her name. "I'm sorry, I didn't hear you come in. What's going on?" she asked, her concerned frown matching his dour expression. "Is everything okay?"

"No, it is definitely not okay," he said, gesturing to her office. "Let's go somewhere private to talk."

"I can't just leave the shop unattended, Fletcher," she said in a low tone, but she was worried about whatever was eating Fletcher to put that look on his face. She motioned for him to follow as she retreated deeper into the Self-Help aisle, which was sadly not the most popular book section. "What's going on?"

"You know how you asked me to look into your friend Dante?"

Her friend. She swallowed, embarrassed that she'd even

asked, but now, given the circumstances, maybe it was wise. "Yeah, did you find something?" *Please say no.*

"He lied to you."

Oh, God.

Frannie stared, unable to process what Fletcher had just said. After a long moment, she asked in a strained tone, "What do you mean, he lied to me? About what?"

"His name, who he is…why he's here…the man can't be trusted. I don't want you around him anymore."

This was all happening too fast. "Hold up, what? I don't understand. What's his name and how do you know all this? Are you sure you have the right man?"

She knew she sounded desperate, but her world was collapsing, and she was grasping at straws.

Realizing she was sinking, Fletcher tried to soften the blow, but there was no easy way to deliver a crap sandwich. "I'm sorry, Frannie, but he's up to no good. Only people with something to hide lie about their identity. His name is Dante Santoro, not Sinclair, and he's part of a dangerous Italian family—the kind that gets away with shady behavior because they have enough money to make problems go away. You know what I'm talking about?"

Those red flags that she'd been ignoring…well, they were practically slapping her in the face now, but she couldn't reconcile what she knew about Dante with what Fletcher was saying. It was like he was describing a stranger.

"You have to have the wrong guy," she protested. "I know Dante. He's the kindest, most compassionate person I've ever met." She felt as if she couldn't breathe. "I'm sorry but you're wrong."

"Frannie, I know it's hard to accept but I asked Max for help because he has access to databases that I don't. The FBI has a file on the Santoro family a mile long but because they're Italian citizens, the FBI has no jurisdiction unless they commit a crime here in the States. They're too good to get caught doing something stupid here, so there's nothing they can tie back to the family, but their hands aren't clean. I'm telling you, Dante isn't safe to be around."

Is that why his car landed in a lake? Is someone after him?

Frannie drew a deep breath, trying to calm her racing heart. "Wait, wait, I need a minute to think," she said, fanning her face as tears crowded her sinuses. What nightmare was she in right now? Two days ago, she'd been wondering if she and Dante should put in an offer on a house together, and now Fletcher was telling her that the man she thought she knew—didn't exist!

"Are you saying he's part of the mob?" Frannie asked, trying to make sense of everything.

Fletcher exhaled a short breath, clearly hating to be the bearer of bad news but wasn't willing to back down. "Look, according to Max, the Santoro family isn't connected to the mafia but they're just as powerful. They're obscenely wealthy and that kind of money creates power. You've seen the movies about powerful families—they always manage to get what they want because enough money makes every problem go away. And sometimes that means people, too."

She couldn't make her brain connect the dots with what Fletcher was saying and what she thought she knew about Dante. "If he's part of this powerful family, why is he here in Owl Creek of all places? It's not as if our town is a hotbed of international intrigue. It's literally the most Mayberry of places on the map."

"Frannie, every place has its dark corners, you know that. Even Owl Creek. We have drugs, crime, you name it."

"Yeah, I know that," Frannie shot back, exasperated. "But Dante doesn't do any of those things. The man goes out of his way to make sure I have food in his fridge that won't send my stomach into a tizzy. He opens doors and is super protective. I didn't tell you because it didn't seem like a big deal, but I had a mysterious flower delivery two weeks ago that came from an anonymous buyer and then another flower placed on my bed a few days later... Dante has been my shadow making sure that I'm safe. Does that sound like a man who's dangerous?"

Fletcher stared. "What are you talking about...what flowers? And why didn't you report this?"

Frannie groaned, shaking her head. "Because it's not that important, more weird than anything else, and I didn't want to bother you with stupid stuff. I mean, it was flowers, not anything scary. But that's not the point. The point is, Dante's been by my side, determined to keep me safe, even if it was from imaginary threats."

"Frannie...did it ever occur to you that maybe he's acting like there's something dangerous out there because he knows exactly who sent those flowers and it spooked him?"

Frannie stilled. No, she hadn't thought of that possibility, but she did now. It made more sense than her random stranger theory. "I have to talk to Dante."

"No. I'll talk to him. I'll bring him in for questioning."

"For what? He hasn't committed a crime," Frannie balked. "You can't arrest someone for using a different name to rent a vacation house."

"We have no idea what he's doing here, or why. He might be an international criminal hiding out until the heat passes."

"That seems a little far-fetched," Frannie said, but her voice lacked conviction. *Helloooo, his car landed in a lake!* That internal voice was practically jumping up and down, gesturing emphatically.

The fact was...she didn't know what was true anymore.

Dante had lied to her.

That was the only indisputable fact.

And her stupid, gullible heart was broken.

Chapter Twenty-Three

Dante walked into the bookstore and felt the unwelcome, hostile chill coming from the police officer standing beside Frannie. He knew something was up.

"Dante…" Frannie looked crushed, and he felt he was at the epicenter of that devastation. "I—"

"Is everything okay?" he asked, feigning confusion.

But the man cut in with a protective stance, his hand resting on his sidepiece as if Dante were a dangerous threat to Frannie. "I'm going to have to ask you to step outside for a minute, *Mr. Santoro.*"

They knew his real name.

Dante caught Frannie's wounded gaze, knowing this man must be one of her brothers. Had she asked her brother to look into his background? He'd never had to hide his identity before, and it was a foreign, uncomfortable feeling knowing they were judging him for being deceptive.

He couldn't blame them.

But he couldn't let Frannie think he was a bad person. He ignored the officer for a minute, directing his attention straight at the woman he loved more than anything. "Can we talk for a minute? I'll explain everything."

But the man wasn't having it. "Outside. Now."

Frannie asked him point-blank, "Is it true?"

The time for lies was over. "Yes." But he was oddly relieved. "And I'm glad you know. But you don't know everything. Let me tell you why."

"There's never a good reason for pretending to be someone you're not," the man replied, his tone hard. "Now, we can do this the easy way or the hard way. Your choice, Mr. Santoro."

Frannie held his stare. "How do I know you won't just keep lying to me?"

"Because now I have no reason to lie and when I tell you why I lied, you'll understand."

"Okay, hard way it is," Fletcher said, grabbing Dante's arm.

"Get your hands off me," Dante growled, stiffening against the man's grip. "I'm assuming you're one of her many brothers and I don't want to make things awkward but if you don't take your hands off me, you and I are going to have an issue."

The man seemed to find Dante's threat amusing. "I don't know how things work in Italy, but here in the United States, threatening an officer of the law is going to land your ass in hot water." He pulled Dante's arms behind his back and zip-tied his wrists together. "We'll finish this conversation down at the station."

But Frannie shocked him by intervening. "Fletcher... wait."

The man looked at his sister in frustration, shaking his head. "Frannie, you have no idea who this man is."

"As far as we know, he hasn't broken the law," Frannie murmured, still conflicted yet shooting dark looks Dante's way.

Dante saw his window, speaking directly to Frannie. "My name is Dante Santoro, I'm heir to one of the most influential and ruthless families in Italy. I changed my name because I didn't want to be found…by my family. I didn't tell you because I didn't want you to be involved with anything as ugly as what I'm dealing with. I haven't killed anyone or committed any kind of crime aside from using a fake name and I never would—which is another reason why I left Italy."

Fletcher quipped, "Great story, let's go."

They managed two steps to the door before Frannie said, "Fletcher, let him go."

"Excuse me?"

"Let me handle this. Dante isn't a threat. This is personal between him and me."

"The hell it is. This man is using an assumed identity. That's fraud."

Frannie couldn't argue that point, but he could tell she was weighing the morality of the situation against what he'd shared already, and she was wavering.

"All I need is a chance to explain," he said, pressing his advantage. He needed her to understand that he wasn't the villain he looked to be.

"Every criminal I know has a sob story—and usually, they're lying about that, too." Fletcher wasn't moved. "A trip to the station is all you're getting today."

This time it was Frannie who was exasperated. "Fletcher, you don't have to do that. He hasn't committed any *real* crime and he pretty much just came clean. Also, he's a lawyer, so he knows the law. Don't waste your time processing paperwork that's not going to go anywhere."

"Frannie…" Fletcher stared long and hard at his sister, but he was digesting her information. Finally, he glanced at Dante, exhaled and shook his head, muttering as he snipped the ties, "I swear to God, if you hurt my sister, I'll show you American justice with extreme prejudice."

Dante rubbed his wrists, nodding. "You're a good brother."

"Yes, I am," he growled, pointing to Frannie, "If he so much as blinks wrong, you better call me."

"I will," Frannie assured Fletcher. "I'll be okay. Thank you, though."

With one final stern glare Dante's way, he exited the bookstore slowly, as if reluctant to take his eyes off Dante. Finally, he climbed into his squad car and drove away.

"So that's Fletcher?" he supposed.

"Yes."

"He seems like a good guy."

"Stop it," she ordered, marching to her front door and locking it, flipping the sign to Closed. "You don't get to blow my world to bits and then try to chitchat about my family. I need you to spill your guts right now."

It was time to be honest—and he was ready for it. Lying to Frannie had become a bigger burden than he ever imagined, and he was relieved to finally be able to come clean.

"In the interest of saving time, what do you know?"

"I know enough. Your family is rich, connected and dangerous. My cousin Max works for the FBI, and they have a file a mile long on your family. But they don't have anything they can pin on the Santoro connection here in the States."

"Sounds accurate," he confirmed. "My family legacy is a checkered quilt of vice and infamy—and I wanted no more part of it once I realized the cost to my soul. I wanted out, Frannie. I swear to you, that's my reason for running away."

"Why'd you have to run away? Are you in danger from your own family?"

"Yes."

Her eyes widened as if she couldn't fathom such a thing, and he knew it was a lot to take in, especially for someone like Frannie, who'd never had to walk side by side with the devil.

She narrowed her gaze with dawning fear. "Your car…

did your family have something to do with your car landing in the lake?"

"I don't have proof, but I believe so."

She gasped. "I don't understand…why?"

He sighed, levering himself into the oversize reading chair. "You're going to want to sit down," he said, preparing to tell her the whole sordid story. "There's no happy ending to this story."

FRANNIE'S HEAD WAS SPINNING, and she felt spun on her axis.

Dante's story was something out of a movie—these things didn't happen to actual people, did they?

Everything Dante had been through—from losing his father and mother to being drawn in by the uncle now trying to kill him—was more than she could process in one breath. She took a long minute to try and sort the facts into manageable cubes, but tears threatened to fall as she failed miserably.

"How are you handling this? My family has its problems, but they seem minuscule in comparison to what you're dealing with. Oh, God, you must think I'm so naive for going on about my family drama when it doesn't even compare to what you're faced with."

"I've never thought you were naive—kind and compassionate—but never naive," he said, trying to make her feel better. "That's why I think you're incredible. That generous heart of yours is a beautiful thing, and your love has made me realize what I needed most in my life."

Frannie wiped at a tear tracking down her cheek. "My biggest fear after my breakup with my ex was finding someone like him who would break my heart by cheating on me." A small bubble of laughter erupted as she realized there were much worse things. "Instead, I fell in love with an international fugitive with a murderous family. I think that's much worse, don't you?"

He fell silent.

She stared at her hands, slipping into a dark place as her heart wept. What was she supposed to do? Break up with him when he needed someone who wasn't trying to kill him? But then, what did that mean for her? Was she in danger, too? "Is that why you kept asking me to go away for the weekend?" she asked.

He looked miserable—and scared—as he admitted, "I'm not sure if either of us are safe here."

Frannie gasped. "What do you mean?"

"I never should've encouraged anything between us, but I did. And in doing so, I selfishly put your life in danger. I can't take back what I've done but I can do everything in my power to keep you safe. I have enough money to take us anywhere in the world and I have contacts that can create a new identity—"

"No!" She didn't want to be someone else. She liked her life here in Owl Creek. "You can't ask me to change everything about my life in the blink of an eye and expect me to skip after you. Honestly, do you really think that's fair?"

"It's not fair at all," he agreed, his eyes flashing. "And I hate having to ask but the thought of you being hurt because of me—it's more than I can handle! I won't have it happen again!"

Again? "What do you mean?"

Dante rose sharply from the chair, startling her with the sudden movement. Tension radiated from his solid frame. She'd never seen him so worked up, and it was a little jarring. She'd only ever seen the calm, cool-headed man who always seemed to have quiet wisdom to share. Not this man who seemed eaten up by an internal fire he couldn't escape.

"My ex—Belinda—the one I don't like to talk about...

there's a reason I'm putting all my cards on the table so there's no more secrets between us. Are you ready for the full truth?"

"I think so," she answered, wary. *It gets worse?* In for a penny, in for a pound, as her grandmother used to say. "What happened to your ex?"

"Belinda was a top pediatric surgeon. Her skill was in her deft work on tiny babies. She had a gift that drew people from around the world to have her in the operating room. She could've handpicked any hospital on this planet as her primary residency, but she loved her home country and always wanted to remain in Italy."

"She sounds like a superstar," Frannie said, feeling insecure at an inappropriate moment. How could she possibly stack up against a résumé like that? Dante's ex probably looked like a supermodel, too.

Dante must've sensed her insecurity. He immediately soothed it in a way only he could. "She was incredible— but she wasn't you. Never forget that."

In that split second, Frannie felt a hot wave pass between them as if their chemistry couldn't be contained, even in moments such as this when the world seemed to be collapsing. A rush of powerful emotion nearly sent her to her knees.

As far as she knew, no one planned to fall in love—it just happened.

And sometimes, it happened with the person who seemed a lousy bet on paper. All the reasons to walk away were scrawled in big, bold letters, but she knew she wouldn't.

Couldn't.

She would stand by him. No matter what happened.

Even if that meant leaving behind everything she'd ever known.

"Tell me what happened to Belinda," she said bravely. "I need to know everything."

Dante nodded, understanding what was unspoken. His eyes watered, but he choked back the tears.

And then he held her hand and unloaded the most horrific story she'd ever heard. His voice broke at times as he recounted how he'd nursed Belinda back to health and then spirited her away when she could travel, leaving her in Switzerland to rebuild. How he'd been chased by the guilt he couldn't dodge.

She saw the pain in his eyes.

Felt the remorse.

And she knew that no matter who his family was, Dante was cut from a different cloth and would never do anything that led him down the same path. His only choice had been running, and she couldn't fault him for that.

Desperate times called for desperate measures, and it was easy to say but harder to follow through. Most people wouldn't have had the strength of character to do what Dante had done to protect himself and his loved ones, but Dante was one of a kind.

There was no way in hell she'd make him walk that path alone.

"I love you, Dante," she said, holding his gaze. "We'll figure this out together."

"Are you sure? Now is the time to cut your losses. I'll help you no matter what."

She heard the desperate note in his voice, battling a war she couldn't possibly understand, and it hurt her heart.

"I'm not going anywhere," she replied firmly. "But I think we should tell my brother and cousin Max. They might be able to help."

Dante shook his head, clearly opposed to that idea. "The fewer people I put in harm's way, the better. We need to keep our circle small. I know you're close to your family, but you have to trust me on this. Please keep this information between us."

Frannie didn't like it, but she agreed. *For the time being.* Everything was too new to start rocking the boat, but she knew Dante was too close to the situation to see that he couldn't do this alone.

Dante, relieved, pulled her close and sealed his mouth to hers in a passionate kiss that they usually reserved for private moments, away from public view.

But it was as if he wanted the world to know they belonged together. Frannie melted against him, loving how well they seemed to fit, but a chill slithered down her spine at the unpleasant sensation of being watched.

Maybe it was because they'd been so careful to keep their relationship private, or perhaps it was because a seed of paranoia had been planted about his family, but she couldn't escape the feeling that someone was watching.

And it scared her more than she wanted to admit.

Chapter Twenty-Four

It took some doing, but Frannie talked Dante into not doing anything rash until they'd had time to make a plan. For one, she couldn't skip town without making arrangements for her shop and at least talking to her mom about an extended vacation as a cover story.

Dante conceded, but he was understandably jumpy.

Even though she promised to keep the situation between them, Franny knew she would at least have to talk to Darla. Someone in her circle had to understand what was truly going on just in case things went south in a bad way. Plus, Darla was getting married soon, and it didn't seem fair to not let her know what was happening in case her maid of honor disappeared.

Darla showed up at the shop the next day with a frown. "Okay, you're going to have to explain that very cryptic voice mail you left because I can't make head or tail of what you said."

"Sorry about that. I was nervous about leaving too much detail on the message."

"Yeah, see, when you say things like that my anxiety just gets worse. What is going on?"

Frannie drew a deep breath, still unable to believe she was in the middle of something this complicated. She tried to prepare Darla. "I'm going to need you to suspend your disbelief and listen to what I have to say because I can guarantee you, you aren't going to believe me at first."

Darla's eyes widened with interest. "You've got my attention. Shoot."

With something this big, it was probably best to throw it all out there and sort the details later. "Dante is part of a dangerous wealthy family—not the mob—but rich and powerful enough to bend the rules to their benefit, and they're after him. His name is Dante Santoro, and we'll probably leave town soon. I wanted to let you know so that you don't worry."

Frannie realized Darla couldn't process all of that as fact because who could? These kinds of things didn't happen to ordinary people. Particularly people who lived in Owl Creek, a town known for its pristine lake and quaint downtown. Darla proved she was right with her reply. "I'm sorry, what?"

Frannie tried again. "I told you it was a lot. Here's the thing. Dante changed his name so he could get away from his family, but they may have found him already. Dante thinks they're the reason he ended up in the lake. They tried to kill him by cutting the brakes on his car."

"That *actually* happens?" Darla said, incredulous. "I thought that only happened in spy movies. I wouldn't even know how to find a brake line, much less cut one."

"You barely know where to put the gas in your car," Frannie quipped. "But I had the same reaction as you. I'm still having a hard time wrapping my head around everything, but it's very real—and very dangerous."

Even though Dante had asked Frannie to keep details private, she couldn't keep that intel from her best friend.

Frannie shared what had happened to Belinda and how

she was starting a new life in Switzerland, but not as a pediatric surgeon any longer.

Darla stared for a long moment, then snapped out of it and declared, "You have to break up with him."

"I'm not going to do that," Frannie said, shaking her head. "I love him."

"And I love strawberries but I'm deathly allergic and if I eat one, I'll most certainly die a horrible death. Sometimes we have to give up things that are bad for our health."

"It's not Dante's fault that his family is awful. He's trying to do the right thing."

"Yeah, and brownie points for his moral victory. But if you end up dead as collateral damage, I could not care less about his emotional growth. Catch my drift? His ex-girlfriend was beaten almost to death and then maimed for life. Dante's got bigger problems than most people and you're too sweet and loving to see that he's going to get you killed—and then if that happens, I'm going to have to go to prison for killing Dante. See how all of that is bad?"

Frannie loved Darla's bold declaration, but she recognized it for what it was—fear. "Nothing is going to happen to me. Dante is determined to keep me safe, which is why we probably have to leave Owl Creek."

"This is ridiculous. What are you even saying? Leave town with a guy who has killers after him? No, let *him* leave and have him send you a postcard when the heat dies down and you don't have to worry about eating a bullet during dinner."

It was sensible, but she knew she couldn't let Dante deal with this alone.

"If Tom were in the same situation, you wouldn't hesitate to do whatever you could to help."

"Tom would never be in a situation like this," Darla countered, shaking her head. "Tom lines up and color coordinates his socks. He would never end up on the run for any reason—and I like him that way. Come to think of it, your situation has me rethinking all the times I called him boring. I like boring."

"Yes, you love Tom. That's the point, Darla."

At that, Darla fell quiet.

"See? We do what we have to for the people we love—and I love Dante."

"Are you sure? You barely know him," Darla returned in a plaintive tone. "This is the premise of a true-crime documentary in the making. No one in their right mind would just leave everything behind for someone who's being chased by dangerous people. What can I do to change your mind?"

"Nothing."

Darla groaned. "This is a nightmare."

"It's not great," she agreed. "But I wanted someone in my circle to know in case things go south."

"Not to sound like a dick, but how are you going to be my maid of honor if you're fleeing the country? And what about your family? It's not like they're going to be fine with you disappearing. Hell, Max will have the FBI chasing after you and then your lover boy will have two people after him."

Frannie laughed, even though it wasn't funny, but it was because it was so Darla. "Yeah, about that… You might want to replace me in your wedding. As for my family, I'll think of something so they don't worry."

"You're irreplaceable."

Darla's deadpan answer was about more than the wedding, and Frannie's eyes teared up. "Nothing is going to happen to me." It was a promise she didn't have the right to offer because she didn't know what the future held, but Darla needed some reassurance, or she might fall apart.

"With any luck, the situation will resolve itself, and this will all be an unpleasant memory."

"Unpleasant is one word for it."

"I don't like what's happening either, but I can't ignore how I feel about him. This is the real deal—the kind of love that only comes once in a lifetime—and I'm not going to walk away. We need each other."

Darla sighed, giving up even though she didn't seem convinced. But at least she didn't keep pressing, and Frannie was grateful. She couldn't fight her best friend and still have the strength to be Dante's support.

The fact that Darla intuitively knew that was why they'd been best friends since the third grade.

They understood each other. They loved each other.

And that love was why Frannie had to tell her.

DANTE FELT LIGHTER but no less anxious. He had hated lying to Frannie—each time he saw that questioning look in her eyes, knowing she was sensing his dishonesty, he'd wanted to break down and lay it all on the line, but he'd known he couldn't.

Now that part was done. He'd told her everything—down to the grittiest detail—and she was determined to stand by his side, which humbled him in ways he couldn't even put into words.

No one had ever been so steadfast, so loyal, and he vowed to make sure she never had reason to question his integrity.

His phone rang, and he checked the caller ID this time before answering. It was Nick, his PI.

"Dante, I thought you might want to know…that guy you had me watching just got flagged on some suspicious purchases with his credit card. It could be nothing, but it was out of pocket enough to warrant a second look."

"Yeah? What kind of purchases?"

"Zip ties, chlorine bleach, ethanol and acetone, and an industrial-size bag of cloth towels. Purchased this morning."

He didn't like the sound of that. "Why would a gig driver need those chemicals?"

"He wouldn't. Unless he was planning to make home-made chloroform to knock out one of his passengers."

A warning bell went off in Dante's head, urging him to check on Frannie at the shop. "I have to go," he said abruptly, clicking off. He immediately rang Frannie. She picked up on the second ring, and relief followed. "Are you okay?"

"I'm fine," she said, chuckling quizzically. "You told me to act normal, so I'm just doing my usual shelving. Darla stopped by earlier but it's just me now."

"No customers in the shop?"

"No, it's nice and quiet. Gives me a chance to catch up on my paperwork. I was thinking of maybe asking Darla to cover the shop while we're gone on 'vacation.'"

"Yeah, sure, good idea," he said, distracted. He still had a bad feeling. "I think you should close early today."

"I can't do that. I have a shipment coming today."

"Frannie—"

"Oh! I gotta go, looks like someone's heading my way. I'll see you later. Let's have dinner with my mom tonight."

And then she clicked off like danger wasn't pressing in on them from all sides—and some danger she didn't even know was coming.

FRANNIE PLACED HER cell phone on the counter just as the front door opened and a man walked through. There was a tingle of recognition, but it took a minute for her to realize she was staring at Allen Burns. However, he didn't look like the same guy she'd shared a few classes with in college.

The years had been rough.

His reedy frame had become soft and doughy, his complexion splotchy and uneven, but his vibe threw her off the most.

Where he'd once been shy and quiet, preferring his plants to people, now there was a disordered air of chaos around him, an anger that pulsated beneath the surface of his seemingly approachable veneer.

Don't be so judgy, a voice admonished. Allen had spent his life being bullied by people who made assumptions. She couldn't do that to him, too.

"Allen? Oh, gosh, I almost didn't recognize you! How are you?" she asked, trying to be polite and engaging as she would with anyone who entered her store. "I haven't seen you since graduation. What have you been up to?"

"Frannie…it's so good to see you," Allen said, licking his lips and glancing around the shop. "This…uh, your place?"

"Yep. Bought and paid for—well, not exactly paid for yet, but I'm doing my best, despite the economy."

"You always did love books," he said, stepping a little closer in a way that made her twitchy. "Anyone else here?"

During her freshman year at Boise State, the campus had hosted a women's safety course with the cooperation of the local police. During one class, the instructor had brought a convicted rapist to talk about how he would pick his victims. He'd look for a woman alone, with hair in a ponytail or a single braid because it was easier to grab and pull the victim off-balance, and he'd look for someone who didn't make eye contact because it suggested a level of humility that he could subdue. But going above and beyond those practical tips, most of his victims shared a commonality— they ignored their intuition because they didn't want to come off as rude.

Frannie stepped back as if heading to her counter to grab the short stack of books waiting for her to shelve, her mind moving quickly. *Keep him talking.* Someone was bound to walk in at some point, and likely he'd leave. "So, what's new with you? What brings you to Owl Creek?"

"Where you going? No hug? I haven't seen you in ages, and you're treating me like I got the plague." His tone was joking, but there was an odd gleam in his eye, and his left hand had moved to his jean pocket.

"Actually, I've got a little summer cold. I better keep my distance, or you'll end up with the sniffles, too."

His gaze narrowed with cold suspicion. "Oh, I get it. You're too good to say hello to an old friend now that you've got your fancy boyfriend."

Frannie stilled. How did he know about Dante? "Allen... how'd you know I was engaged?" she asked, stretching the truth a bit.

Allen ignored the question and slowly advanced toward her. "You know, I always thought you were better than most girls. Always so nice. You never made me feel like a freak like the other girls. I liked you."

"I liked you, too, Allen," she said, careful to keep her tone soft and calming, but her heart raced. "But I'm confused by how you knew I was engaged. I haven't seen you in years."

"I've seen you."

She swallowed. "Oh yeah? When?"

He ignored that question, too, but added something else that froze her blood. "I know what you like. More than he ever could. I know you, Frannie."

"Allen, you're starting to scare me. Tone it down, okay?"

"You like to sleep naked with the ceiling fan on medium and only a light sheet for when it gets too breezy."

"Allen!" She felt exposed. "Have you been watching me?"

"You like to eat dairy when you know you shouldn't because it hurts your stomach something awful, yet you do it anyway. I get it, I do things I shouldn't, too. But I can take care of you, make sure you stop doing things that aren't good for you."

"I don't need anyone to take care of me. I need you to get a hold of yourself and stop acting like this or I will call the police."

"I can't have you do that," he said, moving with a swiftness she hadn't realized possible to jerk her toward him. She slammed into him with an *ooof*, and something acrid and chemically pungent went over her mouth and nose as Allen held her with an iron grip.

Instinct made her scream, but she realized too late she should've held her breath and stomped on his instep instead. Her head started pounding as the chemical smell choked out her breath. No matter how she struggled, Allen's grip held her tight. Her fingernails dug into his arm, but he didn't waver. Within a few minutes, her muscles lost their strength, her vision started to blacken, and she slumped in his arms, passed out cold.

Chapter Twenty-Five

Dante jumped out of the old truck and ran into the shop just in time to see a thick, doughy man grunting with the difficulty of dragging Frannie's inert body out the shop's back door. Sprinting toward them, he caught the man off guard and punched him hard, causing him to drop Frannie and stumble back.

He grabbed the man by his shirt and drove his fist into his face again, breaking his nose. Shaking him like a rag doll, he yelled, "What did you do to her?"

The man glared up at him through the blood, bubbles of red snot dribbling from his nose and mixing with the drool. "She was supposed to be mine," he said with hot resentment. "Not yours. You took her from me!"

"You're a nutjob," Dante said, shoving him with disgust. The man tried to roll away and scramble to his feet, but Dante drove his foot into the man's soft gut and sent him sprawling, gasping for air. "Don't move," he ordered in a thunderous roar, grabbing the first thing he could find to tie the man's hands together. He remembered seeing Frannie stash a roll of duct tape in a utility box beneath the counter. Winding the tape around the man's hands and legs so tight it probably cut the circulation off, he called 911 while checking on Frannie.

She was still breathing, slow and steady. Just as Nick had surmised, the asshole had made his own chloroform. Dante could only imagine what he'd had in mind for Frannie once he got her loaded into his car. He had to stop thinking about the what-ifs, or else he might do something he regretted.

Picking her up gently, he carried her to the oversize reading chair that was her favorite and gently stroked her face, trying to wake her up.

Within a minute, Owl Creek PD showed up with lights and sirens. Frannie's brother was first on the scene. He quickly saw Frannie unconscious and started yelling, but Dante cut him off. "The man you want is behind the counter, near the back door. I've got him tied up with duct tape. I think he used chloroform on her."

"Get a medic in here!" Fletcher yelled before moving toward the back where Dante had left the man trussed up like a Christmas turkey.

Paramedics poured into the building, and Dante stepped out of their way while they checked her vitals.

"BP is stable, but her oxygen is low. Let's get her loaded up for transport," the paramedic instructed as he fixed an oxygen mask over her face.

Another officer bagged the cloth that the man had dropped on the ground when he tried to drag Frannie's body out the back door, and Fletcher confirmed it was chloroform. "Who the hell is this guy? Is he one of yours?" he asked Dante, glaring with accusation. "I told you if you hurt my sister—"

"He's a guy Frannie went to school with at Boise State," Dante barked to shut Fletcher up, following paramedics as they loaded her onto a stretcher. "His name is Allen Burns. Look him up. I'm heading to the hospital with Frannie."

He didn't explain to Fletcher how he knew. That wasn't

his problem, and he sure as hell wasn't staying behind while the ambulance took Frannie away.

When she woke up, he wanted to be by her side.

But Fletcher wasn't finished. "Hold up, where the hell you think you're going? We're not done here."

"The hell we aren't. That ambulance is taking the woman I love, and I'll be damned if I'm going to sit around and wait for your permission to be there when she wakes up. If you want to talk later, fine, but for now, I'm following that ambulance."

The two men had a short stare-down, but Fletcher grudgingly backed down when he realized Dante wasn't playing chicken with him. "Fine, go. But there will be questions later."

"Fine," he growled back, jumped into the truck and chased after the ambulance. All he could say was that if that asshole had somehow hurt Frannie with his bathtub chemistry set, he'd break all the laws to make sure he never had use of his fingers again.

He pulled into the parking lot and sprinted into the lobby, bypassed the registration and went straight to the ER bay. A flabbergasted receptionist hurried after him, screeching about calling security, but Dante wouldn't let anyone stop him from seeing Frannie.

He found Frannie's bed just as her eyes were opening sluggishly. One nurse was finishing a blood draw and another was adjusting her oxygen flow. The doctor, startled by the commotion Dante had created, saw the concern on Dante's face and waved off the security team that had started piling in after him. "I'm assuming you know Frannie Colton," the doctor said.

"Yes, she's my girl," he answered, wishing he could say she was his wife. "Is she going to be okay?"

"Your name?"

"Dante Sinclair," he said, using his fake identity. The fewer people knowing his real name, the better.

Frannie weakly pulled at the oxygen mask so she could speak, and both men swiveled to protest, but she batted at both of them with a frown. "My head feels like it's full of rocks, and my mouth tastes like a stinky sock smells."

Dante's sudden relief was palpable as he leaned forward and kissed her forehead. "There's my brave girl. How are you feeling?"

"Not great," she answered, looking to the doctor. "Hi, Doc, am I going to live?"

The doctor chuckled, shaking his head. "It'll take more than a clumsy chemical attempt to drag you down. We're running some blood tests to check for any other possible toxins, but your oxygen levels are already returning to normal. I think you're going to be fine, aside from a monster headache. We'll get you some Tylenol for the pain."

But Frannie declined, saying, "I think I've had enough chemicals in my body for the day." To Dante, she said, "I'd rather just go home and lie down in a dark room, sleep it off."

"I will happily arrange that," he said, but then people he could only assume were more family anxiously burst into the room.

Two women who looked similar enough ignored Dante and went straight to Frannie.

"Oh my God, Fletcher group-texted us to let us know someone had attacked you in the store," the first one said, shocked. "What happened?"

Frannie sighed, clearly still processing what had happened, but she took a minute to make quick introductions. "Dante, these are my sisters, Ruby and Hannah, and yes, I was attacked by a guy I used to know. If it weren't for Dante... I don't know what he had planned."

The women spun on their heels to rush Dante, crushing him in a surprise hug that startled him. "Thank you!" Ruby said, squeezing him hard. "You saved our baby sister. You're a freaking hero."

The one named Hannah wiped away tears. "I'm literally in shock right now. How does something like this happen in our little town?"

"He's been watching me for a while, I guess," Frannie said, swallowing. "He...he...ugh, he watched me sleep. I feel so damn violated right now and icky. Like my skin is crawling at the thought."

Dante wanted to punch the man all over again. Speaking of... "I should probably talk to your brother and give him an official statement. I didn't give him an option of holding me at the scene, but now that I know you're safe..."

Frannie understood immediately, nodding. "Yes, please go talk to my brother. Let him know what happened. Ruby or Hannah can take me home. I'll see you back at my place when you're done."

It was a solid plan, even though he hated the idea of leaving her side. However, seeing her with her sisters, he knew she was in good hands.

"All right, but only because I don't want your brother showing up at your place trying to put me in handcuffs for refusing to answer questions at the scene."

"Fletcher can be stubborn like that," Ruby agreed. "Don't worry, we'll get her home safely."

"Nice to meet you," Hannah said. "Though I wish it were under better circumstances."

"Yes, indeed," he murmured. Stealing another glance at Frannie as her sister smoothed the hair back from her crown with such love, he suffered a moment of envy for never knowing what that was like.

That's how a family is supposed to act with each other.

Backing away, he left Frannie in the able care of her sisters and headed to the police station.

FRANNIE LOVED HER SISTERS, but she was bothered by the odd expression on Dante's face before he slipped out. Before she could dwell too deeply, Ruby was peppering her with questions.

"Okay, I need details. What the hell?"

Frannie knew they wouldn't rest until she spilled the beans, so she drew a deep breath and shared every detail, down to the weird tingle in her gut that warned her that something was wrong.

"It's so strange. At first I was really happy to see him because I haven't seen him since graduation and I thought we were pretty close, but there was just something weird about his vibe, the energy was off. I think it was something in his eyes. I don't know, but I definitely listened to my intuition, and I tried to put space between us. Unfortunately, I did not do so well at remembering to hold my breath when he put the cloth over my face. Within minutes I was blacking out. If Dante hadn't showed up when he did, I don't know what would've happened."

Ruby shuddered. "I don't even want to think about it, but obviously he was up to no good."

Hannah looked disturbed. "Why were you friends with him in the first place?"

Frannie frowned. "Because I don't like it when people are bullied just because they're different. He wasn't like this when we were in school. When I knew him, he was quiet and shy, and really sweet. I don't know what happened to him between graduation and now but he's definitely not the same person."

Hannah nodded but switched gears. "And who is your

knight in shining armor? The chemistry between you is obviously not platonic, so…new boyfriend?"

"Um, yes," Frannie admitted. "We were taking it slow so I didn't want to prematurely share that I was seeing someone, but we've recently agreed to make it official." *Right before planning to skip town because his family is trying to kill him.* Better to leave that part out. "His name is Dante Sinclair and I'm crazy about him."

"Well, he saved your life so he's automatically my favorite person right now," Ruby said.

Frannie smiled, wishing they had more time to get to know Dante under better circumstances. "He's really great," she murmured.

"I definitely get a better vibe from him than your last guy," Hannah admitted. "I mean, I always wanted to be supportive but your ex…seemed smarmy from the start. Good riddance to that guy. Tell us more about Dante. That accent is so yummy."

"He's…um, from Italy." Maybe she shouldn't have shared that? It was hard to censor herself with her sisters but denying the obvious would've been a red flag. "And yes, that accent was the first thing to grab my attention. Followed by his obvious good looks," she added with a blush.

"Can't blame you. Who isn't a sucker for a good accent?" Ruby said. "Well, it's official, you have to bring him to family dinner soon. Mom is going to want to meet him, and it sounds like he and Fletcher have gotten off to a rocky start? So, sooner rather than later would be great so we can help smooth out any bumps."

Rocky wasn't the word for it, Frannie thought, shifting with discomfort. Fletcher knew the whole truth about Dante, and she hoped he kept that information private.

She was nervous about Fletcher and Dante talking without a buffer, but she could only hope her brother kept a level head and Dante didn't say or do anything to make Fletcher regret trusting him.

Chapter Twenty-Six

Dante walked into the small police station, determined to resolve this without creating more problems between himself and Frannie's brother. She was so close to her family he didn't want to become a wedge, even though he knew it was probably inevitable.

They weren't going to be happy when he and Frannie split town. He would look like the bad guy, and there was no getting around that.

But he didn't have to hasten that opinion by creating friction with Fletcher.

He checked in at the front desk, but Fletcher saw him come in and waved him over to his desk.

"You showed up," Fletcher said with surprise, hitting him with the full measure of suspicion he probably deserved.

"I told you I would."

"Well, forgive me if I don't exactly trust your word right now," Fletcher said. "Have a seat."

Dante bit his tongue and levered himself into the uncomfortable metal chair opposite Fletcher. "I'll tell you everything I know."

"You're damn right you will," Fletcher said. "Start at the beginning. How'd you know that guy was at the shop?"

"I didn't." If he told Fletcher that his PI had been following the guy, he'd ask why and that would open a can of worms. Instead, he said, "I usually stop in to see Frannie at some point during the day. It's part of our routine."

Fletcher didn't seem to like any mention of Dante and Frannie's relationship, which made Dante wonder if he'd been this protective when her ex-boyfriend was out there cheating on her or if he was reserving this attitude just for Dante.

"Then what happened?"

"I saw a guy dragging Frannie down the short hallway to the back door and chased him down, punched him in the face and then subdued him. After I realized he wasn't going anywhere, I checked on Frannie while calling 911. Then you guys arrived. That's the long and short of it."

"How'd you know it was a guy from Frannie's college?"

"She'd mentioned him."

"Did you know him?"

"No."

"Then how'd you know it was him?"

My PI told me. "A hunch."

"Guess it was a pretty solid hunch."

"Guess so."

"Also pretty lucky."

Dante leaned forward, finished with the tough cop routine when he wasn't the enemy. "Look, we can be enemies if you want but it'll just make things harder on Frannie and I don't think either of us want that. I love your sister. Seeing that asshole try to drag her unconscious body down a hallway made me see red. I've never been a violent man, but in that moment, I was willing to go to hell if he hurt her. I'm just grateful that I caught him in time before he managed to get her into his car."

At Dante's blunt statement, Fletcher stilled, as if the importance of what mattered just slammed him upside the temple. All this male posturing was immaterial after realizing they'd all come too close to losing the woman they all loved.

That was the thing, Frannie was a gem. She was kind, compassionate, funny and wise—it was hard to find anyone who didn't find her delightful—which made him feel ugly for selfishly needing her to leave with him.

Fletcher exhaled a heavy breath, frowning as he admitted, "I get that you care about my sister. That much I can see is true. But I can't wrap my head around the other stuff. I'm an officer of the law—integrity matters—and when someone's guilty of lying about something big, chances are, they'll lie about something small. And I make it a point to avoid entertaining liars in my life. But when my baby sister loves someone who's admitted to lying…it puts me in a bad spot. Do you get what I'm saying?"

It was the first honest dialogue between him and Fletcher, and Dante sensed taking advantage of the fragile moment was necessary. "I don't blame you. If I had a sister, I'd feel similarly protective. You already know my family is problematic and I was trying to distance myself from their influence. But it doesn't wipe away the fact that I did lie— to many people for many reasons—and I understand your knee-jerk reaction to keep Frannie away from me."

"Great. So at least we understand each other. But where does that leave the situation?"

The situation would resolve itself as soon as he and Frannie left town, but for now, he wanted justice. "How about we focus on the guy who tried to kidnap Frannie? We can figure out the rest later."

"The investigation is just starting but we've got a detective chasing down the man's background, etc. He's in custody and that's where he'll stay until he's arraigned."

"Unless he posts bail."

"Not likely. Frannie used to babysit for the judge's family. Once this case crosses his desk, he'll set the bail as high as possible and I doubt the guy is rolling in a family trust. He can cool his jets in a jail cell until then."

That was good news, at least. Small-town connections could be a blessing at times.

"If you're running from your family, my guess is you're not planning to stay in Owl Creek for long. What happens then? You gonna break my sister's heart when you bail? Or are you trying to talk my sister into bailing with you?"

The man was too clever. He saw more than he shared and used his "country cop" routine to create the illusion of a dull-minded man—which he was not.

When Dante remained silent, Fletcher shook his head. "Look, man, I'll level with you. Frannie is an adult and she's capable of making her own decisions. But her heart is soft, possibly too soft for what you've got planned and I don't want to see her get hurt. Understand? So, if you're planning to leave town…do it when she's at the shop and just go. Let her move on with her life if you can't offer her a real chance at happiness. Because my sister deserves more than scraps from a man who can't offer nothing but pain and heartache."

Dante swallowed, knowing that Fletcher was right. What was he offering Frannie? Asking her to leave everything she knew for an uncertain future as he ran from his family, leapfrogging from one town to another, only one step ahead of his uncle each day? Was that fair?

That was no life for a woman like her. She deserved the best kind of life where she was cherished *and* safe.

"I would never hurt her," Dante said, though the promise tasted hollow.

"Maybe not intentionally, but you already admitted you're on the run. I don't see how this ends any way but bad."

"I never meant to fall in love with her," he said as if that improved the situation. "I tried to keep some distance between us."

Fletcher seemed sympathetic, saying with a knowing glance, "Oh, I know Frannie can be persistent when she gets something in her head—trust me, I know—but sometimes she doesn't know what kind of trouble she's stepping into because she only sees the good in people. It's one of her best qualities but it sure keeps her family on their toes."

Dante chuckled, Fletcher's words giving him a rare glimpse into what may have been young Frannie's life—protected by a wall of siblings, all the while skipping right into trouble without a second thought. "That's probably what drew that creep straight to her," Dante murmured.

"Likely. Frannie always did love championing an underdog."

Was that what he was to Frannie? The underdog in her eyes? Someone she needed to champion?

He ought to be the one being the champion for her.

Again, he was struck by the fear that he was repeating a loop from his parents.

His father had dragged his mother down a path littered with thorns, not realizing how each step left his mother cut and bruised until she was willing to do anything to be safe again.

The desk phone rang, and Fletcher gestured for Dante to hold up a minute, then answered. His expression darkened as he listened, his jaw hardening. "You're kidding me," he said, shaking his head. Blowing a long breath, he said, "Thanks for letting me know, man. Keep me posted." He hung up and turned to Dante. "That was the detective assigned to Frannie's case."

Dante waited, instantly tense. "What did he find out?"

"That was one helluva hunch," he repeated, eyeing Dante with fresh speculation. "The detective just found a fortified room in Allen Burns's house. Looks like he was planning for a reluctant guest."

"What does that mean?" Dante asked.

"It means that man planned on kidnapping Frannie and holding her hostage for a long time. The sick bastard had shackles bolted into the wall and a bucket in the corner. Holy hell…"

Just like Fletcher, Dante reeled from that intel. He wouldn't have known to get to the shop if he'd missed Nick's call. A delay of even a few minutes could have doomed Frannie to a nightmarish hellscape.

"Tell me how you knew."

Dante didn't want to lie to Fletcher. He was walking the razor's edge with the truth, and it didn't matter that he had a good reason—because more lies just made him look more guilty than he already did in Fletcher's eyes.

"Take a walk with me," Dante said, rising.

Fletcher frowned but agreed, motioning toward the back door. He punched in the security code and stepped outside the building. Once alone in the vehicle yard, Fletcher asked, "Okay, what's with the field trip?"

"My dishonesty has only ever been grounded in necessity. The fewer people who know what's going on, the safer they'll be. You're Frannie's favorite brother. I didn't want to put you in a dangerous position, but it looks like there's no way to fully clear the air between us without the full truth."

"Seems about right," Fletcher agreed, waiting. "So what's the full truth?"

"I knew about Allen Burns because I had my PI looking into him when Frannie started getting weird flower deliveries."

"Go on."

"First, it was a bouquet delivered to her shop. She thought they were from me. When I told her I hadn't sent the flowers, we tried to find out who sent them, but they were sent anonymously through an internet company using a local florist. Frannie waved it off, thinking it was a harmless mistake or maybe even from one of her friends who thought it might be funny to prank her. I didn't find the humor and wanted her to report it, but she said she didn't want to put more on your plate given what your family has been going through."

"That's Frannie, always looking out for everyone else."

"Then, after spending the day on the lake, we got back to her place and there was a single flower laid on her pillow, deliberately placed there for her to find. That was the final straw for me. I didn't want her staying alone after that, but she still didn't want to make a report."

"Damn it, Frannie," Fletcher swore under his breath. "Yeah, those were definite red flags. I knew that was a mistake but Frannie can be real stubborn when she wants to be."

"Well, hindsight and all that. Now we know Allen was the one stalking her, waiting for the right moment to grab her."

Fletcher nodded. "So, why the secrecy? Why'd we have to come outside for you to tell me this?"

"There's more."

Fletcher braced himself. "All right, go ahead."

"The reason my PI was looking into Burns was to either confirm or rule him out. The thing is, Owl Creek isn't safe anymore—for me or Frannie. After my brake line was cut—"

"Hold up, there hasn't been a report completed yet about

your car. How do you know it wasn't just a faulty manufacturer issue?"

"Because my PI got a hold of the mechanic shop contracted to go over the vehicle and there was a clear cut in the line. It was deliberately sabotaged. There's only one reason that could happen and it has everything to do with my family. They won't stop until they get what they want."

"What do they want, exactly?"

"Either I come home with my tail between my legs and agree to rejoin the Santoro family or die. There are no in-betweens with my uncle."

Fletcher whistled low. "And I thought *my* dad was a prick. Your uncle sounds like a peach."

"Yeah, that's one word for him. But my point is, he won't stop. Not until he gets what he wants."

"What's stopped him to this point?"

"Aside from the fact that I keep staying one step ahead? I have something of great value to him with the power to destroy the Santoro reputation. My uncle will do anything to get that piece of leverage back."

"I'm dying to know what it is that you've got but my sense of self-preservation keeps my curiosity in check. All I'm gonna say is, I hope you have it in a safe place."

"I do."

Fletcher sighed, shaking his head as if unsure what to do with all that information, but at least he'd lost that suspicion in his stare. That was something.

"Okay, here's the deal," Fletcher said after a pause. "I don't know why—and I hope it doesn't bite me in the ass—but I'll take a chance and trust you're being truthful this time. I don't know how to solve your problem with your family. But I can tell you if you want to have a life with my sister, you'd better find a solution more solid than being on the run until the end of your days, because Frannie isn't cut out for that life."

Dante knew that. God, he knew.

All he could say was, "I'm working on it," because it was the truth, but even Dante knew that wasn't nearly good enough.

Chapter Twenty-Seven

Frannie finished getting dressed. She was folding her hospital gown neatly when her mother's voice nearly made all three Colton sisters jump like guilty schoolchildren caught sneaking candy from the teacher's desk.

"Francesca!"

"Mom!" Frannie's hand flew to her chest to keep it from plopping from her sternum. "You scared the crap out of me."

To her shock, Jenny pulled Frannie straight to her for a tight hug as if she were terrified to let go. "I just heard what happened." She released Frannie only to glare at her other two daughters. "And why did I have to hear about it from Hettie Long, the biggest gossip in town, while picking up a package at the post office? Hmm? Neither of you could've picked up the phone and let me know what happened to my youngest daughter? Honestly, shame on you both."

"Mom, it happened so fast... I was going to call but I thought maybe it was something Frannie should tell you in person," Ruby said, looking to her sisters for help. "It wasn't like we weren't going to tell you."

Frannie came to Ruby's rescue. "Beyond a nasty headache and the sudden urge to take some self-defense classes, I'm fine. Don't be mad at Ruby and Hannah."

"Yeah, don't be mad at us," Hannah piped in.

"I'm not mad, I'm just…gosh darn it, Francesca, don't you ever worry me like that again!"

And then Frannie saw the misplaced anger for what it truly was—fear. She swallowed, softening. "Mama, I'm okay and the guy responsible is sitting in jail. Don't worry, crisis averted."

A tear escaped Jenny's eye, and she wiped at it quickly, nodding. "Yes, of course. I'm just rattled, is all. Hettie made it sound so…" she huffed a short breath, looking for clarification "…well, dramatic."

"To be fair, it was kinda dramatic," Ruby said. "Some weirdo tried to kidnap Frannie by knocking her out with chloroform."

Frannie swallowed, flushing with the terrible memory. "Yeah, definitely in my top three most horrible experiences. Zero stars—I do not recommend."

"This isn't funny. Don't you dare make jokes," Jenny scolded with an appalled expression. "This kind of thing isn't a laughing matter. Who is this man who rescued you? I need to personally thank him."

Oh, boy, she thought introducing Dante to her mom would go a lot differently, but there was no escaping the moment. "Mom, I would love for you to meet Dante. He's my, um, boyfriend."

Jenny's eyes widened. "Boyfriend? You're seeing someone?"

"That's what she just said," Hannah quipped.

"You pipe down. I'm not in the mood for any sass," Jenny returned sharply.

Hannah shared a look with Ruby and said, "Well, if there's no sass allowed, I'm out because that's pretty much what I'm made of." Despite her statement, she brushed Jenny's cheek with a quick kiss and made her exit. But not before making a telephone gesture to Frannie, mouthing, "Call me," and blowing her an air kiss.

"Good going, Mom, you chased off Hannah," Ruby said dryly. "Are you happy?"

Jenny waved off Ruby's comment, more concerned with Frannie. "Darling, are you sure you're okay?"

"I'm fine."

Ruby looked at her watch. "Mom, if you want to drive Frannie home, I'll go back to the clinic."

Jenny shook her head. "I wish I could but I'm filling in for a night-shift nurse tonight. I have a private patient in Connors."

"Travel nursing now?" Frannie asked, surprised.

"Only here and there. I'm only doing this as a personal favor for a friend. If I could cancel I would. I don't think you should be alone."

"I won't be alone," she assured her mom, returning to the subject of Dante. "My knight in shining armor will be with me and he won't let anything happen."

"He stays the night?" Jenny asked, mildly troubled, as if Frannie hadn't lived with her ex-boyfriend before he became a cheating turd. "Francesca, is that wise? How well do you know this man?"

"I know him well enough to know that he's the real deal and I think I'm going to marry him. Don't worry, Mom, you'll love him. He's terrific."

Jenny looked like she didn't know what to say—caught between gratitude for Dante saving her daughter's life and the discomfort of acknowledging her daughter had an adult sex life—but she accepted Frannie's decision. She looked at Ruby. "You've met this man?"

"Yes. Today, actually. He's really good-looking," Ruby said with an approving wink at Frannie.

"That's the least important thing," Jenny said, dismissing Ruby's assessment. "Character matters more than what's on the outside."

"Yes, because character was what you were most concerned with when you met Dad," Ruby retorted, calling Jenny out for her hypocrisy.

Jenny had the grace to blush as she settled her purse more securely on her shoulder, preparing to leave. "Please take it easy. You've been chemically assaulted. You need to rest."

"I will," Frannie promised.

"I'll expect to meet this knight at Sunday dinner, yes?"

"Can't wait."

Jenny kissed Frannie on the cheek, then Ruby, and left.

Ruby exhaled a long breath, shaking her head. "Will I ever understand our mother?"

"I don't think any of us will. It's part of her charm—the mystery."

"Is that what that's called?" Ruby pretended to consider Frannie's answer, then remarked, "No, I think it's called 'emotionally distant.'"

"Cut her some slack, Ruby. She's going through a lot. Hell, I think we're all going through a lot."

"Yeah, but you officially win with the 'almost kidnapped' thing. No one else had that on their Bingo card. You're so damn competitive," Ruby teased, poking at Frannie gently. "Okay, let's get out of here."

"Sounds good to me. Can we get a milkshake on the way home? I'm craving sugar."

"Anything you want, sissy."

Frannie smiled, refusing to let any bit of sadness pull at her knowing that she had no idea if Sunday dinner would happen. For all she knew, Dante would have them on the road before the weekend hit.

And she had mixed feelings about that.

She loved Dante—but she loved her family, too.

Fate was cruel to make her choose who she loved more.

DANTE FINISHED WITH FLETCHER, still at odds at how easily the tables might've turned the opposite way, and the tension cording his shoulders made him want to punch something. The fact that Frannie had been in danger was more than he could stomach.

He loved her more than anyone.

It was an odd thing to love another human being more than yourself. He thought he'd known true love with Belinda, but now, he knew what he'd felt with Belinda had only been a test run for the real thing.

He'd always care for Belinda, but his feelings for Frannie made him want things he had no business daring to dream about.

Marriage. Kids. A home.

None of that was in his future—even with Frannie by his side, he couldn't give her those things.

It wouldn't be fair to any children they might bring into this world.

But Frannie as a mother? His heart stuttered as fresh longing made the pain of future loss worse.

If he weren't such a bastard, he'd walk away now, but he couldn't.

He'd do anything to make her happy, but it would always be temporary, with a life on the run.

What was he doing?

What was he asking of her?

To leave everything she knew? To go where?

He didn't have the goddamn answers, and it killed him that he couldn't offer much more than his body at night and a promise that he would love her forever, even if he couldn't provide the beautiful life she deserved.

Detouring sharply, he ran into the local florist shop and purchased their biggest bouquet. The last time Frannie had received flowers was from that lunatic. He wanted her to have something beautiful from him to wipe away the terrible memory.

His cell rang. He picked up as soon as he saw it was Nick.

"They have him in custody. Thank you," he said with gratitude. "If it weren't for your call…" He didn't like to finish the thought. It tortured him enough. "Anyway, I appreciate your diligence."

"I'm glad it all worked out," Nick said, switching gears quickly. "I got something you're going to want to know. It's about your parents."

"What is it?"

"On a hunch, I did a deep dive into your mother's finances before she died. I found something that you might find upsetting."

Dante braced himself. "Go on."

"I think your mother had a relationship with your uncle long before your father died."

"What do you mean?"

"I found deposits going back two years from an international bank account in an account only registered to your mother. I traced the deposits, and they are registered to an account owned by your uncle. Do you know of any reason why your uncle would be sending your mother money?"

He didn't, but he was beginning to realize his mother had many secrets.

Was there anything from his childhood that rang true anymore?

His father had been troubled, but he always assumed it was caused by the burden of staying on the run.

Now he wondered if his father had known that his wife regretted choosing a life with him.

Adult relationships were complex, but in his young heart, he'd just wanted his parents to love each other as they once had.

Too bad it didn't always work out that way.

With both of his parents gone, only one person could answer his questions—but even when he was on good terms with his uncle, Lorenzo had refused to answer anything about the past.

Particularly about his brother.

Dante didn't know how to think about any of this anymore.

"Thank you," he said, needing to think. "I'll be in touch."

He clicked off and headed to Frannie's.

But as he pulled onto the street, he saw a car he didn't recognize parked in the driveway.

Perhaps Ruby had stayed until he returned?

His gut tingled in warning. Something felt off.

The old truck rumbled to a stop, and he left the flowers behind until he could ensure that all was well.

His paranoia was on full alert.

He couldn't explain it, but each step closer to the front door filled him with cold dread.

It was probably one of her many family members, he tried to reason, but as he opened the front door, he realized his first instinct had been right.

His uncle's men had found him.

And they were screwed.

The situation had just escalated to panic, and he didn't know how to save Frannie.

Time to find a way.

Chapter Twenty-Eight

Frannie waved as Ruby pulled out of her driveway and disappeared. Her stomach was full of vanilla milkshake, and her headache had subsided slightly, but there remained a dull ache that she assumed sleep would take care of.

As she watched Ruby drive away, she noted how right Dante was about her neighborhood. It really was a ghost town of empty houses. She'd never noticed before, but now she felt suddenly insecure. Letting her blinds down, she went to lock the front door, hoping Dante would show up soon.

Don't be a ninny, she told herself when goose bumps rioted along her forearm for no good reason. Except...all those times when she'd talked herself down in the past and felt watched, it had been valid because Allen *had* been watching.

She still couldn't shake the heebie-jeebies knowing that Allen had watched her sleep, had seen her naked, peeping through her bedroom window while she slept.

Like she'd told her sisters, the man who'd walked into her shop hadn't been the man she'd befriended all those years ago. What had happened to curdle an otherwise nice man? Human psychology had always fascinated her, but she hadn't wanted to face a genuinely disturbed person like she had today.

Rubbing her arms briskly, suffering a chill even though it was warm outside, she couldn't shake her jumpiness. She headed to the kitchen for a glass of water, her mouth still tasting like she'd drunk a chemical martini. But before she got there, a large, square-shaped man stepped into view, shocking the sense out of her.

Before she could scream, an arm clamped around her throat and cut off her airway like an iron bar was pressing against her windpipe. "No screaming," a voice instructed in a thick Italian accent that left no room for misunderstanding. "I can snap your neck before you take another breath," he warned.

I'm having the worst day of my life, she thought desperately. Surely there was some universal rule that you couldn't face mortal peril twice in one day?

"Stop wriggling and I'll let you breathe."

Compelling offer. She stopped struggling, and the grip around her neck loosened, allowing her to draw a gasping breath.

The man from the kitchen gestured for his accomplice to bring Frannie to the dining room. She was forcibly shoved into a chair, her hands and feet tied tightly, while he roughly emptied her purse on the kitchen table, pawing through her belongings as if he had the right.

"I don't have any money," she said, pretending to be ignorant of who they were.

He ignored her, grabbing her cell phone and pulling the SIM card to snap it in half before tossing the remnants to the floor.

Frannie cried in outrage, "Hey! That phone is new!" but he didn't seem to care about personal property. As she started to call him out, he pulled a gun from his back waistband, and her rebuke died on her tongue.

He checked his watch as if he had more pressing things to

do than terrorize small-town bookstore owners, and asked sharply, "When will Mr. Santoro arrive?"

"Um, who?" Frannie feigned confusion. It was a long shot, but Frannie wasn't above trying every angle she could think of to buy time or delay a truly awful end. "I don't know—"

"Your lover, Dante," the man cut in, annoyed with her clumsy attempt at deception. She'd make a terrible spy. It always looked so much easier in the movies. Also, she wished she'd paid better attention to how to escape a dangerous situation. "We know he stays with you every night. When will he be here?"

"And how would you know that?" she asked, wrinkling her nose. "Are you some kind of pervert? Were you peeping through the windows, too?"

"Answer the question."

"I don't know," she lied, wishing he hadn't broken her phone. Although she wasn't sure how she could warn Dante away, given her current situation.

"Have you ever experienced the exquisite agony of toothpicks shoved beneath the nail bed?"

She felt the blood drain from her face. "Um, can't say that I have. Doesn't sound like something I would be into. You do you, though. I try not to judge."

"You think you can joke your way out of this?" the man asked, unamused.

"Judging by the stone-cold look on your face, probably not," she admitted. "But you can't blame me for trying. Sometimes a good laugh can ease the tension." *And I tend to ramble when I'm nervous.*

"My patience is growing thin. When is Mr. Santoro coming?"

She could play stupid for a few more minutes or just cut to the chase. "You're... Dante's family?" she pretend-guessed.

A dark brow went up. "Family? No. Hired by the family to bring Dante home. His family is quite concerned about his absence."

That's a crock of crap. "In my experience, family doesn't try to force members to come home if they don't want to."

The man shrugged. "Different kind of family."

Frannie bit her lip before asking, "Are you going to kill me?" Might as well end the suspense.

"Depends."

The simple answer belied the horror of the moment. Her life meant next to nothing to this man. She was no more significant than an ant beneath his shoe. *Well, screw him.* If she were going down, she'd go down without begging. Hopefully, the end was fast and didn't make a huge mess. Lifting her chin, she said, "I believe in reincarnation. I plan to come back as something with very sharp teeth and will hunt you down like a monster out of a horror movie. Just letting you know—so choose wisely."

"Either you are mentally unhinged, or you have a lot of spirit. I cannot decide which."

"And I can't decide if that's a compliment," she returned, refusing to be cowed, even though she was trembling inside. The thing about facing down your potential death twice in one day, it did something to you. Maybe she was still reeling from the chemicals in her system, but she felt oddly detached from everything, which gave her a different level of clarity bordering on recklessness. "Dante is a good man. He doesn't want any part of the Santoro legacy. Why can't you leave him alone?"

"Not my business. I was hired to bring him home. Nothing was said about a plus-one, so either shut up or offer something useful."

"You're a bully," Frannie muttered but pressed her lips together when the man shot her a dangerous look. She sensed she'd end up in a ditch if she pushed her luck any further.

"I'm a businessman," he clarified, going to stand by the window to watch for Dante.

"So, you're in the business of terrorizing people?" she asked.

"I'm in the business of solutions."

"And Dante is a problem that needs solving?"

"Quiet," he ordered, stepping away from the blinds to stand closer to Frannie. "Your lover is here. If you're wise, you'll encourage Mr. Santoro to come quietly without trouble. I'd rather not make a mess that will require substantial cleanup."

Cleanup. She swallowed, imagining her insides painting her living room from the close-range impact of the bullet sending her soul into the hereafter. "Yeah, that would suck for you," she murmured caustically. "Or, you could just turn over a new leaf and walk away from a life of soul-stealing crime and spend the rest of your days atoning for all of the terrible things you've probably done under the guise of 'following orders.' Life is about choices—"

The sudden pain of her hair being ripped from her scalp as his associate buried his hand in her hair, yanking it hard, stole her breath. "You were told to be silent," the man reminded her in disgust. "American women do not know when to shut up."

Son of a bitch, that hurt. She blinked back tears as her scalp throbbed in time with the fresh pain in her skull. This had to be the worst day of her life.

And then the door opened—and Dante walked in.

"Hello, Mr. Santoro."

DANTE FROZE, HIS blood turning instantly to ice as he took in the situation.

"Hi, honey, we have guests," Frannie said with a pained smile, her neck pulled at an uncomfortable angle.

Dante recognized Benito Ricci, the man holding the gun and watching his every move, as one of his uncle's hired men.

"You are a hard man to find," Benito said conversationally.

"Get your man's hand off my girl," he growled.

"You're not in a position to make demands," Benito said. "You've caused much trouble."

Dante held Benito's stare, promising violence without saying a word. After a long moment, Benito nodded to his associate, who released Frannie's hair. "What do you want?"

"It's very simple. Time to stop playing games and come home."

"My home is here."

"Your home is with your family."

"My family died."

Benito looked annoyed at this back-and-forth. "I'm tired of this ugly country—the language, the customs, the mouthy women, the terrible food—all trash. I cannot imagine what you find here more appealing than Italy."

"We're not exactly jumping for joy having you on American soil, either," Frannie muttered. "You're ruining Italian culture for me, buddy. Previously, I was a big fan."

Benito ignored Frannie, returning to Dante. "You will come with us with zero fuss. Your uncle has arranged for a private plane transport in Boise. He is most eager to put all this nastiness behind him, but first, I need you to procure what you stole."

"That's what he really wants, isn't it? Not me."

Benito shrugged as if that didn't matter to him either way. "The job is to bring you and the item you stole, home. That's what I intend to do."

"And if I don't want to return with you?"

"Then, things get *less* civilized," he answered, shifting his gaze pointedly to Frannie, and Dante knew how precarious Frannie's life was in that moment. "Aside from her constant yapping, she's not offensive to the eye. Perhaps with time, she could be trained to be a suitable Santoro wife, but my guess is that it's more efficient to start fresh with a good Italian woman."

"If anyone's offensive, it's you," Frannie shot back, mindless of the danger but making the situation much more difficult for Dante to save her life. "Also, you dress like a B-movie goon. I thought Italians had more style."

"I could cut out her tongue," Benito suggested as if he found that option more enticing by the minute. "Or perhaps a finger..."

Belinda's ruined hands flashed in his memory, and it took everything in Dante not to spring at the man's throat and rip it out with his bare hands.

Frannie's eyes widened as she swallowed, but she wisely remained quiet.

His options were slim for success. If his only play was to do what he could to keep Frannie safe, he'd take it.

He mentally calculated the odds of success if he rushed Benito for the gun in his hand and found them dismally small. He didn't want Frannie to get hurt, but he had a sinking suspicion that Frannie wouldn't leave this place alive if he didn't use his head to negotiate.

Purposefully relaxing his shoulders, he shoved his hands in his pockets as if casually discussing the latest stock news. "Civilized, eh? Sure, let's discuss how this might enfold if I were open to negotiating terms. Perhaps I'm tired of running and I'm ready to put this all behind me, but not until I know the terms are beneficial."

"Negotiate?" Benito wagged the gun. "Does it look like you're in a position to negotiate? I hold all the cards."

The hell you do. "Call Pietro."

Benito narrowed his gaze with suspicion. "And why would I do that?"

"Because you have no authority to make deals—he does."

"No, you'll get your things, and we'll leave as planned or I'll put a bullet in your lover's annoying head."

Dante held his ground. "Call Pietro. Now."

"Or what?" Benito asked, looking bored.

"Just do it."

Benito's arrogant confidence faltered as he met Dante's unwavering stare. The Santoro stare was legendary—Dante had certainly perfected it before discovering how deep his family's corruption went and why the stare instilled fear in anyone on the receiving end. Benito swore under his breath before tucking his gun in his back waistband and punching a number on his cell. "He wants to speak to you," he said when Pietro picked up, then handed Dante the cell.

"Yes?"

"I'll come home on one condition—Frannie isn't harmed, not a single hair on her head, got it?"

"You'll bring the documents?"

The evidence in his safety-deposit box was his only ace and leverage, but he wouldn't let Frannie get hurt over this. "Yes," he answered tersely. "But I swear if anything happens to Frannie…"

"You have my word, she'll be unharmed—as long as you hold up your end of the bargain. Your uncle is eager to end this."

"Yeah, I bet he is," he growled, hating that his uncle had won, no matter what. "Tell my uncle's men." He shoved the phone back at Benito.

Benito listened, clicking off with a curt, "Yes, sir," his

annoyance probably marred with misgiving at leaving a loose end. That was not how things were done in his line of work. "Untie her," he said, shaking his head. "I'll be in the car. Make your goodbyes quick. I want to be on the road in five minutes."

Dante watched them leave, then went to Frannie as she rubbed her raw wrists, scowling even as she jumped into his arms, whispering, "Good thinking! We can slip out the back—"

"No, Frannie," he said firmly, pulling her free to stare into her beautiful eyes, memorizing the sight of her so he'd never forget he'd once been lucky enough to be loved by her. "I have to go with them."

"What? No! That was just a ruse, right? You can't go with them. You said your uncle wants you *dead*. I won't let you go. That's suicide!"

"I love you, Frannie," he said, ignoring her protests. "I always knew it would come down to this, but I never imagined I might fall in love with someone like you along the way. You deserved so much better—"

"No! Stop it, I won't listen to that crap," she whispered fiercely, her eyes tearing up. "I won't let you go. You're not thinking clearly. We can slip out the back…and… I don't know, run to the neighbor's house and call 911 or something."

"Listen to me," he said, gripping her arms and giving her a sharp shake to get her attention. "They will *kill* you and I'll still have to go with them. Don't you understand? I'm out of options. I'm purchasing your safety by leaving with them. It's the only thing I can do to ensure that you're not hurt. Let me do this for you. If something happened to you… I couldn't live with myself. Please, Frannie."

She crumpled at his pleading, wrapping her arms around

him as she started to sob. "Please, Dante…please don't do this!"

He knew there was no other way. His uncle played by rules Frannie couldn't even fathom. She was part of a soft and kind world, whereas his was cruel and manipulative.

Dante felt the ticking clock. Gently disengaging Frannie's grip around his neck, he kissed her deeply, then cupped her face, leaving her with firm instructions. "Do not try to follow us, and do not give my uncle any reason to even think of you after this moment. Promise me."

"I can't," she cried, shaking her head.

"You must promise me, Frannie," he said, blinking back his tears. "I can't live with the thought of you being in danger. I need to know you'll be safe. Please do this for me."

Frannie didn't want to, but she slowly nodded with a choked, "I promise."

Walk away, the voice told him, and he dragged himself away from Frannie. Turning on his heel, he walked out the door, afraid to look back and see her crushed expression, knowing she might grow to hate him because of this moment, but she'd be alive.

And that had to be enough.

He was returning to Italy.

Time to put an end to all of this.

Once and for all.

Chapter Twenty-Nine

Frannie didn't know how long she sat in the dark of her living room, reliving the moment Dante had walked away, but her toes were numb from the cramped position, and the crusted salt from her dried tears made her face feel tight and gritty.

Rising with the stiff gait of an eighty-year-old woman with arthritis, she hobbled to the kitchen to rinse her face and drink a glass of water. Her brain wasn't working, but her heart was working overtime. Waves of pain and grief washed over her as she ran headlong into the realization that Dante wasn't coming back.

Worse, he'd sacrificed himself to save her.

Her head throbbed, reminding her she'd been attacked twice in one day, but the physical pain was nothing compared to the emotional anguish crushing her soul.

She didn't know what to do. Dante had made her promise, but she didn't care about promises made under duress. Except she knew next to nothing about Dante's family besides what he'd told her—and that had been as little as possible due to the circumstances.

She knew relatively little about Dante besides how he liked to sleep, how he brushed his teeth and loved to make her feel special and cherished.

A trapped sob threatened to burst from her chest as she leaned over the sink, bracing herself as she tried to weather the pain.

She had to talk to someone. Damn it, her phone was in pieces, and she didn't have a landline. With shaking hands, she scooped up the spilled contents of her purse, slid them back into her bag, grabbed her keys and left the house.

She could not sleep in that bed tonight when it smelled like Dante. His absence would only remind her that he was truly gone.

Driving straight to Darla's house, she pounded on the front door, not caring that she was a mess and making a racket when everyone else in the neighborhood was trying to sleep.

Tom, Darla's fiancé, opened the door holding a bat, ready to use whoever's head to hit a home run, but when he saw Frannie, he immediately set the bat down and ushered her inside. "Darla!" he called out, adding with concern, "Frannie needs you!"

Darla came around the corner with an anxious frown, wearing a robe, her hair tucked in a silk hair wrap and a mint green face mask slathered on her face. "What's going on?" she asked, collecting Frannie in a hug as she sagged against her.

She smelled of coconut and pinto beans, which was an odd combination and made Frannie think of the time in junior high when they'd tried to tie-dye their shirts using all-natural ingredients instead of the actual dye. It had been a mess, and all they'd accomplished was a muddy mess that ruined two T-shirts.

"He's gone," Frannie sobbed, her body shaking as she let it all out. Tom left the room and silently returned with a washcloth so Darla could wipe away the gunk. There'd be no time for beauty rituals tonight.

"What do you mean?" she asked, casting Tom a grateful look as she quickly wiped her face. "Who's gone?"

"Dante," Frannie answered mournfully.

"Gone where?"

"Back to Italy."

"That jerk!"

"No," she said. "He was practically kidnapped, and there's nothing I can do about it because I promised I wouldn't."

"I'm sorry, run that by me again?"

Frannie didn't have the energy to go into details, so she gave the TL;DR version. "Dante was on the run from his big, scary family in Italy, but they found him and sent two awful goons to bring him back, using me as leverage." She sniffed back tears, which only made her head want to explode. She winced, adding, "Getting attacked twice in one day is overkill in the karma department. I swear I must've done something awful in a past life to be getting served up this plate of doo-doo in this one."

"*Attacked?* You were attacked?"

"Yeah, I was going to tell you tomorrow, but I never imagined that I might be ambushed when I got home. Allen Burns tried to kidnap me earlier today. Dante saved me, it was a whole thing…but in hindsight that was nothing in comparison to what was waiting for me when I got home."

"Are you kidding me right now? I can't wrap my head around any of this." Darla was visibly reeling, and Frannie didn't blame her, but she was too mentally strung out to soften the delivery.

"Me either, but it happened and let me tell you, stuff like this makes for great movies but it really sucks when it happens in real life!"

Tom, who usually left them to their conversations, had returned with a bottled water for Frannie and caught the tail end of her comment. He handed her the water and sat beside Darla. "Are you okay?" he asked tentatively. "Did they...hurt you?"

"No, nothing like that but the one guy nearly ripped the hair from my head and the other one threatened to cut my tongue out if I didn't stop talking. He, apparently, doesn't think much of our country and was really rude about it."

"And Dante just left with them?"

"He didn't have a choice. It was either leave with them, or they'd start breaking parts of me like they did to his ex-girlfriend."

"Geemini Christmas," Darla exclaimed in a horrified tone. "I can't believe this happened to you. Did you call Fletcher and make a report?"

"No, Dante made me promise not to," she said, feeling sheepish for not calling the police at the very least.

"Well, we can rectify that right now," Tom said, grabbing the phone. "How do you know they won't return and finish the job?"

"Because Dante talked to someone in charge and basically told them to stand down or else he wouldn't give his uncle something he wants really bad."

"Which is?"

"I have no idea."

"This is, like, spy shit," Darla said with the tiniest spark of wonder, as if she found it a little exhilarating even though she shouldn't, but Frannie didn't begrudge her fascination. She would've felt the same if she hadn't been living through it. "So, what happens now?"

"I don't know."

Darla grasped her hand and squeezed it. "No matter what, we're here for you."

"I know. I'm sorry I ruined your night. I couldn't stay at the house...not with Dante gone."

"You fell hook, line and sinker for him, didn't you?" Darla asked, shaking her head with sorrow at Frannie's suddenly watering eyes. She nodded, and Darla's expression melted with pure understanding and compassion. "Well, we just have to find a way to get him back."

"How?" Frannie asked plaintively. "Do you know anyone with the power to strong-arm one of the most dangerous families in Italy to return my boyfriend?"

"No, but you do have a cousin in the FBI. I'd start there. They might be interested in knowing what went down."

"But I promised Dante I wouldn't."

"Some promises aren't meant to be kept," Darla said, shrugging. "I know nothing would keep me from trying to rescue this guy," she said, reaching over to rub Tom's arm. "So, that's what you're going to do for your guy. Everything and anything. It might not work but it's worth a try. At least then you can say you did what you could."

Darla was right. She couldn't give up. Not yet.

"I'll call Max," she said, nodding firmly even though she couldn't quite see straight anymore. Fatigue, chemical warfare and emotional exhaustion had taken their toll, and the bill was due.

Darla took control, saying, "Absolutely—first thing tomorrow morning."

Tom rose. "I'll get the spare bedroom ready."

Frannie started to protest, but a yawn garbled her attempts, and all she could do was stare blearily at her best friend as her eyelids felt weighted with cement. "I suppose you're right," she conceded. "Tomorrow is a better plan."

Darla helped her up, and they walked together to the spare bedroom. Tom had just finished turning down the sheets like the most hospitable host at the most exclusive hotel, and she thanked Darla with a look.

And that was all that was needed.

Frannie crawled into the bed and dropped off before her head hit the pillow.

AFTER A TWELVE-HOUR FLIGHT, Dante was back on home soil, and within the next hour, he was walking into his uncle's stately home.

Even though his eyes burned from lack of sleep, he went straight to his uncle's office, pushing open the door ahead of Benito and his accomplice, leaving them in his wake.

At one time, this had been his home—he'd had full run of the house—and it had been the first time he'd felt safe and secure.

He pushed away those memories and stared hard at his uncle Lorenzo, who, despite the circumstance, seemed pleased to see him.

"You're home."

"Don't," Dante warned.

Lorenzo's expression lost warmth, and he gestured for Benito and his accomplice to leave. Wordlessly, they exited the office and closed the double doors softly behind them.

"You've caused much trouble and strife, Dante," Lorenzo admonished as if he were lecturing an errant schoolboy caught breaking the rules. "I'm displeased with your lack of civility and loyalty to family. Your mother would be crushed to see what you've done."

At the mention of his mother, Dante stiffened, remembering the suspicious deposits over the years to his mother's account. "I need answers," he said coldly. "You wanted me home? Well, here I am. But this time, I want the truth."

"The truth about what?" Lorenzo asked, holding his stare unflinchingly.

"Did you have my father killed?"

"No."

Lorenzo didn't hesitate, nor did he react in a way that would suggest he was lying, but Dante had the evidence suggesting that someone had paid the investigating officer for a doctored investigation. "You're lying," he said to gauge his reaction.

"I'm not." Lorenzo sighed, leaning back in his soft leather chair as if resigned to the long overdue conversation. "Ask the question you're afraid to ask."

Fatigue burned behind his eyes, but he wouldn't leave his uncle's office until he had the answers to the questions eating him alive.

"If you didn't kill him…who did?"

"Your mother."

His world stopped turning. All he could do was stare, uncomprehending yet violently resisting the implication of his uncle's statement.

"No, she would never…"

"I'd hoped that you'd never ask this question. It's not something one should know about their parent. Your mother was a good woman but when pushed to the edge, even good people break."

"What would you know about good people?" Dante asked bitterly, reeling beneath the weight of the information.

"Just because I can't afford the luxury of goodness doesn't mean I don't know it in others," Lorenzo said quietly.

At that moment, Dante remembered how it felt to love this man, believe in him and wish he'd been his father instead of Matteo. After discovering the depth of Lorenzo's crimes, he'd been ashamed of ever wishing such a thing.

Now he didn't know what to think. He dropped heavily into the thick chair opposite his uncle, his brain swimming in a fog. "I don't understand," he said, trying to fit the pieces of this hellish puzzle together. "My mother loved my father."

"She did, but she'd wanted out long before your father's

accident. He wouldn't let her. He threatened to take you and run, so that she never saw you again. She stayed for you. Not Matteo."

"My father ran because of you," he shot back, blaming Lorenzo. "He'd wanted a better life, a clean life for his family."

Lorenzo shrugged as if the reasons were immaterial to the outcome. "Whatever reasons he had, Georgia had lost any shared conviction, and soon after, her love for Matteo died. Behind closed doors, Matteo had become abusive—"

"My father wasn't a violent man," Dante retorted, refusing to believe it. Though a hazy memory of his mother crying behind closed doors and his father storming from the house returned to make him question what he thought he knew about his parents. He'd only been a kid—and a kid's memory was colored by the inexperience of their youth and a forgiving love for their parents.

"She wanted to get away from your father, but he kept you on the move so frequently that she couldn't save enough money to make it happen. She wrote me, asking for help."

"So you started sending her money," he surmised.

Lorenzo nodded.

"But why?"

"Isn't it obvious by now?" Lorenzo asked.

Yes, it was now. "You loved her," Dante said, closing his eyes, feeling sick. "You were in love with my mother."

"I could never refuse her anything."

"Did you conspire with her to kill my father?"

"No. There are some lines even I won't cross." He sighed. "Your mother called me, told me what she'd done, and I helped take care of the problem."

That was the late-night phone call his mother received the night his father died—and why they were on a plane the following morning.

"Have I not given you everything Matteo should have?" Lorenzo asked stiffly, revealing a rare glimpse of his hidden wound. "I loved you as a son, and you betrayed me."

His uncle was right—he'd taken him in, treated him like a son, given him the best education and opportunity—but he'd hidden the true cost of that privilege until it was too late to refuse.

"You used my love for you as a weapon to keep me doing things that went against my conscience.'

To his surprise, Lorenzo conceded Dante's point. "Perhaps." He spread his hands in a conciliatory gesture, "I made mistakes in the moment that I wish I could take back."

It was the closest he would get to an apology from Lorenzo Santoro. Knowing what he knew now, there was no way Lorenzo had anything to do with his mother's accident. A cruel twist of fate had been responsible for the accident that had taken Georgia, or perhaps, karma had come for its due and delivered justice for her part in Matteo's death.

Either way, Lorenzo was guilty of many crimes, but neither Georgia's nor Matteo's death was one of them.

Dante pulled the envelope he'd taken from his uncle's vault and slid it over to him.

Lorenzo glanced at the envelope as if hating the contents but relieved to have it back in his possession, saying, "What happens now?"

Dante knew he couldn't stay. He didn't want the life Lorenzo had created for him, and he could never be like Lorenzo.

His uncle seemed to understand without Dante having to say the words.

Since Dante had left Italy, his uncle seemed to have aged ten years. Lorenzo had always been active and formidable, a robust man for his age. Now he appeared to be a shell of himself. Losing Georgia and now Dante was a blow he couldn't seem to recover from, and he'd lost the will to fight.

"I'm not cut out for the life you wanted for me," Dante said. "I'm not like you and I don't want to be."

"You're the Santoro heir," Lorenzo said as if that should matter to him. "You have an obligation—"

"No," Dante cut in, shaking his head. "Then, disown me. Cut me off. I don't care about the money. I will walk away from all of it, to be free of everything the Santoro name is attached to."

"You really mean that?" Lorenzo asked with a stiff upper lip. "You would walk away from your birthright?"

"Yes. If that's what it takes."

"What if I changed? Would that make you reconsider?"

Oddly, the offer hit Dante in a tender place, perhaps that place where fond memories of his uncle still lived. But he knew that even if Lorenzo's offer was sincere, his uncle was too set in his ways to make those kinds of changes in a meaningful way, and eventually, perhaps slowly, he'd revert to his old ways.

And he couldn't expose Frannie to this life.

"I've met someone. I want to make a life with her. A normal life, one where she doesn't have to look over her shoulder, wary of someone using her as leverage to get to you or me. She owns a bookstore and she's sweet and kind and compassionate—and not cut out for the cost of shouldering the Santoro legacy."

Lorenzo considered Dante's admission, and something shifted in his expression. Perhaps he was thinking about how Georgia would've handled Dante's request, or maybe he was too tired to put up too much more of a fight to hold on to him.

"I will free you of your Santoro name so you can live your life as you choose," he said sighing heavily. "Your happiness is what your mother would've wanted. And if this is the only way I can give that to you… I will."

Dante swallowed, realizing what his uncle was sacrificing and why.

What may have begun as love for Georgia all those years ago had also changed into love for Dante.

Even if Lorenzo had shown it in ways that weren't all that loving.

Speaking of. "What you had done to Belinda…"

"Say no more." Lorenzo waved off any need to continue, shame in his eyes. "I'll ensure she's taken care of. She'll need for nothing. I swear it."

Dante believed him.

There was nothing more to say.

The rage that had lived in his heart for so long had burned away, leaving an empty hole that quickly filled with sadness and grief.

When he left Italy this time, he'd never return.

When he said his goodbyes this time, it was for good.

And they both understood what that meant.

"Thank you, *lo zio.*"

Lorenzo gave an imperceptible nod, and Dante rose, walking away for one last time.

His uncle would never be a good man—but at one time, he'd been the best man in Dante's life.

And for that, there would always be a piece of Dante that loved Lorenzo like the father Matteo should've been.

Chapter Thirty

Frannie stared at Max, confused. "There has to be something you can do. Dante was practically kidnapped by his uncle's men, on American soil! Surely that's a crime? You said that the FBI had a file a mile long on the Santoro family. Here's your chance to bring them in, throw the book at them. Show them how America deals with international terrorists!"

"I'm not saying that a crime wasn't committed, but you said Dante went willingly with them. That doesn't sound like he was kidnapped."

Frannie glared. "They *forced* him to leave."

"At gunpoint?"

"No, but one of them *did* have a gun—and the other guy pulled my hair and threatened to cut out my tongue."

Max tried not to chuckle. It wasn't funny, but maybe in another situation, it would've been a little comical. However, there was nothing humorous about it in Frannie's eyes. "Look, you need to call the National Guard, the Army, or call the freaking president, for all I care. All I know is that I'm not going to sit here and do nothing while the future father of my children is being tortured by his awful, villainous uncle, okay? If I have to fly to Italy and find him myself, I will."

"I have no doubt you would try and in doing so, probably get yourself killed," Max said dryly. "Have you tried calling him?"

"I don't have his number and that stupid goon broke my SIM card." She perked up, remembering, "Hey, that's right, he broke my phone. That's a crime! Use that to extradite that jerk."

"Frannie... I can't deport a man for breaking your SIM card," Max said, trying to talk sense into her, but she had long since left rational behavior behind. She was frantic with worry and ready to hop on a plane to do something reckless if someone didn't help her rescue Dante.

"Please, Max..." she pleaded, needing something to calm her brain. "I'm losing it. I'm so worried."

Max relented, saying, "I'll make some calls, okay, but in the meantime, go home, take a long shower or a bath or something, and try to relax. You stewing isn't going to help Dante, okay?"

Of course, Max was right, but logic was not living in her head right now. She wanted action—she wanted the armed forces to storm the shores of Italy and rescue her beautiful Italian man. Yes, it was irrational and not grounded in reality, but she didn't care.

She just wanted Dante back.

"You don't understand. Dante told me what his uncle did to his ex-girlfriend and now she's living in Switzerland— no, *hiding* in Switzerland—trying to rebuild her life after she was maimed by Dante's uncle's goons! Now try and tell me that I'm overreacting."

Max sobered at this new information but was limited in what he could do. "Listen, I believe you. Dante is part of a dangerous family, but he willingly left the country. I can't just call up the Italian government and demand they hand over one of their citizens without a pretty big reason, and as much as I would love to help in any way possible, I don't know how."

"So that's it? I'm just supposed to sit back, hope for the best and basically move on with my life?"

Max tried a different perspective. "Maybe this is a blessing in disguise. Do you really want to be involved with someone who has ties to such dangerous people?"

It was solid advice—and if she were thinking straight, maybe it might've made a difference, but who could say they were thinking straight when they were in love? "Max... I love him, and I'm terrified. Please. Try and help him. I'll never ask another favor again if you do me this one solid."

Max took a long breath, shaking his head, but he agreed. "I'll make some calls, but I don't know if they'll go anywhere, okay?"

Frannie knew that when Max gave his word, he was good for it. She nodded. This was the best she could get. She had to hope it was enough.

Leaving Max's office, she headed back to Owl Creek to open the shop. The last thing she wanted to do was track inventory and smile with customers as if her world wasn't cracking apart, but it would provide a distraction, at the very least.

The practical side of her nature appeared, reminding her that she couldn't afford to let her business fold, no matter how her heart might be broken.

Just as she finished shelving her newest shipment—*How to Be a Boss Babe in 30 Days or Less*—her landline rang.

"Book Mark It," she answered, and smiled as she heard Darla's voice.

"Calling a landline is like being transported back to junior high before we had our cell phones and our parents insisted on keeping their old number for emergency services," Darla recalled with a nostalgic chuckle. "I kinda miss not being at everyone's beck and call. Anyway, any luck with Max?"

"It doesn't look promising. Max says the FBI can't just extradite from another country on the grounds of kidnapping if the kidnappee went willingly."

"Isn't coercion a thing?" Darla asked, incredulous. "Seems like that would be a thing."

"I thought so, but what do I know?"

"Well, if Max is on it, I feel confident he'll do his best."

Frannie agreed, though it felt hopeless. "In the meantime, I'm trying to distract myself with work."

"How's that going?"

"Not great."

"Hang in there, something will work out."

"How?"

"I don't know but it seems like the right thing to say in a situation like this."

Leave it to Darla to coax a reluctant smile out of Frannie when she didn't want to laugh. "Thanks for letting me crash at your place last night. I slept like the dead."

"No problem. *Mi casa, su casa.*"

"Our senior Spanish teacher would be so proud you retained something from his class," Frannie quipped.

"Hey, I also retained a love of chile relleno, so I call that an educational win."

"Stop trying to cheer me up. It won't work."

"It's kinda working. I know you're trying not to laugh."

Caught. Darla knew her too well. "Okay, fine. But it feels wrong to laugh or feel any kind of joy right now when my boyfriend could be suffering unimaginable torment at the hands of his villainous uncle."

"Right, of course, but sometimes inappropriate laughter is the only thing that keeps us from running screaming into the streets when all hell breaks loose."

Fair point. "What would I do without you?"

"Aside from collapse into a dramatic heap, weeping and wailing, cursing the heavens for the cruel twist of fate? I haven't a clue. Thankfully, you'll never have to figure that out because you're stuck with me—and there is a bright side to all this drama..."

"Which is?"

"Since you're not skipping town and going on the run... you're back on maid-of-honor detail."

Frannie burst into laughter, realizing this was very true. "And what an honor it is," she replied with a roll of her eyes, but Darla was right. Life wasn't going to stop just because her heart was in pieces.

And it wasn't fair of her to ask Darla to put her life on hold because Frannie had fallen in love with a man who'd never been in a position to offer his heart.

Frannie ended the call and sat for a long moment, just trying to find her center again. *Breathe in, breathe out.* Calm and rational was her jam.

But one thought kept jamming her chill frequency.

Please be okay, Dante. Please find a way back to me.

IT TOOK SEVERAL days for Pietro to finalize details of Dante's disownment, and in that time, he and his father's secretary had long talks about how things would work once he returned to the States.

"You're sure about this?" Pietro asked with a disapproving frown. "There's no turning back once this is done."

Dante knew what he was doing, and he was ready. "I am."

Pietro shook his head but finished putting the paperwork in order. "You will forfeit your inheritance aside from what your mother has already bequeathed, which is substantial but not enough for a lifetime. You'll have to go back to work."

"I don't have a problem with that. I hate being idle."

"Yes, you've always been industrious," Pietro said approvingly. "But why this dramatic move? Your uncle has agreed to change his ways…be the man you want him to be."

"Because it wouldn't last. He is who he is and he's too old to change his stripes—and it's not right of me to ask. Besides, the life I want to build with Frannie…is incompatible with my former life, and I choose her."

"What will you do in this new life?"

"Get my law degree to practice in the States, and maybe go into family law. Something that actually helps people instead of tearing them apart. I'm looking forward to being on the right side for once."

"A little idealistic but then, I suppose, that fits you."

Dante chuckled, but the lingering sadness at leaving everything he knew tugged at him. "You were good to me, growing up," he said. "I'll miss our talks."

"You were easy to be good to," Pietro said, pushing a manila envelope toward him across the desk. "Your new identity, fully vetted and legal. Unlike the documents you created, these should hold up against any search."

Dante opened the envelope and saw a large wad of cash as well. "What is this?" he asked, confused.

Pietro shrugged. "A little seed money for your new adventures."

"That's not necessary—"

"Please, let him do this one last thing," Pietro said. "You're the son he never had and he's allowing you to walk away. You have no idea how much this is costing him but he's willing to honor your request. The old Lorenzo would've found a way to force you to his will, no matter the cost. He is changing, bit by bit."

Dante closed the envelope, accepting the gift. He knew

exactly how he'd put the money to good use. "Thank him for me."

Pietro nodded. "I will," he said, shaking Dante's hand. "It's been a pleasure watching you grow up to be a good man. Your plane leaves in two hours. A car is waiting to take you to the airport. I've arranged your final travel ticket. Flying economy…as is appropriate for your new identity."

Dante met Pietro's stare and saw the banked amusement. He grinned. *Cheeky bastard.* A sixteen-hour flight with multiple layovers and zero legroom. He'd done that on purpose. "Can't wait," Dante said.

And then he walked out, leaving behind everything he'd known since he was ten, to make a new life with the woman who'd changed his path forever.

Sixteen hours until he felt Frannie in his arms and vowed never to let her go again.

Maybe he'd see if he could upgrade his flight when he got to the airport—because sixteen hours was too long.

Chapter Thirty-One

Frannie did a final wipe-down of the counters at the café, shut down the machines, set the alarm on the bookstore and locked up. It was a week since Dante had been kidnapped— yes, she was still calling it a kidnapping—and Max had not received news.

Either no news was good news, or Dante was in a ditch somewhere.

She'd returned to some routine, but only by pretending that everything would work out somehow, no matter how unlikely that scenario was.

She spent a lot of time visualizing Dante walking through the bookstore door with a smile and a promise that he would never leave her again and that his family wouldn't keep trying to terrorize them.

What if—

"Ciao, bella."

Frannie's heart stopped at the familiar voice behind her. She squeezed her eyes shut as her heart leaped into her throat. Had she manifested so hard that she was hallucinating Dante's voice?

"Frannie?"

No, that was definitely Dante. She whirled around, afraid

that no one would be standing behind her and that she was losing her mind to grief.

But it was her beloved Dante, standing there as if nothing had happened, as if he hadn't been carted off by those gangsters, breaking her heart into a million pieces, scrambling her thoughts into porridge as the miles stretched between them.

"Dante?" Her voice broke as she ran full tilt into his arms, squeezing so hard she might've cracked a rib or two, but she was afraid to let go as if he might be a figment of her imagination. "Is it really you? Am I losing my mind? How are you here? Did you escape?" Her eyes widened as she rushed to add, "I kept a bag packed in the car with some cash and clothes in preparation of this very scenario—"

"Frannie," he laughed, swinging her around before setting her on her feet to meet her astonished gaze. "I'm not going anywhere. I'm here to stay. There's no need to run."

"I don't understand…what happened?" she asked, confused. "The last I saw, you were being kidnapped—and I don't care what my cousin says, they coerced you into leaving—and you said…well, your uncle wanted you dead! How are you alive?"

"It's a long, sad story and I will tell you every detail but first, just let me taste you." He brushed his mouth across hers in a tender kiss that stole the strength from her knees, reminding her that she was putty in his capable hands and always would be. "God, I missed you so much. A week was an eternity without you."

She felt the same. "Don't ever do that to me again," she said tearfully with a happy smile. "I don't care what happens in the future, you're not leaving without me."

"My love, you will never have cause to worry about that happening. I am yours and you are mine. And now I can offer you what I couldn't before. My uncle and I came to an agreement and I'm free from my Santoro ties. I'm going to get my law degree to practice in the States and we're going to do it right. I want to marry you, Frannie. Now, if possible, but if not, I'll wait until you're ready. I have some money burning a hole in my pocket and I want to buy the home we'll raise our kids in."

"Did you just propose?" Frannie asked, tears welling in her eyes again.

"In a very clumsy and inarticulate way, but yes," he said, laughing. "Please don't hold that against me. I just can't wait to make a life with you."

"I would never hold that against you," she murmured, rising on her toes to kiss him again. "My answer is yes. I will absolutely marry the hell out of you, Dante. I will marry you so hard it leaves a mark on your soul."

"Perfect," he murmured with hunger in his eyes as he lifted her off her feet, deepening the kiss between them as if they weren't in the middle of the sidewalk, putting on a show for everyone to see, but Frannie didn't care. She wanted everyone to know that Dante was her knight in shining armor—no matter what the world threw at them.

And she couldn't wait to start her new life as Mrs. Dante Sinclair.

Or whatever new name identity he'd traded for his Santoro legacy.

As long as her hand was in his…nothing else mattered.

They'd figure it out.

Chapter Thirty-Two

Dante held Frannie in his arms, stroking the smooth flesh of her side as she cuddled against him. The darkness around them was a private blanket of security as he shared everything that had happened when he returned to Italy.

He left nothing out—even revealing the sordid secret that he'd stolen from his uncle. The papers Lorenzo had been desperate to keep hidden.

"I'd always known about the aunt who took her life when she was very young, but when I discovered it was to hide the shame of her child's paternity, I was sick to my stomach. My grandfather was a terrible man. To father a child with his own daughter...well, it was a shameful secret my uncle wanted to hide from the world."

Frannie was understandably shaken but compassionate, as always.

"Family secrets are a cancer," she said. "Discovering my dad had a big secret has made me realize that no one is immune to temptation."

Dante held her more tightly, determined to ensure the Santoro legacy never touched their children. He wanted them to know only love and happiness.

"I'm not legally allowed to practice law in the States yet,

but I'll do whatever I can to help you with your family's situation," he said.

Frannie sighed, her fingers tracing small circles on his chest as she said, "Thank you. We can certainly use any insight you can share. My mom and Chase are heading to court next week to deal with Aunt Jessie's claim. I don't know how that's going to shake out, but I know Mom would appreciate the support. Oh, about that, my family wants to officially meet you this Sunday at family dinner. Are you okay with that? My family can be a lot."

"I can't wait."

And he wasn't just saying that. He wanted the whole experience of what it meant to have a big family, and since he was officially an orphan…he was ready to adopt the Coltons as his new family.

He was all in—and couldn't wait to start.

A mischievous smile curved his lips as he murmured against the crown of her head. "How do you feel about being a pregnant bride?"

Frannie gasped in fake outrage, "Dante Sinclair, are you trying to give my poor mother a heart attack?" She rolled on top, staring at him with an equally flirty smile, looking like a goddess in the moonlight. "However, accidents happen…"

And he knew at that moment his heart would forever be safe with Frannie as his partner in love, life and laughter.

In all things. Just as it should be.

* * * * *

COMING SOON!

We really hope you enjoyed reading this book.
If you're looking for more romance
be sure to head to the shops when
new books are available on

Thursday 11th
April

To see which titles are coming soon, please visit
millsandboon.co.uk/nextmonth

MILLS & BOON

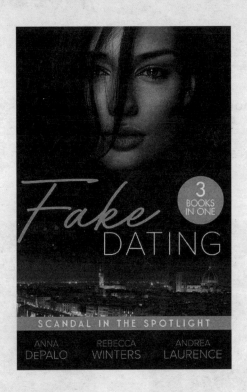